Secrets

Sins

&

Revenge

D. L. Bourassa

Copyright © 2014 D. L. Bourassa

Secrets, Sins & Revenge is a work of fiction. Any references to real people, events, establishments, organizations, or locales are intended only to give the fiction a sense of reality and authenticity. Other names, characters, places, and incidents portrayed herein are either the product of the author's imagination or are used fictionally.

ISBN-13: 978-1502826169
ISBN-10: 150282616X

Author's Note

I write fiction because I want the freedom to invent characters, dialogue and events of my own personal vision. Writing fiction is not much of a task, or a chore, it is a joyful endeavor that I undertake to fulfill my creative impulses. I do not choose my characters: they choose me. Their lives appear to me in glimpses like a movie playing before my mind's eye. Characters come into my head, and I simply put them into motion with my writing so that the reader may see them, too. It is not my intention to create a mirror image of actuality. All the characters in my novel are products of my **imagination**. I gave them faces, created situations and dialogue that fit my own interpretation of what may have taken place if these events had actually happened. I imagined what they might have thought and what others would have thought of them. Any event depicted in my novel that may resemble actual events is purely accidental. I know the difference between fact and fiction and hope my readers know the difference as well. No reader should assume that characters portrayed in my novel are real people or that any of the events ever actually occurred. This is a work of fiction.

D. L. Bourassa
October, 2014

CONTENTS

BOOK ONE

Secrets

CHAPTER 1

BAREFOOT BAY: A picturesque adult retirement community nestled on the East Coast of Florida; a perfect place to enjoy your retirement; a place where seniors are less anxious and more comfortable with love, sex, and intimate relationships.

OR IS IT?

People are still talking about the winter of 2012 and the murder of Phil Gagnon. Seniors gathered in back yards and screened rooms, sharing opinions, exaggerated the few facts they read in the newspaper, while casting judgment without knowing what could have possibly gone wrong, wondering who had killed their neighbor and why. Stricken with fear, residents of this once quiet community retreated to the safety of their homes and locked the doors behind them.

It should never have happened here, but it did.

No one remembers that winter more vividly than Chief of Police, Raymond "Ray" Barrett. The Barefoot Bay Retirement Community was gripped in fear, and for Barrett, it's a nightmare he will never forget. Being the Police Chief in this sleepy little town called Micco, with a crime rate lower than a Pennsylvania Amish community, gave him little to do and a lot of time to do it in. Being involved in a murder was the last thing he wanted, or needed, in his life.

The night Phil Gagnon was murdered started out no different than any other Friday night. Ray had stumbled home about eleven o'clock after spending the night at Bottoms Up, a typical small town bar, populated with blue-collar workers sidling up to the bar, discussing work, sharing jokes, and talking sports while drinking an endless supply of draft beers.

Micco's Chief of Police would be the last to admit he's a functioning alcoholic. He spends his off duty hours hanging out at Bottoms Up, his home away from home, and drinking his constant companion. It's like his whole meaningless life is plainly written out for the whole world to see on a huge blackboard, and booze was the eraser that temporarily made it all go away. With no family and few friends, there was no reason to stay home at night, so he spent his nights drinking at the neighborhood watering hole where he lingered in a place of solitude and escape, keeping himself entertained by staring at the television above the bar, while carefully peeling the labels of his Budweiser bottles. All in all he doesn't believe anything is wrong with his life, except that it has a big gaping hole in it, an enormous emptiness, and he doesn't know how to fill it, or even what belongs there.

Beer is his drink of choice. He believes as long as he is just drinking beer he's in control. He feels drinking beer is a hell of a lot better than drinking wine out of a brown paper bag, which is worse than downing the hard stuff alone behind closed doors.

Several years ago he quit for ten days before breaking down, which was long enough to convince him he was in control of his addiction. But he hated every miserable, sober minute of it and had no intention of going through that again. He knows it would take strength and endurance to completely overcome his addiction before his addiction overcomes him, but lacks the willpower to do anything about it.

It was 11:25 when Ray staggered into his bedroom, stripped off his clothes, letting them fall in a heap on the floor. He turned off the light and dropped back on the bed he has all to himself. Lying in bed at night without a woman isn't unusual; he long ago traded in sex for the bottle.

He immediately fell asleep. But it wasn't long before the same recurring nightmare he had experienced in the past jolted him awake. He awoke imagining black and gray spiders, hundreds of them, crawling across his face. He could feel their hairy tentacles sinking into his flesh, while the creatures relentlessly attacked his eyes, his nose and mouth, determined to enter at every available opening.

He bolted upright, gasping, and began rubbing his face furiously with both hands, attempting to erase the invisible enemy. His heart pounded, his skin felt clammy, and his forehead was covered in a cold sweat.

"Oh, Christ!" he moaned fearfully. "Oh, Christ, somebody help me."

He inhaled deeply, suppressing a rising wave of nausea. With both hands pressed firmly against his face, he spread two fingers apart and stared out between the slits, watching and listening intently for any small movement. Nothing moved, yet he couldn't shake the feeling the spiders were still here, lurking somewhere in the shadows of the room, behind the curtains, under the bed or maybe in the closets.

Lately his life has begun spiraling out of control. Chief Barrett doesn't want to admit he has a problem, but these recurring dreams had become more and more frequent, and he was worried.

After tossing and turning for what seemed like an eternity, watching and waiting for the spiders to return, out of pure exhaustion, he finally dozed-off for the second time shortly after midnight. His trailer home was now as quiet as a cemetery, except for the faint sounds drifting through the open window as he settled into a deep sleep.

Then the phone rang.

The ringing seemed to be coming from a faraway place, in some adjacent universe, a part of a dream he wanted nothing to do with. As it drew closer and closer, Ray slowly opened his eyes and realized it was no dream. In no mood or condition to carry on a conversation, he pulled the sheets over his head, ignoring the ringing.

But it wouldn't stop. The more he ignored it, the more the phone sounded like a jackhammer in his head and actually seemed to be picking up speed. But Barrett was determined to ignore it. He rolled onto his stomach and pulled his pillow over his head. He just wanted to be left alone.

There was a time Ray could drink all night without getting drunk. He didn't have blackouts or nightmares, and his occasional hangover never amounted to much more than a slight headache. All it took was a glass of water and two Extra Strength Tylenols, and he was good to go, but those days were over.

Finally he gave up, realizing if he was ever going to get any sleep, he had no choice but to answer the phone. Slowly opening his eyes, he yelled, "I'm coming . . . goddammit . . . I'm coming."

Raising his head off the pillow, Ray tossed it on the floor, rolled flat on his back, threw off the sheet, and lay staring at the ceiling fan with the bamboo blades slowly moving the air around the room, barely making a sound. The turning motion of the fan was making him dizzy and doing strange things to his thought process while he struggled to gather the strength to sit up.

With a great deal of effort, he slung his legs over the side of the bed and sat up. It was hotter than hell in the bedroom, and he could feel the sweat dripping from his armpits. Bringing both hands to his head, he applied pressure, massaging his scalp with his fingertips, hoping to ease the unrelenting pounding.

The phone kept calling. "Damn it. I'm comin'," he hollered again into the dark, his voice echoing off the walls. "Damn," he said.

With sheer determination, he gathered all his strength and tried to stand; the room began moving, he became dizzy and started wobbling, so he sat back down. On his second attempt, he pushed hard with both hands on the mattress. This time he made it, but just barely. He staggered into the kitchen barefoot, feeling like he was wearing cement boots, being careful not to stumble over clothes scattered on the 1980s era linoleum bedroom floor, its edges torn and turned up. The air was stagnant, and the house was in total darkness, except for a night light under the kitchen cabinets making his shadow glide along the walls. Finally, he managed to make it to the wall phone next to the refrigerator.

Struggling to maintain his balance, wearing only boxer shorts and a sleeveless undershirt, it was evident that Micco's Chief of Police was not in the greatest shape. Ray had a face that resembled an over-the-hill street brawler, with a flat nose spread across his face like an ex-prizefighter that's taken too many jabs, sitting on top of narrow shoulders, skinny arms, a small sunken chest, and ballerina legs, all of which was situated around a swollen beer belly.

With one outstretched arm firmly placed on the wall, he grabbed the phone, placed it next to his ear and said, "Yeah," in a tired, gruff voice.

"Ray, this is Andy. Hate to bother you, but I think this might be important," night Patrolman Callahan said anxiously.

Ray asked, "What time is it?"

"1:15. I know it's late, but . . ."

"No shit. I know it's late, too," Ray interrupted. "What I want to know is why you're calling me at this time?"

"Sir, if you'll calm down, I'll tell you."

Ray's head was throbbing. "So what's going on? And this better be goddamn good."

"Like I've been trying to tell you, I'm in Barefoot Bay. The guys from EMT called and said they had a possible homicide. When I got here, I found a guy lying on his living room floor, dead. The medics at first thought he'd had a heart attack, but after looking closer, they think he might have been beaten," Callahan reported.

Trying desperately to make sense out of this, Ray said, "You must be kidding!"

There'd never been a murder in all the years he'd been a police officer in Micco; even suggesting someone had been beaten to death, especially in the Retirement Community, was unthinkable.

"Kidding? You think I'd call at this hour if it was a joke. Are you all right? You don't sound good."

"No. I'm not all right," Ray snapped.

"Sir, I'm just telling you what they told me. Do you want to talk to them?"

"No. Listen, I better not be going over there for nothing," Ray insisted, looking up at the ceiling.

"Hey, don't get pissed off at me."

"Yeah, okay. Sorry. My head is a little screwed up right now, that's all."

"Well, what do you want me to do, sir? I really think you should come over here."

"I guess I'll have to. Tell the EMTs to hang around until I get there. I'll talk to them then," Chief Barrett instructed. "Where about in the Bay are you?"

"Dolphin Drive. Do you want me to wait until you get here?"

"Yes. I'll get there as quick as I can," Ray said, slamming the phone into the cradle.

He removed his hand from the wall and immediately started feeling unsteady. The room started to spin. He looked for something to hold onto. Grabbing the refrigerator door handle, he inhaled a deep breath and waited until the room stopped spinning.

Ray's headache was getting worse by the minute. Holding tightly to the refrigerator handle, he opened the door, leaned in and grabbed a cold Budweiser. He stumbled over to the kitchen table, collapsed onto a chair, pulled the tab and began pouring the cold liquid down his throat in a long, deep swallow. A pleasant, relaxing feeling began flowing through his body. The only sound was coming from the faint hum of the Frigidaire that kicked on right where it left off a few minutes ago.

Ray was having trouble clearing his head. He needed time to make sense out of this senseless situation, then, his best friend and companion, Elvis, sensing something was wrong, came out of the bedroom, his jangling tags echoing sharply. The dog stepped between his knees, laid his head on Ray's thigh, shoving his nose deep into his crotch. He looked up with big brown adoring liquid eyes that didn't blink, while Ray stroked his head idly.

Looking down at his scraggy mutt, Ray couldn't resist a smile. "What the fuck's going on around here, Elvis; waking a man at this hour about some goddamn murder? Don't sound right to me, how about you?" Ray said, causing the dog's ears to perk up.

Ray often spoke to his dog like he was human, even though he never received any response. Elvis continued staring up with a blank expression. His ears were standing straight up and his head was slightly tilted while listening to Ray rambling on about a possible murder in Barefoot Bay.

Sipping his beer, reflecting on the possibility he could have a murder case on his hands sent a shiver down Ray's spine. The room suddenly felt cold and clammy. If this turned out to be a murder, Barrett knew he wouldn't be able to ignore the problem like he ignored most other problems, by buying a case of beer, locking himself in and getting hammered. He knew the residents of the retirement community would want this matter taken care of, and taken care of quickly.

Finishing his beer, he was about to stand up when he noticed the same blacker than black Florida cockroach, also known as a palmetto bug, that he had been trying to kill for weeks, sitting on the edge of the sink staring him down. It was at least an inch long. It was making a crackling sound with its wings, challenging Ray. He raised the empty can, took careful aim, then, threw the beer can in the direction of the enormous critter. He missed his target by several inches, then watched the can bounce around the floor until it came to rest against the wall. In the wink of an eye, the critter vanished among the mound of dirty dishes in the sink.

Ray shook his head. "You black bastard; I'll get you one of these days," Ray said, a forced smile covering his face, secretly enjoying the game that had been going on for weeks.

Confident he could act sober enough to handle whatever was going on in the Bay, and realizing he had no choice anyway, Ray reluctantly went into the bedroom to get dressed.

Deciding not to go through the trouble of getting into his uniform, he looked at last night's clothes lying in a heap at his feet. He put them back on. They were soiled, rumpled, and reeked with the smell of day old cigarettes and beer from Bottoms Up, but there was nothing cleaner.

Once dressed, he walked back into the kitchen. Elvis remained sitting in the middle of the room watching him closely. "Hold down the fort until I get back," he told him.

Before leaving, Ray went to the refrigerator and took out a traveler for the road. He knew he needed to somehow get through tonight and believed another beer would help clear his head. With any luck, Patrolman Callahan and the Emergency Medical Team were mistaken about this being a homicide. If they were, and he believed that was the only sensible explanation, he'd come back home, drink a couple more beers, crawl beneath the sheets and hope the spiders will leave him alone.

CHAPTER 2

THERE WAS VERY little traffic on Route 1. Ray was driving with the window down, the cool night air helping to clear his head, while the headlights from his beat up Ford Focus cut through the darkness with the ragged image of the moon reflected in the running water of the Indian River on his right. The beer he grabbed for the ride was doing the trick. Between sips he held the icy can to his aching forehead. The coolness of the metal was beginning to ease his pain. After the last gulp, he threw the empty can into the back seat amongst a pile of old newspapers, seldom used tools, coffee cups, and other empty beer cans scattered across the floorboard.

With trembling hands, he grabbed the steering wheel tightly as he forced himself to take shallow, deep breaths in order to better concentrate on what might be waiting for him at the retirement community. Except for a freight train rumbling in the distance that blew three long, lonely blasts when it approached a railroad crossing, the night appeared to be spooky quiet.

Once the five digit security code was punched in, the metal framed gate slid open. Chief Barrett continued down Barefoot Bay Boulevard. Most of the homes were in complete darkness. Residents in the Bay retired early and got up with the sun. Ray being familiar with the community drove directly to Dolphin Drive.

Manufactured homes in Barefoot Bay look alike. The homes are well maintained with look-alike carports and look-alike lawns that are mowed regularly. The yards have an abundance of look-alike, eye-pleasing potted roses, among flaming hibiscus, bougainvillea and azaleas.

Barefoot Bay residents are good people. The person living next door isn't a stranger. They speak to one another regularly, almost to the point of being nosy, and never forget to ask about your health in a friendly manner. Whenever anyone needs assistance there's never any shortage of volunteers.

Rounding the corner onto Dolphin Drive, the first vehicle Ray saw was a large red-and-white box-shaped EMT truck, its motor idling, with lights flashing. Directly behind the EMT truck was the Town of Micco's only cruiser, its blue and red bar lights streaking into the night sky.

Barrett noticed while driving down Dolphin Drive, unlike the rest of the homes he passed, these houses were lit up. Groups of people were gathered in clusters of four and six along the street, wearing pajamas and bathrobes, whispering like their attending a wake and pointing in the direction of the house where all the commotion was going on, wondering what the hell was happening.

Ray pulled his ten-year-old Focus with over one-hundred-fifty thousand miles on it, behind the patrol car, turned off the headlights, cut the engine and reluctantly got out. He marched unsteadily up the cement driveway.

Finding the front door open, he entered and was immediately greeted by Bob Thurston of the Emergency Medical Team, and Bob's assistant, Paul McGrath. Both wore identical light blue shirts with EMT patches on their sleeves. Thurston was someone Ray was familiar with; over the years their paths had crossed when called on to answer other emergency situations, but with his head pounding, the Chief couldn't remember his name.

On the floor, lying directly in front of him was the lifeless body of a man.

Thurston's memory was better than Barrett's. "Hi, Ray. Hate to disturb you so late at night. I thought you should be notified about what I think happened here. I don't like the looks of this," Bob said, shaking his head, then, began walking toward the corpse.

Chief Barrett hesitated, then followed.

Bob shook his head. "When we got the call, I figured just another routine heart attack. After looking closer, I doubt this guy had a heart attack. Come closer. I'll show you what I mean," Thurston said, taking out a pair of glasses from the leather case in his shirt pocket. Getting down on one knee, he pointed at the bruises about the face and neck of the victim.

Barrett kept a comfortable distance, his hands shaking and feeling nauseated, looked through bleary eyes where Thurston was pointing.

"See those purple bruises on the side of his jaw?"

"Yeah."

"It looks like he was hit with a blunt instrument, possibly a fist. If you look over here, you'll notice some discoloration and bruises around his neck. That's not normal."

"Couldn't that have happened when he fell?" Barrett asked.

Thurston turned toward Ray. "You all right, Ray? You look awfully white."

"Think I'm coming down with something," Ray said, avoiding eye contact.

Thurston nodded, smelling the beer on his breath, and continued. "I don't think the bruises happened by falling," he explained. "There's also a large bump on the back of his head. That could have been caused by a fall, but not the other two injuries."

"What you're saying is this was done intentionally. That's hard to believe. Things like that just don't happen here."

Thurston stood, took off his glasses and returned them to the leather case. "All I'm saying is I've seen more than my share of heart attack victims. This guy didn't die from a heart attack. I think you should at least have the County Medical Examiner have a look at him before I remove the body."

Ray's shoulders sagged. "Suppose it won't hurt to make sure," Ray conceded, lacking the energy to argue. "Who called you guys?"

"We got the call from the dispatcher shortly after eleven. Someone called in a 911, and they in turn called us. I don't know who originally called. I'm sure it had to be one of the women at the neighbor's house next door. I understand this guy's wife is over there," Thurston said, glancing down at the body, then back to Ray.

Chief Barrett was not happy. Regrettably, he said, "I suppose I better get in touch with the county and get a Medical Examiner out here to find out what we're dealing with."

The EMT nodded in agreement. "I'd feel better if you did. I'll hang around and wait until he arrives."

Finally remembering his name, Ray said, "Okay, Bob."

Ray walked outside to where Patrolman Callahan was leaning against the cruiser. The Chief walked over and instructed him to radio the County Sheriff's Department. "Explain that we have a suspicious death and need the assistance of a Medical Examiner."

Patrolman Callahan immediately got into the cruiser and made the call, while Ray returned to the house to look around. There was something uncomfortably eerie about walking through a house while the person that lived here was lying dead on the floor. It was quiet. It felt as if the house itself had stopped breathing. He kept his hands by his sides, as if touching anything would be a violation . . . of what, he didn't know.

A quick glance told him the people living here had excellent taste and plenty of money. The living room was done in light beige with two long, low couches covered in oatmeal tweed fabric. Between the couches was a large square coffee table with a thick glass top. On each end table there was an antique looking Floridian lamp. Expensive reproductions hung on the walls. The house appeared clean and organized, with high quality furniture.

Nothing seemed to be out of place. No windows were broken. No sign of forced entry. It was obvious if it was a homicide there hadn't been much of a struggle. The master bedroom was done in light green. A large poster bed dominated by a large green checked bedspread was against the far wall. There were two large Spanish dressers, one with a mirror spread across the top, both with brass fittings. Drawers hadn't been ransacked. Clothes were still hung neatly in the closets. The computer desk in the corner hadn't been tampered with. It was apparent that if a crime had been committed that robbery wasn't the motive. He couldn't find anything in any of the rooms that might yield an explanation to what might have transpired.

"The Sheriff's Department is sending a Medical Examiner. They suggested we don't touch anything until he gets here," Patrolman Callahan said, entering the bedroom unexpectedly, startling Ray.

"They don't have to worry about that. I have no intention of touching anything, especially that guy," Ray said, nodding in the direction of the body as they walked back into the living room.

"What's the problem? He's dead! He can't hurt you," Andy said, looking amused.

"I don't care. I don't like dead people." Barrett said as he continued walking out the front door, ignoring the corpse.

"They're also sending a photographer," Callahan explained.

Standing outside, Ray said, "Thurston said he thinks the wife is next door. That right, Andy?"

"Yes sir. From what I been told, his wife was playing bingo with her friends at St. Luke's. One of the women called 911. She thinks her husband had a heart attack."

"He might have. As far as I'm concerned, until I hear differently, he had a heart attack," Ray said hopefully. "Let's wait until the Medical Examiner gives us a report before jumping to any conclusions."

Ray's headache was getting worse. "Any idea what the guy's name is?"

"According to the name on the mailbox, it's Gagnon." Callahan was anxious to get going. "If you don't need me, I should be getting back out on the road, sir."

"Okay, Andy."

The words were no sooner out of Ray's mouth when Callahan got in his patrol car, said goodbye to the EMTs who were standing next to their boxed ambulance, turned off the red and blue blinking lights, and disappeared down Dolphin Drive.

CHAPTER 3

WHILE WAITING for the Sheriff's Department, Chief Barrett decided to go next door and talk to the wife. The crowd on the sidewalk that had assembled earlier had mostly dispersed. Bob Thurston and his assistant were now sitting in the ambulance waiting for further instructions. The night air smelled damp and musty, as Ray made his way across the damp grass to the house next door. Walking up the driveway, he could see into the living room through the large picture window. He noticed about a half dozen people scattered throughout the room.

Approaching the side entrance by way of the unlit carport, he observed a large man leaning against the side of the building. He decided to speak to him. "You live here?" Ray asked.

The stranger was about to light his cigarette. Ray's question momentarily stopped him. He remained motionless for a second while the match burned down. Before answering, he lit the cigarette before the flame scorched his fingers. The red eye flashed when he took a puff, then he dropped the match. He exhaled a stream of smoke through his nose before answering. "No. I live down the street."

Because of darkness, Ray couldn't get a good look at him. From what he could observe, the man appeared to be huge, over six feet tall, enormous shoulders with a football player's body that had over time turned soft. The glow from the cigarette showed the face of someone with rugged features, intimidating dark eyes and squared jaw.

Ray disliked this man immediately. Even in the darkness, he felt the man's eyes staring at him in a threatening manner. "What's your name?" he asked.

After taking a long drag on his cigarette, the stranger tilted his head back and exhaled into the night. "Who wants to know?"

Ray didn't like the comment. He was the Chief of Police, for Christ sake. People were supposed to respect him. "I should have introduced myself. I'm Chief Barrett, Micco police," he said sarcastically, reaching for his wallet, flipping it open and displaying his badge.

Realizing who he was talking to, the stranger's attitude changed.

"Nick Pappas."

Even with a slight evening breeze, sweat appeared on Ray's forehead; his heart was pumping like a piston while thinking, *I wish to Christ I had a drink.* "You a friend of the Gagnon's next door?"

"Betty's good friend's with Kathy. We get together with them once in a while."

"I'm sorry, but I don't know any of these people. Who's Betty and who's Kathy?"

"Betty's my wife. Kathy's married to Phil, the guy that had the heart attack."

Chief Barrett saw no sense in mentioning what he suspected. Seeing no reason to continue this conversation, Ray said, "I better get inside and talk to Mrs. Gagnon. I'm sure I'll be talking to you again," he said, eyes squinting, attempting to get a better look at the man who called himself Nick Pappas.

Before Ray walked away, Pappas dropped his cigarette, crushing it with his foot, his eyes never leaving Ray. There was something about this stranger that bothered Barrett. He had a hunch about this guy that didn't feel right. He didn't know why. It wasn't always easy to explain how his hunches work. They seem to exist in an emotional no-man's-land. It was just a feeling that came over him.

Entering the house, Ray was greeted with concerned stares. There were four women and two men in the room. Off to his left stood a man and woman; they appeared married from the way they were leaning against each other, as if keeping each other from falling. The woman was crying quietly. The man was talking softly to her.

On the opposite side of the room sat a large man in an oversized leather recliner. He appeared soft and flabby. A man who liked his food rich and often and needed to lose some serious weight. Even seated, Ray estimated him to be well over six feet tall and around three hundred pounds. Unlike the man he encountered outside, this man didn't look at all threatening. Although something about him looked wrong. He appeared unconcerned, bored and distant with what was happening around him.

In the center of the room, three women were sitting on a large leather couch. The woman seated on the left was extremely attractive, wearing plaid shorts and a white sleeveless blouse. She appeared to be in her late fifties. She had beautiful blue eyes, a light tan complexion with skin that had yet to show signs of aging. Her hair was a nice shade of grayish silver and neatly combed. The more Ray stared at her, the more familiar she became. Any woman this attractive wasn't someone he was likely to forget. He began searching his memory for where they had met, but with his head throbbing, drew a blank.

The woman sitting on the right was the complete opposite from the woman on the left. This lady had strong, rugged facial features, broad shoulders and a stout, compact body. Her straight brown hair was cut short, showing signs of turning gray. She had brown eyes and no makeup on. She wore men's khaki slacks and a dark blue golf shirt opened at the collar. Her right arm was draped securely around the shoulders of the woman in the middle who was crying openly, while leaning into her, muttering words of comfort. The crying woman in the middle, Ray assumed was the wife of the dead man lying on the floor next door.

The room suddenly went quiet. Chief Barrett stood in the center of the living room on shaky legs, painfully aware of the slight, uncontrollable trembling of his hands. He began speaking, hoping the involuntary quivering wasn't noticeable. "Mrs. Gagnon."

"I'm Mrs. Gagnon," the crying woman answered, while twisting a damp Kleenex nervously between her fingers, occasionally wiping her eyes.

"I'm Chief Raymond Barrett. I'm with the Micco police. I'm very sorry about your husband."

Struggling to control her emotions, she took a moment to pull herself together. "Thank you."

Everyone continued staring, listening attentively with a blank expression on their faces; except the attractive woman with the silver hair who was squinting slightly. A faint look of recognition flickered in her eyes as if she knew him from somewhere.

"Mrs. Gagnon, I just want to inform you I've gotten in touch with the Sheriff's Department in Melbourne. They're sending people to examine your husband's body."

Her eyes widened a bit. "I don't understand. Why would you do that? Is something wrong?" she asked, her Kleenex wiping away a tear.

Everyone being under the impression Phil had died from a heart attack, now hearing the police officer indicating there might be more to Phil's death were listening attentively. "The EMTs found a large bump on the back of your husband's head. They also found bruises on his face and neck. These bruises are cause for concern. In situations where we have questions about the cause of death, we're required to check them out."

"Are you saying that Phil didn't have a heart attack?"

"No . . . not at all. I'm not saying that. I just have to be sure foul play wasn't involved. It's a routine procedure. I'm sure everything will be fine," he explained.

"Well, I'm sure nothing like that happened," Mrs. Gagnon said, looking around the room for support from her neighbors.

"I'm sure that's the case. Like I said, we just have to be sure, that's all."

After spending a half-hour consoling and assuring Mrs. Gagnon there was no need to be concerned, Ray heard an automobile arriving next door. Realizing it was the Sheriff's Department, he took this opportunity to leave, or escape; he wasn't sure which. "It sounds like they're here. I'll be in touch. I'll let you know what's going on, Mrs. Gagnon," Chief Barrett said, then hurried out the door.

While walking out, Ray noticed the man he encountered in the carport, now standing inside, leaning against the wall next to the open door. His arms were folded defiantly across his chest. He appeared more threatening in the light of the living room than outside under the cover of darkness. Although he had a slight smile on his face, his steady gaze showed no signs of friendship, while his eyes appeared full of anger and rage.

Looking beyond him, avoiding his uncomfortable stare, Ray walked out into the refreshing night air, the coolness helping to clear his throbbing headache. He made his way across the lawn to where there was a Sheriff's cruiser parked in the driveway next to the Gagnon's BMW. When Ray approached, he said, "Thanks for coming."

Ray hadn't bothered putting his uniform on when he hurried out of his house earlier, so, the man paid him little attention. "I'm Chief Ray Barrett. I'm the one in charge here," he said, pulling his wallet out, showing his badge that was attached to the worn, imitation leather.

After a quick glance, the tall, stately looking man extended his hand and said, "Sorry, I didn't recognize you. I'm Barry Whiting, Medical Examiner, from the Sheriff's Department. What do we have inside?"

"Not sure. I think it's a heart attack, but I noticed bruises on his neck and face. They don't look right. I figured it'd be best to have him checked out."

"Let's have a look."

Just then another car pulled up. A short, stocky man got out and began walking at a leisurely pace, carrying a camera, and followed the parade into the house without speaking. Once inside, the Medical Examiner knelt down and began examining the corpse. After carefully examining the bruises, he agreed with Ray. "Think you might be right. Those marks don't look right." Turning to the man with the camera, the Medical Examiner said, "Is anyone else coming, Matt?"

"Not unless you think it's necessary. The officer that radioed in the request for assistance reported the guy most likely had a heart attack. They didn't think it was necessary. What do you think?"

"It's hard to say. It doesn't look like much of a crime scene. I think we can wait until the autopsy is done before we call it a homicide. But since you're here, why don't you take your pictures so we can get the body removed and get the hell out of here. I was supposed to be off hours ago."

Ray, wanting nothing to do with the investigation, stepped off to the side and watched while the photographer worked efficiently without hesitation. He apparently encountered this kind of situation on a regular basis. He knew exactly what he was doing. He began waltzing around the body, shooting pictures like the corpse was a fashion model. Getting down on one knee he took several close-up pictures of the victim's head and neck from different angles, then took several more of the area surrounding the corpse, never wasting a move. Within minutes the photographer completed his work.

Before leaving, Barry Whiting informed Ray not to touch anything inside the house. He said, as a precaution, he was going to request the department send a crew from homicide in the morning to look around in case it did turn out to be a homicide, but it didn't look like there was much to uncover. He also said he wouldn't be doing the autopsy. He informed Chief Barrett the Coroner's Office would be in touch but suggested he call them, rather than wait for them to call him with the results, then the Medical Examiner got in his cruiser and left, following the photographer down Dolphin Drive.

Bob Thurston and his assistant, who had been waiting patiently outside, were told by Chief Barrett, "You're going to be transporting the body. The coroner is going to do an autopsy to determine the cause of death. Hopefully they'll find the guy had a heart attack, and that'll be the end of it."

Anxious to get started and on their way, the two men grabbed the gurney from the back of the EMT truck and hurried up the driveway, pushing the gurney in front of them. They slid the corpse into a zippered body bag, lifted it onto the gurney and covered it with a white sheet. Once the body was securely strapped on, they wheeled it out the door and down the carport. Without much effort, the men slid the metal gurney into the back of the EMT truck, slammed the door and quickly drove away.

It was now after 2 a.m. Ray's head was pounding relentlessly, unaccustomed to being awakened in the middle of the night after spending several hours at Bottoms Up to investigate a possible homicide. There wasn't anything he could do without the results from the autopsy, determining if there was any reason to believe he had a homicide on his hands. He walked back to the neighbor's house and informed Mrs.

Gagnon it would be best if she didn't return home tonight. The stout woman who had been consoling her assured Ray that Kathy would be spending the night with her.

After relating this information, Barrett walked back to his car and collapsed behind the steering wheel and told himself to relax. He sat motionless for a moment, rubbing his face absentmindedly, letting his head fall back, and began staring through the windshield.

A large cloud passed in front of the nearly full moon. Ray took a deep breath, then slowly let it out, the taste of stale beer still in his mouth. The night had not gone well.

He turned the key and the out-of-tune engine started on the second try, the clicking of a sticking valve echoing in the air. Totally exhausted, he found an all-night country music station on the radio and turned it up loud so the music would keep him awake and listened to Johnny Cash singing *Ring Of Fire*. All he wanted to do was drive back to his trailer home where a cold beer and Elvis would be waiting.

He would deal with the suspicious death of Phil Gagnon in the morning.

CHAPTER 4

Phil & Kathy (Hennessey) Gagnon

Married June 5, 1966

PHIL SAT AT THE kitchen table. It was still early. The sun hadn't fully risen over the tops of the large, old oak trees in the back yard, its reflection not yet revealing its blinding glare. It was not even seven o'clock, but he was already feeling tired, angry and sad; tired of seeing his mother this way; angry because she didn't seem to care; sad because he had to stand helplessly by, knowing it was only matter of time before her drinking would destroy her.

He watched her shake her head the way a dog would shake water from its back, clearing her mind, getting prepared to face another day. She stood in front of the kitchen sink, staring into the back yard, her premature gray hair disarranged, her body sagging, the burden of life weighing heavily on her shoulders.

Being the mother of five children and living with a husband that she no longer loved had taken its toll. She had lost the will to go on. Things seemed to get worse with each passing day and she knew getting through today would be a bigger challenge than yesterday.

Philip sat at the kitchen table, moving the cereal around with his spoon. He could see the lines of age streaking down her neck, her skin hanging loosely from her bones; she appeared to be shrinking like a beach ball that was losing air from an invisible leak. He was confused, confused between feelings of sorrow and hatred. It frightened him to think it sometimes came into his mind that he wished his mother dead, wanted her out of his life.

She inhaled the last drag from her cigarette, stuck the burning end under the dripping faucet and dropped the butt into the sink. Then she slowly turned, squinting through red, wet eyes, and said, "Shouldn't you be getting ready for school?"

"Still got plenty of time; the bus doesn't come for another hour."

"Kids up?"

"They're getting dressed."

She lifted the glass to her lips and took a swallow. "Make sure they eat breakfast before they leave for school," she said. "Their lunches are made and in the refrigerator. Make sure they don't run out and forget them. Think you can do that?"

"Don't I every morning?" he mumbled, looking off in the distance, pretending he didn't see her sticking the bottle into her purse.

"I appreciate your helping out like this, Philip. Don't know what I'd do without you," she said, while turning towards the sink, rinsing her glass under the running faucet, then dropped it in the sink, where several flies suddenly scattered from amongst the dirty dishes.

She jumped and began shaking her head wildly. She hated flies with a vengeance. "Jesus Christ, these goddamn flies are going to drive me crazy. You'd think that lazy bastard could at least fix the screen," she spat out, her face twisted with anger, glaring at the hole in the screen.

"Just close the window."

"Close the window? It feels like a hundred degrees in here. Why can't he just fix the goddamn thing? Is that so much to ask?"

Phil knew better than to continue this conversation while she was in such an angry mood. It seemed lately she was always angry. "Going to work?" he said.

She stared at him for a moment. She didn't like the question. "Yes, I'm going to work. And what goddamn business is it of yours if I do or if I don't," she spat out.

He cast his eyes toward the floor. He felt an uncontrollable pressure rising in his chest, fighting the pull of depression which was trying to suck him down like he was caught up in an ocean undertow.

Many mornings it looked like she was about to leave for work; then, she would decide not to go. During these alcoholic episodes, she would spend the day in bed, getting up only to pour another drink. By afternoon, she would be tossing and turning, and begin sobbing, deep down from the pit of her stomach sobs, then, suddenly stop. Soon after, the sobbing would be replaced by a crazy, screaming, hysterical rage that frightened the living daylights out of him and his brothers and sisters.

"I've got to get going or I'll be late," she said, grabbing her pocketbook and tattered sweater from the back of the kitchen chair before hurrying out of the house, banging the screen door behind her. It wasn't until Phil heard the car start up and pull out of the driveway before he felt comfortable enough to relax.

Now that she was gone, Philip slowly stood, looked up at the long crack running zigzag across the ceiling and shook his head, feeling years older than his thirteen years and wondering why couldn't his mother be like other kids' mothers who remained sober, who were cheerful and friendly? For as long as he could remember, he had wanted a different mother, like the mothers on television shows, mothers who wore aprons while cleaning the house, cooked meals and looked after their children. Like Mrs. Cleaver on *Leave It To Beaver.*

He was confused; confused between feelings of sorrow and hatred. It frightened him to think it sometimes came into his mind that he wished her dead, wanted her out of his life. At times he felt pity for her; but other times he thought he loved her because she was the only mother he had, however painful it was, then, his feelings would turn back to shame and regret and then back to hatred, and he asked himself, *is it possible to both love someone and also hate them?*

It was time to get the kids ready for school. He was responsible for seeing that they ate breakfast, were dressed, and had their school assignments securely in their backpacks along with their lunches. He would get no help from his father, James "Big Jim" Gagnon, who made sure he was gone before anyone woke up, avoiding any contact with his family.

The situation became worse when his mother arrived home. She was in no mood to put up with her children. It wouldn't be until she had her hands around a glass of vodka that she could function and tolerate her life. It was evident watching her hurrying around the kitchen preparing supper, banging pots on the stove—ding-bang, slamming the refrigerator door—wham-thump, that there was no doubt she did not enjoy being the caretaker of five children.

Philip wished he could walk away and never return. But he knew he could not. Being the oldest, taking care of his younger brothers and sisters had become his cross to bear. He knew that if he didn't look after them, nobody else would.

Philip was sixteen when the ambulance arrived. The children stood helplessly by, looking at their mother's shrunken body as the gurney passed by; her face was wrinkled, her cheeks hollow and sunken, giving her the appearance of an old woman who had long ago lost the will to live. His younger sister, Pamela, was holding tightly to Phil's hand, listening to her mother's screaming and cursing.

"Get your fuckin' hands off me; why can't you just leave me alone? Somebody please help me," she screamed.

"She's got the DTs," one EMT said while wheeling her out of the house where the neighbors had gathered across the street, shaking their heads.

"I don't want to go. Oh, Christ! Why can't you leave me the fuck alone?" She continued to scream as attendants easily slid the gurney into the back of the ambulance, slamming the door shut before rushing her to the hospital as Pamela watched, then, buried her face against Phil's side, tears sliding down her cheeks.

Once admitted, after a series of tests, it was determined her liver was severely damaged beyond repair. The doctors said it could be months, weeks or even days, but her dying was inevitable. Two days after she was admitted to the detoxification clinic, she passed away. By then, Phillip had convinced himself that he didn't care and never even bothered to visit her in the clinic to say goodbye. Phil couldn't help himself; his first thought when he was told she had died was *Thank God*.

If losing his wife had any effect on "Big Jim," it never showed. Every day after work, he collapsed, all 6 feet 3 inches of his 260-pound body, onto his favorite, worn and tattered recliner. He spent evenings smoking one cigarette after another, drinking beer, reading the newspaper, and watching whatever sporting event was on television. He appeared content with his life and didn't seem to care what was going on around him.

Big Jim was employed as a sanitation engineer, picking up trash off the curbs in front of people's houses. It wasn't glamorous work and didn't pay much, just barely enough to pay the bills and keep him in beer and cigarettes.

The Gagnon's house was the eyesore of the neighborhood. Philip's father never found the time to make any repairs. Peeling green shutters were left hanging lopsided next to cracked windows. There were cabinet doors hanging on broken hinges; water dripped from leaking faucets, and nobody seemed to notice, or if they did, they didn't care.

The children grew up knowing they were dirt poor, and accepted these living arrangements as the way things were supposed to be. They learned at an early age to get by with what they had, which wasn't much.

Philip watched his father arrive home from the Public Works Department, looking exhausted and smelling of other people's garbage. In the summer his face looked like weather-beaten raspberry-colored leather from the sun. During winter, even though he wore several layers of clothing, he appeared to be frozen to his bones. Philip decided there had to be an easier way. He didn't consider the old man someone worth emulating; that was definite, and was determined not to follow in his footsteps.

He didn't like growing up in a family that didn't have two nickels to rub together and looked down on by the neighbors. He grew up in poverty, seen it, smelled it, tasted it, and was determined to change things. He wasn't sure how, but he knew the only positive thing about living this close to the bottom was there's only one way to go from here. He knew it wouldn't take much to turn everything around.

Once his mother passed away, running the house was his responsibility. It was up to him to see to the needs of his brothers and sisters, which he reluctantly did out of necessity and without complaining. He learned at a young age to be responsible, and by maintaining a positive attitude, he became stronger and determined to do whatever he had to get ahead.

Entering high school Phil had grown to be tall and strong. He walked the corridors with an attitude of superiority, his muscular shoulders moving slightly, making eye contact with everyone he passed, and greeting them with a broad smile on his handsome face, masking the pain, loneliness and anger that lingered just below the surface.

He was an outstanding athlete and serious competitor. He had a reputation for never losing gracefully. He always gave a hundred percent and expected his teammates to do the same. Giving up never entered his mind, not even for a moment.

Phil was a winner, born with the killer instinct. He believed the kids who played to win wanted to beat their opponent's brains in, showed no mercy—those were the ones who won. Every time his team lost, Phil would get upset and never hesitated to let his teammates know that losing was unacceptable.

The high school athletic director, Coach Murphy, a man with a barrel chest, wide shoulders, sparkling blue eyes, and one continuous bushy eyebrow, wearing a big brush moustache that twitched when he got excited, often commented, "This lad will give ya' his best. He's a winna', that one. No give-up in him."

Phil never let his troubled home life or inner emotion show around other people. It was difficult to understand what went on beneath the surface of his handsome face. One thing was obvious: he knew how to turn on the charm when it was to his advantage. He was extremely bright and blessed with the gift of gab whenever the need arrived. He refused to accept the disadvantages of being poor as an excuse for failure. He was determined to overcome whatever obstacles were put in his way and he never doubted he would make something of himself.

Growing up, Phil developed two different, separate identities. There was the congenial Phil, who was humorous, unpretentious, easy going and friendly toward everyone. Then there was the other Phil Gagnon, the efficient machine that seldom made mistakes. He could be standoffish and often withdrew into himself, caring about no one but himself. He questioned everything. He was convinced that God didn't care about the poor, and the meek would not inherit the earth. It was all a bunch of bullshit.

He and he alone would take charge of his destiny.

CHAPTER 5

HE LEANED FORWARD and paused, his reading glasses on the tip of his nose. Looking over them, elbows firmly placed on his desk, he said, "This is very serious. I can't stress enough the importance of getting plenty of bed rest."

The voice belonged to Dr. Swanson, his tone brisk and businesslike. "We're fortunate to have discovered it early. If you get plenty of rest and follow my instructions, there's no reason why you and the baby won't be fine," he said, keeping them calm by speaking so positively.

"I don't understand. I've been feeling good. Then, for no reason my legs began swelling and I'm suddenly tired all the time," Susan explained, first glancing at her husband, then back to the doctor.

Dr. Swanson was an attractive, freckled-faced, middle-aged man with reddish-brown hair, bright alert eyes, bushy eyebrows and a no-nonsense attitude. "You were lucky. Few women are aware they have a problem this early in their pregnancy."

"Preeclampsia; I've never heard of it," Bill interrupted, his brow wrinkled with confusion.

Doctor Swanson nodded. "It's fairly rare. Preeclampsia is a disorder that occasionally occurs during pregnancy. If not caught and treated, it can lead to seizures, strokes, and possibly, in some cases, the mother could lose the baby."

"Well, we'll do whatever you say doctor. We've been waiting for this baby for a long time. We don't want to lose it now," Bill Hennessey said, glancing sideways and smiling at his wife.

"Good! I expect you to keep an eye on her, Bill. If Susan starts getting restless and decides she feels well enough to do a wash, I expect you to get after her," the doctor instructed.

The doctor got up from his chair, indicating the office visit was over.

"Don't worry, Doctor, I'll keep an eye on her," Bill said in a calm reassuring voice.

He and Susan also got up, thanked the doctor for his time, and walked out with optimistic concern written on both their faces.

Four months later

Katherine Marie Hennessey was a gorgeous baby. From the moment Susan nestled her newborn daughter to her bosom, she realized the pain and suffering she endured was worth it.

Susan Hennessey had had an extremely difficult pregnancy. There had been moments when she wondered if she had the strength to make it, spending hours praying to God to help her get through the days and months of boredom, frustration and occasional bouts of pain, lying in bed, waiting to give birth.

The first five months everything seemed fine. Mrs. Hennessey loved being pregnant. Her oversized belly stuck out like a trophy, making her feel special. She walked around with a glow on her face, displaying her pregnancy for the whole world to admire.

Unfortunately, her situation unexpectedly took a turn for the worse. She developed a condition called preeclampsia. A situation caused by a toxic substance circulating in the maternal blood stream.

On the advice of Doctor Swanson, she was confined to bed for the remaining four months of her pregnancy. The doctor went to great lengths to explain that, *"if this condition was not treated, it could threaten Susan's life, as well as the child's"* He insisted on absolute bed rest. The only time Susan was allowed out of bed was to go to the bathroom or take a shower, then back into bed.

As a precaution the doctor suggested having the baby by caesarean birth. Susan wouldn't hear of it. She wanted to experience the feeling of giving birth naturally. So with Dr. Swanson assistance and Susan undertaking a great deal of pain, she had a successful but difficult natural delivery. Even though everything had gone well, Doctor Swanson nevertheless realized how fortunate Susan was to deliver her baby with few complications. He strongly advised against any future pregnancies. Several years later, Kathy asked her mother why she didn't have any brothers or sisters, Susan told her, "God had only given her one child, but it was the best child he had." After hearing that, she never mentioned it again and never complained about being an only child. Taking Doctor Swanson's advice, Kathy would remain an only child.

The Hennessey family lived in the best section of the city. Number 28 Maple Street was an oversized Colonial-style house with a front porch that ran its entire length, clean and elegant in appearance. The lawn was large and well maintained. Flower beds lined the front porch, with irises and peonies. The back yard was spacious with two, large, older elm trees with lumpy trunks and fat leaves that touched each other overhead, providing plenty of shade.

Both sides of Maple Street were lined with similar homes where children flowed in and out of one another's houses; bikes and strollers were left unattended out front on the sidewalks, and the constant sound of family life was evident throughout the neighborhood. Between the street and the sidewalk was a strip of grass with beautiful, old New England maple trees. Each year from late September through the end of October, the leaves would change colors, lighting up the entire area with brilliant red, yellow, and orange leaves.

This area was referred to as the Upper Highlands where the affluent lived.

Kathy's father was a tall, stately looking man. Mr. Hennessey had a warmth and kindness in his face that radiated trust. Everyone felt comfortable doing business with him. He owned the *Hennessey Insurance Agency*. Bill originally opened his business in a storefront in downtown Lowell, Massachusetts. With hard work and long hours he managed to build the business into the leading independent insurance agency in the city. His reputation for honesty, combined with a commitment to make sure each customer received reliable, independent service, was the reason his list of clients continued to grow year after year.

Because they were financially secure, Kathy's mother remained a stay-at-home mom. There wasn't anything exciting about being a maid, short-order cook, or chauffeur, but she loved the life she shared with Bill and Kathy. She had a smile for everyone she met, and never spoke ill of anyone. She was content and wanted nothing more than to keep her daughter safe and happy.

CHAPTER 6

Sixteen years later

"WHAT'S WRONG WITH ME? I'm a junior in high school and look at me," Kathy said.

"Honestly, Kathy, I hope you're not going to start that again. Nothing's wrong with you," her mother explained. She was clearing off the supper dishes from the table and placing them in the sink when her daughter asked the question.

"Well, it's true. Do you think I'm fat?" Kathy asked.

After tying her apron around her waist, her mother filled the sink with hot water and began washing plates and rinsing them under the faucet. "Of course you're not fat," she lectured.

"You're just saying that to make me feel better, aren't you. I am fat, aren't I," Kathy insisted.

"You're still young. You're still in high school. Besides, you don't want to have one of those stick figures. Stop worrying."

"So in other words, I am fat. And how come if I am fat, I'm not getting boobs like the other girls?"

Susan smiled. "You're worrying over nothing. Don't be in such a hurry. You will."

They had just started their nightly ritual. Her mother washed and Kathy dried. "I look like a freak; a fat girl without boobs. No wonder I never get asked out on a date. Every guy in school wants to date Marilyn Peters because she's really built."

Kathy was noticing how her classmates were changing all around her. The boy's voices were getting deeper; they were sprouting facial hair, quickly developing into young men. And it seemed overnight her girlfriends turned into beautiful young ladies. She watched as their breasts blossomed and they looked taller, many shooting up four inches in what seemed like weeks. Kathy felt like she was being left behind, believing she was unattractive, plump in the wrong places, flat in the wrong places, short in the legs, with oily hair and drab looking skin that needed constant attention to keep the pimples away.

"Honey, I know what you're going through. I was a late bloomer. You're going to be fine. Don't be jealous of Marilyn. Girls that develop that early usually end up battling their weight their entire lives. What about the boy you said you liked. Do you think he might ask you to the junior prom?" she asked, reaching up and placing a pile of dishes in the cupboard.

"Jimmy Martin?"

"Yes. I think that's his name. You said he often talks to you. Do you think he might ask?"

"He talks to me every day between classes. Sometimes I think he likes me, but he's kinda shy. I don't know if he will or not."

"Why don't you ask him?"

"Ma . . . you want me to ask a boy to the junior prom?"

"Why not?"

"What if he says no? I'll just die if I don't get asked to the prom," Kathy moaned.

Her mother continued washing, watching her daughter struggling with the problems of growing up and smiled. "Everything's going to be fine, dear."

Two weeks later

Kathy was walking to her next class, talking with Marilyn Peters when Jimmy Martin stopped her unexpectedly in the corridor. Blushing slightly and acting nervous, he asked, "Kathy, I'm sure you know the junior prom is coming up. Well, I was wondering if you don't already have a date . . . well, do you think you might want to go with me?"

Kathy's heart began beating rapidly. She hesitated for a moment, her throat suddenly feeling dry, then in a slightly higher pitched voice than normal, said, "No, I don't already have a date. That would be great. I'd love to go with you, Jimmy. Thanks for asking."

"Well . . . I guess we have a date," Jimmy stammered awkwardly. "I'll talk to you later," he said and quickly walked away.

"Congratulations, looks like you're going to the prom. If you want, we could double," Marilyn offered. "Adam has his own car. I don't think Jimmy drives. We could go together."

"Yes, I'll see if Jimmy wants to," Kathy said as she continued down the corridor, a huge smile on her face.

After the prom, Jimmy and Kathy became inseparable. They could be seen walking together between classes, holding hands and laughing as they made their way through the crowded hallways of Lowell High. Kathy was finally feeling good about herself. And as her mother predicted, late into her junior year and during the following summer, she developed quickly, changing from an underdeveloped, overweight teenager into an attractive young lady.

Unlike the Hennessey family, the Martin family was borderline poor, middle class, hard-working people. They also lived in the Highland section of the city. But they were a world apart. There are two completely different areas called the Highlands: the Upper Highlands was where the Hennessey's lived among the more prominent citizens of the city resided. The Martins lived in the Lower Highlands in a second-floor apartment where as soon as you stepped out of your front door, you were competing for space on the public sidewalk.

The Lower Highlands was made up almost entirely of French-Canadians, often referred to as "Canucks." Most of them found employment in the mills along the Merrimack River, working for minimum wages. The French-Canadian are a close knit group, and by living conservatively with each member of the family contributing what they could, they managed to get by.

Jimmy was an average boy with average features who had inherited the smiling brown eyes, unruly dark brown hair common amongst the French-Canadian men. He stood tall and wiry while possessing the natural grace and physical appearance of a well-adjusted, easy going boy.

As the months passed by and their relationship intensified,

Kathy had developed an unsettling curiosity about sex. She wondered how it would feel to make love to Jimmy. Two of her classmates had definitely done it, or claimed they had, and Kathy began feeling like the odd one out. She felt because she hadn't done it yet, she ought to—and soon, and decided she was as ready as she'd ever be, and decided she wasn't going to wait any longer.

Kathy's aunt who lived in Rhode Island was diagnosed with breast cancer. She wasn't doing well. Every weekend her parents would visit her. Because of the long drive, they spent Saturday night in Rhode Island, leaving Kathy home alone. They always asked her if she wanted to come along, but she always said no. Kathy decided the next time they drove to Rhode Island it would create the perfect opportunity to invite Jimmy to spend the night.

They usually went to Paisano's Pizza House and shared a pizza after school on Fridays, located in the Italian section of the city. It was a favorite gathering place for teenagers after school, and this afternoon wasn't any different. The noise level was considerable with kids laughing, talking and chewing on slices of pizza while listening to Ray Charles singing *"Born to Lose"* on the record machine, making it difficult to talk above the noise.

They were seated in a corner booth. Raising her voice above the racket, Kathy got Jimmy's attention. "Remember when I told you about my aunt in Rhode Island that has cancer?"

Jimmy finished taking a sip of his Coke and reached for another slice of pizza. "Yeah, I remember. How's she doing?"

Kathy shook her head. "Not good. Mom and Dad are driving down to Rhode Island tomorrow morning to visit her. They won't be back until Sunday afternoon. She's pretty sick, I guess."

"That's too bad. Are you going with them?"

"No."

Jimmy looked up after taking a bite of his pizza. "They don't mind you staying home alone?"

"No. They trust me. There's nothing for me to do there. Besides, I didn't know her all that well. The only time I ever saw her was Christmas or during the summer when she would drive up here during her vacation. She isn't married and doesn't have any kids or anything," Kathy said, sounding unconcerned.

"She must be getting really bad if your parents keep driving all the way down there every weekend."

"I'm not exactly sure how bad she is. I heard Dad tell my Mom she could last for months, or she might die anytime. Anyways, since I'm gonna be home alone tomorrow night, I was wondering if you wanted to spend the night at my house?"

Jimmy stopped chewing and stared at her intently. "Do you think it will be all right with your parents?"

"Are you crazy? They'd kill me if they knew. They don't have to know," Kathy said, a smile covering her face while taking a sip from her coke through her straw.

There was a moment of silence, then in a low voice but loud enough to be heard above the noise, Jimmy said, "I don't know. If our parents ever found out . . . I'm not sure that's a good idea, Kathy."

Jimmy was having the same feelings about sex that Kathy had been experiencing lately. He knew exactly what she was suggesting and felt a warm, tingling rush of adrenaline race through his body, but was nervous and uncomfortable with what she was suggesting.

Kathy noticed his hesitation. Her lips became tight against her teeth. She narrowed her eyes. "Well . . . if you don't want to . . . then don't."

Jimmy didn't like seeing her upset, but was still uncertain. "Don't be like that, Kathy. I just don't want you to get into trouble, that's all."

"I won't get in trouble," she insisted, pouting openly.

Taking his napkin and wiping his mouth, he crumbled the tissue into a ball and threw it on the empty pizza platter. "You sure you want to do this?" he asked, already knowing the answer.

Kathy smiled. Victory was within sight. She leaned toward him. Her eyes fixed on his, watching him closely over the rim of her Coke, sucking the last of her soda noisily through her straw. "I'm positive."

"Okay. I'll have to tell my Mom that I'm staying at Joey's house. If I tell her I'm staying at your house, she'll blow a gasket and never let me go."

It was eight o'clock when Jimmy arrived. Kathy had been

ready for more than an hour. Without her parents around, she moved around freely. She had bathed, brushed her hair, and dabbed on a small amount of her mother's perfume. After trying on several nightgowns and nightshirts, she had chosen a pink, loose fitting, cotton housecoat that buttoned in the front. She wore nothing beneath it.

Kathy had been dreaming of this night for months. She wanted to be sure she was ready physically. The talk among the girls at school was it could be painful if you didn't get wet enough. *"You could get ripped apart down there,"* they joked. Earlier, while taking her bath, dreaming of Jimmy, she made sure she was wet enough *down there* and wouldn't get *ripped apart.* When his knock came, she was ready. She welcomed Jimmy with a gentle kiss and a seductive smile.

Jimmy was uncomfortable, timid and unsure. Watching him, Kathy knew she would have to be the aggressor and savoring the power, knowing she would be in complete control. Without any chance of her parents returning, she had no intention of rushing. She intended on enjoying every minute of what would be her first time. She knew he would be at her beck and call once he saw her naked body and do whatever she asked. There wasn't one ounce of regret or doubt in her mind.

For nearly a half-hour they sat quietly and watched television, but Kathy was getting anxious. She kept looking at Jimmy out of the corner of her eye. After another awkward half-hour passed, she decided she waited long enough. She moved closer and whispered in his ear, "I've been thinking about this for a long time."

Jimmy continued staring at the television screen, but didn't speak. Getting no response, she continued. "Kiss me, Jimmy," she urged. When he still didn't respond, she placed her hand on the side of his face and brought his lips down to hers. She kissed him passionately. "When I tell you to kiss me, I want to be kissed," she demanded.

Jimmy was unsure of what he should do, or say. Kathy knew exactly what to do. She took his hand, "Let's go to my bedroom," she said, then led him up the stairs. He followed obediently. When they entered her bedroom, Kathy kissed him again, while taking his hand and placing it on her breast.

Jimmy now became the aggressor. His body felt like it was on fire. He wanted her, needed her and couldn't wait any longer. He began grinding his penis against her, while fondling her nipples with his fingers through her cotton housecoat.

Without warning, Kathy suddenly pushed him away. She felt she was losing control. She wanted to be in control. "Don't be in such a hurry," she said, pushing his hand away.

Stepping back, he said, confusion in his voice, "I thought you wanted me to."

"I do, but not until I tell you to," she instructed. This would be the biggest night of her life. She intended on doing it her way, under her terms and at her own pace.

"Take off your clothes. I want to look at you," she commanded, loving the hungry look of confusion on his face as she slowly slid onto the bed, spread her legs slightly apart, bent her knees up and lifted the housecoat to her waist.

Jimmy began unbuttoning his shirt with trembling fingers before slipping it off his shoulders. Within seconds his pants followed, then his underpants. Standing in front of her completely naked, his penis bulging, his face red with embarrassment, shivering slightly from the coolness of the bedroom, he stared at her near naked body and was instantly a slave to her every demand.

She had never seen a naked boy before. Staring directly at his erection, she said, "It looks funny."

"It does?"

She began to giggle. "Yes."

She enjoyed the way she was able to control the situation. It was the power over him that intrigued her the most. Feeling like she was in control, she instructed, "I'm waiting."

Nervously, he walked over to the side of the bed and was overwhelmed with her beauty. She lay naked, and returning his gaze, slowly spread her legs apart, her eyes filled with desire. She motioned him onto the bed with her open hand. Jimmy slipped onto the bed and began stroking her breast tenderly, then, he was on top of her. Kathy stretched her arms above her head and grabbed hold of the pillow and sucked in her breath when he entered her.

At first it hurt. She was about to tell him to stop, but before she could say anything, it no longer hurt. She started having feelings like she never experienced before. She hadn't expected it to be this intense; it was wonderful. Kathy found her first time having sex with Jimmy to be the most thrilling moment in her young life.

Early the next morning when the sun peeked around the window shade, Kathy Hennessey was no longer a virgin. She knew she had crossed the line. Going from a teenage girl to a woman was an exciting experience. Except for a small amount of bleeding, which she wasn't even aware of at the time, her first sexual experience turned out to be everything she hoped it would be; not disappointment, not anticlimactic like she feared it might be.

"I'll never forget this," she told Jimmy while lying next to him, enjoying the pleasant smile on his face, knowing she had made him happy.

Lying side by side, they were both excited, believing they had taken a big step towards growing up. They were no longer children. They had entered a new beginning in their lives and there was no turning back.

Jimmy looked into her eyes, and after his breathing eased, said, "I love you."

She smiled and whispered, "I love you, too, Jimmy."

After that first night, sex became a routine occurrence. Kathy had discovered what her body was for. She was amazed at the pleasure and power it possessed. Jimmy awoke a sexual excitement in her she couldn't control. Her desire for sex took on an urgency that bordered on obsession. Her need for sex brought about a form of joy, an inexplicable thrill, and she had no intention of suppressing it.

CHAPTER 7

AFTER GRADUATING high school, Kathy headed off to Middlesex Community College. Jimmy didn't have the grades, finances, or desire to continue his education, so, he looked for work, eventually finding a job, like his father and uncles, in the mills along the Merrimack River.

Although they went in different directions, and many things were changing in Kathy's life, she knew she would always love Jimmy. They spent countless hours making plans for their future, believing they were meant to be together. Nothing would ever come between them.

"In case you haven't noticed, this school is loaded with great-looking guys. I'm sure this Jimmy is a nice guy, but you're in college. It's time to move on," she said. The lecture was being given by Helen Richards, a rather plain looking girl Kathy had become friends with shortly after entering college. Helen was a bundle of energy, had a great sense of humor and a contagious laugh that was easily recognizable from across the room.

Kathy, wearing her usual garb, faded blue-jeans, loose fitting cotton blouse with the sleeves rolled up and penny-loafers with white socks, was weaving her way through the hallway cradling her books with both arms folded securely against her body, hurrying to her next class when Helen started giving her the lecture about her social life, or rather the lack of any social life.

Kathy listened attentively, while stepping from side to side without looking up, avoiding a collision with other students. "I'm okay. I'm really not interested in going out with anyone else. I'm happy being with Jimmy. Besides, I've never even gone out with anyone else," ,she said, raising her voice to be heard over the noise in the crowded hallway.

Helen shook her head. "Friday night there's a fraternity party. Come with me just this once. You don't have to have a date. I guarantee you'll have a great time."

"I really can't. I've got studying to do," she lied. Friday nights were pizza night with Jimmy, and she knew he would be disappointed if she didn't go with him.

Helen thought Kathy was missing out on many school activities and tried to convince her friend to get with the college scene. "This is college. You're supposed to be having fun, not just studying all the time." Helen continued watching closely, looking for any sign of encouragement, but getting none.

Listening to Helen was beginning to take its toll. Kathy found herself wondering if in fact she was missing out on some great school activities. While she spent her weekends studying and going to Paisano's with Jimmy, Helen and her friends were going to fraternity parties, Saturday afternoon football games and occasionally, going with a group of classmates into Boston. She was beginning to feel left out.

Helen, not one to be easily put off, continued. "There's something else I haven't told you. Someone's been asking about you," she said matter-of-factly.

"Really? Who?"

"His name is Phil Gagnon. I'm sure you've seen him around. He's knockout gorgeous!"

"I don't think I know him. What's he look like?"

After Helen described Phil, she remembered him. "I know who you mean. Kind of a punk, isn't he?"

"Not really. He comes on a little strong, but he's all right once you get to know him."

Kathy stopped walking, casually placing her hand on Helen's arm. "Every time he passes me in the hallways, he stares right at my chest," she said, speaking softly.

They continued to walk. "So what, all the boys do that. You know what I do? I look them right back straight in the eyes. When they look up and see me staring at them, they look away, embarrassed,"

Kathy shook her head. "This guy's different. I feel like he's undressing me with his eyes."

Helen looked at her sideways and gave her a smile. "How can you not like a guy like that? I'll admit he's little bit cocky, definitely conceited, but he's absolutely gorgeous. What more could you ask for?" she asked. "Want me to fix you up?"

Kathy didn't answer. She had to admit it sounded tempting, but she was convinced she loved Jimmy and was determined to remain faithful.

"Well, what do you say?"

"I've already got a boyfriend, remember?"

"Really, Kathy, you've got to get over that guy. Why don't you let me fix you up with Phil? Just one date, okay," Helen persisted.

They turned a corner and arrived at Kathy's American history class.

"Thanks, Helen, but I really can't," she explained, then walked into the classroom, leaving her friend in the hallway, totally frustrated.

It started out to be just an ordinary school day, shortly after Christmas break when Phil Gagnon arrived in her life. Kathy and Helen were in the cafeteria having lunch when Phil suddenly appeared out of nowhere and stepped over the long bench directly across from Kathy. He was wearing a snug fitting T-shirt with the school insignia above the letters MCC covering his broad shoulders. Casually carrying a doughnut in one hand and a Styrofoam cup of coffee in the other, he put the coffee down, but continued holding the doughnut.

"Hi, Helen, okay if I join you guys?" he asked, speaking to Helen but smiling at Kathy.

His smile at her caused Kathy to feel an unexpected shiver of excitement run through her body. She found him to be irresistibly handsome. He had strong facial features, with mischievous, hypnotic sparkling brown eyes with long lashes. Phil Gagnon was obviously someone who was in control and would never hesitate to flaunt his good looks and intelligence, with enough confidence to teach a Dale Carnegie course.

"Hi, Phil, have you ever met Kathy?" Helen asked, nodding in Kathy's direction.

"No, we've never met; hi, Kathy."

"Hi," Kathy replied meekly.

Phil didn't hesitated, "I don't know if Helen told you, but I was asking her about you. I was wondering if you were going out with anyone. She told me you were kinda going with someone, but it wasn't anything serious. That right?"

"Yes," she said, glaring sideways at Helen.

"Going steady?"

"Kinda. We've been friends since high school." The words were no sooner out of her mouth, when Kathy regretted referring to Jimmy as just a *friend*. She should have told him they were going steady. But she didn't. She suddenly felt trapped and knew what was coming.

Phil, sensing an opportunity, said "Friends? So you're not going steady. That's great. Listen, there's a party Friday night at the Gamma Phi Frat House. How about going with me?"

Helen jumped in. "Hey, that's a great idea. I'm going with Randy. We could double."

"No. I don't think I should," Kathy said, trying hard to sound convincing, but somehow her response came out sounding weak and unsure.

D.L.BOURASSA

Helen, eyes darting back and forth, feeling encouraged, sensing the hesitation in Kathy's voice, said, "Come on, Kathy, we'll have a great time."

"Helen's right, I think you'll have a good time," Phil said in a soft, pleading voice.

Kathy, feeling a layer of nervous sweat on her skin, hesitated, then deciding under no circumstances could she be unfaithful to Jimmy. But, then, shocking even herself, she heard a voice that sounded like it was coming from someone off in the distance, the words tumbling out of her mouth before she could stop them, "I suppose it might be fun."

Kathy's life was about to change. It would be the beginning of a whole new, crazy chapter in her life. She was now dating Phil while trying to keep it a secret from Jimmy. Her life had become a juggling act. She knew eventually something will have to be done, but didn't have the courage to tell Jimmy she no longer loved him. She was an official cheater, sleeping with both boys. She had become what her girlfriends called *easy*. But she's a physical girl who got satisfaction and comfort from touching and being touched, a lover of sex, so she continued seeing both boys, even though she knew it's wrong.

She especially liked the control sex gives her over Jimmy and would miss this feeling of power if she left him. He was obedient, patient, gentle, and considerate. He does exactly as directed, but outside the bedroom, she felt they now have little in common. She knew it was time to move on, but did not know how to tell him.

Unlike Jimmy, being with Phil was fun. It was like dating a rock star. He wasn't just one of the guys, he was *THE GUY*. He was interesting and handsome and smart. Everybody considered her to be Phil's girl. Being Phil's girl meant she was special. Every girl wanted to be special, but every girl wasn't special, only Kathy. And for her, being special was the coolest thing ever. Everywhere they went, students went out of their way to befriend them. Nobody threw a party without inviting Phil and Kathy. They appeared to be the perfect match, the coolest couple on campus. What more could any girl ask for?

There was only one drawback; with Phil the sex was not great. Unlike Jimmy who she had complete control over, she felt Phil was the one in control. They didn't make love, they had sex. It was like he's only interested in himself. He was always in a hurry, treated her roughly and except for an occasional grunt, remained silent while he fucked her. Then once he got what he wanted, disappeared like a puff of smoke. It was like the house had suddenly caught on fire. *"That was great, Kathy. But, I have to get going. I'll give you a call."* Slam, bang, thank you, ma'am.

40

Then he was gone, without even so much as a kiss goodbye, leaving her lying there, thinking *is that all there is?*

Kathy knew she should tell Jimmy about Phil, but she put it off for weeks and weeks, which led to more weeks. As the weeks turned into months, she remained a cheater . . . a cheater with two boys . . . a cheater that knows eventually something will have to be done.

CHAPTER 8

THE VIETNAM WAR was picking up momentum.

Jimmy knew he wasn't going anywhere working in the factory. He was bright and hard- working, but like most smart kids, he soon learned to hate mill work, finding it grinding, boring work, same thing day after day, rain or shine, summer or winter, always the same thing. He was determined not to get trapped in the mills like so many others, working at a dead-end job for wages that only allowed people to get by week to week.

He was aware Kathy was seeing someone else. He had seen them together on more than one occasion, and it bothered him. Actually, it was breaking his heart. He realized it was over between them. He needed to get away.

There was a war being fought over in Vietnam. The country was suddenly full of soldiers strutting around in their sharp new uniforms. He watched as students he went to school with were being transformed from young boys to grown men, soldiers being shipped overseas to fight for their country. Jimmy was feeling left out. He decided joining the Army was what he wanted, giving him a chance to rethink his life.

So he made an appointment with the local Army recruiter. After several meetings, the recruiter explained the many advantages of being in the military and encouraged him to join the other young men that were crossing the ocean and fighting for their country. He decided under the circumstances, this was his best option and immediately signed up.

The following Friday afternoon after signing the papers, he and Kathy were at Paisano's Pizza House when he broke the news to Kathy. "I'm thinking about joining the Army."

Kathy had a slice of pizza half way to her mouth. She stopped, placed the pizza back on the paper plate and pushed the uneaten slice to the center of the table. "You're thinking about doing what?"

"I joined the Army," he admitted.

"So you already joined?" Several weeks earlier she had been shocked by the news that one of her high school classmates had been killed in Vietnam. According to what she had been seeing on television, every day, more and more young American boys were dying over there. She sounded both shocked and concerned when she said, "You're not going to Vietnam, are you? "

"I'm not sure where I'll be stationed. I'm leaving for boot camp Thursday morning."

"This coming Thursday?"

"Yes."

She wanted to tell him that staying home would be safer, smarter. Then she realized he had already signed-up. It was too late to talk him out of it. Looking across the table with a worried look on her face, she said, "Jimmy, if they send you to Vietnam you might get killed over there."

He nodded. He realized she was right, but being safer wasn't always the best way. For some, being a part of something meaningful was worth taking a chance. "Look . . . I joined because I want to fight for my country. I can't just stand by and do nothing. It's just something I have to do."

Kathy hesitated, then, thinking, his leaving would solve her problems. Trying to date both Jimmy and Phil was becoming difficult. She was getting tired of it. She was planning on breaking up with him. His leaving would save her the trouble. It wasn't as if she didn't care for him, because she did. It was just that she knew it wasn't working out. Going their separate ways now rather than later would be best for both of them.

Once they finished their pizza, she invited him back to her house. Kathy's aunt in Rhode Island was still alive but had taken a turn for the worse. Her parents had left early that morning to go to Rhode Island to be with her, making Kathy's house available for them to spend one last night together.

It wasn't long after they arrived at her house that they were in Kathy's bed having unrestricted, anything goes, compassionate sex. Jimmy couldn't get enough of her, and Kathy was anxious to please him. For the first time, he was the one in control. She would do whatever he wanted, aware this would be the last time they would be together.

The next morning after a tearful, but cordial goodbye, Jimmy walked out the door and out of Kathy's life. She had not asked him to keep in touch, and he had not mentioned writing to her either. They both realized it was over. Although she would miss him, her life would be less complicated without him. She was free to spend time with Phil. Everything had worked out for the best.

She could do nothing but wait. It's a terrible thing to wait. Each morning to begin with hope; *maybe it will happen today,* were Kathy's first thoughts each morning. She woke up telling herself she was worried over nothing. But she was becoming more and more concerned with each passing day. She had never been late before. It was now more than six weeks. It was maddening for her to be lying in bed each night hoping she wasn't pregnant, when deep down, she feared she was.

After several weeks of tossing and turning, she woke up one morning feeling sick to her stomach. She jumped out of bed and headed for the bathroom. Wearing only a pair of white underpants and an oversized Boston Red Sox T-shirt, she just barely made it into the bathroom. Holding her hair away from her face with one hand, she gripped the rim of the toilet bowl with the other hand, closed her eyes and let last night's supper gush out. With an awful taste in her mouth and the stench of vomit filling her nostrils, she realized her worst fears had come true; there was no longer any doubt. She was definitely pregnant.

Feeling lightheaded and weak, she flushed the toilet, then, struggled to stand. Kathy stood in front of the bathroom mirror looking strange and different, searching her face for some sign of sanity in what was happening. Slowly she reached out and touched the glass. Maybe it was just a bad dream. She wanted to believe she would soon wake up and discover it wasn't true. But, when her fingers touched the glass, she stared intently at the pale, scared image looking back and knew this was no dream.

Kathy retreated to her bedroom on shaky legs and collapsed into her bed. She lay on her wide, four-poster bed and stared up at the ceiling where the street lights outside made weird shadow figures in the darkness. She pulled the sheets over her head, trying to retreat from the world. She was frightened, knowing she had gotten herself into this mess, and not knowing how to get out of it.

Her first thought was to get rid of it.

She knew her parents would never consent to an abortion. She realized if she decided to have the baby aborted, she would have to do it alone and soon. Kathy had heard horror stories about girls who had gone to an underground abortionist, readily available in the back streets of Lowell.

Just over a month ago, rumors had been circulating about one of her classmates. She didn't know the girl personally, or the details, but the pregnant girl, in a panic, thinking having an abortion was her only option, went to a back-alley butcher who obviously botched it . . . the abortionist cut into her artery, and perforated her uterus, causing her to nearly bleed-out and die. She was rushed to the hospital's emergency room where they performed a partial hysterectomy, and now she no longer could have children.

Thinking about it frightened her. She decided an abortion was out of the question.

Keeping the child was her only option. Her parents would not abandon her; they would be disappointed, but they would not let her go through this alone, she was sure of that. Even with their help, she was concerned if the child grew up without a father, the baby would be branded a bastard. She was determined not to let that happen. She needed to find a father.

She had been having sex with both Jimmy and Phil. Who was the father? She couldn't be sure. Jimmy was no longer around. She had been told he was being sent to Vietnam, so naming Jimmy as the baby's father was out of the question.

After giving her situation a lot of thought, Kathy had only two options. One, bring up a bastard child alone with the help of her parents, or convince Phil he had fathered her baby. She decided to go with her second choice. It wouldn't be like she was lying and misleading him. She honestly didn't know who the father was. Convinced Phil was the only sensible answer to her problem, all she had to do now was convince him he had gotten her pregnant, then, wait and see how things developed.

Phil definitely had a lot to offer. He was intelligent and good looking with a great personality. Her parents liked him right from the first time they met him, and she was sure they would welcome him into their family. Of course, Kathy didn't love Phil, that was definite, but she believed in time, love would come, she hoped. Everything of course depended on whether he would marry her. She had a lot to think about, but not tonight. Tonight she was scared, tired, and uncertain about her future. Tomorrow would be soon enough to put her plan into action.

The following day, Kathy was giving Phil a ride home after school just as she'd done every school day, when he announced he had some good news. He was excited and started talking fast as soon as he got in the car. "Guess what, Randy has Red Sox tickets. They're for this Saturday afternoon. He has four tickets. He's going with Helen and said we can have the other two."

Kathy's fingers tightened around the steering wheel; her eyes glistened with moisture, she ran her tongue over her dry lips, looking like she was about to say something, but pulled out into traffic instead and continued driving without giving a response.

Phil gave her a sideways glance and noticed her lack of enthusiasm. She always loved going to Fenway Park. "Hey, did you hear what I said?"

She continued to drive, staring straight ahead, continued saying nothing.

Phil was now watching her closely. Something was wrong. She had been acting withdrawn and cranky for weeks now, and he didn't know why. But whenever he inquired, she got upset and claimed she was fine. He knew better. "Are you okay?"

Kathy continued driving. When it became evident she wasn't going to respond, Phil continued, "Hey, Kathy, what the hell's going on with you lately?"

She decided this was the right moment. "I'm pregnant!" she abruptly answered, then, waited for his reaction while her statement was left hanging in the air.

Phil wasn't sure he heard right. His shoulders lifted while he took a deep breath, contemplating what she had just said. Then he turned toward her after only a minute, an eternity to Kathy, and asked, "Are you sure? I mean, I thought we'd been careful." His voice quivered slightly.

"All it takes is one mistake," she said, tightening her lips over her teeth.

He thought they had been careful, but maybe he had been careless. But regardless, getting married and having a baby was not anywhere in Phil's plans. He still had three years of college left. He had no idea how he was going to support a wife and child. Quitting school to support a family was the last thing he wanted, or, needed in his life.

A flood of emotions rushed through him while trying to figure out his options, which at the moment didn't seem like many. For one thing, he didn't love Kathy. Like her, yes; love her, no.

His first instinct was to get the fuck out of Dodge. Disappear. Vanish.

"What do you think we should do?" he asked, his voice sounding uncertain.

"Well, I don't want you marrying me if you don't want to. I know my parents will be upset at first, but they'll help me. If you don't want to be a part of the baby's life, I can handle it on my own," she snapped, then the tears that had been on the verge of falling started sliding down her cheeks. Without warning, she abruptly pulled the car over next to the curb. "If you don't care about our baby, then you can go straight to hell. And get the fuck out of my car. You can walk home for all I care," she spat out.

"Hey, wait a minute. Don't get all pissed off. I didn't say I didn't want the baby."

His mind began racing. What she said about her parents caught his attention. Phil Gagnon wasn't anybody's fool. He realized Kathy was the only child of a successful businessman. Her parents had plenty of money. They lived in a beautiful house in the best part of town. They belonged to the best country club in the city. It only took him a minute to figure out as the only son-in-law, he'd be in a good position to eventually take over her father's business and inherit everything that went with it.

He realized this wasn't such a bad idea after all. Phil could hear the knocking on the door of a great opportunity loud and clear. He decided he would be a fool not to answer it.

Then, without any further hesitation, Phil continued, took a deep breath and said, "I'm a little shocked, that's all, Kathy. We'll work this out together. Everything's going to be fine," he said, before reaching over and gently put his hand on her shoulder, giving Kathy an encouraging smile.

This was exactly what Kathy wanted to hear. She wiped away her tears with the back of her hand, then, pulled her car back into traffic. Her plan had worked. Now with that taken care of, there was still the matter of facing her parents. But she was not worried. She knew they would be supportive.

When Kathy broke the news to her parents, they were understanding, and sympathetic, just as she knew they would be. Her father actually seemed happy. He said he was looking forward to becoming a grandfather. He told Kathy that he could tell Phil was a fine young man, and he'd be proud to have him for a son-in-law.

Kathy's mother admitted she was disappointed her daughter wouldn't be having the grand wedding she'd always envisioned, but nevertheless was excited and eager to spoil her soon-to-arrive grandchild.

They decided that Kathy would finish school this year. It was close enough to the end of the school year that she would not show any signs of being pregnant. Next fall when the baby was born, she would take a year off from school to take care of the newborn. The following year, if she wanted to continue her education, her mother volunteered to look after the baby while she went back to school.

Listening to Kathy's father, Philip knew he was making him an offer he couldn't refuse. Mr. Hennessey had offered him a job at his insurance agency. If he was interested, his hours could be scheduled around his schoolwork. After graduation, he would begin fulltime, and eventually take over his business.

Phil couldn't believe his good fortune. Looking around the Hennessey house, he couldn't hide his enthusiasm. What kept going through his mind was this was a hell of a lot better than where he came from. Someday it would all be his. Everything seemed to be falling right into place for Phil, just as he always believed it would.

The wedding was a candlelight ceremony. It was held at St. Margaret's Church, a short distance from Kathy's house, with only close friends and relatives in attendance. After the church ceremony, they had a small reception in Kathy's parent's backyard under a large tent.

Unlike her mother, Kathy had an easy pregnancy. With the assistance of Dr. Swanson, the same doctor who had brought her into the world, Kathy gave birth to a beautiful screaming baby boy. He had a full head of black hair and his hands had curling fingers with wrinkled knuckles and nails that were just dots. With his lips pursed together, making his face appear slightly out of shape, Kathy couldn't help but smile when she noticed he resembled a little old man.

When she took him in her arms, she felt an indescribable numbness unlike anything she'd ever felt before. The pure joy of becoming a mother, combined with a strong sense of relief after giving birth, made her realize this was the most magical moment of her life.

When the nurse placed the newborn on her chest, Kathy closely examined her son's face. Whatever doubt she had immediately disappeared. Kathy realized her son's father was far away in Vietnam, fighting a war. Philip was standing by her bedside with a proud smile covering his face. She realized he could never be told the truth. As she looked down at her child, Kathy was aware that their life together was beginning with a lie, a living lie that she would be reminded of every time she looked into her son's eyes. A secret that would remain unspoken until the day she died.

CHAPTER 9

HE WATCHED the ceiling in his bedroom turn from gray to a pale orange as the sun filtered through the space around the edges of the curtain. His arm was draped across his forehead. He was trying to separate fantasy from reality. As his mind cleared, Ray realized the trip to Barefoot Bay last night had not been a dream. Looking at the digital display numbers on the clock next to his bed telling him it was 9:24; he knew it was time to get moving; as much as he hated to admit it, he had a possible murder investigation waiting for him.

He woke up feeling anxious and confused. His head was throbbing. Every day it was becoming more difficult fighting the battle to stay sober. Each morning he woke up and said, *"Today is the day I'm gonna stop drinking,"* but by five o'clock most afternoons he found himself once again headed for Bottoms Up. He swung his legs over the side of the bed and attempted to stand, but staggered and collapsed back onto the bed. Closing his eyes, he bent forward, took a deep breath and gave a forceful push on the mattress and jerked himself up to a standing position.

He stumbled into the bathroom. The room smelled damp and moldy. His hands were hanging limply by his side, arthritis attacking his lower back, reminding him his best years were just a memory. After stripping off his soiled underwear, letting them drop to the floor, he reached in and adjusted the water temperature in the shower then slowly stepped in. With the steady stream of warm water pelting his body, his mind started to slowly clear. He began going over last night's events and shook his head with disbelief. A murder taking place in Barefoot Bay was unthinkable. *"It just doesn't happen, or, does it?"* Ray mumbled to himself. There had to be a simple explanation for Phil Gagnon's death. *"Seniors just didn't get murdered in the Bay,"* he decided.

After getting dressed he walked into the kitchen and found the same mess that was there last night. The kitchen hadn't been remodeled since he moved in over twenty years ago. The worn linoleum was now faded, cracked and curling up around the edges; cabinets were badly in need of paint, garbage was overflowing the wastebasket, while plates that had been lingering in the sink for days, caked with Ravioli sauce, were lying right along with a collection of dirty cups and glasses.

Ignoring the mess, Ray went looking for a bowl for his morning breakfast. He opened the cabinet door, but there wasn't anything that remotely resembled a clean cereal bowl anywhere in the cupboard. His only option was a bowl left in the sink from yesterday. When he picked the bowl up, a nest of cockroaches began scattering, heading for cover. He rinsed the bowl under warm water, reached into the cabinet for the cereal box, filled the bowl with flakes and added milk from his old round-cornered Frigidaire, then sat down and began eating.

Elvis began whimpering and scratching at the door wanting to be let out. After getting up and opening the door, Ray reached under the sink, took the bag of dog food and filled his bowl. Satisfied Elvis would be okay he reluctantly walked out the door. He was headed for the station to see if the Brevard County Sheriff's Department had called, hoping that the autopsy would come back confirming Gagnon had suffered a heart attack.

Chief Barrett turned west off Route 1 onto County Road 510 toward the center of town. For many years the Town of Micco had been a thriving fishing community, evident by the many empty fishing shacks along Route 1 lining the Indian River Lagoon that were now being left to decay in the Florida sun. The shacks looked old and neglected with their brown weather-beaten exterior with gaping spaces where boards had rotted out. It appeared a strong wind could topple them over and send them into the river. There were still plenty of abandoned skiffs sitting lopsided in dry dock under the cypress trees growing along the river banks, surrounded by broken engine parts. Micco had always been and still was a small out of the way town with little to do; not a town that attracted the well-to-do yuppies driving Volvos and BMWs.

Downtown Micco resembled a small, sleepy-looking village, separated by C.R. 510 which ran right down the middle of the two block business section with only one intersection, a blinker-light constantly flashing yellow on all four sides, hanging over it. On the north side of the street beyond Town Hall stood the Catholic Church with its pointed steeple rising high above the other buildings. On the other side of the church was the Micco Diner with a large Coca Cola sign hanging out front over the entrance where the locals eat breakfast and lunch. Situated in front of the diner on a landing that ran the length of the building was a well-worn bench with a high back with enough room to sit four of the town's old timers who passed the time arguing local politics and discussing sports while watching the daily activities unfold in the square;

not that there's much to look at.

The thing about living in a small town like Micco was you were most likely going to see the same thing at eight on a Saturday morning as you would on any other day. There was Martha, the breakfast waitress standing outside the diner nervously puffing away on a cigarette most mornings, while her customers impatiently waited inside for their refill. Farther down the road is Carl's Auto Repair Shop with its faded sign above two pumps in the service island that read *Shell*, but no longer delivered gas, standing idle out front. The owner Carl, at precisely nine each morning except Sunday, faithfully rolled up the groaning wooden door to announce he was open for business.

On the South side of C.R. 510 was the Indian River National Bank with a clock set into the red brick above the front door, which chimed faithfully on the hour. The other building on this side of the street was Connor's Variety Store with sawdust on the floor where the meats are cut. Connor's also served as the Micco Post Office located in the back left-hand corner where Pete Harris spent three hours each morning sorting and stuffing the mail into individual pigeon holes; next was Ken's Clip Joint, complete with the classic red-and-white spiral pole out front, separated by an alleyway.

The Micco Police Station consisted of two rooms located in the rear of the Micco Town Hall which was the first building you passed when driving through town. The building, although eighty years old, was well maintained and stately looking with a fresh coat of white paint glistening in the sun. Above the double black doors located in the center of the building was a large sign identifying it as the *Micco Town Hall,* the American flag hanging limp out front from the flagpole in the motionless air. Next to the parking lot entrance was a sign shaped like an arrow with the word *POLICE* printed in red letters pointing around back. Over the back entrance is another larger sign which states *Micco Police Station* in bold, gold letters, plainly visible on a black background.

Upon entering, the front room was where Chief Barrett's assistant, Darcy, worked Monday through Friday as dispatcher, file clerk, typist, and anything else that she was asked to do. She was the first person people meet when they arrive in the station. Darcy had this need to know everything before anyone else and loved her job. It gave her access to everything of interest that goes on in town, which until last night wasn't much.

The back room was Ray's office where he spent mornings trying to get over his hangovers, read the newspaper and watched the small TV on top of the file cabinet. It was Darcy's responsibility to bring Ray his paper, a cup of coffee and a donut from Baker's Bagel Shop each morning. Darcy didn't like waiting on her boss; it actually pissed her off, but she reluctantly did it to show she's a team player, hoping it will someday lead to a patrolman's position, something she desperately wanted.

Today being Saturday, when Ray walked in Darcy was nowhere in sight. Darcy refused to work weekends. Anxious to find out what, if anything, the County Coroner uncovered, Ray immediately went to his desk and pulled out his phone directory and located the Brevard County Sheriff's Department's phone number.

He nervously began punching in the numbers. "Brevard County Sheriff's Department," the perky desk person's voice answering the phone stated.

"This is Chief Ray Barrett from Micco. I'm trying to get the results on an autopsy."

"One moment please."

There were two short rings. Then a less cheerful voice came on the line, speaking in a deep, raspy voice, "Coroner's Office."

"Yes, this is Chief Ray Barrett from Micco. I'm calling to see if your men had a chance to do an autopsy on the guy from Barefoot Bay yet."

"Barefoot Bay; I don't see anything. What was the guy's name?"

"Philip Gagnon; it was about two in the morning or shortly after when he would have been brought in," Ray said, while anxiously thumping his fingers on his cluttered desk.

"Well, chances are if it was that late, they didn't get to it last night. There's no one here but me right now. Give me a little time to find out what the hell's going on around here. I'm sure there'll be someone in shortly. I'll call you back."

Disappointed, Ray said, "I would appreciate it. Call me as soon as you find something out."

"Will do; Micco you said?"

"Yes. Thanks. I'll be waiting. If I'm not here when you call, just leave a message," Ray suggested before hanging up.

Without an autopsy report, Ray couldn't be sure he was dealing with a homicide. He decided it would be awhile before he heard anything, so there wasn't any sense hanging around the station. Remembering his mess at home, he decided to go back and start cleaning.

Heading back to his trailer home, driving along Route 1, Ray still couldn't get the image of Nick Pappas out of his thoughts. His mind began racing back to the intimidating Greek he encountered last night standing outside the Gagnon's neighbor's house. There was definitely something about this Nick Pappas that bothered Ray. Every time he pictured him he could see those eyes staring back at him. There was something sinister about him, something scary, making Ray feel uncomfortable. His eyes appeared to be empty and cruel, *"The eyes of a murderer,"* Ray mumbled out loud to himself, *"He looks like a mean son-of-a-bitch. He rubs me the wrong way,"* he kept repeating as he made his way back home. If this did turn out to be a murder case, Ray decided he would start his investigation by checking on Pappas.

CHAPTER 10

Nicholas & Betty (Sullivan) Pappas

Married October 7, 1965

THE FARM WAS alive with activity. Squirrels were busy scampering around, gathering nuts in preparation for the long winter; a grouse suddenly explode with a fearful flapping of its wings, sending already fallen leaves swirling from the ground.

This time of year was special in New England. Indian summer lasts for a short time, then it disappears as quickly as it arrived. The nights appear dark purple; the days have a deep golden glow, and everything feels soft and comfortable. It's a magical time of the year when the hills and woods become a blaze of brilliant colors with the sight of bright red, yellow and fast-paling green leaves spinning and floating through the air, while the sun loses its intense heat but still remains warm, giving a person a sense of peacefulness and serenity.

To some, fall represents the beginning of the end. Summer is behind them and the frigid winter is on its way. But for George and Sophia Pappas, today was the beginning; the beginning of a new life. As they drove into the barnyard, their newborn son lay cradled securely in his mother's arms, his breath soft and steady, almost like a kittens purr.

Young Nicholas spent his childhood growing up on this small New England farm owned by his grandparents in the town of Pembroke, New Hampshire, population less than one thousand. If it wasn't for the pavement on the roads and the telephone poles and wires hanging off them, Pembroke would appear not to have changed in a hundred years. There is a small park in the town square surrounding a white gazebo situated next to a large stone sculpture of a horseman wielding a raised sword. The inscription beneath the rider identifies him as General John Stark, a man that led New Hampshire Minutemen in battle during the Revolutionary War and coined the state's motto, *"Live Free or Die."* It's a community where everyone knows everyone's business. A person's personal life is shared by the entire town, like it or not.

When Nicholas's parents married, his grandparents gave his mother and father a small portion of the one-hundred-fifty acre farm to build the house they called home. The ranch-style house is surrounded by large oak trees situated on top of a hill. On clear winter mornings after the trees shed their leaves, the picture-postcard view of snow-capped Mt. Washington and the White Mountain Range stretching across the horizon is breathtaking.

The soil is dark and fertile, not rocky like most of the land in New Hampshire. It produced an abundance of vegetables which the family sells at a stand located at the bottom of the hill next to the mailbox mounted on a wagon wheel. Vegetables are placed on the stand early in the morning. People driving by take whatever they needed and leave the money in the metal container that sits unattended on the corner of the table. To the best of their knowledge, no one has ever stolen from them. Grandfather Pappas farms the land and does carpentry work to support his family. He is considered the best at his trade. He taught his son, George, the carpentry trade well, and over the years, their reputation for good-quality work at fair prices evolved into *Pappas & Son Construction.*

One bright April day when Nicholas was seven, he and his father were doing chores in the barn. They noticed a pair of old roller skates buried under a pile of lumber, skates his father had used as a child. They decided to build a scooter. When the scooter was completed, Nicholas would travel around the farm with reckless abandon. Before long, they began calling him "Scooter."

One of the proudest days of Scooter's life came on his eighth birthday. He was presented with a pair of Sears, Roebuck work boots, a Levi jacket with brass buttons, and coveralls with plenty of pockets and loops for his tools. He now looked identical to his Dad. What was most important about the outfit was the patch above the breast pocket. In bright red script letters, it announced that he was a partner in *Pappas & Sons Construction.*

Nicholas grew up happy on the farm. He delighted his parents and grandparents with his endless energy. He would constantly follow the older men around, emulating whatever they did. Although at times he would get in the way; neither man complained. They enjoyed having Nicholas with them and patiently showed him how to work with his hands. By the time his thirteenth birthday arrived, he was capable of doing whatever chores were asked of him without complaining. The closes neighbor lived over the hill, nearly a mile away, so Nicholas didn't have many playmates. He spent the hours after school and during the summer vacation working with his father and grandfather.

At thirteen he was five-feet-six inches tall, weighing nearly one hundred forty pounds. He had broad shoulders and muscular arms that were capable of doing the work of most men twice his age. He had no trouble keeping up with his father and grandfather and often kept working when they would be taking a break.

Saturday was a short day. They always knocked off around noon and headed for the firehouse. Both his father and grandfather were members of the Pembroke Volunteer Fire Department. Pembroke was a dry town. The back room of the firehouse served as the local tavern. The men that congregated there were a bunch of down-home, no-nonsense New Englanders who spent Saturday afternoons hanging out, drinking beer, discussing local politics, religion, sports, or whatever else that happened to be of interest to them.

Today's discussion was about the sudden disappearance of the town drunk, Billy Sullivan. He apparently had abandoned his family, running off with a woman he met in a bar in Manchester, leaving his wife and two children.

Billy Sullivan had the entire town talking. Although everyone knew that Billy liked whiskey, whoring and gambling; that was simply a fact, nobody ever expected him to pack up and leave his family. But that's exactly what he did.

Scooter was sitting quietly on the running board of the town's only fire truck, waiting for his father, listening closely to the men discussing the Sullivan family situation. Billy Sullivan's son, Michael, was a classmate of Scooter's. The discussion about his classmate's father running off with a *whore,* that's what the men called her, was of great interest to him.

When four-thirty rolled around, Scooter's father finished his beer, returned the bottle to the case of empties in the corner and said, "Let's go, Scooter, time to head home for supper."

His grandfather had left earlier. It was just father and son in the truck. Scooter sat motionless, staring out the window, unusually quiet. Normally after sitting and listening to the men's conversations at the firehouse, he'd have a thousand questions. He would talk fast, and George would let him say whatever was on his mind. Not until he talked himself out would he settle down and allow his father to answer his questions.

But this afternoon, he said nothing.

Taking his eye off the road momentarily, his father asked, "You're awfully quiet. What's up?"

"Nothing."

His father could see the concerned look on Scooter's face. He knew something was on his mind. "Okay, out with it," he demanded.

Scooter spoke softly; his lips pulled back against his teeth, eyes looking down, fixed on his clenched fist. "I was just thinking about Mr. Sullivan, that's all."

His father shook his head. "Don't know what would make a man do something like that? Nice wife and kids like he has. Don't make sense to me."

Tiny tears began forming in the corners of Scooter's eyes. "You would never leave me and Mom, would you, Dad?"

Scooter's father pulled the truck off the pavement onto the grass. He gave him a sideways glance, then reached over and ruffled his hair. He sat silent for a while. He wanted to be perfectly clear. When he finally spoke his voice was soft and the words came out slowly. With a hint of laughter in his voice, he said, "Don't worry, son, I would never, ever, leave you and Mom, never!"

"Cross your heart," Scooter said, his forehead wrinkled with concern, asking his Dad to take the pledge that they agreed, once taken, could never be broken.

Looking steadily into his son's eyes, he said, "Cross my heart and hope to die," while making an X over his heart with his index finger.

Delighted to see his father had taken the pledge, Scooter looked up at the man he adored, wiping away the small tears with the sleeve of his blue-jean jacket. No one had ever had a more loving and dedicated father. He couldn't help but feel a surge of guilt for doubting his love and felt confident that the ties that bound them were unbreakable and felt reassured his father would never leave him.

George put the shifting lever into drive and returned the truck to the pavement and continued their journey home. With darkness setting in over the tops of the trees, they both felt comfortable that everything had been settled. Nothing would ever come between them.

CHAPTER 11

IT WAS FRIDAY NIGHT, shortly before midnight and only a few days before Christmas, when the Pembroke fire alarm sounded, breaking the silence of this cold December night in New Hampshire, notifying the local volunteer firefighters to drop whatever they were doing and report for duty.

Earlier that evening, with the Christmas tree fully decorated, standing in the corner of the Pappas's living room, the family was in a festive holiday mood. The lights from the tree were being reflected in the window against the blackness of the night. The presents that were to be distributed on Christmas morning were spread beneath it. They were wrapped in bright holiday colors, waiting to be opened.

The weather in New England that winter had been exceptionally cold, even by New Hampshire standards. The Eastern Seacoast had an early snowstorm, and the frigid temperatures that followed kept the snow from melting, creating a winter wonderland that the Farmer's Almanac had predicted would last into spring.

Regardless of how cold it was outside, inside the house everyone was comfortable and cozy. Earlier, Scooter's Dad had stacked the wood in the fireplace and started a fire that was now producing an abundance of heat. The flames were performing a lively dance, giving off spectacular colors of yellow and orange, making the living room bright and cheerful.

Scooter's father was seated in his favorite recliner, watching the Gillette Friday Night Fights on television. His mother was busy knitting an afghan that would eventually find its way to the foot of someone's bed. Scooter was stretched out on his stomach, his head resting on open palms on the floor next to his father's chair, watching the two warriors battling in the ring.

On weekend nights, Scooter was allowed to stay up later than his usual eight o'clock bedtime; when the fight on television ended, he was tired, so he got off the floor, stretched, and said, "I think I'll go to bed."

His father glanced over at him, and said, "Good idea, son. Get a good night's sleep. We have a busy morning tomorrow."

"Good night, son," his mother said, turning her cheek up to receive her good night kiss.

"Good night," Scooter said and went off to his room.

It was Christmas vacation. Scooter had spent the day working with his father on one of their construction jobs and flopped into bed, exhausted. He felt warm and comfortable curled up in the quilt his mother had made and immediately fell into a deep sleep within seconds after his head hit the pillow.

What he wasn't aware of, twenty miles south in the City of Manchester, a fire was smoldering in an abandoned mill complex that would change his life. Just as the living room clock chime the midnight hour, he was jolted awake by the piercing sound of the fire alarm that had sat silent for most of the winter atop the firehouse.

Startled at first, but quickly realizing what it was, Scooter threw back the blankets and dashed out of his room just in time to see his father closing the kitchen door behind him. Going directly to the living room window, he watched his father jump into his truck, his grandfather leaving his house across the barnyard following close behind. Once the engine started, he watched the white stream of smoke beneath the red glow of the trucks taillights disappearing down the driveway. The windowpane was rimmed with frost, and he could see his framed face being reflected in the glass. He remained staring beyond his reflection into the darkness long after the truck's taillights diminished.

When his mother noticed him, she asked, "Scooter, what are you doing up?"

The hair on the back of his neck was prickling, standing erect, and the tight feeling in his stomach was like a clenched fist. He had an uncanny feeling that something was wrong. "Where did Dad go?"

"There's a fire. I'm sure he won't be long."

"Where's the fire?"

"I don't know. Probably just a chimney fire someplace," she said, sounding confident.

"Are you sure?"

"I'm sure everything will be fine. Now why don't you get back to bed; it's getting late."

Unable to get the haunting feeling that something wasn't right out of his mind, he reluctantly walked backed to bed and spent hours tossing and turning. The sheets felt cool and smooth, but even the fresh smell of the linen couldn't relieve the inescapably hopeless feeling that something terrible was happening.

With the morning sun breaking through his bedroom window, Scooter sprang up in bed, recalling last night's fire alarm. Scooter immediately threw the blanket aside and rushed into the living room, anxious to see his father sitting in his chair. But he was nowhere in sight. Instead, his mother was sitting in his recliner, leaning slightly forward, one hand over her mouth the way she did whenever she was worried, watching the television.

Moments before Scooter arrived she had been listening and watching the newscaster reporting on the out of control mill fire that was taking place in Manchester. *"The building continues to burn while the wind rushes across the Merrimack River, fanning the fire, turning it into the worst inferno in the history of the city. Flames and smoke are spiraling over roof tops, while the firemen attempted to shoot water from frozen hydrants in an effort to knock down the flames, but the fire seems to have a mind of its own and gives no indication that it will give in,"* reported the newscaster.

For years before the cloth manufactures moved down South, the mill complex were left vacant, the enormous machines used to produce the cloth had been constantly serviced with generous amounts of oil to keep them running efficiently. Over the years, the oil dripping from the machinery had soaked into the timber flooring, creating a burning inferno once the fire had begun.

"Oh, God, keep them safe," she whispered. She wanted to look away but couldn't. Scooter's mother was hypnotized by the flames, unaware that her son was standing next to her. Catching a glimpse of Scooter out of the corner of her eye, she turned and with a forced smile said, "Good morning, Scooter."

"Is Dad home?"

"Not yet. There's been a terrible fire down in Manchester. A mill caught on fire. The firefighters are still trying to put it out," she explained. She had been awake all night, glued to the television, fingers crossed, waiting to hear news about the firefighters who were believed to have been buried underneath a wall of flaming timbers and bricks.

Scooter stood next to her, watching the burning building on the television. "Is that where Dad is? Is he all right?"

Sensing the fear in her son's voice, she forced herself to speak. "Yes. He's with your grandfather. I'm sure he's fine."

What she didn't tell Scooter was it was reported that a large portion of the mill had collapsed, and several firefighters had been trapped underneath the burning timbers. The reporters weren't confirming or denying if there were any fatalities, but they didn't sound like the outlook was promising.

Not wanting Scooter to hear, she turned off the television, her stomach in knots, and went into the kitchen to begin making breakfast. She was trying to act unconcerned and casual, but it was extremely difficult as she went about preparing Scooters breakfast.

Not having much of an appetite, Scooter only picked at his food. After breakfast he got dressed and went about doing his morning chores, feeding the animals and checking to make sure their water hadn't frozen during the night. By mid-morning snow had begun falling, with large, soft flakes, making the sky appear gray and the sun barely visible.

Scooter was holding securely to a basket of freshly gathered eggs and walking across the barnyard through the falling snow. He had just finished cleaning the chicken coop and was heading for the house to put the eggs in the refrigerator when his father's truck drove into the driveway. His grandfather was behind the wheel. Their neighbor, Ralph Harper was sitting in the passenger's seat. They were followed by two other vehicles driven by volunteer firefighters Scooter recognized from his Saturday afternoons at the fire house.

The vehicles no sooner came to a stop when his mother appeared in the doorway. She began crying hysterically. She knew why they had come. Scooter watched closely through the thick snowflakes as his grandfather and Mr. Harper jumped out of the truck and rushed over to her. His grandfather immediately put his arms around her shoulders; then gently guided her into the house, while she struggled to remain standing.

Scooter stood in the barnyard, facing the bitter cold wind, nose red and runny. He knew by the look on his grandfather's face that he would never see his father again. The horrible feeling he'd had in the pit of his stomach since the fire alarm had blasted its frightening call told him that nothing would ever be the same again. He immediately threw the basket of eggs toward the barn with all his might and watched as they sailed through the snow flakes before smashing against the side of the barn.

After standing like a statue in the barnyard for several minutes, snow gathering on his shoulders, Scooter retreated into the barn. He sat on the stool next to the workbench where his father and he had spent so many wonderful hours. He stared blankly at the yellow Maxwell House coffee cans filled with mismatched nails, bolts and screws. His father's carpenter's belt with the hammer still in the holster lay next to an old band saw blade.

Looking at the forgotten scooter they had built together, leaning against the far wall, made him sick. He could feel his body getting cold, and he began to shake. It started with his hands and moved up his arms to his shoulders. He tried wrapping his arms across his chest to stop from shaking, but the shaking would not stop.

Suddenly the silence became so strong, he couldn't stand it. The veins in his neck stood out, he clenched his fist as hard as rocks and began slamming them on the work bench. He screamed inside his head. He screamed and screamed and screamed until he could not contain it any longer and began screaming out loud. He wanted the whole town to hear him. *"You lied to me! You promised you wouldn't ever leave me! You crossed your heart! I hate you! I hate you!"* he screamed. *"I hate you . . . please don't leave me! . . . I love you!"* Then, unable to stop himself, he emptied his stomach on the floor.

He was confused and angry. He couldn't imagine how he'd survive without the love and companionship of his father. Scooter couldn't stop thinking about when his father had made the sacred sign of the cross over his heart promising never to leave him.

He continued staring blankly at the scooter they made. He was consumed with hatred and mistrust for everything he had only yesterday believed in. Scooter was now convinced that loving someone could only lead to the worst kind of suffering. He made a solemn pledge that he'd never love anyone again.

It took more than a week before the pile of rubble was cool enough so the recovery team could search through the smoldering bricks and timbers for the remains of the missing firefighters. After days of searching, it was determined the raging fire had been so intense, any chance of finding their remains was hopeless.

A memorial service was held the second week in January. It was held at the Greek Orthodox Church in Manchester. Many mourners were forced to stand outside in the cold on this frigid New Hampshire day, because the large crowd far exceeded the seating capacity of the church.

Fire departments throughout the state sent representatives to pay their respects to their fallen brother. There were representatives from area police departments, local and state politicians, friends, neighbors, and people who never met George Pappas, but wanted to show their respect and appreciation to the man who had given his life in the line of duty.

Several eulogies were given by speakers, giving praise to the man who gave so much to his community. Scooter's father was credited with being a loving husband and a wonderful father. He was hailed as a man with a reputation for honesty. One speaker after another commented on how he always had a kind word for whomever he met.

Scooter sat next to his mother, uncomfortably warm, droplets of sweat on his forehead, wearing his new navy blue sports coat and tie, looking pale and weak while trying to appear strong. Things were happening that just a few days before seemed impossible. During the funeral he found it difficult to make eye contact with people, and there wasn't much in the way of conversation from Scooter; *okay, no, yes, maybe;* that was all anyone got from him.

When he looked up at his father's picture on the highly polished mahogany table, surrounded by sprays of baby's breath, a few distinctive irises, and clusters of roses, Scooter felt an overpowering sense of loss. He remained motionless throughout the ceremony, staring blankly at the empty pew in front of him, not hearing much of what was being said. He felt angry, betrayed by the one person he always looked up to for love and guidance. The same person he now believed had lied to him.

A small voice in his head kept repeating, *He promised he'd never leave me, and now he's gone. Shut up,* he would think, and the voice would obey, but only for a moment, and then it would come back. *He promised he'd never leave me, and now he's gone,* kept repeating itself over and over in his head like a sad song he couldn't get out of his mind until he thought his head would explode.

Days eventually turned into weeks, weeks into months, then months into years. But no amount of time could stop the heartache and anger that seemed to never leave him; anger that would consume Scooter like a cancer; but unlike a cancer of the body that eats away at your flesh, this cancer was eating away at his very being, and it would never go away.

CHAPTER 12

IT WASN'T UNUSUAL for small towns in New Hampshire to combine their resources, creating regional high schools to accommodate students from more than one community. After completing grammar school in Pembroke, Scooter attended the Hollis-Pembroke Regional High School in the town of Hollis.

After his father died, Scooter was never the same. He preferred to stay mostly to himself. He grew up fast, and behaved like a boy older than his sixteen years. Scooter had become an introvert, showing little interest in getting involved in any social activities. His mother encouraged him to make friends, but he seldom left the farm. While walking the hallways, Scooter would never look his classmates in the eyes. Instead, he seemed to be gazing beyond them, like they didn't exist.

Without his father to tend to the chores, he'd taken on the role of the man of the house. Unlike other kids who were going on dates, attending school activities during the afternoons and weekends, he spent these hours working with his grandfather in their construction business. He was an excellent craftsman even at the age of sixteen, filling the void his father left. Scooter's grandfather, after the loss of his only son, appeared to have grown old and lost the enthusiasm and energy he needed to run the family business, and appreciated his grandson's assistance.

By his junior year, Scooter had become physically way ahead of other boys in his class. He was nearly six feet tall, weighing 180 pounds of solid muscle; his facial hair had begun sprouting, and he had developed a deep, grown man's voice.

The Hollis-Pembroke Regional High School football team hadn't had a winning season in several years. Coach Abbott, noticing Scooter's size and strength, realized he'd be a tremendous asset to his team and never missed an opportunity to try to recruit Scooter, encouraging him to try out for the team. But his pleading fell on deaf ears until one bright autumn afternoon when Scooter showed up for practice. It didn't take long before the coach realized he had been right, he excelled in every position he played. By the end of the football schedule, Scooter owned every scoring record ever set by a running back in the history of New Hampshire Division II Football. He gained more yards, scored more touchdowns than any other player had in their division. He was credited with single-handedly carrying the school to its first regional championship.

As much enjoyment as Scooter got when he scored a touchdowns, it was on defense that he excelled. He loved the violence of the game. It helped release the pent up anger that was always simmering just below the surface. The sound of shoulder pads crashing viciously into opponents, the feeling he got knocking players to the ground, watching them slowly, painfully, get up, gave him a sadistic kind of satisfaction.

He could hit opponents as hard as he wanted. Instead of being condemned, everyone in the bleachers would stand up and cheer. Once during a game, Scooter landed a hit on one of the opposing players that sounded like a head-on car crash, sending the boy off the field on wobbly legs, needing the assistance of two of his teammates. Coach Abbott shouted, "Great hit, Scooter. Hell of a shot. Keep up the good work."

Scooter's performance on the field brought him a great deal of attention. He became the most popular boy in school; although he still remained a loner. With his strong, dark, handsome features, he became especially popular with the girls, who referred to him as "The Golden Greek." Girls' competed for his attention, but the only girl that Scooter was interested in was a pretty sophomore by the name of Betty Sullivan. But unlike the other girls' Betty was shy and showed little interest in Scooter.

Betty was beautiful. She had naturally blond hair, flawless skin that most schoolgirls could only dream of. Her bright friendly blue eyes looked like two sparkling sapphires. She had a quiet, unthreatening personality that made her classmates take to her. She was petite compared to other girls in school who had developed early, but had the kind of figure that would withstand the burden of time and remain attractive for many years.

Betty appeared to be happy on the outside, but hidden underneath, she suffered from moods of depression. Her father had run off with a woman unexpectedly, abandoning her mother, brother and her. His leaving was something she would never get over.

Whenever she approached her mother about his whereabouts, Betty was never given an answer and met with only an angry stare. Her mother never complained or discussed her problems with others. Her children remained the focus of her life. When the residents in town saw how well Grace was getting along without her husband, they felt she was probably better off without that *drunken, whore chasing bastard.* Grace married her husband knowing he drank. She knew he had an eye for women but never believed her marriage would turn out like this. Nonetheless, she was a strong woman and determined to do whatever necessary to take care of her children without him.

Grace Sullivan was an attractive woman when she wanted to be, which wasn't often. She kept her figure hidden under loose fitting cotton drip-dry dresses, seldom applied makeup, and kept her gray streaked hair pulled into a bun on the back of her head. She was liked by everyone. When she was in need of help, the town came to her assistance offering her a much needed job. The selectmen created a secretarial position for Grace at Town Hall in the Building Department.

It didn't take long after her father's departure that Betty's mother removed everything in the house that reminded her he'd ever lived with them. Every photo, his favorite coffee cup, his shaving things, even the chair he always sat in disappeared.

But, of all the items her mother removed, it was the photo of her father looking tall and handsome in his starched white shirt, a diagonally stripped tie and tuxedo, looking confident, standing proudly next to his bride that Betty missed the most. Her mother was wearing a beautiful flowing silk wedding gown and holding a lovely bouquet of roses. She would look at the picture and think someday she, too, would meet a man as handsome as her father, get married, and be as happy as her parents appeared in the photo. Now, looking at the vacant spot on the wall where the photo had hung, she couldn't understand what happened to the love they must've felt on that special day.

One morning while Grace was standing in front of the kitchen sink washing the breakfast dishes, an apron wrapped around her midriff, staring out the window Betty noticed signs of stress and worry etched on her mother's face. Betty would have liked to give her mother a hug but did nothing but stand by helplessly and watched as a single tear formed in the corner of her mother's eye, then rolled down her cheek.

She overheard her mother mumbling to herself. "The whore can have him. I hope they both burn in Hell." Realizing Betty was standing nearby, she looked down at her daughter and, in a voice as hollow as the hole in her heart, said, "Don't worry, Honey, everything's gonna be all right. We'll be fine."

Betty turned her face up. Speaking softly, she said, "I miss Daddy. What are we gonna do?"

"I promise you, we'll be all right."

For many years after her father left with that *whore,* whenever Betty saw someone with a similar profile or the same color hair, she would stare intently, but it always turned out to be a stranger, all the time wondering . . . *where are you . . . where'd you go?* There was never an answer. Although Betty hadn't done anything wrong, she carried a heavy burden of guilt around in her heart, believing she had somehow contributed to her father's leaving.

Betty was desperate for answers. She had been taught to believe in and trust in God. Her mother had made it real clear that God was looking out for her every minute, and if she prayed to Him whenever she was troubled, God would answer her prayers. But after months of praying, Betty finally accepted the reality that her father was not going to return, and her heart became filled with the kind of hopelessness only a child can experience.

Unlike her daughter, Grace Sullivan had learned over time to appreciate her husband's absence. She did not make many friends, nor did she make any enemies. She kept to herself and carried her burden without regret. It wasn't long before she didn't want him to return today, tomorrow, or ever. She was convinced men were nothing but trouble. As for love, she knew well the tragic results of loving a man.

Grace never cared for sex. She felt relieved she no longer was expected to satisfy his demands for sex when he came home smelling of whiskey and cigarettes, and some whore's cheap perfume on his clothes after spending the night in the bars in Manchester.

If it was her lack of interest in sex that had driven him to those other women, so be it. She didn't care. She was doing just fine without him. Caring for the children and her job in the Building Department were enough to keep her busy. Getting from one pay check to the next was difficult, but she managed to pay her bills, feed her children and live comfortably.

It wasn't much, but that was all she wanted or needed out of life.

CHAPTER 13

BETTY AND MARYANN Riddle, a shy, slightly overweight girl and Betty's best friend were hurrying down the crowded hallway. They had just left their English class and discussing their assignment to read *The Hound of the Baskervilles,* a classic Sherlock Holmes mystery written by Sir Arthur Conan Doyle. Ms. Belanger, their English teacher had given them the assignment, saying it would be part of their mid-year exams. Scooter had been on the lookout for Betty, so when he saw the girls walking in his direction, he made his way through the throng of students and confronted her.

Maryann, not seeing Scooter nearly walked into him. "I'm sorry," Maryann apologized.. "I didn't see you, Scooter."

Scooter completely ignored Maryann. It was Betty he wanted to talk to. "Hi, Betty," he said. His dark wavy hair was combed down over his forehead, wearing a skintight tee-shirt under his blue and white football jacket with the white leather sleeves that covered his broad shoulders.

Scooter Pappas was the last person Betty ever expected to be speaking to her. She hesitated before answering, "Hi, Scooter."

Students passing by were curious and began walking slowly, watching and wondering what in the world Hollis-Pembroke High School's star athlete, Scooter Pappas, could possibly be talking to shy little Betty Sullivan about.

Scooter was nervous and anxious to get what he had to say over with as quickly as possible. "Betty, I know this is kinda short notice, but I was wondering if you don't already have a date for the football banquet Saturday night, if you would go with me."

Betty was feeling self-conscious with the students gawking at them as they walked by. After an uncomfortable moment, she found her voice and spoke. "I don't think I can. My mother doesn't let me go out on dates."

"Maybe she wouldn't mind if she knew that my mother and grandparents are going to be sitting at the same table with us," Scooter explained.

The football banquet was an annual event. It was an opportunity for the school faculty, students and parents to come together so they could pay tribute to their football team. Betty was aware that Scooter would be the center of attention and receive the most sought-after trophy, the "Outstanding Player Award," which he deserved.

She knew it would be exciting to be Scooter's date, but she wasn't sure she could convince her mother to let her go. "Well, I could ask her," Betty said, looking away shyly.

"Could you let me know tomorrow?"

"I'll ask her tonight," Betty promised.

The subject seemed to be exhausted and when neither spoke for an awkward few seconds, Scooter ended the conversation by saying, "Talk to you tomorrow," and walked away as quickly as he'd appeared.

"I can't believe it, Scooter Pappas asking you for a date. You're going to the banquet with Scooter," Maryann said, more excited than Betty appeared.

Betty knew it wasn't a done deal. Her mother had made it perfectly clear that Betty wasn't to start dating until her senior year. "I don't think my mother will let me go," she said almost in a whisper as the two girls continued walking to their next class.

Later that evening while eating supper, Betty explained to her mother that she'd been asked to attend the football banquet by Scooter Pappas. "Ma, you know Scooter Pappas, don't you?"

"Yes, he often comes into the Building Department with his grandfather when they need a building permit. Why do you ask?"

"Well, there's the football banquet next Saturday night, and he asked me if I wanted to go with him."

"You mean, on a date?"

"Kinda."

Her mother stared at her for a moment without comment. Grace always knew this day would come, but wasn't prepared for it to be quite this soon. "Oh, I don't know, Honey. I still think you're still a little young. Didn't we agree you would wait until your senior year before you started dating?"

Betty nodded. "I know, but this is kind of a special occasion. Besides, Scooter said his mother and grandparents would be going with us. It's not like we'd be alone or anything," she explained.

Her mother shook her head at first, then, after giving it more thought, reconsidered. She realized Betty was getting older, and sooner or later she'd have to let go and let her daughter begin doing the things she knew other teenagers were doing. Besides, knowing the children were being escorted by Scooter's mother and grandparents put her mind at ease.

"I didn't realize you were even friendly with him."

Betty shook her head. "I'm really not. I mean, I know him, everyone knows him because he's such a good football player, but I never really talked to him before today."

Grace brushed several stray hairs off her forehead with her fingers, then, took a bite of her salad before replying. "Why would he ask you if you don't know him that well?"

"I don't know."

"You said it's a football banquet and his family would be going with you."

"Yes. That's what he said. They have it every year at the end of the football season. So can I go?" Betty asked tentatively.

Grace hesitated, took a sip of her coffee then put her cup down, "Okay, Honey. I guess it'll be all right."

The night of the banquet everyone couldn't help but notice what a breathtaking couple Betty Sullivan and Scooter Pappas made. His dark, rugged complexion, steel black hair, and intense brown eyes made a stunning contrast as he danced awkwardly with Betty. Having never been to a dance before, Betty looked uncomfortable at first as they made their way around the dance floor, wearing a simple but pretty blue dress that covered her petite figure, which highlighted her clear blue eyes, blond hair and fair complexion.

Betty felt like Cinderella sitting next to Scooter. She realized everyone was watching them. She sat quietly and listened to speaker after speaker praising Scooter for his accomplishments on the football field. She was the envy of every girl attending the banquet when Scooter walked up to receive his well-deserved trophy.

Scooter's family had been courteous throughout the banquet, but Betty felt something was wrong. She could feel their eyes appraising her. There seemed to be a tension in the air that Betty didn't understand. She spent the evening sitting quietly, nervously licking her lips, noticeably uncomfortable.

Scooter continuing to date Betty after the football banquet didn't sit well with his mother, grandfather and grandmother, who never passed up an opportunity to voice their objections. Most of the Greeks in Pembroke took the long ride to Manchester to attend the Greek Orthodox Church. The Greeks were a close knit minority amongst the Irish and French-Canadians in Pembroke. They took their religious beliefs seriously and expected their children to marry within their church.

His mother and grandparents were not happy about Scooter showing an interest in a non-Greek, Irish Catholic girl. Mrs. Pappas constantly tried to encourage her son to date one of the Greek girls from the Orthodox Church they attended in Manchester; fearing that Betty and Scooter's relationship might someday become serious. But Scooter had a mind of his own, and wouldn't listen to his mother's complaints about Betty not being one of them.

Two years later

The first summer after Betty graduated, Scooter decided not to wait any longer. *He* wanted to get married.

Scooter was driving his grandfather's company truck, a 1958 Ford pickup. They were returning from Manchester, driving the winding back roads of Route 3 at a steady but unhurried pace after picking up building supplies at the hardware store.

His stout fingers were drumming the steering wheel, his eyes staring straight ahead. The sky looked threatening, dark gray clouds hovering above, but if he was aware of any upcoming storm, he chose to ignore it. He had other things on his mind.

He turned slightly toward her. "Betty, *I've* decided that we should get married," he told her.

Completely caught off guard, she was at a loss for words and hesitated. "You're not serious, are you?"

"Yes. We've been dating for over two years now. You know we're going to get married someday. Why should we wait?" he insisted.

The light in Betty's eyes dimmed. "But we haven't even discussed getting married. I just turned eighteen. I'm not sure I want to get married right now."

"But, *I've* already talked it over with my mother. At first she didn't think it was a good idea, but she said if *I* really wanted to, she wouldn't object."

"Your mother; what about me; don't I get a chance to say something?' she said, raising her voice slightly, on the verge of crying.

"Don't you love me? You know we're going to get married. Why wait?"

She didn't answer. It was not Betty's nature to be confrontational, but she had been having mixed thoughts lately about her feelings for Scooter. She couldn't decide if she even loved him, and getting married had never crossed her mind.

The rain had started with little more than an annoying period of drizzle saturating the leaves of the oak and birch trees. Betty seemed to be hypnotized by the squeaky rhythmic back-and-forth of the windshield wipers. Speaking into the glass, she said, "I've been thinking about going to nursing school. I think we should wait at least until after I graduate and I become a nurse."

"A nurse? Why would you want to be a nurse? The pay's lousy and you have to work stupid hours; besides, it's better for *me* if you're working in the Building Department."

After graduating high school, Betty had been given a part-time job working with her mother at Town Hall; when her mother retired, it was arranged for Betty to assume her mother's position.

Scooter's forehead became furrowed, and it was evident he was irritated with her lack of enthusiasm with *his* decision to marry her. She didn't want to provoke him anymore than he already was, but she needed time to think about *his* decision. "I don't want to keep working with my mother in the Building Department. I really want to go to nursing school," she said, turning away from the window.

"Why not? When she retires, it's all set for you to take over her job."

Everything was happening too fast. "I just think we should wait awhile, that's all I'm saying."

He shook his head, then *told* her, "*I* don't want to wait. My grandparents said my mother could move in with them, and we could move into my house. *It's all been settled.*"

Lacking the courage to continue arguing, Betty reluctantly turned back toward the window as the truck passed lines of old stone walls, moss covered property boundaries from another time. As they continued to drive, Betty observed an abandoned grave yard tucked back off to the side of the road, mostly hidden by overgrown brush. She was frightened. She did not want to get married, at least not now.

"I don't know, Scooter. I'll have to talk to my mother," she meekly said.

That evening she explained her situation to her mother. She was hoping to get some help but got none. Instead, her mother was happy and enthusiastic and congratulated her, telling her what a fortunate girl she was.

"You're a lucky girl, Betty. Scooter's such a fine, hard-working young man. I can't tell you how happy I am for you."

Realizing she would get no help or sympathy from her mother, she didn't know which way to turn. Once word got out about her engagement, everyone in Pembroke kept reminding her how fortunate she was to be marrying someone from such a fine family. They told her how lucky she was to have a hard working man as handsome as Scooter to share her life with, but Betty felt like she was on a runaway merry-go-round ride, but lacked the courage to jump off. Settling down on the Pappas farm in Pembroke was not the future she had envisioned for herself.

Two days before the wedding, Betty and her mother drove down to Manchester to pick up her wedding gown at The Bridal Shoppe. After entering the shop, she was trying her gown on before a full-length mirror, turning slowly, examining her petite figure, delicate features and youthful appearance, and began to frown. She looked more like a child preparing for her confirmation rather than a woman about to get married.

While driving back to Pembroke with her wedding dress draped across the back seat, Betty once again wanted to explain how she felt, but couldn't gather up the nerve to say what had been bothering her ever since Scooter informed her of *his* plans.

With both hands securely on the wheel while glancing over proudly at her daughter, her mother noticed how quiet Betty had been all evening. She asked, "You've been awful quiet tonight. Aren't you feeling okay?"

Betty was sitting up rigid and tense, holding onto the door handle like she was waiting for the right opportunity to jump and run away. She desperately wanting to explain what was on her mind. Finally gathered up all her courage, she said through trembling lips, "Remember how I used to say how much I've always wanted to be a nurse?"

"Of course I remember. What makes you bring that up now?"

"Last year in school, Mrs. McFadden, the guidance counselor, had some brochures from the nursing school in Manchester. After reading them, I decided what I really would like to do is go to nursing school to become a nurse," she explained, then looked over to see her mother's reaction.

"Have you discussed this with Nicholas? I don't know why in the world you want to be a nurse. You already have a good job at Town Hall working with me. When I retire, it's all set for you to take my place."

"I've already mentioned it to him."

"And?"

"He said I was being stupid to even think about going into nursing because it didn't pay anything. He feels the same way you do. He told me to forget it. But I don't want to forget it. I don't want to spend my life working in the Building Department and I don't want to stay in Pembroke for the rest of my life. I'm not even sure I want to get married," she said. Her eyebrows rose with a what-to-do look of desperation on her face.

Mrs. Sullivan's eyes kept shifting from Betty to the road, then back to her daughter. She had listened closely and didn't like what she was hearing. After a minute she glanced at her daughter with a warning in her stern, tight face and explained as clearly as she could exactly what Betty didn't want to hear.

"Listen to me. You have everything a girl could ask for right here in Pembroke. Nicholas is a fine young man, and you're damn lucky to have him. After his father died in that awful fire, he worked on the family farm, helping out his mother. On weekends and during school vacations, he worked construction with his grandfather. He's hard-working and dependable. Something your father wasn't I might add. I don't know what's gotten into you. You're going to marry Nicholas and behave the way I expect you to. Now, I don't want to hear another word of this crazy talk about becoming a nurse or moving to some god-forsaken place. Do you understand what I'm saying?"

Betty watched her mother with little darting glances and listened attentively. All she wanted was to follow her ambitions—feel normal, to live her life like everyone else, to grow, to learn, but her dreams were being beaten out of her by everyone she knew.

Staring out the window she could feel her mother's eyes boring into the back of her head with such intensity it frightened her. Betty wanted to believe her, wanted to believe she was doing the right thing, but deep down nothing about it seemed right. She felt trapped, alone and frightened. But she also knew she had never disobeyed her mother, and would not disobey her now.

Elizabeth "Betty" Sullivan reluctantly but obediently became Mrs. Nicholas "Scooter" Pappas the following weekend. Throughout the ceremony she felt like she was on the verge of breaking down and would begin crying at any moment. While taking her vows, when she uttered the four words *"for better for worse,"* she didn't realize at the time that her life would consist mainly in the latter.

Immediately after the wedding ceremony the newlyweds walked outside into the sunlight, stood on the sidewalk and greeted their guests while a gathering of pigeons waddled and pecked in the grass nearby. Everyone shook hands and commented on how beautiful Betty looked with her veil fluttering in the breeze and small tears of happiness sliding down her cheeks.

But her tears were not tears of happiness. It was hot and her head ached; spells of dizziness whirled before her eyes. She felt a longing to be someplace else. She was frightened about marrying a boy she did not love, and begin living a life she did not want.

It was a long time before the Pappas family reluctantly accepted Betty. She quickly learned that it would take more than a wedding ring to be forgiven for not being born a Greek. Scooter had been brought up in the Greek Orthodox religion. It had been assumed he would someday marry a Greek girl within his faith. When he chose Betty, an Irish Catholic to be his wife, Scooters' family felt hurt and betrayed, and as time went on it became apparent that Betty would never be completely accepted as one of their family.

CHAPTER 14

AFTER CLEANING HIS trailer home Chief Barrett headed for Bottoms Up. When he arrived he pulled up next to a fender-bent Dodge Ram pickup truck loaded down with building materials with a gun rack and a Confederate flag on the back window belonging to Butch and Billy Cunningham, brothers who made their living doing odd jobs. The only other vehicle in the parking lot was a fifteen-year-old Chevy Impala convertible belonging to Walter *"Winky"* Byrd. Winky got his nickname because of an out-of-control twitch in his right eye, which only got worse when he drank, which was every day.

Barrett turned the ignition off and listened to the engine ticking as it cooled. The view across the water of the slow moving Indian River and the clear blue sky above was a beautiful sight. Ray watched as a lone sailboat, sails furled, motored upon the water, creating a low wake on the dazzling liquid sunlight being reflected on the surface.

His empty stomach began growling, reminding him he needed to get inside and get his hands around a cold bottle of beer and a juicy hamburger. It was hot and he could feel lots of midday sun beating down on his neck while making his way across the gravel and weed-infested parking lot while a group of seagulls perched on the edge of the roof began screeching at him for no apparent reason.

Once inside it took a minute for Ray's eyes to adjust to the darkness. The familiar barroom sounds and smells of stale beer and cigarettes greeted him as soon as he opened the door. He took in a deep breath, enjoying the aroma that all true bar-flies know and love. Noticing a seat opposite the sign that read *"Free Drinks All Day Tomorrow"* was vacant, he walked over and sat down, dropping his keys on the bar.

Bottoms Up is located across the street from the Indian River and has the look of a functioning fishing shack. On the ceiling hangs a fisherman's net supporting a life preserver, plastic lobsters, driftwood and an assortment of nautical junk; a large harpoon hung above the bathroom doors that were clearly labeled BUOYS and GULLS. Across the back wall on a shelf are several kinds of rums, whiskies, bottles of Scotch, and various brands of vodka. At the very end of the shelf sits a bottle of pig's feet, next to the pickled eggs, floating in a murky yellow liquid, pressing against the glass, looking like huge eyeballs staring at you.

Ray sat impatiently under the ceiling fan that kept the warm, humid air moving while waiting for Sandy. She was busy on the other side of the swinging doors that led directly into the kitchen. He could smell the aroma of grilled hamburgers filtering through the food delivery opening in the wall behind the bar.

He sat quietly examining himself carefully in the mirror with a string of Christmas lights strung along the top of it, running the length of the bar. Several lights are burned out. The Christmas decorations had been put up three years ago and never taken down. The radio behind the bar was playing quiet country music turned down low the way it is when no one is listening.

On workdays during "Happy Hour" or on weekends, it was standing room only at Bottoms Up. The men who frequented the bar were a loud, enthusiastic bunch, but seldom started any trouble. It just took a quick glance from Sandy if someone stepped out of line to quiet them down.

Sandy was an attractive, middle-aged, busty blonde. She had clear skin and keen green eyes that doesn't miss much. She also had a crooked front tooth, but it didn't prevent her from smiling. She moved effortlessly behind the bar with the grace and confidence of a ballroom dancer for a woman twenty-five pounds overweight. She knew her customers well and easily flowed up and down the bar effortlessly, calling everyone *"Hon"* or *"Honey."* It didn't make any difference if the person was male or female, tall or short, black or white. When business was slow, it's *"Honey;"* when she's busy, it's *"Hon."*

Ray was observing Winky sitting on his usual stool at the far end of the long mahogany bar dressed in a dark blue *Barefoot Bay Golf Course* maintenance uniform, drinking his first, but definitely not his last beer of the day. Seated a few stools closer were Butch and Billy, darkly tanned and looking like twins, although they are not, wearing identical John Deere caps and laborer's jeans. Both men were drinking bottles of Coors held securely in their fingers, elbows firmly planted on the bar waiting for Sandy to deliver them their lunch.

Ray looked down the length of the bar and saw Winky picking at a scab on his sunburned arm. He was a man you'd remember if you saw him just once. He appeared to be one of those people born old, with stringy white-gray hair hanging down below his collar, surrounding a weather-beaten face.

Ray shouted, "How's things goin', Winky?"

Slowly looking up from his bleeding sore while reached for the napkin holder, Winky withdrew a tissue and began blotting his wound. Winky was never one for conversation and spoke only when spoken too. When he did speak it was from the corners of his mouth, revealing teeth that were a little yellow and crooked, hardly moving his lips at all. "Same old shit," he said, in an expressionless voice.

"You happen to know that fella that died last night in the Bay, Winky?"

Knowing he worked Saturday mornings at the golf course, he would have heard about Phil Gagnon's death. Word spread quickly in Barefoot Bay and Ray had observed several golfing trophies and magazines scattered about the Gagnon's house last night and assumed he was a golfer.

He nodded his head. "Yup, I knew him. A real asshole," he said, continuing to blot at his scabs, never looking up.

"Asshole; what do you mean by that?" Ray asked, shooing away a pestering fly.

"You know, one of them guys who thinks' his shit don't stink. Acts like he's God's gift to women."

"What makes you say that?"

"Just the way he acts, that's all," Winky concluded, taking a sip of his beer, turning his back to Ray, indicating their conversation was over.

Sandy suddenly appeared from the kitchen, a cheerful smile on her face carrying two plates of food for the Cunningham boys. When she spotted Ray she dropped the plates carelessly in front of the men, then came directly over, drying her hands on a white bar towel, anxious to get the low-down on the murder in the Bay. "Ready?" she asked, pointing at the cooler.

He gave her the thumbs up. "Might as well."

Reaching down deep in the cooler, she came up with a Budweiser and placed it on the bar. Then she got right down to finding out what the hell all the talk was about. "I heard some guy got himself murdered last night. That right, Honey?" Sandy asked while wiping a greasy smudge from the bar

The rumor started when Patrolman Callahan mentioned to his wife, after getting home at two o'clock in the morning, there had been a suspicious death in Barefoot Bay that could turn out to be a murder. First thing in the morning his wife called her sister. Her sister in turned called her neighbor, setting off a ripple of phones ringing from house to house until the rumors were spreading around the Town of Micco with the speed of a brush fire on a windy day in the Florida Everglades. The rumors would be repeated and enlarged again and then again until everyone felt they had gotten the whole story.

Whenever anything of interest happened in Micco, Sandy got the inside scoop from Ray. She tried to make it her business to know everything that went on in town. The possibility of a murder being committed in the Barefoot Bay Retirement Community was the most exciting news to pass through the bar in years.

Not liking being questioned, Ray glared at Sandy over the rim of the bottle. "Who the hell said anything about a murder?"

"Winky told me. He said the guy was fooling around with some guy's wife. That right, Honey? It's hard to believe them old people over there screw around like that."

Ray set the bottle on the bar. "Don't believe everything you hear. Especially don't believe anything Winky tells you. I'm asking you . . . no . . . I'm telling you . . . don't start rumors that ain't true. People are always starting rumors, Sandy. I don't know what the guy died from yet; could have been natural causes. I'm still looking into it."

Sandy listened closely, then, decided she didn't like what she was hearing. "For Christ sake, Ray, something happened over there. Winky works there. He said everybody says the guy was murdered. Why would people be saying that if it's not true?'

He picked up his beer, took a large swallow, after which he pulled the bottle away from his lips and wiped his mouth with the back of his hand, then put his elbows on the bar and glared at her. "I don't want to talk about it. How about getting me a burger and some fries and minding your own goddamn business."

Sandy was not used to being put off. A flicker of anger appeared on her face, but only for a moment. If something was going on in Barefoot Bay, she wanted to know about it. She hesitated for a moment, then staring directly back at him through tight lips, said, "Coming right up, Hon, but don't forget, we're supposed to be friends. I ain't gonna forget it if you don't let me know what the hell happened over there; I want to be the first to hear about it, understand?"

Deciding he had better things to do than sit here arguing with her, he decided to tell her what she wanted to hear. "Okay, as soon as I find out anything you'll be the first to know, I promise. Now, can I get something to eat?"

After eating his lunch and finishing his beer, Ray casually dropped a ten dollar bill on the bar and left. With Bottoms Up in his rear view mirror, glad to be out of there, he decided to take another look at the Gagnon house, in case he'd missed something last night.

With over five thousand homes in Barefoot Bay, anyone unfamiliar with the layout could easily get lost. All the homes are spaced exactly the same distance apart, painted in light pastel shades. The driveways become carports with utility sheds attached. Ray, being familiar with the layout, and after punching in the five-digit security code, entered and drove directly to Dolphin Drive. The Bay was unusually quiet. After rumors of a possible homicide in their neighborhood, he assumed residents were afraid to venture far from home.

Barefoot Bay has often been referred to as Heaven's Waiting Room, a quiet community in which to live out your remaining years in peace and harmony. That would no longer be the case. If a murderer was lurking the residents would be sure to make the rounds each night, locking every window and door up tight before heading for bed.

Turning onto Dolphin Drive Ray noticed there was a large man bending over and retrieving his folded newspaper from the driveway next door to the Gagnon's. He unfolded it and was glancing at the front page as he walked toward the house. It was now after one o'clock. The man was still dressed in pajamas and bathrobe. Ray watched him as he ambled up the driveway. He was over six feet tall and nearly three hundred pounds. It was the same man who had been sitting quietly on the recliner in the living room last night.

Ray pulled in front of the driveway, hit the button that lowered the window and it worked, which wasn't always the case. "Hey, can I talk to you for a minute?" Ray hollered.

Stanley Kloski hadn't noticed Ray drive up. "Hey, Buddy, got a minute?" Ray repeated louder.

Stanley slowly turned, squinting his eyes against the sun but didn't recognize Chief Barrett at first. Curiously, he shuffled closer, holding the paper tightly in his fist, his eyes a dark gray, looking vacant and strange, the whites appearing too shallow for a healthy man.

"What do you want?" Stanley asked, stifling a yawn.

"I'm Chief Ray Barrett."

"Yes, I remember," Stanley said, finally recognizing him.

"You live here?"

Stanley stared back at him. "Yeah . . ."

"What's your name?"

"Stanley."

"You know the Gagnons, Stanley?"

"Yeah, I know them."

"I'm kind a curious. Can you tell me anything about them?"

The big man looked confused. "Like what?"

"Anything at all; like where they're from, what the husband did for a living? What kind of guy he was, anything at all?"

"They're all right, I guess. At least Kathy was nice. They own some kind of an insurance agency up in Massachusetts. I understand Kathy's father started the business. When the old man died, Phil took over. They have a son who runs it for his father while he's in Florida. That's all I know."

"Did they get along with everyone?"

"Yeah, as far as I know they did."

"How long have the Gagnons lived here?"

"They don't live here all year. They just come down in the winter. Kathy's father owned the house before he died. He left it to them. I never met the father. He died before we moved here."

"How long have you lived here?"

"Two years. It was Carol's idea to move here. I would've just as soon stayed in Pennsylvania."

"Who's Carol, your wife?"

"Yes."

"How did you get along with Mr. Gagnon?'

"Okay. It was mostly the women that hung around together."

"Would it be possible to talk to your wife? Maybe she could answer a few questions for me."

"Not a good idea right now. Carol and Kathy went to bed late. They were up most of the night talking. You know, with what happened to Phil and all. Maybe if you came back later," Stanley suggested, straightening up and backing away from the car, indicating he wanted to end the conversation.

"That's right. I remember now. Mrs. Gagnon was going to stay here last night."

"Yes. Carol didn't think she should be left alone," he said. "Some men were in there earlier this morning. Looked like policemen," Stanley continued, nodding toward the Gagnon's house while slowly walking backwards.

"They must have been from the Sheriff's Department. They were just checking to see if they could uncover anything."

"Uncover something? What could they be looking for?" Stanley asked, looking intently at Ray while edging back toward the car.

"It's just a routine procedure. We have to be sure exactly what caused his death. If Mrs. Gagnon just went to bed I'll come back another time."

Feeling he'd gotten all the useless information he would get from Stanley and anxious to get back to the station and see if Sheriff's Department had called, Ray finished, "Tell Mrs. Gagnon I'll be in touch."

"Okay," the huge man said, then turned and continued up his driveway.

Realizing no one would be in the Gagnon house Ray decided to have another look. The door was still unlocked. Once inside, Ray scoured the house for clues for a reasonable explanation for Phil Gagnon's untimely death, but like last night could fine nothing disturbed or broken. It was obvious if he was murdered in the course of a botched robbery, the intruder, or intruders, must have known exactly what they were looking for. Nothing seemed out of place.

Noticing a collage of family pictures on the living room wall he walked over and closely examined them. The photos were mostly of a young boy. In one, the boy was wearing a baseball uniform with a bat casually sitting on his shoulder, his father standing beside him grinning like a maniac. In another, the same young boy was beaming while holding a fish several inches long in one hand, his fishing pole in the other. Still another picture showed him in a soccer outfit, displaying a trophy on the ground in front of him, kneeling next to a soccer ball.

In two other photographs the Gagnons were standing side by side; Mr. Gagnon's arm encircling his wife's waist and holding her elbow. They both appeared stiff with forced smiles. The only other photo was a picture of a younger Mr. and Mrs. Gagnon. The man was holding an infant, grinning from ear to ear, obviously a proud father while the wife looked on, also smiling.

After walking from room to room, satisfied there was nothing further he could do here, and with Mrs. Gagnon still sleeping next door at the Kloskis, Ray decided to head to the station and see if the coroner had called with the results from the autopsy.

CHAPTER 15

Stanley & Carol (Johnson) Kloski

Married October 12, 1968

STANLEY KLOSKI'S MOTHER never married.

A situation she blamed on her bastard son. Doris always felt that Stanley had been cruelly forced upon her, just like the boys at the fraternity house had forced themselves on her that horrible night they had taken turns gang raping her.

Three generations of Kloskis lived in a large house high on the hill in the best area of South Orange, New Jersey. It had been built around the turn of the century with a distinctive Victorian style, consisting of three floors, a large porch that wrapped around two sides and painted white with black trim. It was an old, elegant neighborhood with stunning panoramic views that reached out across the Hudson River where the towering skyscrapers of New York and the Empire State Building were clearly visible. It was where the well-to-do lived, and the Kloskis were well-to-do.

Doris's father, Joseph Kloski was president of the South Orange Savings Bank. He and his wife Constance and their daughter, Doris, and her bastard son Stanley, lived together in this exclusive neighborhood.

But Doris's son would always serve as a constant reminder of that horrible night she had been raped. It occurred shortly before she graduated from Seton Hall University. She had been repeatedly raped by three or maybe four of her classmates whom she had considered, before that night to be her friends.

The night started out no different from most other Friday nights. Many of Doris's fellow students had gathered on campus in the cellar of the brick, ivy-covered Georgian-looking, fraternity house to drink beer and socialize.

Everyone in the smoke-hazed, dimly lit basement was in their early twenties. It was the usual scene: students in a festive mood, standing around telling stories that ended with an occasional burst of laughing, others gathered in groups having intense conversations, their faces bent toward each other, shoulders hunched, discussing Roosevelt's recent death and the haberdasher from Missouri, President Truman's, recent decision to drop the atomic bomb on Hiroshima and Nagasaki, ending World War II. Doris had attended many of these frat parties in the past. Until tonight she never had any reason to be concerned with her safety. But before this night was over her life would be changed forever.

Doris was rather plain looking and wasn't somebody that got many second looks from the boys. She had a flat face, small nose, beady eyes, and was slightly overweight, and didn't get asked out often. But she was outgoing and there were not many school activities that Doris wasn't involved in.

By the time Doris arrived the gathering was in full swing. She greeted her many friends with a smile while making her way through the crowded basement on her way to get a beer. She had grabbed a plastic cup off the table next to the beer keg and was waiting her turn when Paul said, "Hey, Doris, do me a favor and pour me a beer, will you?"

When he handed her his empty cup, she said. "Sure. That's if Cookie will move his ass," nodding toward her classmate, John Cook, who was busy pouring himself a beer.

Cookie overhearing her, handed her the beer he had just poured and took Paul's empty from her hand. "Here, take this one," he said, then began filling Paul's cup. Without hesitation Doris snatched the plastic container from his hand, thanked him, took a small sip and walked away.

Paul took the now filled cup from Cookie and followed Doris. "You're looking especially attractive tonight," he said, sliding his eyes seductively down her body, then back up to her eyes.

She was wearing a worn and tattered New York Giants T-shirt, cut-off dungarees and sneakers, and knew she didn't look especially attractive tonight. "How many beers have you had, Paul. I think it's time to shut you off," she said, with a good natured smile.

Doris knew bullshit when she heard it, but was nevertheless thrilled by the unexpected attention Paul Reynolds, the handsome president of the fraternity was showing her. They remained leaning against the wall, making small talk for over an hour with Paul quickly going over and refilling her cup whenever it was empty. After consuming several beers it was time for Doris to head for the girls room, so, she excused herself and hurried off to pee. Once she was out of sight, Paul glanced around, realizing no one was watching withdrew a small plastic container from his pants pocket. He carefully took two white capsules containing diazepam from the container and slipped them into Doris's half-filled cup of beer. Confident he had gone undetected he closed the container and returned the remaining tablets to his pocket, then walked over to the beer keg and refilled her cup.

It would just be a matter of time. When she returned he handed her the beer and said, "Drink up, Doris, the nights young."

She willingly took it and said, "Thanks."

The chitchatting went on, but gradually nothing was making sense to Doris. She began feeling lightheaded. She couldn't understand why the room suddenly started pitching and rolling. Unable to focus clearly and finding it difficult to keep her balance, she reached out for Paul's arm, missed, and fell backwards against the wall. Paul quickly placed his arm firmly around her waist, then suggested, "Doris, I think you've had one too many. I think you better lie down for a while."

"Don't know what's wrong, Paul. I feel all screwed up."

"You'll be fine."

"I think I'm gonna be sick."

"Come on now, you're not going to be sick. No one is in my room. You can use it to lie down for a little while, until you're feeling better."

In no condition to object, she agreed. "Okay."

With some difficulty, and Paul's hand on the small of her back, encouraging her along, they climbed the three flights to

Paul's bedroom. When they arrived at the top of the stairs Doris was struggling to breathe and held tightly onto Paul's arm, unaware that there were three boys following close behind. Paul glanced back at his friends standing on the landing below, winked and gave an encouraging thumbs-up.

Entering the bedroom, Doris collapsed with a thump onto Paul's bed, then, she rolled face down on the mattress and closed her eyes. The room smelled of stale beer and cigarettes, with musty clothes scattered haphazardly on the mattress. A small lamp on the desk against the wall provided the only light.

Paul joined her. "No, no, Doris, don't lie on your stomach," he instructed, grabbing her shoulder and forcing her to roll over. "You'll feel better if you're on your back."

From that moment on Doris remember almost nothing. The little she did recall was Paul kissing her, his beery breath tasting uninviting and foul. Then the kissing stopped. He began fumbling nervously, rushing to push her T-shirt and bra up over her breast. "Just relax, everything's going to be fine, everything's okay," he kept repeating. Doris at first tried to protest, but it wasn't long before she gave up and lay motionless, helpless to stop him.

"Now that's what I call a great pair of tits," Paul announced to the three boys that had entered the room while leering at her exposed chest, before reaching over and grabbing one breast and squeezing it roughly. "Well, if you gentlemen would excuse me, I have business to take care of," Paul said. "You guys can pick straws, flip a coin, or do whatever you want to see whose next, but I'm going first," he insisted, while boldly getting up and pushing Cookie and the other two boys toward the open door.

Alone now with Doris completely unconscious and unable to protest, Paul began pulling at her cutoffs and panties, working feverously, determined to claim his prize. After a few moments of tugging and pulling, she lay nearly naked, ripe for the taking. *Yes,* he thought to himself, *oh yes.*

When Paul was finished, he announced loudly, "Next."

The boys filed back into the room one after another, taking turns fucking her.

Cookie was last. After he had finished, the other boys reassembled in the bedroom. Paul sat on the side of the bed, reached down and spread her legs apart and announced with a hardy laugh, while grabbing her mound firmly, "Not a bad piece of ass, guys; not a lot of enthusiasm on her part, but not bad," he said, with a broad smile on his face "She was awful tight; I think she might have been my first virgin," he announced proudly.

"If she was, she's sure as hell not a virgin now," Cookie boosted. "She looks a little sticky Paul. You've got cum all over your hands," he continued, looking where Paul had grabbed her.

Paul took a tissue from his pocket and wiped his hand. "Anyone want sloppy seconds?" Paul asked, throwing the wet tissue in the direction of the waste basket. "Anyone want a smell?" Paul said, extending the hand he had just wiped towards the three boys.

Cookie's face squinted. "No thanks. I'll pass. I've had enough; besides, I can't make up my mind which is uglier, her pussy or her face."

"What difference does it make, as long as there's a hole to stick your dick into," Paul said. All the boys thought his comment was hilarious and laughed hardily.

With no takers for a last smell or sloppy seconds, Paul turned off the small light on the desk and the group single file left the room satisfied and marched downstairs to the basement to rejoin the party.

Hours later, Doris slowly opened her eyes. Everything appeared woozy and unreal. She struggled to clear her mind. Eventually the hazy image of drinking with Paul, her lying in bed with him, his groping her breast started coming back. Franticly looking around the dark room, the only sound came from a small alarm clock ticking away the seconds. She was confused and scared and wanted someone to explain what had happened, but found she was alone.

Feeling an uncomfortable throbbing between her legs, she turned the desk light on, looked at the clock and noticed it was after four in the morning. Looking down she was embarrassed to see her T-shirt and bra pushed up over her breasts. Her panties were rolled into a twisted, tangled mess around one ankle. Her cutoffs were lying in a heap on the floor next to the bed. It only took a moment to realize what had happened. She knew she had been raped.

Fearing Paul might return; Doris wanted to get out of there. She began sobbing and gasping, trying to control her breathing while frantically gathering up her clothes. Her vision was blurred with tears. She squeezed her eyes shut, but the tears couldn't be contained. They dribbled down her cheeks while she struggled to pull her T-shirt and bra down over her breasts. With trembling fingers she reached down and untangled her panties and pulled her underpants up before retrieving her cutoffs from the floor and putting them on.

She needed air, needed to breathe. As soon as the last button was secured on her cutoffs, Doris bolted out of the room, only to find Paul standing in the hallway with an odd glint in his eyes that showed no guilt or fear. His face trembled slightly as if deciding if he should speak. He moved his lips but changed his mind and said nothing. Doris could detect a half-smile, half-smirk on Paul's face as he looked past her, before flattening himself against the wall, allowing her to pass.

She didn't want to talk to him. She just wanted to be away from him. Petrified he might reach out and touch her, she tried not to stumble while running down the stairs and out into the cool spring night. Making it to her car she leaned against the fender and consumed with a wave of shame and humility, became sick and emptied her stomach. When the vomiting finally stopped, icy chills shuttered throughout her body.

Doris couldn't stop shaking. She carefully stepped around the sour smelling pile of vomit and got into her car. Once inside, she fumbled with her keys and found it difficult getting the key into the ignition. Finally, when the engine roared to life, she put the car in drive, rolled down the window, then, sped away, desperate to get home. She felt unclean. Her crotch ached and burned. There was a foul taste of stale beer in her mouth from vomiting. She needed to take a bath. She needed to wash away her shame and humiliation.

Safely in her bedroom, she looked in the mirror at her bloodshot eyes. She knew her life had forever changed. She was no longer a virgin, a condition she had always secretly been proud of. It had been important to her that someday she would present herself to the man she would marry untouched. That day would no longer be possible.

After getting undressed, she looked down and noticed the hair between her legs was matted and sticky. Her legs turned to jelly and she quickly grabbed hold of the bureau to prevent her from sprawling onto the bedroom floor. She staggered into the bathroom, leaning heavily on the wall, turned on the faucets and filled the tub with hot water. Doris winced and held her breath while she slowly submerged her body into the bath water, watching the warm steam float up between her open legs, turning her inner thighs a bright pink.

Bending her head back, staring at the ceiling, her mind returned to Paul's room. She wasn't sure, but she seemed to recall there were other boys in the room. She was almost sure of it. She believed she could hear the sound of their voices off in the distance. She could almost feel the weight of their bodies on top of her. The vague image of what had taken place was slowly materializing like a ghost story taking place in a fog. She kept thinking *they raped me. I was raped. Why? What have I done to deserve this?*

Then, a feeling of guilt began seeping into her head. She began wondering if she had done something to encourage them? Hadn't she gone to Paul's room willingly? Hadn't she drunk too many beers? Had she led them on?

She couldn't remember. She was confused and ashamed, finding it difficult to focus on her life right now. She didn't want to think about it. She wanted this nightmare to go away. She wanted to go back in time and redo what she had done. She felt like the whore she now believed she was. Doris pressed her fingers over her eyes, slid down in the bathtub and couldn't stop crying. She picked up the wash cloth and began washing her body but knew no matter how much she scrubbed, she would never be able to wash the memory of this night out of her life.

CHAPTER 16

Several weeks later

THE VOICE OF ANGER was evident, coming from her father as he paced back and forth in their richly furnished living room. Both Doris and her mother sat silent, eyes cast toward the floor. Her mother, wearing a long skirt and Victorian era blouse was rolling one of the dark, smooth beads between her thumb and forefinger of her rosary beads, while she rocked back and forth, mumbling: *"Hail Mary, full of grace, the Lord is with thee . . . "* under her breath, keeping her head bowed, barely moving her lips and never interrupting while her husband continued to rant and rave about his daughter's unforgivable behavior.

Doris refusing to tell who the father was infuriated him. "What do you mean you can't tell us?" he roared.

After informing her parents that she was pregnant, her father had been trying unsuccessfully since to get to the bottom of who had fathered the child. Doris was unable to look up at him, she wanted desperately to explain what had happen, but couldn't. She couldn't tell him that three or maybe four boys had raped her, and had no way of knowing who the father was.

Tears were running down her cheeks. She attempted to wipe them away with her damp tissue. "I'm sorry. I can't say. I'm so sorry," she mumbled, only infuriating him further, while her mother continued praying; *"Blessed is the fruit of thy womb . . . "*

Doris knew if she told him she had been raped, he would confront Paul, press charges and would not relent until justice was done. Paul was the president of his fraternity; all his friends would come to his defense. It would surely turn into a she-says/he-says situation. If the police were called in to investigate, it would be disclosed that she had gone to Paul's bedroom willingly. She could plainly hear the police asking, *"What did you do to encourage them?"*

Doris's father took off his glasses and began pacing as he continued his rampage, his eyes bulging. The determination in his voice sent shivers down Doris's spine. He stopped walking, stood rigid inches in front of her, and shouted, "Just what do you expect to do with this bastard child?"

Joseph Kloski had a reputation to uphold. He was highly respected in the community. His daughter having a bastard child was devastating. "I hope you realize you've disgraced me and your mother, Doris. Don't expect any help from me in bringing up your child. The child will be your responsibility and yours alone," he hollered, his voice echoing throughout the house.

The weight of Doris's grief felt inescapable, heavy and hopeless. Doris pleaded with him to consider giving the baby up for adoption, but her request was rejected. Her father, after careful consideration, felt that the Kloskis didn't run from their responsibilities. They were of the Catholic faith, and an abortion was never even discussed. He decided his daughter would keep the child. A decision Doris was forced to abide by, and a decision she would regret for the rest of her life.

Stanley spent his childhood alone in the corner bedroom of his grandparents' house a lonely castaway. Joseph Kloski never completely forgave his daughter, and would have nothing to do with his bastard grandson. Stanley was considered an unfortunate embarrassment that was to be kept out of sight. Doris purposely avoided him, keeping herself busy building her career at the bank. She didn't have the love, time, desire or the patience to behave like a mother.

Stanley lived an isolated childhood. One that creates the kind of uselessness a child in solitude starts believing when he thinks he doesn't matter . . . to anyone. After spending years of being ignored, the idea of an absentee mother shouldn't have concerned him, but it did. There were times when Stanley was alone in the house, when he'd turn the volume up on his radio and began screaming, the screams vibrating off the bedroom walls, releasing the pressure of waves of anger and frustration he felt from being unwanted.

When Stanley was twelve years old, his grandfather suffered a heart attack and died while working at the bank. The Kloski family owned the largest percentage of the bank shares, which consisted of more than fifty-five percent of the total assets now held jointly by Doris and her mother. During the next shareholders meeting, Doris was unanimously voted acting president. Once she took over the corner office, Doris kept herself occupied doing the bank's business, leaving even less time for her son.

With no adults or playmates Stanley's age to associate with, his only outlet was to live in a world of pretend and make-believe. He began creating imaginary friends. He would spend hours upon hours alone in his bedroom, unbearably lonely, conversing with imaginary playmates that existed only in his mind. It would be the beginning of a fine line between reality and fantasy that grew irrevocably blurred, creating how vast the difference Stanley saw the world and how it truly was.

School didn't provide any relief. Although he study hard and received good grades, he had few friends and did his best to appear invisible in the classroom. *Weird* Stanley they called him. He was picked on, teased mercilessly and often beaten. When confronted, he would put his hands in front of his face and cry, but never fought back.

It was May, and Stanley was looking forward to the end of the school year. He was alone in his bedroom finishing up the homework he hadn't done the night before. Unaware of the time, he was startled when his grandmother began knocking on his door. In a no nonsense voice, she informing him, "Stanley, you're going be late unless you get moving."

Stanley gathered up the papers off his desk, grabbed his schoolbooks, said goodbye to his imaginary friends, and ran down the stairs and out of the house. He needed to be in his classroom before Tony got his hands on him. Tony was the toughest boy in school, and he didn't like Stanley one bit.

Walking quickly but not running, Stanley was unprepared for the voice that spoke to him. *Think Tony will be waiting for you?* The question was being asked, in the deep voice he used in his make-believe conversations with his imaginary friend, *Rocky.*

"What?" Stanley asked, in a state of panic, unsure of what he heard.

Why do you let Tony pick on you? The voice continued talking in his head.

"He's the toughest boy in school. He doesn't like me," Stanley said, gasping for breath as he hurried along.

You shouldn't let him push you around, Stanley. You know what would happen if he ever picked on me, don't you?

Stanley knew exactly what would happen. But he wasn't anywhere near as tough as his imaginary hero, Rocky. So he had no choice but to avoid Tony at all cost. When the schoolyard came into view, Stanley's greatest fears were confirmed. Tony was leaning against the fence and spotted him. He watched as Tony pushed himself away from the fence and began walking in his direction.

Thinking it might be smart to remain on the opposite side of the street until he could cross directly in front of the main entrance, he quickened his pace; but he was not fast enough. His heart began beating rapidly when Tony approached. "Hey, lard ass, you're late, aren't you?"

Tony said, resting his arm on Stanley's shoulder and wrapping it around his neck.

Stanley looked down at the pavement, but didn't dare speak.

"What's the matter, cat got your tongue, fat ass," Tony continued, tightening his hold, then, slapping Stanley's face lightly.

Unexpectedly, Rocky spoke out from inside his head. *"Get your hands off him"*, the voice demanded.

"What did you say?" Tony asked.

"You heard me. Get your hands off him," the deep, gruff voice repeated.

Tony released his grip and stood directly in front of him, then slapped Stanley hard across the face. "Are you talking to me, asshole?"

Rocky never hesitated. He hit Tony flush in the mouth with such force that his knees began to wobble, then they buckled, sending Tony reeling backwards onto the ground with Rocky in close pursuit. Now sitting on top of Tony, knees firmly planted on each side of his chest, Rocky delivered blow after blow to his victim's face, causing his head to slam backwards onto the hard pavement, before bouncing back again and again, just to receive another blow. *"Don't you ever do that to him again . . . I'll kill you . . . Do you hear me?"* Rocky began screaming over and over again.

The schoolyard crowd couldn't believe what they were seeing. They watched in shock as the blood flowed freely from the nose and mouth of the toughest boy in school, while the biggest coward, Weird Stanley Kloski, relentlessly delivered one blow after another.

A short time later, sitting outside the principal's office, crying, his shoulders rising and falling as he gasped for air, listening to the ambulance coming to take Tony away, Stanley realized he was in trouble, even though it had been Rocky, not he who had beaten Tony. He knew he would be held responsible for beating the schoolyard bully. Nevertheless, he felt a great deal of pride in *Rocky,* knowing his hero had come to his assistance.

Because of the seriousness of the injuries, the police had no choice but to press charges in juvenile court. When Stanley appeared in front of the judge, the judge decided because Stanley had never been in trouble before, to put him on probation for six months. If after six months he didn't get into any more trouble, the charges would be dropped, and his record would remain sealed.

As added punishment, the school committee decided it would be in everyone's best interest if Stanley didn't return to school, so he finished eighth grade being tutored at home by his grandmother. In June when the rest of his classmates received their diplomas, Stanley was not sitting amongst his classmates on stage in the auditorium. Instead, he received his diploma one week later in the mail.

By the time Stanley entered South Orange High School in the fall of 1960, his reputation had preceded him and had actually grown. He was no longer someone the other students taunted or teased. He walked the hallways of school with newfound respect after word of his fight with Tony had been repeated and exaggerated over and over.

Entering high school, Stanley was just two inches short of six feet. He was overweight at nearly two hundred thirty pounds and uncoordinated. Whatever he wore looked several sizes too small. When he walked, his feet dragged and his arms hung loosely at his side, extending from massive slopping shoulders. But nobody dared make any comments about his oversized body. The students no longer called him *Weird Stanley*. Instead it was *Crazy Stanley* that they feared, capable of exploding at any time.

Stanley had no more incidents like the situation with Tony throughout high school. His past court record was forgotten and wasn't an issue. He began feeling better about himself and anxious to get on with his life. After graduating from high school, he applied for admittance, and was accepted at Seton Hall University, the same school where his grandfather and mother had previously attended.

CHAPTER 17

IT WAS FRIDAY, May 12th, four-thirty-five in the afternoon when Carol discovered she was a lesbian.

She was lying on the floor in the family room, elbows firmly planted, holding tightly to her history book, reading her class assignment covering the Civil War, when the subject of Todd Bryant came up. Her two older brothers, Danny and Michael, were watching television when Danny began telling his younger brother about the incident that had taken place in the school gym that caused Carol to abandon her studying and listen closely.

Todd was believed to be queer. Although no one was one-hundred-percent sure, everyone in school suspected it. Todd was a slight child, small for his age, with delicate, almost pretty facial features, a high pitched girlish voice and he had an odd way of walking. He was extremely sensitive; making him the perfect target for constant harassment and humiliation delivered by the other students, who traveled in a group like a pack of wolf's, acting like animals, attacking the weakest member of the herd, knowing he would not retaliate, or go to the guidance counselor and complain.

What had taken place was a group of boys had surrounded Todd in the gymnasium, forming a circle of hatred that there was no escape from. He was forced to submit to their demands, and had no choice but to let them have their moments of triumph, while all he felt was dread and a deep imbedded form of panic. Ronnie, the ringleader of the group and most vocal, was standing in the center of the circle, smiling triumphantly. He held Todd's hair in his fist, forcing his head backwards, while tears fell from his victim's eyes. The spectators, thinking this was entertaining, laughed and encouraged Ronnie to keep up the torturous humiliation of Todd Bryant.

Danny was relating these events to Michael, while Carol pretending not to be paying attention, but actually listening attentively. "You should've seen the look on Todd's face when Ronnie snuck up behind him and pulled his gym shorts down. Then, Ronnie grabbed him by the hair, forced him to his knees and made him admit he was a faggot. The queer started crying like a baby. At first he denied it, but then he admitted he was queer. Everyone heard him say it. It was a riot," Danny said, laughing hysterically.

Carol had remained silent, hypnotized by the conversation. Finally, unable to remain quiet any longer, she asked, "Why does Ronnie always pick on Todd? He never bothers anyone."

Danny hesitated for a moment, then, continued. "I told you, because he's queer. All the kids pick on him. It's fun. Todd's nothing but a faggot."

Michael was intrigued by the story, but wasn't exactly sure what a faggot was. "What's a faggot?"

Both Michael and Carol had heard the expressions, *faggot, homo,* and *queer* many times, but didn't fully understand the meaning.

Danny looked around the room, being sure no one else was listening. "Queers and faggots are guys that have sex with another guy. You know, men that love other men."

The air in the room suddenly felt thick. Carol was finding it difficult to breathe. She didn't know anything about men that loved other men, but she had been struggling lately with mixed feelings about her own sudden interest in sex, and her recent attraction to Rhonda, a beautiful girl she was attracted too.

Carol was frightened. She always felt she was different from other girls, but it wasn't anything she was concerned about. It was just the way things had always been. After listening to Danny, she was starting to understand why. "Is it just guys that are queers, Danny? Are girls like that, too?" Carol asked meekly, holding her breath, waiting for the answer she feared was coming.

Danny explained. "Girls are lesbians."

"Are queers and lesbians the same thing?"

"Yes. Except girls that are lesbians have sex with other girls."

As Michael and Danny continued talking about Todd Bryant, Carol kept looking from Danny, then to Michael, then back to Danny, while they continued to talk about Todd and how other kids pick on him because he was a *queer.*

Growing up wishing she had been born a boy was one thing, now realizing she actually was a boy in a girl's body was quite something else. She often wondered why she was never interested in playing with dolls, but would much rather be hanging around the ball field with her brothers, playing baseball or doing other things the boys liked doing. She no longer wondered *who* she was, she was now concerned with *what* she was.

Everything changed that afternoon. She would remember this day forever. She felt she was moving toward the truth, her new identity, the end of her old life, and the beginning of a new life, but she wished it was anyone's life but hers.

Until that afternoon, being labeled a *tomboy*, a title her father Ralph Johnson proudly gave her, was a title Carol was extremely proud of. He loved sports. And she loved him. Making him smile whenever she made an exceptionally good play on the ball field or the basketball court, knowing he was watching gave her a great deal of pleasure.

But, being a *tomboy* was one thing, being a *lesbian* was an altogether different story. In the past she had overheard her father making cruel remarks about gays and lesbians, and knew by the sarcasm in his voice that he didn't like them. If he was to discover her secret, it would break his heart. She was determined to keep her secret, just that, a secret.

It didn't take long for Carol to realize that if her secret was ever revealed, if her brothers, her mother, her father, or if the kids at school found out she was a lesbian, they would have nothing to do with her. She would be shunned. She would be subjected to the same kind of harassment and humiliation that Todd Bryant constantly received.

Throughout the family room chat, Carol's body went from hot to cold, then back to hot. She couldn't get over her feelings of uneasiness, making her cringe with fear, heart beating rapidly and her whole body breaking out in a sweat. She was not crying, but she was on the verge. She knew she was trapped. Trapped inside her own body, knowing she would never be allowed to be herself ever again. She would have to keep her secret inside forever.

She continued carrying the burden of being an outcast hidden inside, and would often cry herself to sleep at night. She was in a state of constant fear that her classmates would discover her secret. Alone in her bed at night, Carol would slide beneath the sheets and pray to God to change who she was. But when she awoke in the morning, nothing would be changed. She was doomed to spend her life pretending to be someone she wasn't.

At fourteen, Carol remained unattractive. She had big bones, short stout legs, and a flat chest, unlike her classmates who were developing breasts, getting tall and filling out their hips. There was one girl in particular, Rhonda, the most attractive girl in Trenton High, who was fully developed and extremely beautiful for her age, a girl Carol could not keep out of her mind.

Rhonda had hips that curved out from her tiny waist and her breasts appeared stunning, straining against her tight-fitting sweaters she wore almost daily. Her perfectly even white teeth and bright hazel eyes always appeared to be smiling. Carol would spend nights in bed tossing and turning, wishing Rhonda was beside her, wondering what it would feel like to touch her breasts, or kiss her bright, red lips.

The most embarrassing day in Carol's life happened while sitting next to Rhonda in the cafeteria. Carol was quietly eating her lunch, speaking to no one, but unable to stop staring at Rhonda out of the corner of her eye, when an uncontrollable urge to reach over and touch her face overwhelmed her, so she did. Before realizing what she was doing, she gently ran her fingers against her cheek. Rhonda's face turned scarlet red. She got a mean look in her eyes and slapped her hand away.

"Get your hands off me, queer," she spat out, hatred in her eyes.

The look of anger, disgust and contempt on Rhonda's face as she quickly got up, leaving her unfinished lunch on the table, as she stormed away, made Carol feel more rejected and humiliated than at any other time in her life. She couldn't stop shaking, fighting back the urge to cry. Her gut feeling being: *Crawl into a deep, dark hole, and never come out.* After that, Rhonda treated her like a leper, and Carol knew enough to stay away.

For the remainder of her high school career, Carol was successful in staying in the background. Fearing her secret would be discovered caused her to be especially discrete. She didn't want to be this way. She wanted to be like everyone else. But, as much as she wanted to be 'normal,' there was nothing she could do that would change who she was.

Stanley Kloski was overweight, uncoordinated, lazy, and lacked the slightest bit of competitiveness in his personality. These were the reasons Stanley's involvement in sports activities were limited to being a spectator, rather than a participant. Although he never played sports, he could be seen at almost all of the school sporting events cheering enthusiastically from the side lines.

Unlike Stanley, Carol Johnson was a gifted athlete. She had a win-at-all-cost attitude whenever on the field and the athletic ability to make sure that happened. In her senior year, she had been voted, uncontested, by her teammates to represent them as Captain of the Seton Hall Girls Softball Team.

These two complete opposites unexpectedly found themselves sitting next to each other one afternoon in the bleachers at the boy's gym, watching the varsity team practicing for the upcoming basketball game against the much larger and more powerful University of Connecticut. Seton Hall, being a smaller school than U-Conn. was usually not considered a threat, but this year the Pirates were playing exceptionally well and were planning on pulling off an upset.

Carol spoke first. "Do you think they have a chance?"

Not used to having anyone speak to him, Stanley ignored her, and continued watching the players passing the ball around and shooting baskets on the court.

When he didn't respond, Carol continued. "Hey, I'm talking to you."

Startled and unsure what she had said, Stanley turned and asked, nervously. "What?"

Carol continued looking at him with raised eyebrows in a who-do-you-think I'm talking to, sort of way. "Do you think we can beat U-Conn Saturday?"

"No. But it certainly would be a big upset if we did."

"By the way, I'm Carol Johnson," she said, extending her hand.

"Stanley Kloski," he replied, shaking her hand weakly, avoiding eye contact.

Carol shook her head. "I've gone to all of the home games this year. With the biggest game of the year coming up, it would have to be away and I'm gonna' miss it."

"You're not going? Half the school will be there. Tickets are already sold out."

"That's the problem. I waited too long. I couldn't get a ticket. I have no way of getting there even if I did have a ticket," she said, sounding disappointed.

"There's a guy in my math class that might have a ticket for sale. Said he needed to spend the weekend studying. I can see if he wants to sell it," Stanley offered.

"Even if I get a ticket, I don't have a ride. The buses are already full."

"I'll give you a ride."

"Are you serious? Do you really think you can get me a ticket? If you can and don't mind my tagging along, I'd really like to go," Carol said, inching closer and beaming with enthusiasm.

"Do you have a number that I can call later?"

Carol quickly tore a page from her notebook, wrote down a number and handed it to him. "I'm headed back to the dorm shortly. You can call anytime today and I'll be in."

Stanley stood and began stumbling between the bleachers as he headed out to find the ticket holder. "I'll call as soon as I know something," he said, speaking over his shoulder.

Two hours later, Stanley called and gave Carol the good news. They made arrangements for him to pick her up in front of her dorm at nine o'clock, Saturday morning to drive to Connecticut and watch the Seton Hall Pirates, hopefully upset U-Conn.

Unfortunately that didn't happen. The Pirates were soundly beaten, 86-74.

Driving home from the game, they talked freely about many things, especially sports. They discovered they had a lot in common, both being diehard Yankee and Giants fans. Before dropping Carol off, they had made plans to get together again. Stanley asked her if she would be interested in spending Sunday afternoon at a local pub to drink beer and watch the Giants play the Dolphins in a playoff game on television. Carol said she would love to.

It wasn't long before they were frequently seen walking the corridors together at school. As a couple, they found they were more accepted by the other students. They began getting invited to parties at fraternity houses where they had never been invited before.

For the first time in both their lives they began feeling normal and accepted. They were truly enjoying their new found popularity. Stanley was anxious to introduce Carol to his mother, not knowing what to expect from the woman he hardly knew. When they met, she acted delighted, and said to Stanley privately later, "She may be exactly what you need."

Their relationship moved along quickly. It wasn't long before Carol was spending nights at Stanley's apartment. Sex was awkward and infrequent. But Stanley was truly happy for the first time in his life.

Although Carol liked Stanley and enjoyed his company, she had an alternative motive to wanting their relationship to evolve. Carol was studying to be a physical education teacher. She hoped to find employment teaching Phys Ed at the high school level once she graduated. She was aware if it was known she was a lesbian, any chance of getting a job working with teenage girls was almost impossible. Marrying Stanley was the answer; she just had to talk him into it.

On many occasions, she had heard the words *dyke, lesbian* and *gay* whispered behind her back. Unlike her classmates in high school, students in college were more sophisticated and knowledgeable about gays and lesbians and were suspicious about her identity. She wanted to put a stop to it. It was the vast, lonely distance from everyone that bothered her about being a lesbian. She was sick and tired of being alone, walking around with a constant knot in the pit of her stomach, believing she was some kind of freak of nature, knowing it would have been better to be a leper than to be born a lesbian.

Nobody was aware of what a combination of fear, anger and sadness she had consumed throughout her life. Until she had met Stanley, she often felt her situation was hopeless, and often thought *If I had a gun, I'd stick it in my mouth and blow my head off.*

All that heartache and pain was going to disappear if she could convince Stanley to marry her. Carol wanted nothing more than to be like everyone else. Get married, have a family and be accepted by the straight community. She thought of her two brothers, Danny and Michael, who were going about their business living normal lives, and wanted to be able to live the same kind of life. She also knew if her macho father, whom she adored and had always admired her *tomboyish* athletic ability, found out it was because she was actually a boy hiding in a girls' body, he would go ballistic.

She wanted to believe that once she married Stanley, it would be the answer to her prayers. She wanted to believe she could change. She wanted to believe it was just a matter of determination and dedication to her new life. She wanted to believe if she worked at it, she could control these feeling she harbored for other women. She wanted to believe in time she would learn to love Stanley.

She was convinced anything was possible if she wanted it bad enough. And she did. She wanted to be accepted by society more than she wanted anything before in her life, and believed marrying Stanley was the way to get the respectability she needed. She also knew when you were keeping a secret, you had to do it alone, keep it out of sight and buried in the darkest corner of the closet.

Stanley Kloski and Carol Ann Johnson were married shortly after graduating from college in a simple ceremony in the chapel on the campus of Seton Hall University, before a small crowd of relatives and friends.

CHAPTER 18

AFTER TALKING TO Stanley in his driveway and leaving the Gagnon's house after a quick walk through without any more information than when he walked in, he drove out of Barefoot Bay, headed for the station. The afternoon heat created a dank and musty, stale odor from discarded beer cans scattered on the floorboard behind him. The smell was making his stomach turn and he felt like he was going to throw-up. He considered pulling over, but didn't. He didn't want to be seen puking on the side of the road by the Barefoot Bay residents.

He turned left onto Route 1. Unable to stop shaking and suddenly craving a drink; he reached over and turned on the air-conditioner to maximum cool. Whenever he felt sick, with the shakes, alcohol was his only cure. Ray desperately wanted to drive to Bottoms Up, belly up to the bar and take his medicine, but couldn't. He needed to find out the results of the autopsy.

Walking into his office, Barrett noticing the red light blinking on his answering machine, Ray threw his keys onto his desk and quickly pressed the play button. A pre-recorded voice informed him, "You have one message." Then, after a short pause, "This is Detective Bill Pennie from the Sheriff's Department. I've got your autopsy results. Call me anytime today. The number is 331-772-5345, extension 310."

Taking a deep breath, his stomach in knots, Ray punched in the numbers and asked for extension 310. He was patched straight through. "This is Chief Barrett. I got your message," he said, as soon as Detective Pennie picked up.

"Yes, Barrett, the coroner finally got around to doing the autopsy," the detective said.

"So, what did he find out?"

"Bottom line; according to the report, your guy was strangled."

"I was afraid of that. Can you give me any details?"

"Well, he was banged-up pretty bad. The official cause of death resulted from asphyxiation." There was a slight pause while Detective Pennie caught his breath. "There was internal trauma in his neck and throat. The subject had also bitten his tongue; all this is consistent with cases involving strangulation."

"It looks like I can forget about natural causes," Ray said, speaking more to himself than the detective, while picking up a pencil and nervously tapping it on his desk.

"No way did this guy die from natural causes."

"You're sure."

"Positive, but that's not all of it. I'm sure you noticed the bruises on the left side of his jaw. He was either punched or hit with a blunt instrument. It appears it was a fist from the looks of the bruises," Detective Pennie continued.

"You don't think those bruises could have happened while falling?"

"Not a chance. This might be helpful. It appears from the location and the direction the blow came from; whoever hit him was right handed. The victim also suffered a slight concussion from blunt force trauma to the back of his head. That could've happen when he fell, but not the bruises around his neck and jaw," he explained.

Barrett's stomach started churning. He felt he needed a beer and he needed it now. "You said whoever did this was right handed. Are you sure?" Ray asked, his eyes rolling back in his head.

"Reasonably sure; if it was a fist, it had to come from someone right handed, according to the coroner's report, he seemed to be sure about that."

"The guy looked to be in good shape. I imagine it would've taken a powerful man to do something like this," Chief Barrett said, visualizing Nick Pappas.

"You're definitely looking for a man. A couple of men were sent out this morning to look around. From what I can see from their report the place was clean. No sign of forced entry. If you want my opinion, I don't think the victim was picked randomly. He must have known whoever did this and let him in."

"I agree. I walked around the house earlier myself. Nothing looked out of place," he said.

"These kinds of situations are almost never random. Family problems, spurned lovers, people close to the victim; that's where you should start looking," the detective suggested.

"That's what I was thinking, too."

"I guess that's about it. Where do you want the body sent?"

"I'm not sure. He's from up North. I imagine the wife will want his remains sent back up there. I'll have her give you a call."

"If you have any other questions, don't hesitate to contact us. I'll email you the report."

"Thanks for everything," Ray said, hung up and slammed his fist on his desk.

There was no longer any doubt. Chief Barrett had his first homicide case. His only suspect was Nick Pappas. Pappas was certainly big enough and looked mean enough to commit murder, but that wasn't enough to build a case on. He needed more.

It was late afternoon when Ray walked out of the station. He needed to inform Mrs. Gagnon about what he had found out, but decided there wasn't any sense in waking her while she was sleeping at her neighbors. It could wait until tomorrow. Going to Bottoms Up was out of the question. Rumors spread quickly around Micco, and now that it was officially a murder, it wouldn't be long before stories of a killer lurking inside the gates of Barefoot Bay would be circulating. He knew everyone would be hounding him with questions if he went to the bar. He was in no mood to answer their stupid questions, especially since he didn't have any answers.

Ray decided to head home. He was feeling a little better, but still hadn't completely gotten over the shakes. He needed a few beers to settle his stomach. He knew if he didn't have a drink soon, he would start dry-heaving. He hated the dry-heaves. He decided he would stop at Winn-Dixie on his way home and picked up a case of beer, a steak for the grill, and ingredients for a salad.

He planned on spending the remainder of the afternoon eating steak and drinking beer, while explaining that he was in the middle of a murder case that he wanted nothing to do with, in great detail to Elvis, who would listen, pay close attention, but never ask dumb questions.

CHAPTER 19

SUNDAY MORNING, Ray woke up at 8:30 with a white glare of sunlight shining in his face. He reached up, pulled the curtain tight, moaned loudly, then fell back onto the bed and went back to sleep. He remained lying motionless for the remainder of the morning. It was after 11 o'clock when he managed to drag himself out of bed.

It felt like his head was about to explode. Sitting on his stained, lumpy mattress, rubbing his swollen, glazed eyes, he made the same promise he made yesterday morning, the morning before, and many mornings before that. He was going to stop drinking. He had to change his ways. He couldn't continue waking up every morning with a sour stomach and a Budweiser hangover.

Before moving to Florida, Ray was a policeman in Hartford, Connecticut. He thought being a cop would be glamorous work, walking around in a handsome uniform, protecting the good guys from the bad guys. But he wasn't on the job long before realizing he could never be one of those macho men who loved breaking up brawls, kicking in doors, and trying to settle domestic disputes. He had seen more than his share of women who'd been worked over by the loser husbands they had married, who used them for punching bags. Once while chasing some guy down a dark alley, he nearly broke a leg jumping off a fence, trying to catch the bum. He never did catch him and to this day couldn't even remember why he was chasing him.

Being a cop in a big city like Hartford could get a guy seriously hurt. So in a desperate attempt to outrun, rewrite and change his past, Ray started looking for a way out. After reading a want ad in the *Police Gazette* that a town on the east coast of Florida was advertising for a police officer, he decided to apply. It sounded peaceful, a town where he wouldn't be chasing bad guys down dark alleys and jumping over fences.

Two weeks later, he was in Micco for the interview. He got hired, went back to Connecticut and packed up his few belongings, moved to Florida and never went back. Years have gone by since leaving Hartford, and he couldn't tell you where they'd gone; twenty-five plus years and twelve-hundred miles due North, in another world, in another life.

He soon discovered being unmarried, with no relatives and few friends, there's little to do in Micco. In order to fill his off duty hours, Ray began spending his leisure hours drinking at the local saloons, feeling lonely and ignored, neither hated or loved, just feeling a deep sense of self-pity, where he found alcohol helped block out the emptiness of his life.

But today would be the day he was going to turn his life around. He was determined. He couldn't go on like this. He knew people were talking about his drinking. He was the Chief of Police, for Christ-sake. He was definitely going on the wagon, and this time he meant it, he really meant it. Now that the decision had been made, he had to get moving. He needed to speak to Mrs. Gagnon and tell her that her husband had been murdered, and he needed to sober up if he was going to solve this murder case.

Ray stood, wavered, but managed to stumble into the bathroom without falling. He hovered over the toilet and relieved himself. He reached into the medicine cabinet, took two Tylenol tablets with a glass of water, then, struggled to shave and get dressed, before going into the kitchen. He forced himself to eat several mouthfuls of cereal, threw the half-full bowl into the sink, reached under the counter for Elvis' food, fed the dog and left for Barefoot Bay.

Walking down his carport into the bright Florida afternoon, breathing in the slightly humid air, Ray opened the car door and was about to get in. The aroma of discarded beer cans caused him to gag. Opening the back door of his Focus, he reached down and began throwing the empty cans onto the driveway, next to yesterday's cans that were scattered around the grille, were a swarm of flies were feasting on the grease from last night's steak. He shooed them away before slamming the cover down. Getting into his car, he backed down the driveway, while listening to beer cans being crushed beneath the tires.

Remembering Mrs. Gagnon spent Friday night at her neighbors, he drove directly there. He turned into the driveway and walked up the driveway on shaky legs and rang the doorbell. He was rubbing his forehead when Stanley answered the door.

"Hello, Stanley. It is Stanley, isn't it?"

"Yes, come in," Stanley offered, stepping aside.

"I was hoping to speak to Mrs. Gagnon."

Just then, a masculine-looking woman came out of the back bedroom, closing her bathrobe and tying the cord tightly around her waist. Her eyes were having difficulty adjusting to the daylight, and her hair was still uncombed. Squinting slightly, she said, "Kathy decided to stay at her house last night," Carol Kloski explained.

"You must be Stanley's wife. I'm Chief Barrett," Ray said, stepping forward and extending his outstretched hand.

She took several steps forward to meet him. "Yes, I know. I remember you from Friday night."

"Yes, that's right."

"Sorry about my appearance. So, what can we do for you?"

"I was just saying to Stanley that I was hoping to speak with Mrs. Gagnon."

"Like I just said, Kathy not here."

"She's not; well, if you don't mind, since I'm here, would you mind answering a couple of questions?"

"Ask anything you want."

"I presume you're close to the Gagnon's, that right?"

"I don't know what you mean by close, but yes, we're friends."

"Are you aware of any problems in their marriage?" Ray inquired, squinting through bloodshot eyes.

"Why are you asking questions about how they got along? What does that have to do with Phil having a heart attack?" Carol asked, eyeing Ray suspiciously.

"I'm just curious, that's all."

"I don't know about any problems. I think I would have known if they were having problems," Carol said defensively.

"I'm sure you would have. Going back to last Friday night, I noticed two other couples. I talked to one man outside in the carport. His name was Pappas. Is he married to the woman that was sitting on the couch with you and Mrs. Gagnon?"

"Yes. Her name is Betty."

"I see. There was another couple standing off to the side. Who are they?" Ray asked, his knees getting weak, wishing he could sit down.

"Jimmy and Rita Martin, they live across the street. They're renting the house for the winter."

"I understand all four of you women were together Friday night," Ray said, his legs getting weaker by the minute.

"That's right. We went to bingo at St. Luke's."

"How does everyone get along?"

"Everyone gets along fine. We girls go to bingo, the gym, and shopping together. The guys occasionally play golf," Carol answered, wondering why all the questions.

"Have all of you known each other for long?"

"We all met here in Barefoot Bay, except for Jimmy and Kathy. They used to date back in high school." Kathy had told Carol weeks before that she and Jimmy had dated, but had asked her not to say anything. Carol, not fully awake, had forgotten her promise.

"That's unusual, them getting together here in Barefoot Bay after all these years."

"Yes, Kathy was surprised when they rented the house across the street. Would you like to sit down, officer? You don't look good," Carol finally offered.

Ray was feeling weak but declined. "No thanks. Since Mrs. Gagnon's not here, I'll be going. Do you think she'll be awake?"

"I'm not sure. Knock on her door and find out."

"I'll do that. Thanks for your time," Ray said, then quickly left.

Leaving his car in the Kloski's driveway, Ray walked across a perfectly manicured lawn, with neatly clipped boxwoods lining the walkway and front of the house. He could feel his headache spreading into his eyes as he made his way across the grass.

He was greeted by Mrs. Gagnon, who was standing next to her frosted, beveled glass front doorway, the image of a flowering iris etched into the glass. She was dressed in her housecoat, but unlike her neighbor, she had taken time to put on makeup. She looked tired, but considering what she'd been through, managed a strained smile as Ray approached. "Good morning. I saw you were at Carol's house. I figured you'd be coming over here next."

"I thought you might still be staying with them."

"Carol invited me to stay, but I decided there was no sense in imposing any longer. Come in, officer," she said, stepping aside. "Have a seat."

"Thanks," Ray said.

"I'm glad you stopped by, officer. I can't stop wondering why you felt it necessary to take Philip's body to Melbourne to be examined."

"Whenever we suspect foul play, we're required to have an autopsy performed."

"It's hard to believe Phil had a heart attack. He never complained about having any problems," she said, her voice sounding unsteady.

"That's why it's important that I had the autopsy done."

"Have you finished?" Kathy asked. Then realizing what he had just said about, *whenever we suspect foul play,* asked, "What do you mean by foul play?"

"Before I get to that, Detective Pennie from the Sheriff's Department said if you give his office a call, they can assist you in having your husband's remains shipped up North. If that's what your intentions are."

"I'll have my son call. He's flying in this afternoon. Do you have the detective's number?"

"Not with me. I'll have my secretary, Darcy, call you tomorrow morning, or you could call the County Sheriff's Department yourself. Ask for Detective Pennie."

Ray hesitated for a moment. He was impressed at how in control Kathy seemed to be, waiting for him to explain what had happened to her husband. But he knew she wouldn't be much longer, once he delivered the news. "Mrs. Gagnon, your husband didn't have a heart attack!"

Everything became still, like the air gets before a thunderstorm. "He didn't? What happened?"

He could see uncertainty and fear spreading across her face. He knew it was about to get worse. "Your husband was assaulted by someone. I'm not sure who or why, but he was definitely beaten," he said, purposely avoiding the word murdered.

Kathy's appearance changed. She appeared confused. Her body began shaking nervously. She tried to remain still by grasping her knees but continued to tremble. Losing her husband hurt terribly, but discovering he'd been beaten in the sanctuary of her home was devastating.

The sense of reality at what the officer was telling her was overwhelming. For a long moment she remained motionless, frozen with confusion. Her eyes darted from his face to her hands, then back to his face. "Are you sure? Why? I can't believe that someone would do such a thing to Philip! Officer, you must be mistaken!" She had always felt so safe and protected here. Things like this happened to other people, but never to her and especially not in Barefoot Bay.

Chief Barrett didn't know exactly what Kathy Gagnon was feeling. Panic probably, but fear and insecurity for her future, absolutely. "There's no mistake. The autopsy definitely concluded that your husband was beaten and strangled."

"Who could have done such a terrible thing? Especially right in our home," Kathy asked.

Ray's head was pounding, and he wasn't comfortable giving her this information. "I don't know, but every effort will be made to find out," Ray assured her. "Was there someone your husband might not have gotten along with?"

"No. I can't imagine anyone doing anything like that. What will my son think? How am I going to tell him? Oh, my God, I can't believe this," Kathy said, her forehead wrinkled, her eyes shut tightly.

"I'm sorry, Mrs. Gagnon. I know this comes as quite a shock."

"Quite a shock; Officer, are you sure? Phil didn't have any enemies," she said, tears beginning to flow freely.

"Yes, I'm sure."

"It doesn't make sense."

"No, it doesn't. Do you feel up to answering a couple more questions?" When she didn't answer, Ray continued. "Is there anything missing in the house, jewelry, money?"

"No. Nothing."

"Have you noticed anything unusual lately, strangers in the neighborhood for instance, maybe a car you didn't recognize driving by?"

"This is a large community. There're always different people and cars coming and going. I haven't notice anything out of the ordinary."

"You said your son's arriving today. Will you be staying up North for the remainder of the year?"

"I'm going home. I doubt I'll be coming back this year. I'm not sure now if I'll ever be back. So much is going on right now. I don't know what to think," she concluded, tears streaking down her cheeks.

"If you'll give my secretary your home address when she calls in the morning, I would appreciate it. I'm sure I'll have to get in touch with you eventually. Once again, I'm sorry, Mrs. Gagnon. I know this is a shock. I'll do what I can to get to the bottom of it. I'll keep in touch," he said, getting up and walking backwards toward the door, anxious to get the hell out of there.

"Oh, my God, I can't believe . . . ," were the last words Ray heard before quietly closing the door behind him.

Later that afternoon, Ray was sitting in his office going over his earlier conversation with Carol Kloski and Kathy Gagnon. He had things he needed to do. First: get the names and hometown addresses of the Gagnon's neighbors. Second: call the local police departments from each of their hometowns to see if there was anything suspicious about their backgrounds that he should know about, especially that Greek, Pappas. He was Ray's prime suspect, and he intended on watching him closely.

Third: the situation with Kathy Gagnon and Jimmy Martin being sweethearts back in high school. Their supposedly unexpected meeting again after all these years in Barefoot Bay seemed suspicious. That would have to be checked out. Tomorrow morning he would have Darcy call Mrs. Gagnon and get her Massachusetts address. If there was any connection between Jimmy Martin, Kathy Gagnon and her husband's death he needed to know where to locate her.

It was now late Sunday afternoon. Monday would be soon enough to start his investigation. Realizing he had done everything he could today, he was heading to Bottoms Up for happy hour. He hoped he would be left alone once he got there. He needed a couple of beers to clear his head and time to go over the events involving his first murder case. He was remembering his pledge to quit drinking, but there were just too many things going on right now to quit today. Tomorrow, definitely tomorrow he would stop drinking, and this time he meant it, he really meant it.

CHAPTER 20

James & Rita (Magliano) Martin

Married November 15, 1969

STARING OUT THE port window of the C-130 transport aircraft that was due to land shortly on an isolated airstrip in Da Nang, Jimmy looked below in awe, taking in the beauty of the lush green, oceanfront coastline that was Vietnam.

From high above he could see a narrow river cutting its way through the rice fields, and without a cloud in the sky to hinder the view of the aqua-marine ocean water and white costal sands, it appeared more like a tropical resort than the dangerous country it was.

Already thousands of American soldiers had lost their lives, and many more would follow. Jimmy realized he too could die and become just another statistic, arriving home in a body bag as so many other young men already had. During boot camp his Drill Instructor had informed him that *"If it was your time to die, there's not a hell of a lot you could do about it."*

It was 1965. The Vietnam conflict was not popular with many Americans. College students were out in droves protesting the United States' involvement, chanting *"Make love not war."* Colleges such as Brandeis University were turning out radical students such as Jerry Rubin, Angelia Davis and Abbie Hoffman who were spreading their message to other campuses across the country about ending our involvement in a war they believed we had no business being in.

Hippies were smoking pot on the streets of San Francisco and listening to Janis Joplin, Jimi Hendrix and Joan Baez using the stage and their microphones as a platform to protest the war. Barry McGuire's popular antiwar recording of *"Eve of Destruction,"* along with Bob

Dylan singing *"Times They Are A-Changing"* was being played on every campus in the country, causing unrest and uprising amongst students.

It was a crazy time in the United States. The country was divided as it had never been divided before. Many Americans thought we had no business sticking our nose in the affairs of a foreign country, fighting a war that posed no threat to the United States.

All these thoughts were going through Jimmy's mind as he continued looking out the window of the C-130 cargo plane as it started its descent, pitching and rocking in the dense tropical air. The plane appeared as if it was about to crash into the overgrown jungle, but at the last minute he heard the landing gear drop from the belly of the plane and snap into place as a small asphalt runway appeared.

Once the aircraft engines went silent, Jimmy Martin turned and gazed about the plane at the thirty-six men in his platoon, a hundred pounds of gear lay at their feet. He believed every soldier was contemplating the reality of the situation and praying for the same thing; to somehow survive their tour of duty and return home safely to their families.

Jimmy was starting to have second thoughts. He felt himself moving farther and farther away from everyone and everything he knew. His mind was wandering back to the day at Paisano's Pizza House when he talked to his friend, Joey Magliano, about his reasons for joining the Marines.

Jimmy and Joey were best friends since they met in the first grade and still remained close. Joey was leaving for boot camp in less than two days when this conversation took place. "Why the hell did you decide to join the Marines?" Jimmy asked, looking puzzled.

"It was just a matter of time before they would have drafted me. I felt I might as well join now and beat them to the punch. Besides, I don't agree with all those draft-dodging, pot-smoking hippies who are running up to Canada, or the college students who are protesting this war. We're Americans; if we want this country to stay free, we have to stop those Communist bastards before they take over the whole fucking world," Joey explained, sounding patriotic.

"I guess a lot of people don't agree. They think there isn't a threat as long as the Communists stay over there."

"Well, they're wrong! The whole purpose of us fighting them in Vietnam is so we don't have to fight the bastards over here."

"What's your mother think about you leaving?"

"She agrees. Rita got a job with my Mom in the dress shop. They should do fine," Joey said. "Don't forget, my Mom comes from the old country. She thinks America is the best place on earth and worth fighting for. What about you? Ever think about joining?"

Jimmy hadn't given any thought to joining the Army, Marines or any other branch of the service. But now that Joey brought it up, he started thinking this might not be a bad idea.

He had just turned nineteen. His life was going nowhere working in the mills for minimum wage. It was just a matter of time before he'd be getting his draft notice. Rather than wait, he began thinking, like Joey, he might as well join.

Kathy was making new friends. The two of them didn't seem to have much in common anymore. He was aware that Kathy was spending a lot of time with someone else. He was sure Kathy didn't know he knew, but he'd seen them together. He was having a difficult time coping with it. He felt he still loved her, but with her dating another guy, there wasn't much hope of them staying together much longer, and realized it would be better if he wasn't around.

He decided the Army was what he wanted. The next morning he talked to the Army recruiter. Less than two weeks after talking to Joey at the pizza house, Jimmy joined. Once he made the commitment, there was an unfamiliar sense of excitement about being part of the United States Armed Forces. He believed he'd taken a big step in becoming a man.

The last night he spent with Kathy Hennessey was a night he would not forget. They spent the night making love over and over again. The next morning when he walked out of her house, Jimmy had a lump in his throat. He knew he would miss her and felt he was leaving behind a part of himself that he would never recapture. There had been no mention of keeping in touch.

Jimmy was shipped off to boot camp at Fort Hadley, Georgia, where he was trained as an infantry soldier. It was here that he was given courses on how to survive during guerrilla and psychological warfare before being sent to that hellhole called Vietnam.

His Drill Instructor, Sergeant Baxter, a soldier with a barrel chest, dressed in a khaki uniform with boots so highly polished he could see his reflection in them, told him to forget about everything and everyone he left behind. It didn't take long before his hometown of Lowell, his family, his friends, and Kathy suddenly were pushed to the back of his memory.

When Jimmy was assigned to his regular division, the instructors from the Third Division Special Forces Group had said it was not only their right but their duty to kill the hated Vietnamese Communists. He vividly remembered when he came face to face with Drill Instructor Baxter at boot camp, being told more than once with a smirk on his face, *"Don't worry, they can't kill you if it's not your time. But if it is your time, there's not a hell of a lot you can do about it.*" If that was supposed to make Jimmy feel better, it didn't.

It didn't take long after he arrived in Vietnam that Jimmy found himself in the middle of the horrors of fighting a war, living through sleepless nights, hunger, young men screaming for help, their body parts blown away, dragging the bodies from the battlefield of those that didn't make it.

The first time Jimmy was confronted by one of the enemy was when he became separated from his company. It had been raining since early morning. The storm had slackened, then turned to a drizzle. The ground was saturated, and the weather was hot, steaming with humidity, causing sweat to pour down his face, stinging his eyes.

He was quietly crawling through the brush in what his platoon leader thought was unoccupied jungle. He was inching forward through the brush, arms aching, tired, hungry and scared, dragging his rifle with one hand, trembling badly. Unexpectedly, only twenty feet in front of him, he found himself staring down the barrel of the rifle of a young Viet Cong soldier

The enemy lifted his rifle, aimed and fired. For a moment he experienced paralyzing fear, the mother of all emotions. The bullet missed its target. Jimmy was able to retaliate. He raised his rifle and took dead aim at the enemy's chest. He started to squeeze the trigger, then, realized he couldn't do it. He couldn't murder another human being in cold blood, even one of the hated Viet Cong.

The enemy looked at him with pleading eyes, his gaze begging him not to do it.

Then he did it.

The bullet found its mark in the center of the enemy's chest. He watched as the sniper slumped to the ground. He slowly edged over through the leaves and branches. The young soldier was laying there, his hand clutching his chest, covering his wound dripping with blood, as he began gasping for breath.

Jimmy could see the frightening look of confusion in the enemy's eyes, like he didn't understand what had happened to him. *I guess today was his time,* he thought while gazing down at the young boy he'd killed. The twisted look of terror on the young Vietnamese soldier's face would haunt him for the rest of his life.

Vietnam had become hell on earth. Death and dying was all around him. But his drill sergeant, who at the time he thought was his worst nightmare, had been right; when it came to you or someone else, you killed someone else before he killed you.

Over time, he began seeing death so routinely he became numbed by it. He no longer felt the sense of duty and obligation to fight for the country that brought him here, but the killing went on. He didn't want to die in this God-forsaken place. Jimmy wanted to go home.

Jimmy Martin survived his three years in Vietnam. In the spring of 1968 his mother's prayers were answered. Unlike the thousands of soldiers arriving home to a hostile, ungrateful country, his family welcomed Jimmy with open arms, considering him a hero.

While in Vietnam, Jimmy's mother kept him informed about what was happening in his hometown. She notified him his old girlfriend, Kathy Hennessey, had gotten married and had had a baby. Without any correspondence between them while spending three years in Vietnam, trying to stay alive, any feelings of love he felt for Kathy Hennessey had dissolved into nothing more than a fond memory.

Of all the newspaper clippings he did receive from home, the one item that upset him the most was the obituary about his best friend Joey Magliano. It simply stated that Joey had died in Vietnam fighting for his country and commended him for making the ultimate sacrifice. Along with so many other young Americans who died fighting for what turned out to be a losing cause, Jimmy's best friend, Joseph Magliano returned home in one of those United States issued stainless steel coffins that Drill Instructor Baxter had talked about in boot camp. It apparently had been Joey's time to die, and there wasn't a hell of a lot he could do about it.

CHAPTER 21

LOWELL, MASSACHUSETTS isn't much different than any other large New England city. The neighborhoods are broken up into sections by nationalities. The French, Polish, Irish, Italians, and Greeks had settled in various sections of the city, establishing schools, churches, and social clubs that represented their individual cultures. People of all nationalities worked hard to adapt to their new surroundings and learn the American ways.

The Italian section of the city is referred to as Little Italy and has its own distinct look and feel. Running down the middle of Little Italy is Canal Street, famous for its unique restaurants. The aroma of pasta, sweet sausages, and Italian meat sauce is blown outside by unseen kitchen fans somewhere down the alleyways between buildings, drifting out onto the sidewalks, tempting the appetites of people strolling by. If a person was to take a picture of Canal Street and any street in Napoli, it would be difficult to identify which one was taken in Italy.

People living there have their own dialect, combined with the local slang. If you don't understand what comes out of their mouths, you can usually pick it up from their hand gestures. It's a neighborhood of mostly three-story wooden rental properties occupied by the working class Italians.

Jimmy was walking through these familiar surroundings, reminiscing about the days when he'd been a youngster on his way to his friend Joey's house, remembering the times when life was uncomplicated and carefree. He was looking at his past from a distance where many things changed, yet, in a way, nothing really changed at all.

Today was going to be anything but uncomplicated or carefree. Jimmy wanted to express to Mrs. Magliano how sorry he was about the loss of his best friend Joey, and her only son. He couldn't think of any way to explain why he'd come home safely, honorably discharged, his whole life ahead of him, while her son had died needlessly in some jungle on the other side of the world.

Arriving in front of the three-family apartment house where the Maglianos lived, he stopped and took a deep breath. Gathering his courage, he entered the dimly lit hallway. He slowly walked up to the second-floor apartment where the Maglianos lived.

Jimmy knocked gently on the familiar, faded brown door. After a moment, Joey's younger sister Rita opened the door. Jimmy wasn't sure if he had the right apartment. Rita had grown into an attractive young woman with big, sparkling brown eyes and smooth olive skin. She was still small and petite, but nevertheless had developed nicely, with a figure that could best be described as wholesome.

"Oh, my God, Jimmy Martin!" she exclaimed, smiling brightly. "Come on in, what a wonderful surprise. Mom, Jimmy Martin's here," she announced enthusiastically, turning slightly, looking in the direction of a closed bedroom door off the kitchen. When Rita looked up at him she couldn't help but admire how he had grown into a handsome man, not Clark Gable handsome, but handsome in a way women would feel comfortable with, and even men could admire.

Mrs. Magliano soon appeared from her bedroom wearing a pair of white cotton socks on her feet, while tying a twisted knot beneath her ample bosom, from a ratty old terry cloth housecoat that appeared to have had years of use. Her face looked so much older than he remembered. Her hair was completely gray and pulled back, except for several strands that had become lose and fallen down next to her ear.

She took her glasses out of her pocket and slipped them on, made the sign of the cross, then with arms extended, crossed the room and embraced him. "Oh, my a God! It's a Jimmy Martin," she said with a welcoming smile.

It appeared he'd disturbed her nap. "I hope I didn't come at a bad time."

"No! I'm a so happy to see a you," she assured him.

Feeling uncomfortable but not wanting to put off what he had come to say, Jimmy took a deep breath and exhaled his words slowly. His face nestled against her ear, his voice quivering slightly, he whispered, "I'm very, very sorry about Joey. When I heard what happened, I couldn't stop thinking about him. I had to come by and see if there's anything I can do."

The old woman could see Jimmy was struggling with the death of her son. Leaving her arms around him, embracing him with the love and affection she would have shown her own son had he come home alive, she assured him she understood.

When she spoke, she spoke so softly Jimmy bent down, bringing his ear closer. "Thank you so a much for comin' a by. You a good boy. I know you a love Joey, just a like me and a Rita," she whispered. "Thank a God you a come home safe. I a pray every night for you and Joey. I don't understand why a God does these a things he a does, but it's not a right I should question him. Come. You sit a down. I'm a glad you visit."

Jimmy took off his jacket, hung it over the back of the chair and sat at the kitchen table. After being offered a cup of coffee and sitting and talking for a while, he started to relax. They remained around the kitchen table all afternoon reminiscing about all the wonderful memories they had of Joey.

It was refreshing for Mrs. Magliano to have someone who wasn't hesitant to talk about Joey. You don't think about how awful something is; you're in shock at first, but she still remembers how beautiful the funeral was. The playing of Taps, the firing of three volleys from the rifles of the spiffy looking soldiers, how proud she was to accept the three cornered flag that had covered her son's coffin, the flag that is now proudly displayed on the wall in her parlor.

It was only after the funeral that it got really hard, when people stopped talking about him, behaving like he had never existed. Now, whenever the old woman ran into friends in the market, at church, out on the sidewalk, they acted awkward and uncomfortable mentioning Joey. Everyone was quick to forget him because people hate fear, and people fear death more than anything, so they rarely speak of death.

But, she didn't want people to forget him. She wanted to hear his name and have people talk about how he died heroically for this country. It was as if when they talked about him, it was not the end; it was as if a small part of her son was still alive.

While sitting around the table talking, Jimmy couldn't stop admiring the sweet innocence that Rita projected. She seemed quiet but pleasant with a wholesome look and feel about her that Jimmy admired.

The old woman noticing his interest in her daughter, and took every opportunity to openly boast what an excellent cook and housekeeper she was. "Rita, she make a this delicious cake. Rita's a wonderful a cook," she continued to brag, while Rita kept looking uncomfortably down at the floor, then back up, only to find Jimmy smiling at her.

When it got to be seven o'clock, Jimmy said he'd be going, but promised to call again. Mrs. Magliano assured him he would be welcome anytime. Rita walked him to the door and with that easy, captivating smile, also encouraged him to come back soon.

"Don't be a stranger. Ma and me are almost always home, except for Sunday mornings when we go to church, so just drop in anytime," she said, smiling sincerely.

Jimmy was captivated by Rita. He had every intention of returning. He had seen something in her smile that made him feel she had the ability to replace all the unpleasant memories of Vietnam and turn the war into nothing more than a distant memory.

Sunday afternoons with Rita and her mother had turned into a weekly routine. Jimmy had recently taken the Post Office Civil Service Exam and was waiting for the results. If he got hired, his future looked promising. The job paid well and had excellent benefits. The only thing missing was Rita. Jimmy had fallen in love with her. She remained cordial but gave him no indication she felt the same way about him.

She would purposely avoid him whenever they were left alone, creating an air of tension between them. After eating their Sunday meal, it became a ritual that Jimmy would volunteer to help Rita clean up. Mrs. Magliano would usually remain sitting at the kitchen table sipping her coffee and eating buttered bread. One night, after putting the left over salad in the refrigerator, he picked up a dish towel from the counter and began wiping the dishes from the rack on the side of the sink.

Watching her closely out of the corner of his eye, while moving the dish cloth smoothly over the plates, Jimmy said, "You sure are one heck of a cook, Rita. If I keep eating like this, I'll have to buy new clothes."

"Thank you. I'm glad you enjoyed it," she replied, avoiding eye contact.

They continued working in silence. For weeks now, Jimmy had been trying to get up the courage to ask Rita out on a date. Deciding not to put it off any longer, he took a deep breath and said, "Rita, I was wondering, would you like to go to the movies tonight."

Mrs. Magliano overheard his invitation; before Rita could decline, she got up and rushed over and gave Rita an encouraging hug. "Yes, you a go. It's good you a both get out of the house."

Rita suspected this was coming. She thought she was prepared, but wasn't. She had rehearsed several reasons why she couldn't go out with him, but when he asked, she become confused and tongue tied. "I don't know. The movies don't get out till late. Don't forget, Ma, we have to get up early for work," Rita nervously explained.

Feeling rejected, but determined, Jimmy said, "We still have time to catch the early movie."

Stepping between them, pushing them away from the sink, the old women said, "Yes, you a go, Rita. Leave a the dishes. I'm a gonna finish. You a go to the movies."

Rita was trapped. She didn't want to disappoint her mother or hurt Jimmy's feelings, so she reluctantly accepted. "Well, I guess I could go."

During the movie, Rita couldn't get comfortable. She remained rigid without speaking. She felt at ease with Jimmy at the apartment with her mother present, but couldn't chase away the demons from her past whenever they were alone. What was supposed to be a casual night out had turned into a nightmare for Rita. There was a strange sensation of fear sitting in the dark theater with him that she couldn't overcome.

After the movie, Jimmy suggested they stop for something to eat at Paisano's Pizza House. Rita shyly turned her head away. "I think it's getting late. I really should get home," she said.

Not wanting to upset her, he reluctantly agreed. Earlier in the theater when he attempted to hold her hand, she flinched, then, pulled her hand away. Her reaction had rattled through his brain like ricocheting Ping-Pong balls. They remained quiet for the remainder of the walk back to the apartment.

The sound of their footsteps echoed in the deserted stairway. There was only a small night light on the landing between floors, giving Rita's face a mystical glow. She looked radiant, and Jimmy wanted desperately to kiss her. He was struggling to think of something to say that might break the strangely distant and uncomfortable feeling between them.

"You've been quiet tonight, Rita. Is everything okay?"

Taking several strands of hair between her fingers, she began twirling and tugging nervously, measuring every word she said. "Everything's fine . . . Thank you for taking me to the show."

"Did you really enjoy it? You've been so quiet I was worried something might be wrong."

"Everything's fine," Rita said, glancing up at him for a moment, but quickly looking away.

"If there's anything wrong, something I might have said or done, I'd like to know what it was."

"It's nothing. I'm just tired. I think I better go in. Thanks again for the movie," she said.

Jimmy leaned in to kiss Rita, but she pulled back, turned away and disappeared into the apartment. He stood looking at the closed door, wondering what the hell he could have done that upset her? Feeling rejected he spun and stomped his way down the stairs, slamming the front door behind him.

The apartment was quiet. Her mother, was nowhere in sight. Rita drifted like a zombie around the apartment, shutting off the light over the sink, then, going directly to her bedroom. She brushed her teeth and washed her face before crawling into bed. She closed her eyes. She wasn't going to allow herself to cry. "I'm not going to cry," she said aloud, then, she cried herself to sleep.

When she awoke the next morning, she felt terrible. She wished everything could be different. She doubted it ever could be. Jimmy was the sweetest, nicest guy she had ever met. She knew he was in love with her. She wanted to feel the same way about hm. But she couldn't feel that way. She didn't think she could ever physically love a man, ever. She wished she was a normal girl from a normal family but knew she was not.

He was perfect. Just the kind of guy a nice girl imagined she would fall in love with and marry someday. But she wasn't a nice girl; and Jimmy deserved a nice girl. What would he think of her if he knew? Would he still love her? Of course not!

She wanted desperately to be able to return his affection. But the demons of her past wouldn't allow it. She couldn't block out all the terrible memories. No one could imagine how awful it feels, until it happens to them. Nobody can.

Rita learned early how to shut out her feelings. But, nothing could ease the pain. Maybe the worst pain she would ever feel in her life because she had lost something she could never get back, something that was forever gone. The strains on her life were unspeakable, creating deep emotional wounds that could not be seen, but caused her to think of herself as unclean, spoiled goods.

She was in her bedroom playing with her dolls when she looked up and saw him standing in the doorway. There was just the two of them in the apartment. Her mother wasn't due home from work for several more hours. Her brother Joey was at the ballpark with his friend, Jimmy Martin. He was wearing pants that hung loosely beneath his swollen stomach, his sleeveless undershirt was soiled with cigarette ashes and beer stains. Her father appeared bigger than his five-foot-nine inches, as he stood, legs slightly apart, struggling to maintain his balance, while he glared at her like a hungry animal stocking its prey.

Rita had never seen him look like this before. Something was wrong. At first she thought he was ill. But when he spoke, his words came out slurred and she knew he had been drinking. "What a you doin' a Rita? Playing with you a doll?" her father, Bernardo said, holding tightly onto the door frame for support.

An uncomfortable feeling came over her that something awful was about to happen. Rita turned away and began staring at the crucifix on the wall above her bed. She wanted him to leave, go away, but instead, on unsteady legs he began walking towards her. "You a know, Rita, you a such a pretty girl, just like your a Momma."

Rita didn't respond. She was paralyzed with fear. He continued advancing toward her. She remained frozen, clutched her doll to her chest, afraid to do anything, or say anything that would make him angry, afraid to be disrespectful.

Standing directly above her, he slowly reached down and lifted her off the floor. "You a getting to be a big a girl, Rita. Poppa can a hardly hold you a up." He glanced at the doll clutched tightly in her hands, and continued. "You like a playin' with your a dolls? You wanna play game with a your Poppa? I'm a gonna show you a how to play a grown-up a game," he said, then set her down on the edge of the bed.

She watched as he stood in front of her and unbuckled his belt; a sickening smile on his face. Rita didn't understand what he was doing as she watched his pants and undershorts fall to the floor. In his hand was his stiff penis, long and shiny. It was the ugliest thing she had ever seen. He began stroking himself. "Do you a know what Poppa's doin'? This is a game you can play too, Rita. But you must a not tell a no one. This is a game for you a and Poppa. Now it's a your turn, Rita." he said, then reached down and took her hand and placed it where his had been. She knew this was wrong, terribly wrong. She wanted to run away, wanted to stop playing the game, but the game went on.

That was the first time they played the game, but it would not be the last. Like an animal waiting to pounce on its prey, whenever they were left alone, her father would attack again and again, forcing her to play the grown-up game.

"Listen to a me, you must a never tell a anyone about dis a game, Rita. If you a do, a police man will come and take you away and put a you in a orphanage, and you a never see your a Momma or Joey again," he threatened, and she believed him. "This a gonna be our special a secret."

Unable to speak, she nodded slightly. He bent over and kissed her lightly on the cheek, the foul smell of beer and cigarettes on his breath. "You a good a girl, Rita, Poppa loves a you," he said before stumbling out of her bedroom.

As soon as he was out of her room, Rita jumped up and closed the door behind him, then her knees buckled. She collapsed onto the floor and began sobbing. Curled up in a tight ball, her fingers reached for her doll; finding it, she drew it to her chest.

Her father had turned Rita's life into something ugly and disgusting, ending her childhood innocence. She would play the grown-up game again, and again, and as time went on, the game would change and became more frightening. She began having nightmares. She would wake up in a cold sweat, her dreams ravaged by hands pulling at her, voices calling to her to play the game. She began wetting her bed, causing her humiliation and bringing criticism from her mother, who didn't understand what could be causing her nightmares and accidents. There were times when her mother asked if she was okay. She wanted to tell her what her father had done to her, but she said nothing.

The abuse went from one year into two, then three. Finally one night it ended. Rita was asleep, when without warning she was startled out of a deep sleep. He was half-naked and crawling into bed with her. Groggy and still half asleep, unable to understand what was happening, feeling his hands tugging at her pajama bottoms. Rita grabbed the elastic waistband and held on with all her strength. "It's a okay, sweetie. It's a your Poppa. Don't a be afraid. We're gonna play a the game," he whispered.

He had been at the Italian-American Club all day. He was now very drunk. The way his perspiring, naked body felt against Rita's skin, combined with the smell of day-old beer and cigarettes on his breath, was more than she could endure. Without thinking about the consequences, she let out a horrific, high-pitched, frightful scream. Within seconds her mother came crashing into the bedroom.

Her mother was enraged, standing in the middle of the room she watched her husband frantically stumbled out of her daughter's bed. "What you a doing in a here?" she screamed, not wanting to believe what she was seeing.

"How I'm a get in this a room?" he said, struggling not to fall as he hurried to stand up.

"You a get outta here right a now," Rita's mother demanded.

"I must a got into the wrong a room. I'm a sorry, Rita," he tried to explain.

"Get a your clothes on a and get outta here, you a bastard. Then you get outta this a house," Mrs. Magliano screamed. Behaving like a wild woman, she threw herself at him. She began hitting him with clenched fists. She grabbed him by the arm and dragged him out of the bedroom, his pants tangled below his knees.

Rita's mother had suspected something was wrong. Rita had showed all the classic signs of being sexually molested: unprovoked crying, bed-wetting and sleepwalking, but she was living a life of denial and didn't want to believe that anything like this could be happening in her home.

Rita remained sitting on her bed, shocked to the point of being paralyzed and began sucking her thumb, trembling out of control. Her almond eyes looked frightened, tears began falling freely. She couldn't stop shaking. She could hear her mother clearly through the wall, ordered him out of the house, telling him if he ever returned she'd have him arrested and thrown in jail.

Rita listened to the slamming of the kitchen door, followed by a deafening stillness. The only sound came from outside her bedroom window where an old oak tree switched its branches against the side of the building. Listening closely, Rita could hear the quiet sobbing of her mother. She wanted desperately to go and give her a hug and explain how sorry she was for what she'd done, but she was too ashamed to move.

Rita never saw her father again, and her mother never mentioned him. It was as though he never existed. With him out of her life, the nightmares and bed wetting stopped, but the burden of guilt remained constantly on her mind. She felt somehow responsible. Rita felt that she must've done something to make her father behave the way he did. She would struggle for the rest of her life with this shameful feeling of guilt, knowing she had been a bad girl because she played the game.

Many years had passed since that terrible night, but the demons continued to haunt her. Whenever her mother left her alone in the apartment with Jimmy, memories of her father standing in her bedroom doorway would come flooding back, sending waves of fear throughout her body.

It took over a year before Rita felt comfortable enough with Jimmy to participate in innocent acts of affection. Things as normal as hand holding, good-night kisses, hugs, and playful embraces were difficult for her. Rita truly loved Jimmy and wanted desperately to explain what had happened, but she was too ashamed to tell him her secret.

Jimmy nevertheless remained determined. There were times he didn't think Rita would ever accept him. But with slow, persistent patience, he continued courting her, showing up week after week. Finally, more than a year after Jimmy first visited the Maglianos to pay his respects, Rita told him she loved him and agreed to marry him. As happy and excited as he was, there were times when Rita acted restless and uncomfortable. Whenever Jimmy held her, he could sense there was something dark and unknown about Rita that he didn't understand, and it worried him.

Jimmy Martin married Rita Magliano in a simple ceremony at St. Anthony's Church with a small gathering of relatives and friends in attendance to the delight of Rita's mother who had come to love Jimmy like the son she had lost.

During the ceremony, when the priest announced, *"You may kiss the bride,"* Rita looked up into Jimmy's face and knew she loved him; it was that simple. She realized if Jimmy wanted, needed and loved her, she couldn't be all that bad. She leaned into him, feeling the warmth of his body against hers and for the first time felt comfortable in the arms of a man.

Rita believed now she was married, she could block out her past and begin a new life. *Okay, now I'm going to be fine,* she thought. But Rita would find there are no guarantees or timelines when, or if she would ever be fine again. She knew she would never tell Jimmy about what had happened to her. It's not the kind of secret you want to share with your husband. It was *a secret* she was determined to keep to herself.

BOOK TWO

Sins

CHAPTER 22

Two months earlier

KATHY HAD COMPLETELY lost track of the time. She'd spent more time on the computer, checking her mail and sending her son, Philip, an email than she normally did. She was now rushing to get dressed for her Wednesday morning aerobics class. After pulling her loose-fitting gray sweat suit over her shorts and T-shirt, she was ready. The ride to the gym took approximately twenty minutes. They only had thirty minutes to get there.

As soon as she walked out of the bedroom, the telephone rang. "I'll get it," Kathy announced. These calls had become more frequent the last couple of weeks. She knew who was calling before answering. The conversation was brief. "Hello . . . okay. I'll tell Carol," she said and hung up.

"Don't tell me," Phil said. "That was Betty. She's not going to the gym, right?"

Phil knew exactly who was calling. They had been using this system so Betty could send a signal to Phil that Scooter would be playing softball, meaning she was free to meet him. He had been sitting impatiently reading the morning paper, hoping she'd call. When she did, he was relieved. He needed to talk to her. It was important.

"Well, if I looked as good as Betty, I wouldn't bother going to the gym either," Kathy said.

Betty Pappas was nearly sixty but looked fabulous. Her body remained slim, and her small breasts were firm with a flat stomach above legs that looked great in a pair of shorts; she was the best looking woman in Barefoot Bay, no doubt about it.

"Any plans this morning?" Kathy asked, rushing around looking for her purse.

"Nothing special," Phil said, the lie rolling easily off his tongue. "Probably go over to the golf course, do a little practicing and check on my starting time for Friday. Why do you ask?"

"No reason, just curious. Well, I have to get going," she stated, hurrying out the door without as much as a goodbye.

Carol tapped her index finger against the steering wheel, waiting impatiently in the driveway with the engine of her Jeep Cherokee running. "Betty called and said she wouldn't be joining us," Kathy informed her, while sliding into the passenger seat.

"This is getting to be a habit. You don't suppose she has a boyfriend she's meeting in the mornings, do you?" Carol said, chuckling slightly.

"No. Although, she could have any man in the Bay if she wanted to. I'd kill to look like she does!" Kathy said while securing her seat belt across her plump mid-section.

Carol agreed, then wasted no time backing out of the driveway, and headed down Dolphin Drive.

Minutes after they were out of sight, Phil followed. He jumped into his BMW and also drove down Dolphin Drive. But unlike what he told Kathy, he wasn't going to the golf course.

It wasn't long before Betty Pappas emerged from her house. After glancing around the neighborhood nervously, she got into her Ford Explorer and joined the parade.

Arriving at the gym with only a few minutes to spare, Kathy and Carol hurried inside. They each picked up bright blue rubber mats from the pile next to the wall and looked around for a vacant spot on the floor. After an hour of vigorous aerobics, the class was dismissed. On their way home they made their usual stop at the neighborhood Dunkin' Donuts on Route 1.

After ordering coffee and bagels, they seated themselves in a corner booth.

"If you and Stanley don't have plans later this afternoon, why don't you come over. I'll have Phil throw something on the grill," Kathy suggested.

"Sounds good; always happy to get a free meal," Carol said.

"By the way, how's Stanley adjusting to Florida? Any better?" Kathy asked.

"Still a pain in the ass. But he's gonna have to get used to living here, or he can go back to Barnstead. I'm not going back, that's for sure!"

"You mean to tell me you'd let him go back alone? Are you serious? You'd stay here by yourself?"

"You bet I would. In a heartbeat," Carol said with raised eyebrows.

"You're awful!"

Carol smiled and changed the subject. "Oh, the house across the street finally got rented."

"Well, that's good. It was starting to look like they weren't going to get a tenant."

Carol reached for her coffee, took a sip, and set it back down. "I noticed the "For Rent" sign was gone yesterday. I've been meaning to ask you, how was your trip back home?"

"Good. The golf banquet went off without a hitch. It was good seeing the girls again, but I was happy to get back to Florida. I can't take that cold weather anymore."

"So, are you still the president of the golf league?"

"No. I had my turn," Kathy said.

They continued talking for another half hour, cleaned off the table, then left the donut shop and headed for home. As soon as they turned the corner onto Dolphin Drive, Carol noticed an unfamiliar car in the driveway of the rented house directly across from Kathy's. A man and a woman walked from the car, carrying luggage and clothing into the house.

"Look! Those must be our new neighbors," Carol exclaimed, drawing Kathy's attention across the street.

At first glance, Kathy thought the man looked familiar. As they got closer and just before he disappeared into the house, Kathy got a better look and caught her breath. It couldn't be! Could her eyes be deceiving her? She had only caught a quick glimpse, but she was almost positive that it was her old boyfriend from high school.

"Jimmy Martin," she said in a voice so low Carol didn't understand her.

"What?" Carol said.

"That man, I think I know him."

"Really, someone from your hometown?"

"If that's who I think it is, he used to be my boyfriend. We went to high school together. When I went to college, he joined the army. I haven't seen him since." Her voice trembled slightly.

"Well, that's good. I'm sure you'll have a lot to talk about."

Kathy only caught a brief look at the man and couldn't be a hundred percent sure it was Jimmy. But if it was, it could create an awkward situation.

Just thinking about the possibility of her son's father unexpectedly showing up in her life after all this time was devastating.

Stepping out of Carol's Jeep, Kathy continued staring across the street. She hoped the man would reappear, but he never did. A petite woman, apparently his wife, reemerged from inside and brought in what appeared to be the last of their belongings. Kathy watched carefully as the woman slammed the trunk, picked up the remaining luggage and quickly walked up the carport and disappeared through the side door.

"If you want, later we can do the welcome-wagon thing," Carol offered, while carefully observing her friend.

"Yeah, maybe later," Kathy replied. "Don't forget, we're cooking out later."

"We'll be there. What time?"

"Around three-thirty or four will be fine," Kathy instructed, never taking her eyes off the rented house.

As soon as Kathy walked into her house, she went directly to the large picture window facing the street. Standing off to the side, she watched, hoping if it was Jimmy Martin, he might reappear. After a few minutes with no movement, she decided it was foolish to be spying. If it was him, there wasn't anything she could do about it. She would just have to deal with it. Shrugging her shoulders, she quickly retreated to her bedroom to get out of her sweaty gym outfit.

The more she thought about Jimmy showing up in her life, the more concerned she became. After she'd married and given birth to their son, at first, whenever she'd look at her newborn, she saw Jimmy's face and innumerable times review her secret privately. Years passed, and she had stopped thinking about him. In fact she'd almost forgotten who her son's father really was. She now subconsciously accepted Phil as her son's biological father.

Once completely undressed, she turned on the water, then stopped before getting into the shower to examine herself in the full-length mirror on the back of the bathroom door. Obviously all the dieting and exercise classes she'd participated in hadn't done much good. She still had the same extra twenty-five pounds she was constantly trying to lose. Her breasts had become soft and now lay flat against her chest, with small blue veins showing through the skin. She no longer had the tiny waist that was so becoming in college. Her hips had also put on unwanted inches. Her skin had, nevertheless, stayed smooth and clear, mainly because she faithfully used the most expensive facial creams and body lotions on the market.

The steam from the shower left a slight mist on the mirror, but it couldn't hide the realities reflecting back that she had grown older. She was sixty-two and had regrettably learned over time to accept the fact that she was no longer a young woman.

She wondered why, after all these years, she was so concerned with what Jimmy would think. Would he still find her as attractive and desirable as he had back when they were dating? She didn't have an answer, but it seemed important to her that he still find her attractive.

Even the warm water couldn't stop the surging sense of desire she experienced when she thought of the many times she'd made love with Jimmy. For a long time after marrying Phil, she could not stop comparing the way it was with Phil with the way it had been with Jimmy. She always felt something was missing with Phil.

Over the past several years, sex with Phil had gone from once in a while to nearly nonexistent. It was as if he had grown tired of her. She wasn't sure if it was because he was getting older, a loss of interest in sex that most men experienced with age, or if he no longer found her desirable.

Although Phil was the only other man she'd ever had sex with, Jimmy was the one who had the ability to make her feel special. Throughout her entire married life she'd endured Phil's routine attempts at making love. She had pretended to enjoy having sex with him out of duty, but she knew love had nothing to do with it.

After thirty-five years of marriage, she wasn't sure if she even loved Phil. She recalled how she often woke up in the middle of the night, watching the digital clock ticking off the minutes, thinking she had made a terrible mistake. She found herself closing her eyes and trying to imagine what her life might have been like if she had married her baby's father.

But even if she never loved Phil, they had been close; although she no longer felt that closeness. They had not drifted apart overnight. It happened so gradually she never saw it coming. But the space between them grew wider with each passing year. She realized she cared for him in a strange sort of way but didn't understand how she could be with a man for all these years, share so many intimacies and still feel unconnected; distant in their relationship, like she has been dancing through life without music or a partner.

They seldom touched outside the bedroom, where little went on except for an occasional attempt at meaningless, silent, mechanical sex in the dark. Throughout their marriage, she couldn't remember the last time they made love—or if they had ever made love—they often fucked—but she didn't remember making love. And she lacked the will or interest to do much about it.

Their marriage had turned into no more than a marriage of convenience. He had provided a father for her son. In return, her family had given Phil security, money and the community prominence that was so important to him.

And now, the boy she had loved in high school, the boy that had fathered her son might be living across the street. Kathy couldn't help but wonder once again, what if she had married Jimmy? What if?

When she finished showering, Kathy grabbed a terry cloth towel, dried herself off and quickly got dressed. She heard Phil in the front room and when she walked into the living room, she found him sitting in his recliner, reading Golf Digest.

She looked at him and had to admit he was certainly a handsome man, making her wonder if all these years she had been more impressed with him, than in love with him. She heaved a frustrating sigh. "Just get back from the golf course?"

Startled for a moment, he looked up, closed the magazine and tossed it carelessly on the end table. "Yeah, I went over to the clubhouse to check the schedule for Friday morning. Figured while I was there, I might as well get in a little putting practice," he lied for the second time that morning without flinching.

"When I drove by the parking lot with Carol, I looked for the car, but I didn't see it."

"Really? I was sandwiched between two SUVs. You must have missed it."

"Anyway, did you happen to notice some people have moved in across the street?"

"Yes. They must have just arrived. They weren't there earlier when I drove by."

Kathy at first was reluctant to mention anything about her suspicions, then changed her mind. If it was him, he would find out later, so she might as well mention it now. "Do you remember Jimmy Martin?"

Phil wrinkled his forehead. "Martin . . . Jimmy Martin . . . . No, should I?"

"When we first started dating, I was going out with him. He didn't go to college. I knew him from high school."

"Okay. I remember. I don't think I ever met him. Didn't he go to Vietnam?"

"Yes. Well, if I'm not mistaken, the man moving in across the street could be Jimmy. I only got a quick glance, but it looked exactly like him," she said, then waited for a reaction. Getting none, she continued, "I wonder if it's really him?"

"Just take a walk across the street, say hello and find out."

"That's what Carol suggested. I think I'll wait. Give them a chance to get settled first." She tried not to act overly anxious.

Remembering that she'd invited the Kloski's for dinner, Kathy said, "Oh, by the way, I invited Carol and Stanley over for a cookout later."

Phil closed his eyes, then opened them slowly. "Come on, Kathy! You know I can't stand Stanley. Why do you keep inviting them over here? Now I'll have to spend the whole goddamn evening trying to make conversation with that jerk."

Phil Gagnon and Stanley Kloski were like day and night, salt and pepper. They mixed like oil and water, but Kathy and Carol were good friends, and Phil was forced to endure Stanley's company on many occasions.

"I need a drink!" Phil headed for the portable bar in the living room to make himself an unusual, late morning Scotch and water. He needed a drink to calm him down now that he discovered Stanley would be visiting.

CHAPTER 23

EARLIER THAT MORNING, after calling Kathy, Betty waited by her front window and watched the series of events she knew were about to unfold. Within minutes, Kathy emerged from her house, hurried across her front lawn and got into Carol's waiting Jeep. The two of them immediately drove off. Minutes later Phil followed. She knew Phil had gotten her message.

Confident he would be meeting her, she went to the wall mirror, took one last glance to be sure she looked all right, and as always, she did. There was a sparkle in her eyes, something that had been missing before Phil had come into her life. Giving her reflection a satisfactory smile, she, too, left her house, got into her car, and joined the procession down Dolphin Drive.

Normally the three women went to the aerobics class together every Monday, Wednesday and Friday. Betty's husband, Scooter, played softball on these mornings, which provided a perfect opportunity for Betty to meet Phil at the Captain's Quarters.

Phil had rented a small apartment so they could be together without being seen or interrupted. The Captain's Quarters consisted of twenty efficiency apartments located approximately four miles past Bottoms Up on the banks of the Indian River. The owner, Captain Bill, was a stout, rough looking gentleman with a short neck, and thick forearms covered with tattoos. He got a big draw from clients who paid cash and knew they could count on the Captain to pretend they didn't exist.

While driving with both hands securely on the steering wheel, Betty's heart beat rapidly. She reminisced about how her affair had started with the husband of her best friend. Thinking of the first night they had made love, she remembered how she knew immediately it was more than just a casual affair that had drawn them together. Although they had been meeting for only a short time, she was sure she loved him, and he loved her.

Kathy and Betty met when she and Scooter first arrived in Barefoot Bay. They didn't know a soul in the Bay when Kathy had come over and introduced herself. They'd hit it off immediately, remaining friends ever since. Now she was sleeping with Kathy's husband.

Phil had the uncanny ability to detect the absence of any kind of love between certain married couples he met, even when they went to great lengths to hide it, thus making these women easy targets for seduction. He detected this was the case after only knowing the Pappas for a short time. Phil had been mentally stalking Betty ever since.

The opportunity for Phil to fulfill his fantasies about Betty arrived when one of Scooter's friends, a former coworker on the Pembroke Fire Department back in New Hampshire, had unexpectedly had a heart attack. Because he had been the fire chief and had remained a friend for so long, Scooter was expected to attend the funeral.

It was a coincidence that on that same weekend, Kathy flew back home to Lowell to attend a Christmas banquet held by her golf league at the Pleasant Valley Golf Course, where she and Phil were members. Kathy had served as president of the women's golf league the past summer, and it was her responsibility to oversee the affair.

Unexpectedly that Saturday afternoon while Kathy and Scooter where away, Betty got a call from Phil. "Since we're both going to be alone this evening, why don't we go someplace together to eat?" he suggested casually.

Like most women, when she first met Phil, she found him to be extremely handsome. Betty admired the way he always seemed confident and in charge. No matter what the situation, he always dressed with the best of taste and had a friendly smile for whomever he met. Characteristics her husband, Scooter, never possessed.

His offer was tempting. But she'd been caught off guard. She didn't feel comfortable accepting. "Do you think it would be all right? I mean, Kathy and Scooter aren't around. What will people say if they see us together? You know how people in the Bay like to talk." She sounded uncertain, looking around her living room as if someone might be listening.

"I was thinking of going to Joseph's in Port St. Lucie. Not much chance of running into anyone from Barefoot Bay there," he assured her, speaking clearly in a steady voice.

Momentarily speechless, Betty finally said, "Joseph's! Isn't that kind of expensive?"

"I feel like treating myself tonight. I really would enjoy it if you would join me. Come on, Betty. Don't let me dine alone. Please!"

Although she couldn't see the enthusiasm on his face, she could hear it in his voice. Betty had never been to anyplace like Joseph's. When he first mentioned going out to eat, she assumed he was talking about a place like Applebee's. Joseph's was a completely different matter. An upscale restaurant like that was where people went to celebrate birthdays and anniversaries or when a gentleman wanted to impress a special date.

Betty was confused. She couldn't be sure if she was being asked out on a date by her best friend's husband, or if Phil was just being a good neighbor. She didn't know what to say while she continued looking up to the ceiling for answers.

"I don't know, Phil, I'm not sure this is such a good idea."

"Of course it's a good idea," Phil said confidently. "Have you ever been to Joseph's?"

"No."

"Well, then, you're really in for a treat. I'll come over and get you at six. Okay?" he said, sounding like the matter had been settled.

"Okay, I guess," she agreed, unable to think of anything to say that might discourage him. And not sure she wanted to.

Once she accepted the fact she had a date, and she now really believed she was going on a date, Betty spent the rest of her day getting ready. Three years ago she'd purchased a lovely black cocktail dress at Macy's Department Store in New Hampshire and never had the chance to wear it. The dress hung unused in the back of her closet still draped in the same plastic sheath it came in, waiting for that special occasion. She bought it hoping Scooter might take her to someplace like Joseph's for their anniversary or her birthday, but Scooter's idea of going out on a special occasion was eating at Ruby Tuesday's.

Standing in front of the mirror, holding the dress in front of her, she realized as long as she remained married to Scooter, her dress would never be worn. They did nothing together that made her happy. But tonight she was going to a first class restaurant with a handsome man, and she was more excited than she had been in many, many years, and anxious for tonight to arrive. She intended to take her time getting ready. She wanted to look her best for Phil.

"You look absolutely beautiful," were the first words out of Philip's mouth when he arrived promptly at six. Betty was aware of how attractive she looked, but it still felt wonderful to hear Phil compliment her.

"You look really handsome yourself," she said and meant it.

Phil wore a tan pair of dress pants, dark blue jacket with gold buttons, and light blue oxford shirt with a bit of white woven into the fabric, complemented by a dark blue, silk tie. He had broad shoulders, a solid chin, captivating smile, sparkling brown eyes and perfect hair with a touch of silver around his ears, and he wore just the right amount of cologne. Betty knew they'd make a stunning-looking couple when they arrived at Joseph's.

Joseph's turned out to be even more elaborate than she imagined. As they drove from the main road and approached the restaurant, its splendor was startling. The winding driveway was bordered on both sides with lavishly designed landscaping. Tall palms extended high into the evening sky, surrounded by lush ferns and flowers sprouting everywhere.

When they arrived at the front entrance, a smartly dressed young man opened Betty's door; she exited and stood waiting until Phil walked around his car and led her into the restaurant. Another smartly dressed man slid behind the wheel of Philip's BMW, then quickly drove away.

"Reservations for Gagnon," Phil informed the maître d' as soon as they entered.

"Yes, of course. It should only be a few minutes. If you wish, you may wait in the lounge. I'll notify you as soon as your table is ready," the gentleman in the tuxedo informed Phil while looking down intently at the reservation list.

"I'd really rather not wait. I would also appreciate a table with a little privacy, if that can be arranged," Phil insisted, while casually placing a large bill into his hand.

The money fluidly disappeared into his pocket. The maître d' then said, "Right this way."

They made their way through the waiters and waitresses, who were dressed in white shirts and bow ties, to a table off to one side of the large, dimly lit dining room. Betty walked with confidence, aware, without having to look around, that everyone was watching, wondering who this handsome couple could be.

When they arrived, the maître d' pulled her chair away from the table, placed the menus on the table and said, "Your waiter will be with you shortly," then briskly walked away.

The table setting was breathtaking. The forks, knives, and spoons were sterling silver complete with white linen tablecloth and a small floral centerpiece arrangement lit by a flickering candle. The room was large and elegant with mirrored walls and red velvet draperies.

"Well, what do you think of this place?" Phil asked. He could see she was impressed by the look on her glowing face.

It was obvious that Joseph's was a place where wealthy people came to see and be seen. Betty felt comfortable the odds of running into anyone from the Barefoot Bay Retirement Community were almost nonexistent.

"I've never been to a place like this," Betty admitted, looking around the room, her eyes straining to take in the elegance, but no longer trying to see who in the restaurant they had impressed; she now just wanted to impress him and only him.

Phil could smell her perfume drifting across the table, making her more alluring. "The food here is fabulous. What's your favorite dish?" Philip asked, just as a spiffy-looking waiter, wearing a well-starched pleated white shirt and black bow tie, seemed to appear out of nowhere.

"Good evening. My name is Donald, and I'll be your waiter tonight. Will there be cocktails before dinner?"

"We'll have two tall Scotch and waters," Phil ordered without consulting Betty.

When it was time to order, Betty was undecided. She could hear Scooter's voice saying, "Don't get carried away, we're not made of money." So out of habit, she started scanning the menu for the least expensive meals, but soon realized there were no prices.

Phil noticed her hesitation and immediately took control. He began ordering for both of them. Unlike her husband, prices didn't seem to matter. He instructed the waiter to bring them a grilled Portabello Caesar salad, Maine lobsters, steamed and removed from the shell, served with lemon saffron Mornay sauce.

"And would you care for a bottle of wine with your meal?" the waiter asked.

Without hesitation, Phil replied. "A bottle of Dom Perignon, please."

Betty watched while the waiter listened to Phil's instructions, never writing anything down, simply nodding his acknowledgment. Just as he was about to walk away, Phil also informed him to "Keep the Scotch and waters coming."

"Certainly," the waiter said and quietly walked away.

Betty couldn't help but admire the way Philip seemed to handle everything. He was confident, in control and prepared for any situation. He obviously was very comfortable in places like this, unlike Betty, who felt like a fish out of water.

After the waiter delivered their drinks with quiet professionalism, Phil returned his attention back to Betty. "Are you enjoying this evening?"

"Oh, yes, very much. What about you?"

"How could I not be enjoying this evening when I'm with such a beautiful woman." He raised his glass and seductively raised one eyebrow.

Betty felt as though she was living a dream. The three Scotch and waters she had before dinner were having an effect. She was relaxed and a little lightheaded. It was wonderful.

When the check arrived, Phil glanced at it, tucked what looked like a hundred-dollar bill along with a fifty in the leather wallet, and casually placed it back on the small tray without much interest.

An hour and a half after they arrived, Phil and Betty stood outside waiting for the valet to bring Phil's BMW around to the front entrance, marveling at the display of thousands upon thousands of stars surrounding a full moon. The evening felt cool and refreshing on Betty's naked shoulders. A gentle December breeze moved her hair, and the night sky was clear and smelled so fresh she wanted to drink in the air.

Phil looked over at Betty out of the corner of his eye and noticed her perfect profile in the darkness, silhouetted by the lights of the restaurant. She shivered and crossed her arms over her chest.

"Are you cold?" he asked.

"A little, but I'm fine. This has been a wonderful treat."

Standing close to her, he could see how the soft material of her dress moved slightly against her body with every move. He couldn't help but admire her wholesome beauty. From the satisfied smile on her beautiful face, he knew he had shown her an evening she would cherish for a long time to come.

During the ride home, Betty's cocktail dress worked its way up, exposing more of her slender, firm, tanned thighs than maybe she should have been showing. But she didn't care. In fact, she was enjoying watching Phil trying to avoid looking down at her legs while concentrating on his driving. The drinks had made her relax. Unlike when they left Barefoot Bay, she was the one now talking enthusiastically the entire way back, while Phil tried desperately to keep his mind on the road.

It was eleven o'clock when they arrived in the Bay. They both walked directly to Betty's house from Phil's driveway, even though she hadn't invited him. Somehow it had been taken for granted that he'd be welcome.

Once inside, Betty decided not to use the light switch next to the door, which would've illuminated the entire room. Instead, she snapped on the small light situated on the end table next to the couch, giving the room a much warmer and more intimate, romantic feel. "Can you handle another drink?" she asked while walking over to the CD player and going through her collection of disks, selecting, *"Days of Wine and Roses,"* a song she thought was appropriate.

"Sure, why not?" he said as the music filled the room.

She went into the kitchen and took the bottle of Scotch out of the cabinet above the sink. Taking the ice from her refrigerator freezer, she dropped several cubes in each glass, added the Scotch, ran the drinks under the facet and returned. She handed one to Phil and said in a sultry voice, "Thanks for a wonderful evening."

Phil took off his jacket and tie and draped them over the back of the couch. He stood in front of the bookcase, a book open in his hand. "You're entirely welcome," he assured her. Then each took a small sip while looking into each other's eyes.

"I didn't know you like to read," he said.

Betty had worked her feet out of her shoes and stood next to him, looking at the novel he was holding. "Wally Lamb, *I Know This Much Is True,* any good?"

"Excellent."

He quickly ran his eyes up and down her body. He stared at her as though he was seeing her for the first time. "You looked pretty tonight. The other men in the restaurant couldn't stop looking at you. In fact, neither could I," Phil said, smiling at her.

A smile appeared on her lips. "I felt pretty for a change."

"Don't you always?"

"No."

"Really!" Phil sounded startled. "I would have thought someone as attractive as you would always feel pretty. I was the envy of every man in the restaurant. You must know what effect you have on men."

"It's hard to feel pretty when you feel dead inside."

Phil wasn't sure where this conversation would lead if he pursued it, and he didn't want to find out. He wanted to keep the conversation cheerful. Returning the novel to the bookcase, he placed his drink down on the coffee table, then took her drink and placed it next to his.

Feeling confident she would not resist, he reached over and drew her to him and kissed her lightly on the lips.

They were standing in the middle of the room. Phil took in the aroma of her perfume.

Betty said, "Will you dance with me?"

"Sure."

She moved even closer, and they began to dance. "I can't remember the last time I danced."

"You're doing great."

She looked up into his eyes and moved her body to the music as she hummed the tune. The music filled the room. Their bodies came together, and she leaned into him, feeling their stomachs and legs touching, her breasts flattened against his chest, breathing in the scent of him. She closed her eyes and laid her head on his shoulder.

"You're something . . ." Phil started to say, but Betty cut him off.

"Don't talk. Just hold me, just dance. I just like the feeling that there's someone who cares enough that he wants to dance with me."

Moving awkwardly at first, they soon found their rhythm and moved effortlessly around the room. As they swayed to the music, Phil felt her body was dainty and compact, while listening to the soft rustle of her dress against his body. Betty seemed to relax. The tension of the night began draining from her shoulders as she let Phil lead her to the tempo of the music.

Betty's heart began to beat strongly when she became aware that he was about to kiss her. After a series of short kisses, she lifted her face and looked into his eyes.

Phil's fingers slid down her back and began to unzip her dress. He gently pulled the garment off her shoulders, and the dress collapsed onto the floor as if a statue was being unveiled. She stepped out of it. He easily unfastened her bra. She let it fall next to her dress. Her breasts were beautiful, round and firm. The texture of her skin was smooth and unblemished. Her nipples were erect; he bent his head and playfully teased her with his tongue. She did nothing, said nothing to stop him. She wanted him.

Lifting her up, he effortlessly carried her from the living room into the bedroom. Betty felt as if they simply floated together, holding on to each other, sharing kisses as they both worked with fumbling fingers until they were completely undressed and lying naked in each other's arms.

They continued to kiss. Each kiss brought them to another level of passion. She could smell the light, clean fragrance of his cologne, felt their skin rubbing together, his hands running up and down the entire length of her body. Betty didn't want this feeling to ever stop. She'd never experienced this kind of excitement before in all the years she had been married.

Betty slowly ran her hands over his chest, enjoying the sensation of her fingers running through the thick gray curls. They continued to kiss. He entered her, and they began moving as one.

He immediately slowed her down, stopped her from bucking. He knew this would not be one of those rapid, degrading, over in minutes sex that he had become used to. He continued telling her over and over again how beautiful her naked body was; words she'd longed to hear from her husband, but words that he'd never spoken.

When finally they'd brought their lovemaking to the height of exhilaration, a feeling Betty hadn't felt before, their bodies exploded together, climaxing as one. He was everything she had hoped he would be and more.

Phil remained holding her in a tender embrace, kissed her face, caressed her body, telling her she was beautiful, making her feel special. What they had just done was beyond anything she could have imagined. A short time later she closed his eyes and slept soundly under the sheet, naked, content and relaxed, as if she had been drugged.

When Betty awoke early the next morning, the dawn was peeking through the slats of the Venetian blinds. Phil was no longer in bed. He had gotten dressed while she slept and gone back to his house. She thought he probably wanted to leave before daylight to prevent being detected by early-rising neighbors.

Lying quietly on her side, Betty could still smell the fragrance of Phil's body on the sheets. She imagined she could feel the soft kisses on her breasts, his hands caressing her, the sensation she felt when he made love to her. There was a slight creaking of the bed frame when she shifted her weight, while trying to distinguish if it was lust, or if it was something approaching love. She had never had a man truly make love to her before. Phil had been everything she'd hoped he would be. She believed she had finally discovered the difference between sex and love.

Phil returned the following night. They picked up where they'd left off. The sex was every bit as exciting and passionate as it had been the previous night. But more importantly, Betty thought she had found someone to love and would love her in return.

All these memories came flooding back as she continued down Route 1 on her way to the Captain's Quarters where Phil would be waiting for her. Betty's heart began beating quickly with every passing mile and seemed to pick up speed when she finally pulled into the gravel parking lot next to his BMW. The man she loved was inside anxiously awaiting her arrival.

CHAPTER 24

PHIL WAITED impatiently. He was thinking he had been foolish to get involved with her in the first place, but it was too late to worry about that now. As difficult as it would be, he was anxious to get what needed to be done over with.

The efficiency apartment consisted of two rooms. The walls were paneled in dark oak with two framed tropical prints hanging slightly crooked in well-worn frames. One room had a pullout bed that served as a couch during the day, a television, dark blue chair, floor lamp, and a bureau with a mirror. The remaining room was a kitchenette with a small table, two chairs, compact refrigerator, counter-top stove, definitely not new, a sink with metal cabinets above it next to the door leading into a cramped bathroom. The room smelled slightly stale and musty.

When Betty entered the apartment, she immediately sensed something wasn't right. Glancing around the room, she noticed the couch hadn't yet been converted into a bed like it normally would've been. He hadn't greeted her at the door either, as he'd always done in the past. So she went looking for him.

She found him sitting at the table in the kitchen, a strange, faraway look on his face. It was obvious his mind was preoccupied with something other than her. She didn't like what she was seeing. "Why so glum?" she asked, standing rigid in the kitchen doorway.

"Hi, I didn't hear you come in," he said, jumping slightly.

"You look like you're a million miles away. Is everything all right?"

"Everything's fine."

Unconvinced, she said, "I hope it isn't anything I've done."

Looking at her standing there, he lost his nerve. His mind went blank. Everything he had rehearsed earlier was suddenly gone. "It's nothing that concerns you," he lied, forcing a smile.

He got up and kissed her but not with the same intensity she'd become used to. Betty seductively smiled, put her arms around his neck, looked him straight in the eyes, and said in a teasing tone, "Is there anything I can do to make you feel better?"

With that comment, everything changed; a broad smile appeared on Phil's face. Smelling the scent of her perfume, feeling her familiar body pressing firmly against his, made him forget what he had been rehearsing all morning. He found himself unable to resist her advances. "Oh, I can think of a few things," he said, leaning into her.

Betty had him fully aroused now. Just the way she wanted him.

Of all the women Phil'd had, Betty was the most eager sex partner he'd ever been with. She was anxious to do whatever it took to make him happy. It wasn't long before the couch was no longer a couch, but a bed that squeaked and groaned shortly after they shed their clothing as they romped and rolled with pleasure.

The morning went smoothly with Phil apparently showing no signs of resisting her. They stayed in bed, talking, laughing, and making love again and again. But Betty couldn't help but feel something was missing. Phil had somehow changed. She could sense that something was different. It was like he was beginning to distance himself. She felt that things weren't getting said, and what didn't get said was more significant than what did.

The morning passed quickly. Betty realized it was getting late. Without getting out of bed, she picked up her watch from the end table, glanced at it and said, "It's almost noon. I'd better get going."

Scooter normally got home from his softball game shortly after noon. He would expect her to be home and his lunch waiting. She had little time to waste. She gathered up her clothes and began dressing. Phil remained in bed, smiling whenever she glanced his way. He enjoyed watching her every move. She looked almost as sexy putting her clothes back on, as she did taking them off. It was like watching a reverse striptease.

As he watched her secure the small hooks of her bra, turn the garment around and slip her arms through the straps and pull them over her shoulders, he was disappointed that he hadn't told her these meetings had to come to an end. He knew by the way she had acted, she suspected something. Just before leaving, she asked with a look of concern on her face, "When will I see you again?"

He managed to remain calm, shook his head and answered, "I'm not sure."

Betty watched him closely, unconvinced everything was all right. "You've got me worried. You seemed different this morning. Are you sure everything's all right?"

"Everything's fine. It's just that I'm not certain what's going on the next couple of weeks, that's all."

Betty waited a moment. When he didn't continue, feeling awkward, uncertain what to do next, she said, "Okay. I'll be waiting to hear from you."

"All right, Betty, I'll see you later."

Betty hesitated, still feeling there was more to be said. She was concerned there was something lying just beneath the surface that he wasn't telling her. "Okay. Call me." She kissed him lightly on the cheek, then left, closing the door quietly behind her.

Once Betty had gone, Phil began tidying up. He was upset with himself. Why didn't I just tell her? Get it over with, he scolded himself. He realized he was the one who had initially started this affair. But, Betty had become too serious. It had gone too far. He never intended for her to be anything more than a onetime piece of ass. Phil had no intention of ever leaving his wife. He needed her. It was time to dump Betty but getting rid of her now wasn't going to be easy.

Throughout his married life, Phil never felt guilty about cheating on Kathy. But he was concerned he'd pushed his luck too far this time. Playing around with not only a neighbor, but one of his wife's best friends, was a little too close to home.

It had always been a rule of his to keep his affairs isolated, away from his home life; married women who worked at the office that he had control over and could be counted on to keep their mouths shut were okay; girls he met in bars on business trips were fair game; but never family friends or neighbors. Now, because he had broken this rule, he needed to bring his affair with Betty to an end and the sooner the better.

Phil couldn't help being attracted to her. What man wouldn't be? It had been the thrill of the hunt, the sense of achievement when he succeeded in getting her into bed, and the powerful, satisfying feeling he received whenever he saw Scooter that made it all worthwhile. He always enjoyed the sensation, knowing he'd been successful in fucking other men's wives. It gave him a secret feeling of superiority over them.

When the opportunity presented itself, both Scooter and Kathy being out of town at the same time, it was just too much to pass up. He knew it was dangerous, but it was such an exciting challenge, he couldn't resist. He couldn't help but be proud. He had accomplished his goal, experienced the thrill of victory. But the game had to come to an end before he experienced the agony of defeat. As Kenny Rogers had stated so clearly in his song, "You got to know when to hold 'em, know when to fold 'em." It was time to dump Betty Pappas.

Phil Gagnon was not usually a worrier, but he was worried now. He could not stand to be bested by anyone or anything; it was a simple fact he took for granted, and that was all there was to it. He was well aware that a woman's pussy was the most powerful weapon in the world, more powerful than a nuclear bomb; a weapon that had been responsible for more deaths than any war this country had ever been involved in, destroyed countless marriages, broken up families and ended millions of careers. He wasn't about to fall into that tender trap. After all, there was more to life than a pretty ass and a great set of tits. He definitely was not about to lose everything he had worked for over the years because of Betty.

Phil wasn't stupid. He realized what was at stake. Getting caught could put an end to everything he'd worked so hard for. Early in life he learned that Phil Gagnon took care of Phil Gagnon. Everyone else could take care of themselves. The lack of warmth and love he never received as a child followed him throughout his adult life, so he never completely let down his guard and remained unattached, maintaining that distance from everybody except his son. He always managed to keep people at arm's length. Faced with the potential for wealth and connections, not loving Kathy was never a factor. He did whatever needed to be done to get where he was. He wasn't about to have a meltdown now, especially over a woman.

Without Kathy he could lose everything. He realized he was a kept man, tied to his wife's money. He was often haunted by her mortality, thinking if she was to die, the money and everything that came with it would be his and his alone. He felt he shouldn't think these thoughts, and although he tried to push them out of his mind, realizing the chances of her demise were slim at best, they nevertheless frequently haunted him.

Life had been good ever since Kathy told him that she was pregnant with his son. Getting her pregnant had turned out to be the best thing that had ever happened to him. Within the Gagnon's social circle, Phil appeared to be a self-made man, but the bottom line was, without Kathy he was nobody.

Several years after he married Kathy, her father suffered a serious stroke, needing almost constant attention, which his wife willingly gave him. This created more responsibilities for Phil. Mr. Hennessey was grateful that Phil was responsible enough to run the agency. He never fully recovered and eventually lost all interest in his business. It wasn't long before he decided that winters up north were too harsh, and he and Mrs. Hennessey moved to Barefoot Bay.

This was what Phil had been waiting for. Running the business was entirely in his hands. He was able to start making changes. He didn't hesitate to expand the agency into the suburbs of Lowell—changes his father-in-law had rejected.

Phil saw the opportunities that opened up in the surrounding towns. People were buying cars and moving to the suburbs in droves. Within two years after taking complete control, Phil had opened two new branch offices. The Hennessey Insurance Agency quickly became the largest independent insurance agency in the Greater Lowell area.

There was one problem. Years later, when his father-in-law passed away unexpectedly, Phil discovered at the reading of his will that Mr. Hennessey had left all his assets to Kathy and her mother, and them alone. Two years later Mrs. Hennessey followed her husband, and she, too, had passed away, giving Kathy complete control over the Hennessey Insurance Agency, the house in Lowell and even the home in Barefoot Bay. Phil owned nothing.

Phil tried unsuccessfully to convince Kathy to transfer everything into both their names but to no avail.

Both the old man and Kathy had suspicions that Phil played around. Although they'd never actually caught him, they weren't blind. Kathy was aware he could charm the ladies without having to exert a great deal of effort to be irresistible whenever he wanted. Kathy was no fool.

He thought for a moment about his childhood and had no intentions of going back. Sitting in this small apartment, far from his youth, he recalled the misery growing up that had instilled a hunger, an ambition and a need to never settle for anything but the best, and now this was where that need had brought him. In a motel, having an affair with a woman he hardly knew. He reached for his coat and headed for the door. He wasn't going back by losing all that he had accomplished over Betty Pappas.

While locking the door and leaving the apartment, hopefully for the last time, Phil knew there was no sense in putting it off any longer. He wasn't always right about everything but he was usually right about most things. He certainly knew he was right about ending this affair before losing everything he'd spent his whole career building. Leaving the Captain's Quarters, he promised himself that today would be the last time he would meet Betty.

CHAPTER 25

AFTER LEAVING KATHY in the driveway gawking across the street, wondering if her old boyfriend was in town, Carol went into the house looking for Stanley. She couldn't wait to tell him about being invited to the Gagnon's for a cookout, knowing it would ruin his day. She entered the kitchen, glanced around, but he was nowhere in sight. She knew exactly where to find him.

Dropping her pocketbook and keys on the table, she walked directly to the screen room out back. Sure enough, there he was, all three hundred pounds of him slouching in his lounge chair, reading the newspaper while the television was broadcasting a recap of last night's baseball game.

They had been in Florida for nearly two years, and Stanley hadn't made any friends. Watching him day in and day out, hanging around the house like a useless mass of humanity made her sick to her stomach. A day didn't go by that she hadn't wished she'd left him back in Barnstead.

He had days when he acted completely normal, smiling, taking walks, greeting neighbors with a cheerful good morning. Then his mood would swing. He would become aggressive, cranky and abusive. She was caught between fear and pity, not knowing which Stanley she was dealing with.

"I figured I'd find you out here," she announced, turning off the television.

Stanley slowly looked up from his newspaper. "Where the hell did you think I'd be? Why did you turn the goddamn TV off? I was watching it."

"What were you doing, looking through the paper? Anyway, Kathy invited us over later this afternoon for a cookout," she told him, then waited for his reaction.

Stanley stared blankly at her for a moment. He didn't like Phil Gagnon any more than Phil liked him. Going next door and listening to him brag about his achievements on the golf course wasn't exactly how Stanley wanted to spend his evening.

"What? Why do I have to go? Why don't you go by yourself?"

"Kathy was nice enough to invite both of us; so both of us are going."

Stanley leaned his head back and emptied his lungs of air. If Carol said they were going to the Gagnon's for a cookout, then that's exactly where he was going. "What time?" he reluctantly asked, picking up the remote and turning the TV back on.

"Between four and four-thirty; why, did you have plans?" she asked sarcastically.

He reached down and picked up the paper. "No. Just curious."

That settled, Carol headed for the bedroom to get out of her sweaty gym clothes and take a shower. After throwing her clothes into the laundry basket, she looked at herself in the full-length mirror behind the bedroom door. The picture never changed. After close examination, she shook her head and gave a strained smile to the image looking back. She was not a pretty sight. Today's gym class had changed nothing. She still had the same broad shoulders, large chest and hips that went straight down, with thick muscular legs that she'd always had.

Before turning on the shower, she sat on the side of the tub. She was thinking how different things might have been if Robin hadn't died. When they decided to move to Barefoot Bay after retiring, after spending all those years living a lie, after being careful to hide their feelings for each other in public, they intended on coming out of the closet. Finally, after years of hiding they would be a couple. They would let the whole world know they were in love. But, everything changed that terrible night in Vermont. She now only had Stanley and was caught in a trap of her own making.

Carol met and fell in love with Robin more than twenty years ago.

Shortly after marrying Stanley, Carol drove up to the small town of Barnstead, located in the Pocono Mountains of Pennsylvania, for a job interview. Ever since high school, it had been her dream to be a physical education teacher at the high school level. Unsure if she would get hired, she never mentioned to Stanley that she had applied for this position.

Driving through the Pocono Mountains, windows open, her heart beating a mile a minute, she arrived in the quaint little village of Barnstead and immediately fell in love with the look and feel of the town. She located the school a short distance outside the business district. Carol parked her car, nervously got out and began searching for the principal's office.

"I'm looking for Principal Billingsley," she informed the neat looking receptionist in the administration office.

"I'll check and see if he's available. Who shall I say is here?"

"Carol Kloski. I'm here about the Physical Education position."

"Yes. I believe he's expecting you," the receptionist said. She got up and knocked on the closed door with the words Principal's Office in gold letters. Opening the door she informed the principal of Carol's arrival.

The principal came out and escorted her into his office. After an hour of intense discussions, Carol left satisfied she had given a good account of herself, and drove back to New Jersey thinking she had an excellent chance of finding employment. Two weeks later a letter arrived, saying the position was hers, if she wanted it. She definitely wanted it.

She told Stanley the good news as soon as he came home from the bank. "I've got a job," she exclaimed, waving the letter vigorously in front of him.

He snatched the letter out of her hand, then, read it slowly. He wasn't happy. "For Christ sake, I've got a great job here at the bank. I can't just pull up stakes and move," he argued.

"Stanley, I want this job. I want this job more than anything I've ever wanted before."

"No, Carol. It's just a matter of time before my mother retires. I'll move up to vice president and then president. It's out of the question."

Stanley continued to pout and complained for several days and insisted they would not relocate. But he was no match for Carol once her mind was made up. And her mind was made up. Reluctantly but obediently, Stanley moved to Barnstead, just as she knew he would.

Carol fit right in with her new job. After only two years at Barnstead High, she had successfully improved the girls' athletic program dramatically. Before she had arrived, Barnstead hadn't had a successful season in any of the girls' sports. It didn't take long before she turned things around. Suddenly the girls' softball team, swimming team and basketball team quickly improved and in doing so, she became extremely popular with the kids. The students were attracted to her because she was young and clever and full of enthusiasm. In some ways, she was one of them.

When she was in the gym, Carol watched the girls go through their routines, guiding them through their plays and encouraging them to do their best, and knew she'd made the right career choice. She loved coaching. Everything was going along fine. She was happier now than she had ever been in her life. She couldn't imagine her life getting any better.

Then it did. She met Robin.

June was quickly coming to an end. It was the last day of the school year. Carol had just completed her second year of teaching. The students had already started their summer vacation. Carol was walking down what appeared to be a ridiculously long, empty hallway, not liking the quiet. She preferred it when it was complete chaos with rivers of students flowing through the hallways, girls erupting in shrieks of laughter, clanging lockers, backpacks thrown everywhere and boys jostling one another while hurrying to their next class. She was on her way to turn in her final report of the year before beginning summer vacation.

Carol entered the principal's office and observed an attractive young lady seated against the wall. She was dressed in an expensive, well-tailored woman's business suit with a light gray skirt, matching jacket, and white ruffled blouse.

Trying not to be conspicuous, out of the corner of her eye she glanced over at the attractive young lady with the pretty blue eyes and blond hair cut in a Dutch-boy hairstyle and was impressed with how youthful and innocent she looked. The girl was nervous as she subconsciously tapped on a manila envelope in her lap.

As Carol walked by, Robin looked up, gave a timid smile, then looked away and continued tapping a tune that didn't sound like anything either of them recognized.

Carol had just passed Mary, Mr. Billingsley's secretary, in the hallway. She decided to see if there was anything she could do to help the young lady. "Can I help you with something?"

Robin considered the question. "No thanks. The woman who just left said that Mr. Billingsley would be with me shortly."

After walking around the waist high counter and dropping off her report on Mary's desk, Carol was about to walk out but stopped. "I don't believe I've seen you around school before."

"I'm applying for the teaching position in the Art Department," Robin said.

There had been talk among the teachers that Mrs. Simchuck, the art teacher, had decided to retire. It appeared Mr. Billingsley was interviewing candidates for the position. "So where are you teaching now?" Carol asked, sitting on the vacant seat next to her.

"I've just graduated from the University of Rhode Island. I don't have any teaching experience," Robin confessed. "I'm afraid my lack of experience might be a problem."

"Hey, don't worry. It's gonna be all right. This was my first job. I know other teachers who were also hired right out of college," she said, reaching over and taking Robin's hand, giving it a friendly squeeze.

Just as Carol was about to get up to leave, Principal Billingsley came out of his office. He wasn't especially tall, but there was something about the way he carried himself, very straight, head held high, that made you think he was. Everyone thought the world of him, considered him to be fair and respected his decisions.

"Hi, Carol. Looking forward to the summer vacation?" he asked.

"Yes and no. It'll be nice to be able to sleep in mornings, but I really enjoy the kids, and I'll miss them." She released Robin's hand, then stood.

"Well, I want you to know the school committee couldn't be happier with what you've done with the girls' phys ed. program."

"Thanks," she said.

He turned his attention to Robin. "You must be Miss Pruitt, the young lady interviewing for the position in the art department." Principal Billingsley extended his hand.

Robin quickly stood and shook it weakly. "Yes."

"If you'd allow me to run down to the teachers' lounge to get a coffee, I'll be with you shortly. Would either of you care for one?"

"No, thank you," they both answered, sounding as one.

"Are you sure?"

"I'm all set," Carol said. Robin said nothing, forcing a smile.

"Okay, I'll be right back."

Once alone, Carol said, "Would you do me a favor?"

"Sure."

"Stop in the teachers' lounge after your interview. I'm really interested in how you make out." Carol was eager to continue the conversation with her new friend.

"How do I find it?"

"Right down the hall, first door on the left; you can't miss it."

"Okay. See you as soon as I'm through."

"I'll be waiting, and good luck."

After about forty-five minutes, Robin burst through the teacher's room door.

"From your smile, I take it things went pretty good."

"I think so." Robin sat down in the vacant chair next to Carol. "Mr. Billingsley said my lack of experience wouldn't be a problem. He said that Mrs. Simchuck has been with the school for over twenty-five years, and now that she was retiring, the school committee was looking for someone younger. Someone they hoped would bring some new ideas and energy into the art program."

"Like I explained earlier, I was hired right out of college. I really didn't think that would be a problem."

Carol heard the enthusiasm in Robin's voice. "I hope not. Well, anyway, he said he would have to take my application up with the school committee before any final decision could be made. But he did say he was going to recommend me."

The conversation continued to flow effortlessly. They talked as though they'd been friends for a long time. Carol went into details about the benefits of working in a small community like Barnstead, and Robin listened closely.

Carol sounded more excited about the prospects of her new friend coming on board at Barnstead High than Robin was. There was no doubt she'd met someone special. She didn't know how she knew, she just felt it.

They had been chitchatting for over an hour when Robin realized how much time had passed. "I've got a long ride ahead of me, I'd better be going."

Carol looked at her watch. "Where did the time go? I'm sorry if I've held you up."

"Not at all, I really enjoyed talking with you. I've got my fingers crossed I'll get the job. Wish me luck," Robin said.

"I know everything's going to work out. I've got a good feeling about your coming to Barnstead."

Robin picked up her manila envelope, and they left the teachers room, each feeling they had made a new friend. They walked slowly down the sidewalk to the teachers' parking area, continuing their conversation.

When they arrived at Robin's car, a Volkswagen Jetta, Carol hated to say goodbye. "I'm going to give you my phone number. Give me a call when you hear something. I'm anxious to see how you make out. Do you mind?"

"Of course I don't mind. I'll call as soon as I hear one way or the other," Robin promised.

"I've got a good feeling about today," Carol concluded, handing her the telephone number she had hastily written on a scrap of paper. Then, she gave Robin a casual hug. Her new friend smiled, accepting the hug willingly.

Robin got into her car and backed out of her parking spot. Before driving away, she looked back at Carol and waved. When their eyes met, Carol believed at some level something beyond her control had just happened. Her life was about to change. She returned her wave, feeling a pang of disappointment, knowing it was going to be a long summer before she saw Robin again.

Now, stepping into the shower, Carol couldn't help but think back to the days when her life was so much better. She had come so close to living the life she always dreamt would someday be hers. Sharing it with someone she truly loved. Someone to share her dreams with. Now she was gone!

Moving around the bedroom, selecting the outfit she would wear to the Gagnon's later, Carol's mind flashed back to the long, hot summer before Robin began teaching at Barnstead High.

Since receiving Robin's call telling her she got the job, Carol had been anxious to get the summer break behind her and return to teaching. They kept in touch by phone and made plans to meet the Wednesday before school officially opened.

Arriving in the faculty parking lot, Carol parked her Ford Explorer and immediately looked for Robin's Volkswagen. She located it on the far side of the pavement. Without hesitating, she turned off the ignition, quickly got out and walked into school.

Carol hadn't been able to get Robin out of her mind. She had never felt this kind of closeness with another woman. It had only been a brief encounter, but they had developed something special between them; she couldn't explain it, but she just knew it was there.

Going directly to the art room, she found Robin unloading a carton of art supplies into an open drawer. "Welcome to Barnstead High School. May you spend many happy years trying to instill some kind of culture into the minds of your students," Carol announced with a friendly smile.

"Thank you. I'm so excited. I don't think I slept more than a couple of hours all night," Robin replied.

Carol dropped her leather briefcase on the desk, then embraced Robin, which was accepted with an equal amount of compassion. Carol gently pushed her back, still hanging on at arm's length. "I can't tell you how good it is to see you. Have you been here long?"

"About a half hour. Thanks for coming by. Having a friend is going to make getting started a lot easier. I can't thank you enough."

"Don't mention it. Believe me, I'm happy to do it. Look, after you've put the rest of those supplies away, I'll take you on a tour of the campus."

"Fantastic. I've been driving around town this morning. I was up early, so I figured I might as well spend the time looking around the town."

Carol released her, jumped up and was now sitting on the edge of the desk. "Not much to see. Barnstead's a typical small New England town. You'll get to love it. But like most small towns you have to be on your best behavior in public. Everybody knows everybody's business."

"I'll try to keep a low profile. Oh, by the way, I didn't get a chance to tell you, I found a nice apartment just outside of town."

"That's wonderful. How did you manage that?"

"I drove up last weekend."

"Why didn't you call me? We could have met for lunch."

"I didn't have a lot of time. It's not very large, but it's furnished. It's perfect for me."

"How did you find it?"

"Answered a classified ad. It's a single family house that's been converted into two apartments. I'm going to be living on the second floor. The landlady lives downstairs; she's widowed and seems really nice." Robin sounded excited.

"I can't wait to see it."

"You're welcome to drop by anytime."

"I've got a great idea. After I show you around the school, I'll treat you to lunch. Then we can spend the rest of the afternoon driving around the outskirts of Barnstead. Later you can show me your new apartment."

"Sounds like a plan," Robin said.

Carol couldn't remember a time that she was happier than that autumn afternoon she'd spent driving around Barnstead with Robin. After leaving the school, they drove up to The Shack, high in the Pocono Mountains for lunch. The menu at The Shack was typical of most small restaurants with daily specials of pot roast, stuffed peppers, spaghetti on Wednesday and always fish on Fridays.

What drew most customers to The Shack was the breathtaking mountain views which had resisted the march of time, making it an exceptional eating place for lunch or dinner. After the meal, they drove around the winding back country roads, Robin's Volkswagen cutting through oak, maple and pine trees with the varied shades of green, reds, browns and yellows of autumn. They stopped occasionally, got out of the car and walked along a lake on a beaten path. It was quiet with no sign of activity except for the sound of birds chirping off in the distance. The air was full of the scent of pine trees with only the movement of the wind breaking the silence.

Robin occasionally reached down, picked up a dried maple leaf and crushed it between her fingers. "I've always thought autumn is such a wonderful time. Some people think it's sad because it means the end of summer, but it's much too beautiful to be sad."

While casually walking along a lakeside path, they unexpectedly disturbed a pair of mallard ducks that quacked their complaints as they soared off into the autumn sky. "Oh, what a delightful day. I love the smell of fall," Carol told Robin, and they both smiled, their hair whipped around by the brisk, early September wind.

When it got to be after four-thirty, Robin suggested they head home. "It's getting late. We had better start back. I'd invite you for supper, but my cupboard is bare," she confessed. "Do you know of any place along the way that we can stop? I'll be happy to treat."

"The Kozy Korner is just a short drive from the school. You can drop me off at my car and follow me there. It's not fancy, but the food is plentiful and good," Carol suggested.

"Sounds like my kind of place."

The Kozy Korner was a small, mom-and-pop restaurant and true to its name was located on the corner of Route 3 and Boggy Creek Road. They both ordered fried chicken dinners. They were ravenous and devoured their meals. The chatter never stopped as the food disappeared off their plates, covering everything from religion, politics, sports, favorite movies, which actors they liked, didn't like, they even traded family stories. There was so much they didn't know about each other and they were both anxious to fill in the missing years.

When they arrived at Robin's apartment, Carol glanced around the well-kept, landscaped yard flaming with September colors of yellow, red and golden leaves of autumn from the maple trees, and smelled the scent of burning leaves off in the distance. She followed Robin up the outdoor staircase that led directly into her new apartment. "Looks like a nice quiet neighborhood."

"Last night was the first time I slept here. I think it's going to be fine," Robin said. Inserting the key and turning the knob, she opened the door easily. "This place is a total mess. As you can see, I'm still in the process of getting settled." Robin waved her hand casually toward the clutter that was everywhere. "Well, how do you like it?"

"I love it. It's so cute. The large windows let in so much light. It's bright and cheerful."

"The light is great for my painting," Robin said.

Carol's eyes swept around the living room. Several paintings leaned against the walls. About a dozen more oil paintings of her best seascapes were propped on the floor against the chairs and sofa. An easel with a landscape in progress stood next to one of the windows. A stool was in front of it. On top of a small table, a glass container smelling of turpentine and paint had different size paint brushes sticking out of it.

"I only have a couple of cokes in the refrigerator."

"Coke's fine. I'm not an expert, but your paintings are really good." Carol picked up a seascape from against the sofa.

"Thanks."

"Do you sell them?"

"While I was in college, me and some of my girlfriends would go to the shore and try selling them. You know, looking to make some extra cash. I hope I'm a better teacher than an artist. I'm really just an amateur."

"You're not an amateur. They're wonderful." Carol replaced the canvas back against the sofa.

"I'm maybe a good amateur, but an amateur nevertheless."

Robin handed Carol her Coke. They sat silently on the sofa staring at each other for an awkward moment. With sunlight beginning to fade, it cast a pale orange shadow on the walls, giving the room a warm comfortable feeling.

Unable to break eye contact and with a burning desire for Robin that had been eating away at her all day, Carol leaned over and gently kissed Robin on the lips. Robin's eyes widened, but her gaze didn't waver. Realizing what she had done, Carol drew back. Her heartbeat quickened as she clenched her hands into fists before looking away. When she lifted her head, she put her hand over her mouth.

Their eyes met, and Robin gave her a thin smile that seemed to say, I'm okay; it's okay.

"I'm sorry. I shouldn't have done that," Carol said.

Robin continued to smile, moved closer, grasped her by the shoulders and drew Carol toward her. She began kissing her on her eyelids, then on her mouth and gently started caressing her breast. "I've been waiting for this moment ever since we first met," Robin whispered.

Carol heard angels singing. It felt like the Fourth of July with fireworks exploding in the sky. She looked deep into Robin's eyes, at her beautiful smile and realized her life was just now beginning. Carol had never been with another woman. All the pent up frustration and heartache that had consumed her for most of her life was being released, and she felt free to feel like a human being.

Robin began stroking her throat with her finger tips, then slowly slid them down and began unbuttoning her blouse.

Carol was experiencing for the first time what it was like to be sexually desirable. She put her hand on Robin's thigh, then slid it up between her legs, feeling the fierce heat through her slacks. The thrill and anticipation of what was to come made her quiver all over. Robin unbuttoned Carol's blouse and traced the swell of her breasts above the cup of her bra. Carol pulled Robin on top of her. She felt their breasts being squashed together. Their desire for each other was beyond reason.

Soon they were in Robin's bed. Years of frustration made their bodies ache for fulfillment. Their nipples were firm, and they were being taken to a place that before today, they had only dreamt of. For a while afterward, they lay next to each other, not speaking, holding hands, both physically spent.

Finally Carol spoke. "I was afraid I was going to die without anyone ever making love to me," she whispered.

"I know. I've been hiding my whole life. Pretending to be something I'm not," Robin said.

"This is my first time."

"I know."

Carol smiled. "God, I'm glad I found you. Why couldn't I have found you a long time ago? I've been fighting to keep my sanity. Waiting for someone to come along who would understand what it's been like. I've been so lonely."

"Let's not look back," Robin said.

"Will you hold me?"

"Sure."

"Mmmm, that feels good."

"Just being held?"

"Yes."

"From now on, everything's going to be fine."

"As long as we're together, I know I'll be all right." Carol nestled her head against Robin's shoulder.

"You'll never be alone again," Robin promised.

They spent the remainder of the night snuggled together beneath a quilt.

That was the beginning of a relationship of unconditional love between Carol and Robin. It didn't make them evil, immoral, or sinners. Didn't people know that two women could fall in love? It wasn't just a fling. It wasn't about sex. It was the beginning of real love . . . the kind of love that comes only once in a lifetime.

Dressed, Carol sat on the edge of her bed, weeping silently as she remembered Robin's words, "You'll never be alone again." But she was alone. Moments like this weren't uncommon. When Carol wasn't able to sleep, the memories returned. The tears flowed, knowing she would never see Robin smile again. She found herself thinking in the past rather than the present or the future. She knew it did no good to cry. What happened in Vermont had happened. All the tears in the world were not going to bring Robin back.

CHAPTER 26

WHEN THE KLOSKIS arrived, Phil, wearing loose fitting, green cargo cutoffs and a Boston Patriot's T-shirt, was standing in front of his grill, a beer in one hand and a wooden spatula in the other stirring the onions and peppers. A platter of uncooked Italian sausages was on the table next to the store-bought macaroni salad, a tossed green salad and rolls covered with aluminum foil.

"Hi, Carol, hi, Stan. Welcome to Phil Gagnon's Italian Eatery. The finest Italian sausages in Florida." He waved the spatula around like a conductor.

"Peppers and onions smell great. Sausages, one of your favorites, Stanley," Carol said, unsuccessfully trying to get her husband enthused about being there.

"Yeah, smells good," Stanley replied halfheartedly.

"Well, I haven't started cooking the sausages yet. I'll throw them on whenever we're ready. If you want something to drink, there's plenty of beer and soda in the refrigerator," he offered, motioning toward the house with the spatula.

"Good idea, I think I'll have a Coke," Carol said. "Stanley, you want a beer while I'm going?"

"Okay," he grunted, sitting with a thud at the patio picnic table.

"Be back in a minute," Carol said.

Left alone, Phil inquired, "Where have you been, Stan? Haven't seen you in a while."

"Been around," Stanley answered bluntly.

Examining him closely, Phil couldn't understand how anyone could be as useless as Stanley Kloski. The thing that bothered Phil the most about Stanley was that he didn't seem to have any purpose or agenda to his life. He walked around with a blank expression on his face, with a drowning man's stare, making it impossible to tell what was going on behind those dead man's eyes.

"Still playing golf on Wednesdays with the men's league?" Phil asked, their eyes locking momentarily with the question.

Upset about being here and intimidated by Phil's stare, Stanley couldn't look Phil in the eyes for long and looked away. He was recalling how during the past weeks he'd been awakened by the same recurring nightmare.

In his dream he was running, trying to escape, being chased across an endless field. Phil was dressed like a clown in a red costume with purple and green polka dots, wearing a bald headed wig with long red curls on the sides. Although Phil's face was covered in makeup, Stanley knew it was him. Stanley's legs felt like cement. The harder he tried to escape, the heavier his legs became until he was unable to move.

Once caught, Phil pounced on him, knocking him to the ground. He straddled him and laughed hideously, his face painted in clown make-up, his huge red lips smiling while slapping Stanley again and again. Stanley tried to scream, but when he opened his mouth nothing came out. Phil continued slapping him harder with his large gloved hands until Stanley was jolted awake and lying on the floor.

Realizing he had fallen out of bed, he crawled across the room and sat in the corner. Consumed with fear, he pressed his fists against his eyes and moaned like a lunatic, the clown's hideous laugh echoing in his head. He sat there in the corner unable to move, listening to the wind moving against the house, afraid if he crawled out of the corner, the clown would once again attack.

After several minutes passed, he crawled like a dog across the room, then pulled himself onto his bed and collapsed. He pulled the blankets to his neck and lay shaking, his sheets soaked in sweat. The dream slowly faded away as dreams usually do. He glanced at the clock on the bureau. It was 2:20 in the morning. It had been the beginning of what would be another long night.

Now in Phil's company, he was trying to erase the nightmare that was replaying in his mind like a video. "Yeah, I'm still playing once in a while."

"You're a C-player, right Stan?"

"Yeah."

"I'm an A-player so that's why we don't get to play together. They always start the A-players off first in the morning. That way you guys don't hold the better players up. Nothing I hate more that getting stuck behind you C-players."

As Phil rambled on, Stanley looked away. He hated the way Phil always talked down to him in a deliberate no-nonsense voice, putting on an air of superiority whenever they were together, acting like Stanley wasn't fit to wipe his ass. He hadn't been here more than five minutes, and already he was getting a sick feeling in the pit of his stomach. He would love to head back home but knew if he did he'd have to face Carol later, a situation better avoided.

Carol entered the house, but Kathy wasn't in the kitchen, so she went to find her. She was looking out her front living room window, the light beige curtains drawn back, allowing for a clear view of the house across the street. "Any sign of your friend yet?" Carol asked in a strong voice, shattering the silence.

"Oh, my God, Carol, I didn't hear you come in." Kathy turned suddenly, putting her hands to her chest. "You scared the life out of me."

"Boy, you're sure dying to find out if that's your old boyfriend, aren't you?"

"Well, I guess I'm a little curious," she admitted. Kathy was more than a little curious. The thought that her son's father might be living across the street after all these years both frightened her and excited her.

Earlier, while standing in front of the bedroom mirror in her underwear, she kept trying on different outfits. If it was Jimmy, she wanted to look her best if she decided to walk across the street and find out. Unable to decide what to wear, she threw each outfit she tried on in a pile on her bed. If one outfit didn't look right, she tried on something else; if that one wasn't right, she'd find another. After trying on skirts, blouses and dresses for about thirty minutes and deciding they didn't feel right across her breast, skirts were tight around her waist and slacks were too snug, they all ended up on the pile.

A frustrating half-hour later, she finally selected a simple white dress with a red belt, cut just low enough in the front to show off her Florida tan. Slipping it on, she realized it was just slightly snug when she looked at her reflection in the mirror. First turning to the left and then to the right, she nodded her approval, giving herself a confident smile. That's about as good as it gets, she decided.

She couldn't deny the obvious. The passage of time was taking its toll. Her hair roots were showing signs of gray and the flesh of her abdomen was beginning to crease in the usual places, but she now possessed a sense of warmth and grace that came with maturity. She was convinced she looked as good as could be expected for someone over sixty.

"Why don't we just go over and introduce ourselves? We'll say since they just moved in, we wanted to welcome them to Barefoot Bay and invite them over for a cookout. Looks like Phil has plenty," Carol suggested.

"Maybe later." Kathy was nervous and didn't feel quite up to meeting Jimmy just yet, and something deep inside told her it was definitely going to be Jimmy.

"Has Phil started cooking?" Kathy looked over her shoulder, taking one last glance across the street before heading for the kitchen.

"He was stirring the peppers and onions when I left." Carol followed her friend. "I was just coming in for drinks."

"What's your pleasure?" Kathy asked while opening the refrigerator.

"I'm drinking Coke. Stanley's having a beer."

Kathy grabbed enough drinks for everyone. "Let's go join the guys." She followed Carol out the door.

After they finished eating, they remained seated around the table talking. At least Carol, Kathy, and Phil were making conversation. Stanley grunted occasionally when asked a direct question, which wasn't often.

"Did you know Kathy's old school chum?" Carol asked Phil.

"No. I don't think I ever met him, did I, Kathy?"

"No. I only dated him for a little while in high school. When I went to college, we went our separate ways. It really wasn't serious," Kathy said, looking in Phil's direction. "He probably won't even remember me. It's been so long."

"Let's go over there. I'm dying to find out if it's him," Carol insisted.

"Maybe later; they're probably still unpacking," Kathy said.

"How long can it take to unpack?" Carol asked. She couldn't stand the suspense any longer. She was determined to solve the mystery, with or without Kathy. "Okay, I'm going. I'll find out once and for all if it's this Jimmy Martin or not. Kathy, are you coming with me?"

Deciding to get it over with, Kathy reluctantly agreed. "Okay. You guys want to come along?" Kathy asked, looking at Phil, then at Stanley, then back to Phil. She wanted all the support she could get, but soon realized she wasn't about to get any.

"No, thanks. I'll just sit here with Stan," Phil said sarcastically, giving a sideways glance in Stanley's direction.

Walking across the street, Carol was in the lead, moving along like a woman on a mission. Kathy followed close behind. Her stomach was churning, and her heart pounded with stop-start anxiety. Arriving at their neighbor's door, Carol didn't hesitate and rapped with a firm knock that would definitely get the attention of whoever was inside.

Kathy heard a man's voice from inside, "I'll get it, Rita," and recognized it immediately. Within seconds, Jimmy Martin opened the door with a puzzled look on his face. He and Rita didn't know a soul in Barefoot Bay. At least, he thought he didn't know anybody until Kathy Hennessey showed up on his door step.

Unable to think of anything to say for a long moment, Kathy stood in the doorway, feeling awkward, staring at him with a forced smile on her face. The shock of seeing him after all these years ran the length of her body. A feeling of excitement went all the way to her toes. Barely able to speak, she said, "Jimmy! Remember me?"

"Kathy Hennessey!" He sounded surprised. "What in the world are you doing here?"

"I live across the street. This morning when Carol and I got back from our exercise class, I thought I recognized you walking into the house. How in the world are you?"

"I'm just fine."

"You're looking good," Kathy said and meant it.

He looked more handsome now than when they were dating, in a mature sort of way. There was warmth to his face, a gentleness that didn't appear forced or put on. Jimmy was trim. His hair was still dark, although turning slightly gray around his temples, giving him a distinguished look. His voice, his handsome face, the way he moved his body was just as it was so many years ago. She wondered how she looked and subconsciously tightened her stomach and pulled back her shoulders, wanting to look good in her white dress and Florida tan.

"Rita, we have company," Jimmy announced, turning slightly as his wife walked into the living room.

Rita was surprised, but soon realized her husband apparently knew these women. "Honey, this is an old friend from back home. Kathy and I went to high school together," Jimmy said, glancing toward Kathy.

"What a small world. Come in and sit down." Rita stepped aside. Once they were seated, she continued, "I'm sorry I don't have anything to offer you. We just arrived."

"We can only stay a minute. I was telling Jimmy, I saw you moving in this morning. I only got a quick look before Jimmy disappeared into the house. I wasn't sure if it was really him," Kathy explained. "This is my friend and neighbor, Carol Kloski. Carol and her husband also live across the street."

Jimmy kept staring at Kathy, impressed at how attractive Kathy looked. He noticed she had put on weight but had a mature, wholesome look about her. He noticed the sparkle in her eyes was still there. Absent were the small lines that most women get around their eyes and mouths when they get older.

"So, are you still living in Lowell?" Kathy asked, struggling to keep her quivering voice under control.

"No. After we got married we bought a house in Chelmsford. I worked for the Post Office in Chelmsford for over thirty five years. I just retired this past fall," Jimmy informed her. "I see that your family still owns the insurance agency."

"Yes! Both my parents have passed away. Phil and my son run the business now. Actually my son has just about taken over. My husband is semi-retired."

"I've met your son. Whenever I drop in to pay my bill, your son is usually working. I've briefly spoken to him on a couple of occasions but never mentioned I'm an old friend of his mother's."

Mentioning her son brought back the realization of her situation. The past years of pretending Phil was her son's real father suddenly came crashing down on her. Examining Jimmy's features closely, Kathy was confronted with the face of reality; any doubts she might have had vanished when she realized how much Jimmy resembled their son, Philip.

With delicate facial features and an almost childlike innocence, Rita appeared warm and friendly. Her large brown eyes had a twinkle and were highlighted by the clear light cinnamon brown shade of her skin. She wore a pale green blouse with a Peter Pan collar, a tan pair of shorts and dark brown sandals. Jimmy's wife looked like the perfect suburban housewife and a perfect match for him.

"How long are you here for?" Carol asked.

"We rented this house for three months. We'll be going home at the end of March," Rita said.

"That's great. I want both of you to come over for dinner next week and meet our husbands. In fact why don't you come over now and join us?" Kathy suggested.

"Thanks, but we have a million things to do. We still have to go shopping," Rita explained.

"Are you sure?" Kathy said, re-inviting them.

"Yes. We really need to go shopping."

"Well, don't forget you're invited for dinner next week. It'll probably be Monday. I'll invite Betty and Scooter, too. I know how difficult it is when you first move into a new neighborhood getting to meet people."

"Kathy never misses a chance to entertain, as you will find out," Carol informed them.

"Do you play golf by any chance?" Kathy asked.

"Jimmy belonged to the golf league at the Post Office. He and our son, Jason, played occasionally." Rita answered before Jimmy had a chance to respond.

The mention of Jimmy and Rita having a son sent shivers down Kathy's spine. "How many children do you have?"

Rita's face seemed to light up when she spoke of her children. "We have a son Jason and a daughter. Elizabeth is expecting in June so we'll be home in plenty of time for the arrival of our first grandchild. Jason just got married this past summer."

"You sound awfully proud of them," Carol said.

"We are."

"Seeing as you're a golfer, I'll have Phil set up a game. I'm sure Scooter and Stanley will play. That way you'll have a foursome," Kathy suggested.

"That sounds great. I'm dying to play golf and look forward to meeting your husbands," Jimmy said.

"I know you have to go shopping, so we'll run along. The boys will be wondering what happened to us. Don't forget about dinner Monday evening." Kathy stood, immediately followed by Carol.

They slowly made their way to the front door. "It's great to see you again, Jimmy. I can't get over how good you look. Your wife must take good care of you," Kathy said.

"Actually Jimmy's a pretty easy guy to live with. It's a job I really enjoy," Rita stated proudly, looking up affectionately at her husband. "Talk to you girls later," she continued once Carol and Kathy were outside.

"Don't forget dinner Monday evening," Kathy reminded them.

"We won't." Rita closed the door gently behind them. "That was a surprise. How come you never mentioned Kathy to me before?" Rita tilted her head to one side in a playful manner.

Jimmy could only laugh at her remark. "She was only a friend. We went to high school together, that's all," he explained, seeing no reason to elaborate.

"I'm just teasing. I think it was nice of them to come over and welcome us."

"It's sure a small world. I haven't thought of Kathy Hennessey in years, and out of the blue, she's knocking on our door."

"I'm going to finish making out a shopping list."

"Let me know when you're ready," Jimmy said, pickng up "The Florida Survival Handbook" he had purchased when they stopped for gas at a 7-Eleven Store after entering Florida.

Kathy Hennessey was now a stranger, Jimmy told himself as he read the Florida guide. He hadn't thought about her for years. He was a happily married man. A father and soon to be grandfather. Kathy Hennessey meant nothing to him now. But he had to admit, she still looked attractive dressed in that snug fitting white dress.

Her grocery list now complete, Rita called out to Jimmy, "You all set to go?"

Jimmy folded a corner of a page where he had left off and dropped the book on the coffee table. "All set."

"Well, the mystery has been solved. It's Jimmy Martin, Kathy's old boyfriend from high school," Carol announced before sitting down at the picnic table.

"Carol! Now don't start trouble. He was just a good friend. We only dated a couple of times," Kathy lied, blushing slightly. "Promise me you won't say anything to his wife. Maybe Jimmy would rather she didn't know that we dated."

Phil was sitting by himself, reading the daily newspaper, the *Press Journal,* when they returned. Stanley had gone home, claiming he wasn't feeling well. Folding the paper and throwing it on the picnic table, Phil said, "So it really was your friend from school after all."

"Yes, and he looks great. His wife seems really nice. By the way, I told him that you would take him golfing. I was thinking that you, Stanley and Scooter could get together," Kathy explained.

"So he's a golfer! That's good. I'll be happy to show him around," he agreed.

"I'm planning on having a small get-together for dinner Monday evening so everyone can get to know one another," Kathy said.

"That's a good idea," Phil agreed.

It was the middle of winter and darkness came early, so Carol said, "Since the mystery has been solved, and it's beginning to get dark, I'm heading home. See you tomorrow, Kathy."

CHAPTER 27

EVER SINCE INVITING the Martins over for dinner, Kathy had mixed emotions about Jimmy coming back into her life. She knew there was no way to ignore him and wasn't sure she wanted to.

She had notified everyone that dinner would be served at six. She was in the kitchen getting the food ready when the Kloskis arrived, as usual, on time. When Kathy walked out of the kitchen wearing her bib apron, Carol gave her a casual hug and an air kiss. Stanley stood rigid with an uncomfortable look on his face, wishing he was anywhere but here.

The scent of Italian prepared chicken, mingling with the aroma of freshly cooked vegetables, lingered in the air. "Something smells delicious. If it tastes as good as it smells, we're in for a treat," Carol said, inhaling deeply.

"I'm hoping everyone likes it. This is the first time I've tried this recipe," Kathy said.

Within minutes after Carol and Stanley arrived, the Martins showed up, Rita holding tightly onto Jimmy's arm. She looked nervous but smiling. Rita wore beige slacks and a light blue blouse, the only jewelry a plain wedding band. When they were introduced to Stanley, unlike Carol who had been outgoing and friendly when they met earlier in the week, he weakly shook hands and grunted, "Nice to meet you." Then he quickly cast his eyes to the floor.

The Martins weren't surprised when they met Kathy's husband. They had assumed he'd be a handsome, distinguished-looking man. They weren't disappointed. He was one of the fortunate people for whom age was actually a compliment. He was impeccably dressed, wearing a striped IZOD golf shirt over light tan Dockers slacks and dark brown leather Stafford shoes. The frequent trips to the gym kept his body firm, but with muscles that have the kind of motion that makes moving about look effortless with the power that comes from a man who took care of himself, and playing golf ensured he had a tan that complemented his deep brown eyes and perfect teeth.

Phil Gagnon was obviously a man who was most comfortable being in the spotlight. He appeared confident; someone who set his own standards, wanting to impress everyone. "Welcome to Barefoot Bay," Phil said, while shaking Jimmy's hand firmly.

"Thanks. I've wanted to come to Florida for some time now. I finally made it," Jimmy replied.

Phil cleared his throat, then spoke, "I think you'll like it here. You can't beat the weather."

"It took me awhile to convince Rita to come to Florida. I'm hoping she gets to like it," Jimmy said, turning slightly, smiling while he glanced at his wife.

"Maybe in time. We're only here for three months," Rita said.

"Don't worry, Rita, we'll keep you busy, won't we, Carol?" Kathy said.

"Florida grows on you. Eventually I'm sure you'll get to like it," Carol contributed.

Just as Carol and Stanley were always on time, Betty and Scooter could be counted on to be the last to arrive. As expected, they arrived fifteen minutes later.

Rita and Jimmy were surprised and impressed at how attractive Betty Pappas was walking through the door. She was dressed smartly in a casual pair of light green shorts and a yellow sleeveless blouse. When Kathy introduced them, Betty didn't hesitate to give them a warm, inviting smile. "It's so nice to meet you. Welcome to Florida. Kathy tells me you're going be here until the end of March."

"Yes. I'm looking forward to spending the rest of this winter in a warm climate for a change," Jimmy said, looking pleased.

Scooter stood large next to his wife. He had dark, rugged features, piercing eyes and a strong jaw, and looked like someone who must've been a good athlete when he was younger. But like a lot of ex-athletes, he was putting on unwanted weight around his waist. His graying hair hung over his ears and looked unkempt, as if he'd combed his hair with his fingers. Scooter Pappas appeared to be a 'what you see is what you get' kind of guy.

When Kathy introduced him to the Martins, he said, "Hi, nice to meet ya," his greeting lacking any warmth and sounding a little forced with no real feeling behind it. He walked away with an expression on his face that revealed nothing.

"Why don't we all have a seat? Phil, would you see what everyone's drinking?" Kathy turned toward her husband. Phil immediately started taking orders, then walked to their portable bar and began preparing drinks.

While Phil mixed cocktails, Kathy watched Jimmy sitting on the couch, trying to carry on a conversation with Stanley. He was positioned next to the end table with a graduation photo of *their* son, Philip, dressed in his navy blue cap and gown, proudly holding his Brown University diploma. Not having much success getting any response from Stanley, Jimmy turned his attention to the photo. He slowly picked it up and examined it closely.

Eyes wide with discovery, he turned to Rita. "Doesn't their son look a lot like Jason?"

Rita reached over and took the picture. Giving the photograph a quick glance, she said, "My God, he does! If I didn't know better, I'd think they were brothers," she exclaimed. "Kathy, I can't believe how much your son looks like our Jason. The resemblance is uncanny."

Kathy's stomach tightened. For a moment she couldn't breathe, her lungs tight. *My God, is it possible they could realize he's Jimmy son? No, of course not! Get a hold on yourself.* Then slowly the feeling passed. She felt a sense of relief, but only for a moment. Her face turned red, a single bead of sweat ran down between her breasts toward her stomach, while a cold chill ran down her spine.

Kathy tilted her head down and to the side so they wouldn't notice her uneasiness. "Does he really?" she finally managed to say, squeezing her fingers tightly around her glass.

Feeling she needed to do something, not wanting to continue this conversation any longer, she stood up and announced that dinner was about to be served. "Please come to the table, everyone," she instructed through trembling lips.

Kathy knew eventually the subject of her son would come up. She thought she was prepared to handle the situation but realized now that having her son's biological father living across the street was going to be a challenge.

Kathy had planned her table setting carefully. She placed yellow tapered candles in spiral silver holders on the table; the candles were flanked by an arrangement of chrysanthemums. She put the leftover flowers in a vase on the coffee table in the living room so everyone would see them when they arrived. And, as expected, everything looked perfect.

Kathy had a reputation for putting on excellent dinner parties. Tonight would not be any different. She had decided to cook an Italian meal. Her new neighbor, Rita, appeared Italian. She felt this would make her feel at home. On the menu was a tossed green salad, followed by fried calamari with fettuccine and chicken bathed with Italian seasoning.

Throughout dinner, Kathy felt uncomfortable whenever Jimmy made eye contact. She had purposely chosen a seat directly across from the Martins so she could observe Jimmy without being obvious. She now wished she had made other arrangements. The comments about Philip resembling their son had rattled her.

As she watched the Martins, she kept thinking what a handsome couple they made. They appeared to be happily married. Under no circumstances would she ever reveal the secret that she'd been living with for all these years. She didn't want to do anything that might create problems. Nothing good could come out of revealing her secret. She was more determined than ever to take her secret to the grave.

Rita was amazed at how good Kathy's Italian meal had turned out, and complimented her. "It's hard to believe an Irish girl could cook such a delicious Italian meal like the one I've just eaten," she said.

"I hate to admit it, Rita, but I think Kathy could give you a run for your money," Jimmy said. He'd always taken great pride in his wife's cooking.

"Well, maybe Rita will treat us to one of her Italian dishes some evening. Then we can taste a real Italian meal, prepared by an authentic Italian," Carol suggested.

"I don't think I could do much better than you did," Rita admitted.

After everyone had finished the main meal, Kathy cleared the table, went into the kitchen and returned with a New York cheesecake, topped with fresh strawberries.

"Looks like we'll have to work out extra hard at aerobics to work off this cake, Carol," Kathy informed Carol.

"Oh, my God, that looks delicious!" Carol exclaimed, "The hell with the diet. Cut me a piece and don't be bashful," she instructed with bulging eyes.

Wanting to include Rita in their activities, Kathy asked, "Rita, would you be interested in going to aerobics? We go on Monday, Wednesday, and Friday mornings. It's really a lot of fun, although it hasn't helped me lose any weight."

Rita had never been to a gym in her life. One look at her and it was evident there was never any need to. Although she didn't have an outstanding figure like Betty, she never had a problem with her weight. Rita was one of those women who looked basically the same when they aged, without exercising. Her figure could best be described as petite and wholesome, not counting a little bit of tummy that really didn't show that much.

Not wanting to appear antisocial, she replied, "Sure, why not? Sounds like fun."

"It's only three mornings a week, unless you play hooky like some of us do occasionally," Carol said, glancing toward Betty with accusing eyes.

"I know," Betty said. "I guess I just get lazy sometimes."

Looking directly at Betty, Kathy said, "There seems to be something that prevents Betty from showing up lately. Think you can make it Wednesday?"

"I'm not sure. I'll have to check my social calendar. I'll let you know," Betty answered with a strained laugh. Then she glanced down toward Phil, wanting to see his reaction, but he never looked up.

Betty had been getting the impression all evening that Phil was avoiding her. She couldn't escape the concerns that had been troubling her since the last morning they spent together at the Captain's Quarters. She was beginning to feel he was pulling away. Like something had come between them, and it bothered her.

When everyone finished dessert, the men went to sit in the living room to discuss their upcoming golf game. Kathy brought up the subject during dinner, and they made plans to set up a match, while the women cleaned off the table.

"What's convenient for you guys? I'm playing with the men's league on Wednesday. Anytime other than that will be fine with me," Phil said, taking charge as he always did.

"I've got softball on Wednesdays and Fridays. Any other day is fine with me," Scooter volunteered.

"I guess I'm the only one without a life. Any time is fine with me," Jimmy said.

"How about Thursday morning at ten o'clock; is that okay with everyone?" Phil suggested.

Everyone agreed except Stanley who didn't say yes and didn't say no. He would have been happier if they called the whole thing off.

"I'll call the club house tomorrow morning and get a tee time. I'll let you know if I was able to get a ten o'clock start," Phil offered.

Everyone said that would be fine, except Stanley who simply nodded but continued to remain silent.

Whenever Phil played, there had to be a wager involved. He claimed it made the match more interesting. Phil was known for his competitiveness. He did not merely have to win, he had a need that boarded on desperation and enjoyed proving he was better than the other players.

"I'll tell you what. I'm willing to take Stanley," he volunteered.

"You're on," Scooter said,

"I'm not so sure you're getting the best of this deal, Scooter. I'm really not very good," Jimmy admitted.

"Trust me, I've played with Stanley. Scooter is definitely getting the best of this deal. I don't care how bad you are, Stanley's worse," Phil assured Jimmy, breaking out in a hearty laugh.

Stanley's face turned red with embarrassment.

"Don't worry, Stanley, I'm really bad," Jimmy said.

Stanley felt his body tremble with hatred for Phil. He felt uncomfortable and out of place whenever they were together. His dinner lay heavy in his stomach, and his skin was damp with perspiration. He was afraid he might be sick at any minute.

Phil never passed up an opportunity to belittle him. He seemed to find pleasure in taunting him. He wished there was some way of getting out of playing with Phil Thursday morning, but he knew if he didn't show up, Carol wouldn't let him hear the end of it.

"What are we playing for?" Jimmy asked.

"What we'll do is, you two losers pay the bar bill at the 19th Hole after the match," Phil explained.

"We'll see about that," Scooter said.

The match was set.

CHAPTER 28

THURSDAY TURNED OUT to be beautiful. The sky was a light blue with a scattering of white puffy clouds. A constant breeze came across the Indian River from the Atlantic Ocean. January was usually the coldest month in Florida with temperatures frequently dropping into the forties at night, then returning to the low sixties by midday. Today the temperature was an unusual seventy-six degrees, a perfect day for golf.

Phil was first to arrive in the parking lot. He had no sooner driven into the lot when his phone rang. He had purposely avoided her all week. It was Betty. He was hoping she'd get the message that it was over. But she apparently hadn't. He needed to get rid of her. Not because it was wrong . . . it had always been wrong . . . but now it was dangerously wrong.

Before she called, he had been thinking about their affair and something his father, Big Jim, had told him. It was probably the only good advice his father ever gave him. "When a man gets a hard-on, his brain goes soft, and he can't think straight. His pecker starts doing his thinking for him. That's when the trouble starts." And that's exactly what Phil was doing.

Phil had always thought of himself as being cool, relaxed, unfazed by most anything, but the one crack in his armor was he loved the ladies. He knew it had been stupid, but the temptation to conquer Betty had been too great to resist. Like most men, he was a slave to the power of a sexual conquest.

Before answering, he flipped his phone open, checked his caller ID and knew it was her. "Hello," he said, then closed his eyes and waited to hear her speak.

"Hi. You busy?"

"No. I'm getting ready to play golf with your husband, although I think you already know that."

"Scooter just left. I figured we could talk before he got there. I've been trying to get in touch with you all week."

"I've been busy. I didn't want to take a chance calling you. You know we have to be careful."

Betty hesitated a second, considering his answer. "I called your cell phone several times and left messages. I know we have to be careful, but you still could have called me back. I'm getting the feeling you're trying to ignore me. Are you?"

Her bluntness caught him by surprise. A momentary silence stretched out, causing an uncomfortable pause. "No . . . ," he said, letting it hang in the air.

"No, what?" she asked.

"No. Of course not! Like I said, I just don't want to take any chances. That's all," he lied.

His explanation didn't please Betty. She was frowning on the other end of the phone. "I hope not."

Phil had purposely left his phone off all week, and he'd enjoyed her being completely out of his life. That's how he wanted it; no, that's how he needed it. "My phone has been acting crazy lately. I would have called if I knew you were trying to get in touch with me."

"Well, I'll forgive you this time. Can you make it tomorrow?"

"Tomorrow; I don't think so. I've already made plans. I'm going to be busy," he said.

"Is everything all right?" she asked.

"Everything's fine." Phil stared straight ahead, squeezing the steering wheel tightly. "What about Monday? Can you make it next Monday?" He was upset with being questioned but realized he couldn't avoid her forever.

"I think so. Scooter should be playing softball. But he's been having a lot of headaches lately. If he doesn't play, I won't be able to show up."

"We'll do like we always do. If you can make it, call Kathy and tell her you're not going to the gym, then I'll know it's a go."

"Monday's a long way off. I don't know if I can wait that long. I bought a new sexy nightgown just for you," Betty said in a teasing, seductive voice. "It's a naughty one. I think you're going to like it."

He immediately had visions of her modeling her naughty nightgown, and he liked the image. "Waiting will make it better," he said, shaking his head, raising his eyebrows, anxious to get off the phone.

"Hopefully I'll see you Monday at the Captain's."

"I hope so, too," he said.

"Love you," she said.

"Okay," he replied before flipping the phone closed.

She was going to be hard to give up. But he knew he had no choice. One of the things he enjoyed most about fucking Betty was the feeling of danger, the exciting feeling he received every time he saw macho-man Scooter, knowing he was screwing his wife. The problem was, Scooter was one big son-of-a-bitch and a mean looking son-of-a-bitch at that, and he didn't appear to be the sharing kind. There was no telling what the son-of-a-bitch would do if he caught them.

"I must be crazy," Phil mumbled under his breath, looking in his rear view mirror. "You're a crazy bastard," he repeated affectionately, breaking into a smile. He didn't really believe he was crazy; he really thought he was daring, adventurous and bold. He remembered how truly exciting the anticipation was, equal to, or even more thrilling than the conquest. He was aware how addicted to him she was, and how difficult it was going to be to give up the power he had over her. *I'm going to miss the bitch.*

Phil was getting out of his car when Jimmy Martin drove up and parked next to him.

"Welcome to Paradise," Phil said, extending both hands wide toward the sky. "You wouldn't be having weather like this if you were back in Massachusetts," he concluded.

"That's for goddamn sure. I was watching the weather station this morning. They're expecting a snowstorm. The temperature is twenty-eight degrees. That means heavy, wet slush; they can have it."

"I've spent my last winter freezing my ass off, that's for sure," Phil agreed.

"I'm hoping Rita gets to like it here, but the jury's still out on that. Once she sees her grandchild, that will be the end of Florida," Jimmy said.

"I can't tell you how many times I've heard that story."

Just then Scooter drove past, waved and parked a short distance away.

"Here's Scooter. I have to warn you, he comes on a little strong at times. He thinks he's a better golfer than he actually is. After you get to know him, he's really all right," Phil said, preparing him for Scooter's intimidating personality.

"I can't get over what a good-looking woman he's married too," Jimmy said.

Phil smiled an I've-got-secret smile. "Best looking woman in Barefoot Bay, that's for sure," he said, *and probably the best piece of ass in Barefoot Bay,* he was thinking.

"Stanley should be here shortly. Not that playing with him is anything to get excited about."

"He seems quiet. Didn't have much to say at the dinner party," Jimmy said.

"He's a pain in the ass. He reminds me of a fella I occasionally play with. He has an arthritic knee, limps a little. Every time we play he says, You guys go on ahead. Old Peg-leg'll catch up. So everyone walks slower, and you feel like a heel if you beat him."

"Why doesn't he take a cart?"

"Because then he wouldn't have an excuse for losing. Just like Stanley. Instead of admitting he sucks, he makes excuses."

After putting on their golf shoes and getting their clubs secured on their golf carts, they walked over to where Scooter was sitting on the edge of his open trunk, in the process of lighting up a Marlboro. "Hi, guys. Couldn't ask for a better day," he said, looking to the sky.

"Hi, Scooter, haven't seen much of you since Kathy's dinner last Monday. What have you been up to?" Jimmy asked.

Scooter spoke through the cigarette hanging from the corner of his mouth. "Softball mostly; sorry about leaving the party early. I was getting another headache." For the last several months, Scooter had been getting migraine headaches for no apparent reason and had left the Gagnon's dinner party early.

"Feeling all right now?" Phil inquired.

"I'm fine. Today's the day I'm looking forward to whipping your ass, Phil," Scooter said, sounding confident, plucking the cigarette from his mouth between his nicotine-stained fingers.

Phil began to laugh. "The day you beat my ass, Scooter, will be the day I give this game up," he said. "Wonder where the hell Stanley is?"

The words were no sooner out of his mouth when the fourth player showed up. He drove by, never looking in their direction. Stanley parked his car, got out and sat on the edge of his trunk while putting his golf shoes on, placed his clubs on his pull cart, then walked over, his oversized body swaying from side to side. Having no choice, he said, "Hi," without making eye contact.

"Hi, Stan," all three men said.

"Why so glum, Stanley; be happy you're not up north freezing," Jimmy said.

Stanley looked down at the ground without replying. Phil wasn't at all pleased with having Stanley for his partner, but he felt he was good enough to beat Scooter and Jimmy, even with him on his team.

"Are you ready to beat these guys, Stan?" Phil asked.

Still looking down, thinking *fuck you, Phil*, he said instead, "I'll try," in a low tentative voice.

After checking in with the starter, the four men stood on the first tee, flipping a coin to see which team got the honors. Phil and Stanley won the toss. Phil was about to walk onto the tee-box, when he noticed four women out on the fairway.

"Well, isn't that just great. Looks like we have four women in front of us," he said, looking down the fairway where a foursome of ladies was waddling along.

Scooter lit up a Marlboro, inhaled it hard, closed his eyes and let go with a stream of smoke. "Looks like it could be a long, long, long day," he said.

"It won't be that bad," Jimmy said.

"That's what you think. Women belong in the kitchen; or, in the sack with their legs spread apart. Not on the golf course," Phil said, shaking his head.

Three of the men laughed. Stanley wasn't paying attention.

"You guys can hit now," Roger, the starter, called out now that the four women were safely on the first green. "As you can see, you've got a group of ladies ahead of you. Hope you guys aren't in a hurry," he explained, smiling broadly.

"Okay, let's get started," Phil said.

Phil always wanted to go first. His reason was to intimidate the opposition. He casually walked between the blue markers and placed his tee and ball in the ground. After taking a couple of practice swings, he drove his ball nearly two hundred fifty yards straight down the middle of the fairway. Casually bending over, he picked up his tee, turned toward Scooter, nodded and smiled.

Nobody out-drove Phil. They were definitely intimidated. They grabbed their pull carts and began walking down the fairway. Phil was feeling confident. He was sure he could beat Scooter and Jimmy, even with Stanley as his partner.

As predicted, because of the four women, the golf match had progressed slowly. Finally after waiting on every shot, watching the ladies spend more time talking than playing, they made it through fifteen holes with the match all tied up. The next two holes were halved with identical scores. When they arrived on the par three eighteenth green, the golf match was still tied, but Phil and Stanley definitely had the advantage. Phil had come through as would be expected and made a birdie two. Jimmy and Scooter had some difficulties and ended up bogeying the hole for a total of eight.

Stanley, as usual, was having his problems. He was about three feet away for his double bogey five. The putt was straight uphill with no break. If he makes it, he and Phil win the match. "What do you say, guys, how about giving Stanley the putt?" Phil suggested, not having a lot of confidence in his partner.

In a friendlier match the opposing team would've normally conceded the putt. That wasn't about to happen with this group. Stanley was the one making this three-foot putt under pressure. Scooter had played with Stanley in the past. He knew he usually choked under pressure. He wasn't about to let him off the hook, especially with the bar bill at the 19th Hole on the line.

Phil tried to encourage him. "It's impossible to miss, Stanley. Even a blind man couldn't miss that putt. It's straight uphill, no break, just hit it; it has to go in," he said.

The pressure was building. Stanley was getting sick to his stomach. His eyes were straining. His grip became tighter on the golf club. He could feel the sweat starting to run down his back, and his legs were getting shaky. He hated being put in situations like this, knowing how he'd failed so many times in the past. Phil's remark about "It was impossible to miss," only added to the pressure.

"Come on, Stan. Just knock the ball in the hole. I need a drink," Phil said, while glancing at Scooter with a victorious smile on his face.

Stanley couldn't put it off any longer, and decided to get it over with. Drawing the putter back slowly, he could feel a bead of sweat trickling over his brow and drop into his right eye. His hands began shaking like he had Parkinson's. The nervousness that had been building finally pushed him to hurry, get it over with, but when he began moving the putter forward, a voice inside said, STOP.

He had lost his confidence and attempted to stop the putter's forward momentum, but it was too late. Striking the ball timidly, he watched it travel toward the hole. Time stood still; everything moved in slow motion. The ball advanced two feet, nine inches, three inches short of its intended target and victory. Three inches more and he'd have been a hero. But as usual, Stanley Kloski came up a loser.

Phil Gagnon couldn't stand to lose to anyone. It was a simple fact in his personality and that was all there was to it. Phil's shoulders rose and fell. He shook his head from side to side, and right on cue, announced loud and clear, "I don't believe it. Stanley, you have to be the world's worst golfer! How could you possibly miss that fuckin' putt?"

Missing the putt meant that the match was square. That wasn't good enough for Phil. Winning was not all that important to Jimmy and Scooter, but there was no substitute for winning with Phil, and he wasn't about to accept even a tied match without letting Stanley know it was his fault.

The awful look of hopelessness on Stanley's face made Jimmy wish they hadn't played. "Don't worry about it, Stan, it's just a game," he said, and meant it.

"Let's have a beer. I'll buy," Scooter said, trying to ease the tension.

Stanley stood motionless for several seconds, eyes blinked rapidly, a childlike expression on his face like he had just been scolded, trying not to cry. He wished everyone would leave him alone. He wished he could've been a hero. He wished the putt had traveled just three more inches. But all the wishing in the world wouldn't change the fact that Stanley Kloski was born a loser.

After Jimmy replaced the flag, the men walked off the green. Phil continued shaking his head in disbelief, repeating, "I don't fuckin' believe it."

Stanley couldn't take it any longer. His blood pressure shot up and his pulse was acting crazy. His eyes narrowed, he slammed his putter into his golf bag and stormed off. He wasn't going into the 19th Hole and listen to Phil humiliate him. He didn't care what anyone thought. He was headed home wishing things could've been different. But as usual, everything remained the same. Stanley had fucked up again.

After walking over to their cars, Phil, Scooter, and Jimmy took off their golf shoes and returned their clubs and shoes to their trunks. Together they started walking to the 19th Hole when they heard Stanley's car roar to life. Without hesitating, he backed out of his parking space, jammed the shift into drive, stepped down hard on the gas and drove quickly away. Not so much in a hurry to get someplace as he was to be getting away from Phil Gagnon.

Figuring out other people's vulnerabilities and using this power over them was one of Phil's greatest talents. He had always taken pleasure with the loss and pain of others, and watching Stanley suffer after missing the putt, even though it had cost him the match, had given him a secret sense of enjoyment. Other people's misery always gave Phil a sense of superiority. "Well, I guess Stanley's not joining us," Phil said, looking at Stanley's car barreling down Barefoot Boulevard. "What an asshole," he announced, loud and clear.

"He does seem a little strange," Jimmy said.

"I think he likes being an asshole. Some people can't help it, but he works at it. Doesn't do shit all day! Carol told Kathy, he sits on his fat ass and reads the paper or watches television, never goes out, doesn't talk, just grunts and mumbles too himself."

Sticking a Marlboro between his lips, then, lighting it and letting the smoke drift out of his nose, Scooter said, "Always thought there was something wrong with that guy."

The three men continued walking toward the 19th Hole.

"There is. He's an asshole. It's as simple as that. Don't try shooting the shit with him, you won't get any response. He's just an asshole," Phil said, picking up the pace, badly in need of a drink. "Drinks are on me, guys."

CHAPTER 29

AS SOON AS STANLEY arrived home it was obvious the golf match hadn't gone well. Carol's first indication he was upset was the slamming of the car door shortly after pulling into the driveway. Upon entering the house, he walked by her without saying a word, going directly to his sanctuary out back.

After collapsing into his recliner, he began shaking his head like he was trying to chase away whatever demons were haunting him. Then he began slowly rocking back and forth, his body slumped slightly forward, a line of spittle running down his chin, his arms wrapped tight around himself like he was trying to hold himself together. He began moaning, making soft, low-pitched wailing sounds like a wounded dog. It was not a pretty sight, but Carol couldn't look away. There was something awful in his eyes, hurt and anger she supposed, but something more, something deeper making the small hairs on the back of her neck stand up.

She was becoming increasingly concerned about Stanley's behavior. For months now he had spent nearly all of his time sitting in their screen room like a concrete statue, inhaling small parts of his imaginary world, exhaling whatever parts of his world he lived in.

He had never been very outgoing, but at least in Barnstead he managed to keep himself busy by working at the bank. But ever since retiring and moving to Barefoot Bay, he seemed to have isolated himself, remaining practically motionless, did nothing, spoke to no one.

What was a real concern to Carol was lately he would be staring off into space with a strange, vacant look on his face, unaware of his surroundings, sometimes bent forward, sometimes nodding, sometimes smiling, usually deeply involved in a conversation with someone by the name of Rocky who wasn't present.

His strange behavior reminded her of something she'd learned in her psychology class in college. Her professor talked about people who suffered with bouts of schizophrenia and manic-depression. Carol remembered the instructor saying people suffering with schizophrenia often hallucinated and sometimes heard voices that nobody else heard.

They usually preferred to isolate themselves from society, showed little emotion and had limited interest in their surroundings. All these symptoms had been noticeable in Stanley's behavior in the past, but he was now communicating with these imaginary people on a daily basis.

Carol was aware she hadn't been the best wife, but felt it wasn't her fault that she'd been born a lesbian. She was reasonably sure Stanley was aware of what had been going on between her and Robin He had to realize that two women spending this much time together were more than just friends. Stanley was gullible, but he wasn't entirely stupid.

Carol continued to observe Stanley rocking back and forth while moaning softly as her mind began traveling back to a more pleasant, happy time, when she still had Robin in her life. The tears began to well up in her eyes as she recalled those last precious days they had spent together before the tragic accident in Vermont.

Robin and Carol had been teaching in Barnstead for over twenty years and felt it was time to retire; come out of the closet and fulfill their dream of living together. They had been successful in avoiding unwanted attention to their relationship, although there were some teachers that were suspicious, but they'd been successful in keeping their suspicions exactly that, just rumors. They were aware that lesbians teaching their children would never be tolerated by the parents or the school committee, but in all the years they'd taught in Barnstead, the school committee never got a single complaint from any student or parent about their behavior, or their ability as teachers. In fact, they were respected by the faculty and very popular with the students.

One of their favorite destinations during their Christmas vacations was Key West, Florida, the anything-goes, and the fun-never-stop's capital of America. What they enjoyed most about the Keys was they felt unrestricted. Many evenings in late December, they could be found sitting together, arms around each other's shoulders, swaying to the music of Jimmy Buffet's Margaritaville floating through the air at a surfside bar, watching the sun setting over the ocean.

It was while driving back from Key West, when they stopped in the town of Micco and discovered the Barefoot Bay retirement community. They were driving along Route 1, coming back from eating an early dinner at Meg O'Malley's in Melbourne when they came across an "Open House" sign at the entrance of the retirement community.

They called the realtor and made an appointment to visit the community. The next morning they were escorted around the retirement community, and couldn't help but be impressed with what they saw.

There appeared to be plenty of outdoor activity going on. The tennis courts seemed to be getting plenty of use. When they passed the golf course, they observed groups of people scattered throughout the lush fairways. Barefoot Bay seemed to have everything they'd been looking for in a retirement community.

The following day they were drinking draft beer and munching on Buffalo wings while looking out over the Indian River at Squid Lips, a local restaurant famous for casual, friendly dining, built on large wooden pilings situated directly over the river. While chewing on their wings and watching a group of brown pelicans moving in quiet unison over the river, they continued the conversation about relocating in Barefoot Bay where they could live together out in the open as a couple. It was decided they would teach one more year, then, they would retire and move to the Barefoot Bay Retirement Community.

A year later

Realizing this was going to be their last year of wintery weather, they decided to spend their final Christmas vacation skiing.

Stowe, Vermont was their favorite skiing destination. The ski resort had a feeling of timelessness that surrounded them whenever they walked past the small shops with colored lights lining the windows and strolled through the many gift and novelty shops. They loved listening to the Salvation Army bell ringers out front of the stores while Christmas Carols were being piped through speakers into the frigid winter air, created a three-dimension Hallmark Christmas card winter wonderland.

As soon as they arrived, they checked into the Mountain Range Lodge. It was a hotel/motel that they'd frequented many times. They'd made a reservation months ago. It was a good thing they had as the "No Vacancy" sign was already on display when they arrived.

On the last day of their vacation, they were skiing on the novice slope named Spruce Peak. The sun was shining bright in a clear, blue cloudless sky. They were having a wonderful time when the announcement echoed over the loud speakers through the leafless trees that because of approaching darkness, this would be the last run of the day.

Both women felt relieved. It had been three hours since they had taken a break and were looking forward to relaxing and having a glass of wine by the fireplace inside the Powder Keg Lounge at the base of the mountain.

After securing their skis to the top of Carol's Dodge Caravan and stripping off their heavy clothing, they began walking, eyes cast down, across the hard snow packed parking lot, heading for the lounge.

"I think every bone in my body hurts," Carol said.

Stumbling on a loose piece of ice, Robin said, "You're not the only one. My legs are so tired I can hardly pick them up."

Carol was blowing her warm breath into her frigid fingers when she noticed Robin stumble. "We've been skiing for days without breaking any bones. Don't break your leg now," Carol remarked cheerfully.

When they walked into the bar they discovered it was extremely crowded. Fortunately there was a small table for two unoccupied over by the wall in front of the fireplace. They never hesitated and rushed over and sat down.

A pretty waitress with dark brown hair that hung just below her shoulders and small dark eyes was right behind them, carrying a bowl of free popcorn. As soon as they were seated, they took a handful of the fragrant smelling snack and popped several kernels into their mouths before each ordering a glass of Carlo Rossi burgundy red wine. After the waitress walked away, they turned their cold hands to the fire and sat in silence, hypnotized by the flames burning brightly as embers crackled loudly and a piece of wood collapsed with a whoosh, sending sparks up the chimney.

Their complexions were crimson from the afternoon sun and the brisk winter temperatures, combined with the reflection from the fire, created a healthy glow upon their face, while their hair needed the attention of a comb.

"Doesn't the heat feel great?" Robin said, feeling warm enough to unzip her jacket, but didn't remove it, while closing her eyes and leaning her head back. "I feel tired enough to go to sleep right here."

Carol was tugging on the ski pass attached to her jacket zipper. When it broke off, she balled it up and threw it into the fire and watched it turn into black ash. "I'm ready to hang up the skis, What about you?" she asked.

"You've got that right. I can hardly move. I can't wait to take a hot shower," Robin confessed, bending her head back while closing her eyes and rubbing the back of her neck. "It's time we headed to Florida and the sunshine."

Carol picked up her glass and offered a toast, "To us and many happy years together in Barefoot Bay."

"Finally," Robin said. "Just think, this time next year we'll be living together in Barefoot Bay. I've been waiting for this forever," Robin exclaimed, reaching over and squeezing Carol's hand.

"By the way, did you turn in your paperwork to Mark?" Robin asked. Mark Bisson was the union representative who handled the affairs for the teachers.

"I gave Mark my papers two days before school vacation. He said there wouldn't be a problem. By the way, you have to get your papers in before the first of March," Carol informed Robin.

"I haven't even started to fill them out," Robin admitted.

"What do you think the other teachers will say when they find out we're both retiring at the same time? Do you think the great mystery will have been finally solved after all these years?" Carol asked.

"This isn't the fifties. We don't have to hide in the closet anymore. It's time to come out into the sunlight."

"Did you ever think the day would come when we wouldn't have to be afraid that someone would find out we were lesbians?"

"No. I know things are better, but it still bothers me, wondering what people say. When I was a kid, especially in high school, I walked around feeling like I would throw up if anyone even mentioned the words queer, dyke or lesbian."

"Instead of high school being the best years of my life, they were the worst," Robin agreed.

"Even today things aren't much better. I still wouldn't want to be a gay kid in high school. I watched more than one girl in my Phys-Ed class that I was pretty sure was struggling with who she is. The last thing they want is for the other kids to find out," Carol said.

"I've had students, both boys and girls that I would've bet anything were gay. But I couldn't say a thing. I wanted to tell them they weren't alone, that I understood, but it would've cost me my job, so I kept my mouth shut," Robin said.

"I'm sick of living a lie. I'm sick of acting like I'm somebody I'm not. I'm especially sick of living separated from you. Besides, most of the teachers already suspect what's been going on. Now that were retiring together, everyone can say, 'I knew it, I told you they were lesbians.' I can almost hear them talking in the teachers' lounge now," Carol blurted out.

"I think when people see a gay couple they assume their relationship is just about sex. I still can remember when I was young, listening to my older brother Danny explaining to my other brother what gays and lesbians where; he said it was two guys having sex together. As if that was all there is to a gay couple's relationship. And you know, I think people grow up believing that. And it's not true. Why can't people understand two women can fall in love? The way we feel about each other is no different than the way straight couples feel about each other. It isn't just about sex. It's about sharing your life with someone you love," Carol continued.

"You're right, it's not fair. All I've ever wanted was to be treated like everyone else," Robin said.

"But you know what? They can all kiss my big, fat ass. We'll be in Florida and what the other teachers or anyone else says won't make a bit of difference."

"How do you think all the old timers in Barefoot Bay will feel about a couple of old lesbians shacking up together," she remarked.

"Just told you, don't know, don't care! We've been living apart long enough. We have a right to be happy like everyone else. And what do you mean by old? We've got a lot of good years left."

"By the way, have you said anything to Stanley?"

"Not a word. He doesn't have a clue. He'll know when he sees me putting my clothes in the car."

"Are you planning on getting a divorce?"

"No! I'm just taking my clothes and personal belongings and leaving. He can have the house. He's in pretty good shape financially. He inherited a bundle when his mother died," Carol said, her voice sounding tired and strained.

With the wine gone and the popcorn bowl empty, they decided it was time to head back to the lodge. Carol pulled her jacket sleeve up, noticed the time and said, "It's almost six-thirty. I'm hungry. Let's get started."

Robin casually dropped a ten-dollar bill on the table next to the check; then they dragged their tired bodies out of their chairs and started for the door.

"I don't know what I want more, a hot shower or something to eat," Robin mentioned while walking across the frozen parking lot.

The air had turned frigid, causing icy conditions in the parking lot and on the roadways. As soon as Carol was seated, she buckled her seat belt before driving on the slippery surface. Robin was tired and weary, causing her to become careless, choosing to ignore the beeping seat belt alarm until it gave up and went silent.

Carol turned onto Route 108 South and started the drive down the twisting mountain road, heading for the Mountain Range Lodge. Robin reached into the console and took out a number of CDs. Deciding on one of her favorite singers, Michael Ball, she inserted his recording of "Songs of Love" into the CD player and closed her eyes, enjoying the music, and dozed off.

There were no other cars on the steep, winding mountain road, and Carol wasn't paying attention to her speed. She didn't realize her speed had increased to fifty miles an hour. Without warning, she suddenly came upon a sharp curve. Before she knew what was happening, the

Caravan began skidding out of control on black ice. She was helpless to stop the van from sliding toward the steep embankment. In a panic, she immediately turned the wheel and jammed her foot as hard as she could toward the floor, sending the already out-of-control vehicle to fishtail and propel itself on the ice even faster toward the steep ravine.

There was the sound of branches breaking and snapping all around her, followed by the airbag exploding, instantly slamming her back against her seat. For a moment Carol was able to glance over at Robin. Everything seemed to be happening in slow motion, like a time-lapsed film that goes on forever. She was able to make out the look of fear on Robin's face but was helpless to do anything to stop the madness.

The vehicle continued its descent down the embankment, going end over end, bouncing and slamming into one tree after another. The van was completely demolished when it finally came to rest, wedged between a large boulder and a mammoth oak tree, with only the sound of steam hissing from under the hood breaking the silence of the night.

Before Carol lost consciousness, she glanced over and realized that Robin was no longer in the van. She began to panic, yelling "Robin, Robin," at the top of her lungs. She tried frantically to release herself from her seat belt. She wanted desperately to get out of the vehicle. Robin was in trouble and needed her. Then everything went black.

When she came to, people were lifting her onto a stretcher and began carrying her up the steep hillside. Somewhere off in the distance she heard sirens and saw bright lights flashing all around her. She tried to speak, but her lips wouldn't form words. Then she slipped back into the black hole of unconsciousness.

When she awoke in the hospital, she was informed she had suffered a severe concussion, plus numerous bumps and bruises. But the physical pain she felt was nonexistent compared to the heartache she endured when informed of the death of the one person in this world she truly loved.

Looking back, her regrets were difficult to deal with. From the moment she met Robin there was a friendship in her eyes. At some point their friendship had become a deep, binding love . . . the kind she believed would endure throughout the rest of her life. But it hadn't endured throughout her life. Now she was alone.

Robin had taught her what real love was in a way few women would ever experience. She had given her years of happiness and made Carol whole. They had laughed together and cried together. They had danced under the moon on the beach, they'd held hands in bars while listening to Jimmy Buffet sing about the carefree life in Key West, they had made love many times; not the kind of love when people display no interest in intimacy, but powerful, wonderful love in some incredible places. She would never stop thinking of her. Robin would always be there in her heart and mind. Always!

But that was then and this was now.

As she watched Stanley, who had stopped rocking and moaning, and was now staring into space, talking to people who didn't exist, she gave out a long sigh, letting her body relax as if in defeat. A heavy burden settled upon her shoulders, thinking of the future.

Shortly after accepting the reality that Robin was gone and wouldn't be sharing her life in Barefoot Bay, Carol decided to go on with her plans to retire in Florida. Since that time, she realized inviting Stanley to join her had been a terrible mistake. She often asked herself why?

Maybe it was because after losing Robin she was lonely and felt it was better to be with someone she didn't love than to be alone. When she first told Stanley she intended on retiring and would be moving out of Barnstead and relocating to Florida, he hesitated about going. If only she'd taken that opportunity to pack her things and leave before he changed his mind, she wouldn't be putting up with this crazy situation now where Stanley was mumbling to himself and carrying on conversations with thin air.

CHAPTER 30

"RISE AND SHINE; it's another beautiful day in Florida," the weatherman on the Ocean 97.1 FM radio station announced.

It was early Tuesday morning. Jimmy was eating a bowl of cereal while listening to the radio and watching patterns of sunlight streaking across the kitchen floor. He'd been in Florida for nearly two months and was convinced this was the place to be in winter. He'd been watching the weather up north, and how people were struggling with the snow and frigid temperatures, and was happy he wasn't there. Unfortunately, Rita didn't share his enthusiasm.

Everything had been going along fine. Rita seemed to be adjusting to Florida. That was until last evening. They'd received a call from their daughter, Elizabeth, who gave Rita an update on her condition. She claimed she was doing fine, having a perfectly normal pregnancy. She told her mother she'd been to the Chelmsford Pediatric Center that afternoon. The obstetrician told her that she and the baby were in excellent condition. No problems could be foreseen. Regardless of all this positive news, Rita was convinced she was needed at home, helping her daughter get through this important event, and woke up in a foul mood. She was homesick and wanted to leave.

Experience had taught Jimmy whenever his wife was in one of her moods, which was not unusual, it was best to leave her alone to work her way through it, so he was keeping his distance. Not wanting to waste this beautiful morning sitting at home watching his wife pout, he decided to go for a walk. He felt obliged to ask Rita if she wanted to join him, although he knew the answer before he asked.

"I'm going for a walk down by the river. It's too nice a morning to sit around the house. You want to come along?"

"No," she snapped.

"Is there anything you want me to get while I'm out?" he offered.

"No," she snapped once again.

"Okay, then, I'll see you later." He left the house, happy to be getting away.

Driving out of Barefoot Bay, humming to himself, Jimmy noticed how the robin's-egg blue Florida sky stretched above and beyond in every direction into eternity. When he approached the Sebastian River bridge, he crossed over it and turned left and drove down Indian River Drive. About a mile farther he came upon a small strip mall on his right where Baker's Bagel Shop was located.

Deciding he could use a cup of coffee, he parked his car next to a BMW that looked exactly like the Gagnon's car. The air had begun to thicken with humidity, and he felt a line of perspiration forming in a damp line across his forehead as he walked across the road and entered the bagel shop. Kathy Gagnon sat in a corner booth reading a magazine. Without hesitating, he walked over and said, "Good morning," startling her momentarily.

"Stop sneaking up on me like that! You scared me," she said with a nervous laugh, her open hands pressed against her chest.

"Sorry, I didn't mean to scare you," Jimmy said.

"I'm only kidding. I'm really happy to see you. Join me," she said, nodding toward the empty seat across from her.

"Give me a minute. I want to get a coffee. Can you use another cup?"

Glancing down at her nearly empty cup, she accepted. "Okay, regular, cream, no sugar. I'll put my own in."

"Do you want something to eat?"

"No. One bagel a day is enough."

"Be right back," he said, then walked over and got in line.

After getting his coffee, a cinnamon raisin bagel with cream cheese, and Kathy's coffee, Jimmy walked back to Kathy's table.

As soon as he sat down, she asked, "Where's Rita?"

"She's not feeling good this morning."

"She's not sick, I hope. She looked fine yesterday at aerobics class," Kathy said while tearing open two small packets of Sweet & Low and pouring them into her coffee.

"No, she's not physically sick. Last night our daughter called. Rita got homesick. She thinks she should be home playing the part of the expectant grandmother. Hopefully she'll get over it," he explained, shaking his head.

"I'm sure she will. There's no problem with the baby, is there?"

"No, everything's fine. Elizabeth keeps telling her she's all right. Rita still thinks it's her responsibility to look after her little girl, even though her little girl is now a grown woman, pregnant and married."

"Once a mother, always a mother," Kathy assured him. "You seem to have adjusted to Florida."

"I think it's great. You can't beat this weather. Not sure I would want to be here all year. The summers get pretty hot from what I hear," he said.

"That's why we don't come down in the summer."

After a long pause, while staring at him intently, she continued, "Was it a big surprise when I came knocking on your door?" she asked.

"Actually it was," he said in a casual voice.

"You know, Mr. Jimmy Martin, we go back a long way. We did a lot of growing up together," she said, reminding him nonchalantly about those years they'd spent together.

"Yes, I know. It was a long time ago," he said.

"Did you ever think of me in all those years?" she asked.

"Once in a while, I guess." He felt uncomfortable with the question. "But when I met Rita shortly after I got out of the Army, we got married, and I've been busy working and raising a family ever since."

"Rita seems like a wonderful person. From what I've been hearing, it sounds like your children are doing just fine, too."

"They are. I've been lucky. I was fortunate to get a job with the Postal Service. I worked there for over thirty-five years. We bought a house in Chelmsford shortly after we got married."

"And now you're retired and living in Florida."

"Only visiting; I've always wanted to spend winters in Florida. I don't care for the cold weather. I hope Rita gets to likes it enough so we can return next year, but it's not looking good right now," Jimmy said.

"She's just having a bad day. It takes time for some women to adjust. Rita seems happy when I'm with her."

"She can be unpredictable. Many days she gets depressed for no reason. There's something bothering Rita, that even after all these years, I don't understand," Jimmy told her.

"Probably just that time of her life. Some women have a difficult time going through the change," she explained.

"No, it's more than that," he said, then, wondering why he had shared this personal information with Kathy, he changed the subject. "What about you? You and Phil seem to be doing all right."

"Phil and I got married after I finished my freshman year in college. I was pregnant when we got married," she confessed, feeling uncomfortable mentioning it. "Phil stayed in college and got his degree. I decided not to go back. I stayed home, became a full-time mom. After Dad had his heart attack, he lost interest in the business. Phil took over. He's done really well. That about covers the highlights of my life; not very exciting, but I can't complain."

"What about your son? I occasionally see him when I stop in at the insurance agency to pay my bill. It must be satisfying to see him carrying on the business your father started," he said.

A brief, uncomfortable silence came between them as she looked into his face and noticed the remarkable resemblance between father and son. Then, trying to pull herself together, Kathy said softly, "Yes. He's doing just fine."

"I still can't get over how much he looks like my son," Jimmy said.

"Yes, that's what you said," Kathy said, not making eye contact.

"Sitting here reminds me of when we used to stop at that pizza place after school. What was the name of that place?" Jimmy asked.

"Paisano's; I don't think it's there anymore," she said. "I'll always remember the afternoon when you told me you joined the Army."

"My life was pretty much at a standstill. It was just a matter of time before I would have been drafted. I figured I might as well enlist and get it over with."

"I never heard from you after that."

"Well, I was pretty busy trying to stay alive."

Kathy frowned and shook her head, "That was such a terrible war. I still can remember every time I heard that someone from Lowell had died, I thought of you. I was so worried that something would happen to you." Jimmy looked down at his half-filled cup of coffee but didn't reply. "Does it bother you to talk about it?" she asked.

"Yes. But that's in the past. I try not to think about it. The years certainly have been good to you. You still look just as attractive as you did back when we were in high school," he said.

"Thanks for the compliment, but I'm sure I don't look like I did when we were dating. You know, Jimmy, I've never forgotten you. I often thought of you and wondered how you were doing. You were such an important part of my life growing up. And now, here we are. It's odd how some things seem to have happened so long ago, and now with you sitting here, it doesn't seem like that long ago at all. I never realized until now how much you meant to me, and how much I've missed you," Kathy said slowly, in a meaningful voice.

Feeling uncomfortable with the direction of their conversation, Jimmy nervously bit down hard on his dry, lower lip. "Those were good years. It's funny how things turned out. Back then I was so sure that we would end up getting married someday, then we kind of drifted apart and ended up marrying someone else," he said, Rita's image flashing across his mind.

"Your lip's bleeding."

"It is?"

"Yes."

Taking a napkin from the holder, Jimmy touched it to his lip, checked the small smear of blood, dabbed again, then seeing the blood had disappeared, crumpled the napkin and put it aside.

Kathy could feel herself wanting to tell him how much she had been thinking about him since he came back into her life, but decided it was best to change the subject. "I was planning on taking a walk along the river. I guess I better get started."

"Actually that's the same reason I came down here," Jimmy admitted.

Kathy hesitated for a moment, wondering if she should invite him to join her. She was concerned that if she spent any more time alone with him, she might reveal what she was feeling. The safest, wisest, easiest thing to do was say goodbye now. Kathy had always done the safest, wisest, easiest thing; until now. She paused, faced him, realizing she was living dangerously, and said, "If you're going to take a walk, why don't we walk together?"

For some strange reason, Jimmy didn't want to say goodbye, at least not now. "Okay."

The Indian River walkway was across the street from the bagel shop. They left their cars parked at the strip mall and walked across the road and began walking along the winding trail. The wind was blowing slightly across the river. It was warm but they felt comfortable strolling beneath the towering palm trees, magnolias, and evergreens. They couldn't help but admire the beauty of the juniper bushes while watching the geckos dart across the path, then disappear among the overgrown exposed roots of the banyan trees with the Spanish moss hanging gracefully from their branches like a long flowing veil. The sky was a beautiful shade of blue, broken only by an occasional cloud, making it a perfect day to be strolling along the water's edge.

They walked for a while, being cautious to keep enough distance so as not to accidentally touch as they talked about the past. Then they walked in silence for short periods listening to the river, feeling the gentle breeze on their faces with the wind rustling the leaves on the magnolia trees. Several minutes had passed when Kathy nonchalantly reached for Jimmy's hand and directed him down a secluded trail separated from the main path to a bench facing the river. Her hand was warm and moist and trembling slightly. She squeezed his hand a little tighter to stop the trembling but didn't take it away.

"I want to show you something," she said when they arrived at the edge of the water, where the land sloped steeply about twelve feet to the river below. "This is my favorite spot. Don't you just love it?" Kathy said, still firmly holding his hand, looking out over the water.

"It is really nice," he agreed, conscious of her hand in his.

"Let's sit for a minute," she said, leading him to the bench. Immediately upon sitting, Kathy released his hand.

Many people used the bench to rest while enjoying the view. Others idled away the hours reading or just day dreaming. There were hundreds of birds, and the scenery was breathtaking. Often amateur artists came to paint, trying to capture the beauty along the Indian River Lagoon.

The sun, almost directly overhead and reflecting off the water, caused her to use her open hand to shield her eyes from the sunlight dancing on the water like diamonds sprinkled across the surface. Kathy pointed in the direction of the large black bird, posing with outstretched wings. "Look, Jimmy, there's one of those Anhinga birds. They dive in the water for food, then stand on the banks of the river with their wings spread in order to dry their feathers."

The bird remained motionless, standing just above a partially submerged log where turtles rested in the sun, while a hundred yards off shore a small flock of pelicans soared by effortlessly, suspended only a few feet above the water.

Jimmy wiped his forehead with the back of his hand and squinted in the bright sunlight. "So you must come here often," he said, still feeling the sensation of her hand holding his, aware that she was still capable of sending small waves of excitement throughout his body.

"I usually come on Tuesday mornings. I run errands first before the stores get crowded. Then I have a coffee at the bagel shop before taking a walk. Sometimes I sit for hours on this bench, enjoying the view. It's so peaceful this time of the morning!"

"Does Phil ever come with you?"

"Never," she said raising her eyebrows. "He has no trouble walking eighteen holes of golf, chasing a little white ball around, but he doesn't seem to have enough energy to take a walk with his wife."

"Sounds like a typical man to me," Jimmy said.

"Yeah, I guess you're right," she agreed.

There was a slight breeze coming across the water and a little humidity in the air; the top two buttons of Jimmy's shirt was undone, and Kathy could see the top of his chest. She tried to look away but failed. She wondered how it would feel to touch his chest, to kiss his lips. For the first time in many years, she felt warmth between her legs as she watched him. She forced herself to look away, finding it a struggle to breathe evenly.

Guilt surged through Kathy. Not that they had done anything. Yet, she felt guilty, guilty because of the possibilities, and wondered if she was getting herself into something she couldn't handle and might later regret. "I suppose we'd better get going," she suggested.

"Yes. Rita will be wondering what happened to me. I don't want to upset her any more than she already is."

When they stood, Kathy took a last look across the river, inhaled deeply and smiled as she let her breath relax. Leaving the bench behind, they strolled along the walkway, through the fallen twigs and leaves, kicking them aside as they walked. The low hanging oaks and cypress trees lining the path gave them the sensation of looking through a time tunnel. It created an ageless beauty, as if it hadn't changed in a hundred years.

"It's so peaceful here, I almost hate to leave," Jimmy said.

"It is beautiful, isn't it? I don't understand why more people don't use this walkway," Kathy said, looking ahead at the empty path.

When they returned to where they'd parked their cars, Jimmy took a long look at Kathy, realizing how much he was still attracted to her. She was wearing a tasteful light green summer dress with spaghetti straps, accompanied by a simple white belt with matching white sandals. He couldn't help noticing the smooth skin exposed just above her breasts. Her arms and shoulders were heavier than they'd been when she was younger, but she still looked inviting.

She smiled at him. He looked away, embarrassed by what he was thinking. "This has been a wonderful surprise, Jimmy. Thank you so much for keeping me company. I've really enjoyed it."

"I enjoyed it, too."

She smiled, and he felt a strange fluttering inside. "I'll be here next Tuesday morning if you feel like buying me a coffee and taking a walk with me," she said.

"Maybe I will," he answered, unable to make a definite decision while his emotions were on this roller coaster ride. He was torn between wanting to stay and wanting to leave.

The conversation seemed over, but then she paused a second, as if she remembered something. "Jimmy . . . ," she started to say, then shrugged her shoulders and said nothing. He held her eyes and saw what she must have seen in his eyes, a strong physical current of desire. "Well, I'll be here next Tuesday if you decide to take a walk," she concluded.

Later, she would ask herself why? Why she had without thinking, bent her head up and kissed him quickly on the lips? It had been just a friendly, casual kiss, but a kiss nonetheless. It wasn't something she had planned on doing. It just happened. But once she realized what she had done, she felt foolish and immediately started fumbling for her keys in her purse. Finding them, she quickly opened the car door, got in, gave him a strained smiled . . . a smile that came straight from the past . . . through the closed window, backed up, jammed the shift in drive and immediately drove away.

Jimmy's body shivered involuntarily while watching her car disappear down Indian River Drive. His fingers went to the spot on his lips where she had kissed him, as if to capture it and keep it from going away. He was unable to figure out exactly how he felt. His emotions were going in several different directions. He felt himself being drawn into something dangerously intoxicating. He couldn't understand if he was attracted to her because of who she was today, or, was it because of who she used to be?

Well before dawn the following Tuesday, Jimmy was awake in bed, lying next to the woman he loved, staring at the ceiling, listening to the hum of the ceiling fan that clicked with every revolution, thinking about Kathy's kiss and the invitation to take another walk with her along the river. At first he thought it wasn't such a good idea. But the memory of their walk and the way he felt when she kissed him had been haunting him all week. He realized he was being strangely drawn to her and realized his meeting her again was dangerous and could lead to trouble. He couldn't stop the feeling that he was being sucked into an emotional whirlpool, its current powerful and difficult to resist.

Across the street, Kathy was lying in bed tossing and turning, unable to sleep, watching the digital clock on the nightstand tick away the minutes. It was three a.m. Kathy had been thinking and rethinking that spontaneous kiss and shivered every time the scene flashed before her eyes. It was just a crazy impulse on her part. It was a stupid thing she did. What was she thinking? She couldn't imagine what he must have thought. She certainly didn't act like a responsible, mature adult. She knew it was wrong. But being alone with him brought back a flood of memories, and her feelings for him had resurfaced. From the moment their lips met, she hadn't been able to think of anything else but him and wanted desperately to see him again.

Later that morning, Kathy's heart was beating hard while waiting at the bagel shop to see if he would show. She was looking at the local newspaper, staring at the print but not seeing the words, when she felt someone approaching. From the corner of her eye she saw him. It was Jimmy. He was walking toward her, his face strained; he kept glancing around as though afraid someone was following him. She continued to watch his approach and welcomed him with a warm smile when he arrived. The boy she had once loved, the father of their son had not disappointed her.

CHAPTER 31

IT STARTED RAINING during the night. It was still raining at midmorning. Most south Florida rainstorms consisted of sudden torrential downpours—"Forida Car Washes." These storms would suddenly appear in mid-afternoon, last for short periods of time, then quickly stop, but not before completely saturating the ground. Today's rain was more like what you would expect up north where the rain would linger for hours and sometimes days.

Betty saw flashes of lighting in the distance, followed by the grumbling of thunder. Even with the gray skies and soaking rain, nothing could dampen Betty's spirits this Wednesday morning as she drove cautiously down Route 1, her wiper blades pushing aside the rain.

She was on her way to the Captain's Quarters. Betty had bought a new sexy nightgown and was anxious to model it for Phil. She'd been concerned with the way he had been acting lately, like he'd been losing interest in her. She was looking forward to modeling the naughty nightgown for him, convinced it would renew his interest.

When she'd called the other morning before his golf match, Phil at first sounded distant and uncertain but then agreed to meet her. After hanging up, she felt better and realized she had most likely been over reacting and worried over nothing.

She called Kathy earlier to inform her she wouldn't be joining the girls at aerobics class. Kathy was used to getting these calls and said, "You've been doing so good lately. You made it both Wednesday and Friday last week and again this Monday. What's so important that it can't wait until tomorrow?"

"I'm just not in the mood today. Besides, there's something I need to take care of," she said, smiling to herself, thinking if she only knew.

"Okay, I'll tell the girls," Kathy assured her as she looked out her front window and noticed Rita walking over to Carol's. "I see Rita crossing the street. I better run. See you later," Kathy said before hanging up.

Because of the weather, Scooter's softball game had been cancelled. Usually whenever he didn't play ball, Betty didn't want to take a chance that Scooter might suspect something and follow her. Because of the way Phil had been behaving lately, she was anxious to see him; throwing caution to the wind, she decided on taking a chance.

When she went looking for Scooter, she found him sitting out back in the screen room and informed him that she was going out, said she needed to run errands. "I'll probably be gone all morning," she had said.

He never bothered to look up from his newspaper, just grunted, "Yeah . . . okay," and went right on reading. If he had, he might have noticed she had her keys in one hand and a small Victoria's Secret bag in her other hand.

Phil was pacing back and forth. He decided he couldn't put it off any longer. He'd been trying for weeks to get up enough nerve to tell Betty it was over. He decided today was definitely the morning he would end it. He didn't care how insanely good the sex was, enough was enough. To continue meeting her was just too dangerous.

Phil was trying to come up with a reasonable explanation for dumping her. Unfortunately nothing sounded right. He kept repeating different lines over and over in his mind, then repeated them out loud, but nothing sounded convincing.

"You know, Betty, we have other people to consider besides ourselves . . . You know I think the world of you, but we have to be realistic . . . You have Scooter to think about, and I have Kathy, not to mention my son. If he found out I have been unfaithful to his mother, he'd be heartbroken . . . Be sensible Betty, as hard as this is, it's for the best." He was rehearsing these lines when Betty walked in.

Phil watched her shaking the raindrops from her hair while taking off her rain jacket. He knew telling her wasn't going to be easy. She casually threw the raincoat over the arm of a chair, dropped a small bag next to it, and gave him an inviting smile. He immediately forgot everything he'd just rehearsed. She looked irresistible.

"What a miserable day," Betty said, then, walked over, draped her arms around his neck and kissed him passionately.

"Well, you're certainly in a good mood. It doesn't look like the weather's dampened your spirits," Phil said, taking in the aroma of her perfume.

"I couldn't care less if it's raining," Betty said.

"According to the weather forecast, it's gonna rain most of today," Phil said.

Her smile was sleepy and sexy. The kind a woman gave a man she wants to make love to. "Who cares? I don't care if it's raining outside. It's going to be a beautiful day in here," she said in her most sensual voice, leaning hard against his body, kissing him again, more passionately than their first kiss, her tongue probing deep inside his mouth.

"With it raining, I figured Scooter wouldn't be playing ball. I was surprised when you called Kathy," he said when they parted.

"He's not."

"I thought we agreed we wouldn't meet when he wasn't playing.'

"I know, but I couldn't wait to see you. Besides, I've got a surprise for you. I'll be right back," she said, scooping up the Victoria's Secret bag and heading for the bathroom.

When she returned, she held out her arms and turned slowly, putting on a revealing display. With the backlight from the kitchen, her slightly visible, naked body silhouetted through the sheer wine-red negligee revealed her every curve. "Well, what do you think?" she asked.

"Wow, you are incredibly beautiful," he said. Any thought of ending their affair now just a distant memory

It wasn't long before they were beneath the sheets of the hideaway bed. Betty gave herself to him completely. She fucked him like she couldn't get enough of him. She was only interested in making him happy. Exhausted but satisfied, they lay quietly next to each other, covered only by a thin sheet. Betty was feeling warm and comfortable, listening to the rain beating against the building, giving the room a pleasant, comfortable feeling.

Betty snuggled up next to Phil. He draped his arm around her shoulder, drawing her close, making her feel secure. She was once again feeling satisfied that everything was right between them, knowing that whatever it was that had made her feel uncomfortable and insecure in the past, was now just that, in the past.

After several seconds passed without speaking, Phil all of a sudden became restless. With a concerned look on his face and without warning, he turned abruptly toward her, and said, "Betty, there's something we have to talk about."

"I don't want to talk. I just want you to hold me," she said, moving closer, making sure her bare breasts pressed tightly against his naked chest.

For a moment they both lay motionless. Neither of them spoke while Phil gathered up the nerve to go on. When he looked into her eyes, the words caught in his throat. But he knew he had no choice. He had to tell her and right now. He edged away from her and turned further onto his side.

Finally he said, "I'm serious. There's something we have to talk about. I don't think we should keep on seeing each other."

The short period of security and contentment Betty had been feeling, was suddenly shattered. The dam containing her uncertainties these past weeks had without notice burst apart. Her expression changed . . . she felt like she was drowning in self-doubts and fear. "Why? What's wrong?" she asked in a high pitched voice, pleading for answers, unable to believe what he was telling her.

"We have other people to think about. You understand, don't you? I just don't think what we're doing is fair to Scooter and Kathy," he said, their eyes meeting briefly.

Betty reached over and grasped his hand, her eyes moist with tears. She immediately felt him pulling away. "What do you mean? You know how I feel about you. I love you, Phil."

"We can't keep sneaking around like this. I'm still married to Kathy."

"I love you. Don't you love me?" Her voice sounded weak. She wanted to hear something positive, something to give her hope, something to reassure her they had a future together, anything but what he was telling her.

"Love has nothing to do with this. We both have too much to lose. I don't want to keep meeting like this," Phil said.

"Love has everything to do with it. We can't walk away from each other now. Please, Phil, I thought you loved me," Betty begged.

"Things aren't that simple. I wish they were, but . . . they're not," Phil explained.

Betty bit down hard on her lower lip. "This isn't fair!" she spit out through clenched teeth.

"It's not about being fair. It's about doing the right thing," he said.

She stared at him for a long moment, realizing what was happening. She stopped crying. "I feel used. I feel like a stupid, desperate woman who was looking for love, and you took advantage of me and started fucking me because you were bored with your wife."

"That's not true."

"Yes, it is. A convenient piece of ass; that's all I've ever meant to you. I'm right, aren't I?"

Taking a deep breath, Phil continued. "I've made up my mind. I don't want to see you like this again. It's not right for you. It's not right for me. And it's especially not right for our families."

"You're serious! It's over just like that?"

"Yes."

She shook her head. "You're nothing but a self-centered cowardly excuse for a man," she said, the look of contempt and hatred burning from her eyes.

Considering his words carefully and speaking with a tone of finality in his voice, he said, "Betty, I'm sorry if I've hurt you. But it has to end. It's over."

He attempted to reach out to her. She flinched and drew back. It had only been minutes ago that he was inside her and she had been eager to have him, but now she cringed at the thought of him touching her. There were no longer any tears. Her expression changed. She glared at him with contempt in her eyes that made him cringe.

"I understand now what you've been doing; a quick fuck, an occasional blow job; that's what this has all been about. You're no different from Scooter. All the two of you think about is yourselves. An available piece of ass, that's all I ever was to you. Fuck you, Phil!" she said in a purposely controlled, mean tone.

Betty struggled to keep her emotions under control. She was determined not to give him the satisfaction of seeing her cry. Getting out of bed, she gathered up her clothing that was in a pile at the foot of the bed. She hastened to put on her underpants, inside out. She didn't notice. She picked up her bra and slipped it on.

Phil started to explain, "Betty, it's not like that at all . . ."

Betty raised her open hand to him, stopping him in midsentence. "Shut up, Phil. I don't want to hear another word from you, no more of your lies. If you think you're gonna get away with this, you're mistaken. Someday you're gonna pay; take my word for it."

He decided not to say anymore. He knew if he continued it would only make matters worse. He rolled over on his side, facing the wall, listened to her get dressed. All he wanted now was for her to get the rest of her clothes on and get out of his life; to go away, disappear.

Fully dressed, reaching for the door knob, Betty looked over her shoulder at him and realized what a fool she'd been. Then she quietly left the room, gently closing the door behind her, determined not to give him the satisfaction of thinking she cared enough to slam it.

Phil took a deep breath, then letting out a sigh of relief, turned and watched as the door closed behind her, satisfied that it was finally over. He knew the best sex he'd ever had, or ever would have, just walked out the door. She would be missed. But as good a piece of ass as Betty Pappas was, she was never anything more than that, just a piece of ass. She wasn't worth taking a chance on losing everything he'd worked for all these years.

"Thank God that's over with. She was right about one thing. She's a good fuck. I'm gonna miss it," he mumbled with a satisfying, triumphant smile on his face, looking down at the crumbled naughty nightgown on the floor.

The wind was gusting, causing the rain to blow sideways against the windshield. It became nearly impossible to see. Betty found herself trapped behind a trailer truck, its rear wheels sending up a spray, creating moments of watery blindness, causing her to hold the steering wheel with both hands, her knuckles white from her stranglehold. Her face was tight with concentration as she drove on instinct alone. She put on her headlights and slowed to twenty miles an hour, but it was still impossible to see beyond the hood of the car. Her heart raced and she told herself to remain calm.

Suddenly a wide lake appeared in the center of the highway, crashing against the underside of the car. Betty momentarily panicked. She realized going any further would be suicidal. She began looking for some place to pull off to wait for the torrential rainstorm to stop.

Looking for any place safe, she noticed the blurred neon signs in the windows of a bar on the side of the road. Without hesitation, she drove into a parking lot and stopped between a police cruiser and a green pick-up truck. She remained in her car for a few moments, bent over, putting her face in her hands and leaning her forehead against the steering wheel. Then, lifting her head, she looked out over the river into the dark, angry sky. The heavy rain had gone from a downpour to a thunderstorm rattling the car with flashing jigsaws of lightning that lit up the sky, while winds gusted, creating white caps across the surface of the Indian River.

Noticing the bright red and blue blinking neon sign with a tilted yellow cocktail glass in the window of the bar, advertising "HAPPY HOUR, 3 TO 6," Betty decided she needed a drink. Running her hand through her hair, she took a deep breath and got out of the car, running toward the front door just as an enormous streak of horizontal lighting split the sky, followed by a snap of thunder so loud it shook the earth beneath her feet.

Safely inside, Betty found a long mahogany bar on her right, running the whole length of the room. Several good old Southern boys who looked like they made their living working with their hands, wore work clothes streaked with paint smears and sported a combination of John Deere and NASCAR hats, were eating their lunches and drinking beer. They stopped and watched intently as she walked past them and headed for one of the empty booths on her left, where she collapsed.

Betty definitely looked out of place. She felt self-conscious but knew it was standard procedure in all small town bars to give a stranger the once over. Who is she? What's a classy woman doing in here this time of the morning? After a minute of checking her out, the men went back to their lunches.

Once seated, she noticed a police officer sitting by himself at one end of the bar. He was staring at her with suspicion. Betty recognized him from Barefoot Bay, where she'd occasionally seen him driving around in a police cruiser. After a few uncomfortable minutes of watching her closely, he, too, seemed to lose interest and went back to tapping his fingers on the bar, apparently waiting impatiently for his lunch.

Just as Betty was taking off her rain jacket, the busty, blond woman behind the bar hollered over, "What can I get you, honey?" Not realizing the woman was talking to her, Betty hesitated to answer, so the blond repeated, "Honey, you want something to drink?" in a louder voice.

"I'll have a Scotch and water, please," she ordered, realizing the barmaid was talking to her.

"Short or tall . . . honey?"

The men at the bar once again stopped what they were doing and turned toward Betty, apparently interested in what this out of place customer was ordering.

"Tall," she said while opening her purse and placing a ten dollar bill on the table.

"You want anything to eat?" the barmaid asked when she arrived a moment later with her drink.

Although Betty smiled, her smile was only on her stiff lips and obviously forced. "No ,thanks. I'm fine."

"It sounds like it's coming down pretty good out there."

"It's coming down in buckets. I couldn't see ten feet in front of me," Betty said.

"The worst should be over shortly. You all right, honey? You don't look so good," the barmaid asked.

Betty was just about to assure her she was fine, when the police officer yelled out, "Where the hell's my food, Sandy?"

"Hold your horses, Ray. I'm talking to someone, in case you haven't noticed," she immediately shot back in a commanding voice. The police officer turned away without saying another word.

"I'm fine. It's been a rough morning, that's all," Betty said, never making eye contact.

"Okay, if you say so. If you decide you want something to eat, just give a holler, hon," Sandy said. She picked up the ten-dollar bill and walked back behind the bar to get Betty change.

After Sandy returned with the change, Betty was alone with her thoughts. She stared at her drink in silence as the laughter and loud chatter continued around her. Slowly moving the plastic straw around in her drink, creating a miniature whirlpool, she stared blankly at the swirling motion. In a hypnotic trance, her mind drifted back, thinking about how she'd been misled and mistreated by the three men in her life she had given her heart to, and hating them for what they'd done to her.

She felt the beginning of a headache coming on, causing her skin to tighten on her forehead. The same old familiar ache in her heart returned, the same ache she'd experienced so many times before. She couldn't believe she had been so blind. She knew now that Phil had used her, just as Scooter had been abusing her throughout their entire married life. Betty thought about her father, how he abandoned her as a child, leaving her bewildered and wondering how someone who was supposed to love her could just walk away and never return.

Now this! Once she had given Phil what he wanted, once his appetite for sex had been satisfied, he threw her out like a piece of meat that had gone bad.

And then there was Scooter; the man who had murdered her son.

CHAPTER 32

CRADLING THE DRINK between her fingers, Betty let her mind drift back over the years that she'd spent married to a man she not only did not love, but had grown to hate. Heartache had become a constant part of her life. Even before marrying Scooter, she had realized she was making a mistake. Within weeks after she married him, Betty discovered there was a side of him that she'd not seen before. He became extremely possessive and controlling. He wouldn't allow her to do anything without first checking with him. He was going to be the boss. That was definite.

He took pleasure in criticizing her and never passed up an opportunity to say things that would make her feel hopelessly stupid. Unlike husbands who beat the living hell out of their wives, Scooter abused her emotionally, verbally, mentally, and spiritually; things nobody knew about, because, unlike a woman who gets beaten physically, her injuries remained inside, out of sight.

She recalled vividly the morning she woke up and realized she was pregnant. For weeks she had suspected she might be. When it became definite Betty became excited, thinking with Scooter becoming a father he'd change.

She loved being pregnant. She would linger in front of the mirror admiring her image while running her hands over the sight of her swollen belly. She spent her evenings reading every article she could find about pregnancy and childbirth. Nothing in her entire life felt better than the first time the baby kicked. She had never felt so alive. Her life was taken over with the intense feeling that she would be giving birth, and she felt sure a baby was what Scooter needed to make him happy.

But it didn't take long before she discovered how terribly wrong she had been.

Shortly after arriving home with their son, Scooter became restless and irritable, and informed her that Bobby would be their only child. "I don't want any more kids. Things are tough enough around here without any more mouths to feed," he lectured.

Bobby was a cranky baby, waking Scooter in the middle of the night on several occasions. "I haven't had a decent night's sleep since that goddamn kid came into this house. How the hell can I get up and go to work if that kid keeps me up all night? I said no more kids. That's the way it's gonna be. Understand?" he insisted.

Betty was heartbroken. "Bobby's not any trouble. I'll keep him quiet. I really want another baby. Please, Scooter. It's important to me," she pleaded, but to no avail.

She was crushed. Having children to love was what she wanted and needed to give her life purpose, taking some of the loneliness and heartache out of her marriage. But Scooter was relentless and brought it up daily, until Betty reluctantly, but as she had always done throughout her life, did as she was told and obediently agreed to see a doctor and had herself fixed.

Somehow, she accepted her life as the way things were supposed to be, endured Scooter's abuse, trying to make a go of a hopeless situation without anyone to reach out to.

As Bobby grew older, any attempts to get close to his father were quickly rejected. It seemed as if Scooter was afraid to love anyone, even his own son. Betty didn't understand why. Bobby didn't possess the athletic skills that his father had as a youngster. He didn't even look like his father, who was extremely handsome with dark features, *The Golden Greek,* the girls had called him in high school. Bobby looked more like his mother, small in stature with light skin and delicate features, with a beautiful face, a gentle face.

Scooter seldom attended any of his son's baseball games, and when he did, he could be heard making hurtful remarks like, "The kid's awful! Why does he even bother?" Scooter was right. Bobby was the clumsy, gangly, non-athletic kid who was picked on and picked last, the kid no one wanted on their team. The only reason Bobby got to play in any of the games was because the Pembroke Youth Association had a policy that required every child made the team and would play at least a third of each game.

As hard as Bobby tried, he constantly embarrassed himself by striking out or dropping simple routine fly balls. Making matters worse, Bobby was nearsighted and needed to wear glasses, the lenses so thick they made his blue eyes appear large. His glasses were shell-rimmed, and before every game, he would bend the earpieces in so the glasses would stay tight to his head.

Scooter would watch Bobby playing in the outfield, pushing his glasses up the bridge of his nose, casually holding his baseball glove that was too big for his hand, limply by his side. Hardy ever did a ball get hit to Bobby, but whenever one did, and after misjudging or dropping the ball, he would glance toward the fence on the third base side where his father had been standing and watch as Scooter walked away, head bent, mumbling loud enough so the other parents could hear, "I've got better things to do than stand here and watch four-eyes make a fool of himself."

What ended any hope of Betty ever making a go of their marriage happened the night Bobby was to perform with his school band just before Christmas. The memory of that night and what followed was like suffering a severe wound after which you get stitched up, take your medication, and eventually the wound heals, but the scars never go away. Flashes of anger eventually gave over to remorse as she recalled how she had failed as a mother. All the signs were there in plain sight, but she had been too blinded with concern for her own miserable life to see them.

Several weeks before taking his life, Bobby's grades started to go downhill. Up until then he had been a good student; suddenly his homework was left unfinished, tests incomplete and school projects not started. He had become depressed, vague and showed little interest in what was going on around him. She now believed as his mother she should have taken notice of his cry for help.

It was after the funeral when Betty found Bobby's letter, written on paper from his school notebook, buried between the sheets on his bed. The note had been Bobby's way of calling out to her. But by the time she discovered it, it was too late.

Mom

Why does dad hate me? I know I'm not perfect, not even close, but I really try hard. I can't do anything right so why should I even try? I know you care about me. I wish dad did. Sometimes I wish I was dead. I mean it; I really wish I was dead.

Betty had once read an article on children who commit suicide. What she read said that when children tell you they're thinking about dying, what they are really doing is asking you to stop them. But she found the letter. After reading it she crushed it in her hand and threw it across the room. She felt a pang of guilt, enlarged by the reality that she was living through a parent's worst nightmare. She collapsed on Bobby's bed, wrapped herself in the dark blue blanket that had been used to make him feel warm and safe and began crying uncontrollably.

The memories of the day were vivid in Betty's mind as she sat in Bottoms Up, slowly swirling the straw in her drink. Her thoughts drifted back to the past, a past that seemed part of another lifetime.

Bobby was to perform in the auditorium with the school band. Scooter had missed the concert after promising he'd attend. Bobby had looked forward to showing his father how much he'd accomplished with his music. He had become so good at playing the clarinet that Mr. Gendreau, the music teacher, had chosen Bobby over all the other students to do a solo clarinet piece in the middle of the performance. Bobby couldn't wait for this opportunity to impress everyone, especially his Dad, at how good he had become.

The night of his performance it became apparent to young Bobby that his father would be a no-show. The seat in the front row center next to his mother was vacant. Betty was outraged, watching what she didn't want to watch, Bobby's small eyes glistening with tears and listening to the sadness that she could detect in every note. Bobby's small body was limp with rejection, his face had the look of defeat, eyes filled with tears, once again seeing too much disappointment, forced to stare at the empty seat throughout his performance on what was to be the biggest night of his young life.

At the end of the concert, refreshments were served in the cafeteria. All the parents had assembled there, congratulating their sons and daughters on a job well done. Every adult raved about what a fine clarinet player Bobby was and encouraged him to keep up the good work, but all their words of encouragement didn't prevent Bobby from feeling depressed, because the one person he desperately wanted and needed to hear these words from had not bothered to show up.

While driving home, Betty turned and focused on Bobby for the first time since leaving the school. His glasses had slid halfway down his shriveled nose and tiny tears of rejection trickled down her son's cheeks, while he stared blankly out the front window.

"I'm sorry your father couldn't be there tonight. I was very proud of you. You did a great job," she said, forcing a smile.

Bobby slowly turned away from the window, looked at her, creating one of those rare moments between mother and son that would forever be etched in her mind. "I love you, Mommy, you're the best mom in the world," he said.

She responded hesitantly, timidly, her eyes grinned with affection and pride. "I love you, too, Pumpkin." At that moment Betty realized a mother's love for her child was the deepest and most sincere kind of love there was, and there was no greater joy in this world than being a mother. She made a mental note to herself that she would never forget and would cherish those words until the day she died.

"No, really, Mom," he said. "I love you so much. I'll miss you."

"Miss me? I'm not leaving. I'll always be here for you," she said, confused.

When Bobby didn't respond, she turned her attention back to her driving, not understanding what he meant by *I'll miss you*, but decided he had been through enough tonight. She made a terrible mistake and didn't question him further.

When they returned to the farm, Scooter was sitting in front of the television as if nothing unusual had taken place. Bobby went directly to his room. Scooter gave Bobby little more than a glance and continued watching the news on television.

Shaking nervously, fearful of what might follow, but determined nonetheless, as soon as Bobby's bedroom door closed, Betty lashed out, angrier than she'd ever been in her life. She didn't care what the consequences would be. She intended to tell Scooter what she'd been harboring inside for years.

"And just where the hell were you tonight?" she screamed.

"I had to work late," he answered, hardly taking his eyes off the television, brushing her off with a tired, unconcerned glance.

"You promised you'd be there," she spat out.

"I never promised anything. I said I'd try to be there. Didn't I? If I said I'd be there, I'd have been there," he said, sounding disinterested.

"That's a goddamn lie! You told me you'd go, and don't try to deny it."

"I had to work late. I told Pat Murtagh that I'd have his addition done by Christmas. I'm running behind schedule, so I had to work later than I planned," Scooter snapped, finally turning and looking at her with fire in his eyes.

With her hands firmly planted on her hips, she demanded, "Why is it so important to keep your word to Pat Murtagh and not keep your promise to your son?"

Scooter drew a long, deep breath, then lit into her. "Because Pat's going to pay me the money we need to put food on the table. Because Pat's going to pay me the money we need to pay the bills around this fuckin' place; that's why it's important to keep my word and get the job done on time."

Although she could feel her face burning with fear, she continued. "Pay the bills? Is that what you said? For Christ sake, I'm working, you're getting a salary from the town for being the fire chief, even though you're never there; you're making all kinds of money with the construction business, and you make it sound like we're starving."

Knowing she was right, Scooter regretted what he'd said, but only for a moment. "How the hell do you know? I'm the one who pays the bills around this goddamn house."

This was true. Scooter paid the bills and was in complete control of their finances. He went to great lengths to make sure Betty didn't know what their financial situation was. But she wasn't stupid. It wasn't hard to figure out that with three sources of income and the way they lived, never going anywhere or doing anything, they must have plenty of money in the bank, and she was right.

"I don't care about the money. I'm talking about your son. He was heartbroken tonight. He just wants you to be proud of him. He's worked so hard for tonight. He wanted you to be there," she explained, disappointment and anger in her voice.

"Proud of him; proud of him for what; getting up on stage and making a fool of himself, playing that stupid clarinet in front of all those people." Scooter had now gotten up from his chair and was hot with anger. He lunged at her. She attempted to get out of the way, but he grabbed her by the shoulders and pushed her against the wall.

She looked up at him, fearing him but determined to say what was on her mind. "What is it that makes you so mean all the time? You're like a wild animal, always stalking, waiting to lash out for no reason. It seems like you're mad at the whole world, including me. For some reason, you're afraid to feel anything, to love anyone. Why? Whatever it was happened before I ever met you; I've tried to make you happy. I know I haven't been the perfect wife, but Lord knows I've tried. But nothing I do makes you happy. And now you're taking it out on your son." Her stare bore a wounded fierceness as though the years of sadness and anger simmering just below the surface was ready to explode.

Momentarily, looking down into her face, Scooter saw the anguish and pain he was causing her and wanted to be able to feel something but felt empty. It was times like these that he thought he was going mad, slowly but surely, and the worst part was, he couldn't prevent it.

"Nothing happened. You don't know what the hell you're talking about, so shut up."

"Whatever it is happened a long time ago; it's time to get over it. Let me help you."

"I don't want your goddamn help." Scooter lifted his head toward the ceiling and blew air out of his mouth. "You can't help. Nobody can. Because it happened yesterday, the day before, today, and it will happen tomorrow and the day after that. Don't you understand? It never goes away. He's gone, he's gone and he's never coming back," he hollered with a crazed look in his eyes.

Frightened and realizing Bobby must be listening, and not wanting him to hear his father say any more hateful words about him and his performance, Betty wanted to end this argument, at least for now.

She said in a softer voice. "Your son did a wonderful job tonight. Everyone complimented him on his performance. If only you could have been there, Scooter. It would have meant so much to him."

Scooter looked around the room. Tears appeared in the corners of his eyes. He removed his hands from her shoulders and let them fall to his side. His face softened. Betty watched as he struggled to speak, but nothing came out.

"I don't understand what happened before we got married. You're resentful and distant. I keep hoping you might change, but you never will. You're always angry. What is wrong with you, Scooter? He's your son, for God's sake. Don't you even care a little?" she asked, exhausted, not wanting to fight any more, completely disgusted with him and their life together.

Scooter, having a hard time swallowing, soon regained his composure. With renewed anger flashing in his eyes, he said, "Who the hell do you think you are? This is my house. Don't come in here and tell me what I should or shouldn't do. I tell you what to do. Don't you ever forget it, you ungrateful little bitch! And don't you ever talk back to me again, understand? And besides, I never wanted that goddamn kid, anyways."

With his face twisted in rage, his eyes large, he locked his jaw into a snarl, then brought his fist back as if he was about to hit her, but punched the wall instead.

"Fuck you," he screamed, storming out of the room, swiping at the table lamp, sending it crashing to the floor. Then, he stomped down the hall to their bedroom and slammed the door behind him.

Betty stared at the broken lamp, then looked down the hall and opened her mouth to scream after him, but she remained silent.

The house suddenly became quiet, too quiet, as the stillness surrounding her left Betty scared and frightened of what the future held for her and her son. She wondered how much longer she could go on living each day with an ache in her heart that she knew would never get better. Her life was like living inside a metal straight jacket, heavy, hopeless, inescapable.

The pain that Scooter had caused her son was unforgivable. She felt hopelessly trapped, with nowhere to go. Taking Bobby and leaving the farm was out of the question. Where would they go? How would she provide for them? These questions haunted her constantly as she'd tried many times to think of a way to escape. She'd never been outside Pembroke and was scared and uncertain of the unknown.

Feeling totally defeated, she took a deep breath, her knees growing weak and slowly collapsed onto the couch, as if sliding under water.

Bringing her hands to her head, she massaged her temples while remembering the look of desperation and pain on Bobby's face as he played his clarinet on stage.

Exhausted and unable to deal with the situation any longer, she slid out of her shoes and lay down on the couch, not bothering to take off the new red dress she'd bought specifically for this night. Betty's mind was filled with pain and heartache. After turning off the lights she pulled her knees up in a fetal curl and spent the night lying on the couch someplace between wakefulness and sleep, listening to the tick-tock of the grandfather clock while the heater clicked on and off, blowing warm air into the room. She despised her husband with every breath she took. She despised him when she went to sleep at night, and she would despise him when she woke up.

The next morning Betty lay motionless, watching the sun filter in around the curtains, regretting having to start another day. Somehow she knew she would have to make up a lie to explain to Bobby that his father's absence last night was unavoidable. She knew he wouldn't believe her, but felt she needed to say something in the hope of bringing some kind of normalcy back into their lives.

Dragging herself up, she decided the sooner she spoke to him the better. She walked down the short hallway to his bedroom and put her ear close to his bedroom door. Hearing nothing, she was about to knock when she felt a cold blast of air from beneath the door on her bare feet.

Betty immediately had a sick feeling in the pit of her stomach. Something was drastically wrong. She burst into the room and found it empty. The window by Bobby's bed was open, allowing the light blue curtains to flutterer in the wind and the frigid December air to fill the bedroom. Outside his window, past the black, frozen twigs of the lilac bush, the snow blew sideways across the barnyard, the wind forcing it to pile up against the side of the barn. She hurried over to the window, hoping to see him in the barnyard. Bobby was nowhere in sight. She saw small footsteps embedded in the snow leading to the open barn doors; they were never supposed to be left open in winter. Betty panicked.

The whole scene was crazy, wrong. Bobby was in trouble. She needed to find him. Betty ran out of the house in a panic. She never felt the hard, frozen earth beneath the snow on her bare feet, or the stinging ice-cold wind against her face. She ran across the barnyard, stumbled and fell. Ignoring the sharp pain in her knees, she pushed herself up, slipping in the snow and continued while praying to God. *Please let him be safe.*

When she entered the barn, she looked up in horror and found Bobby's lifeless body hanging from a frayed workman's rope attached to a long, single beam that extended the length of the barn. "Oh, my God, no, please, no," she whispered.

Her son's once-beautiful, gentle face was a pale, sickening shade of grayish blue, his neck looked unnatural the way it was twisted and stretched, his head had begun to swell, while he stared into eternity through empty hollow eyes. The gruesome sight sent her into a state of shock, leaving an image forever frozen in her memory.

She gasped, covered her mouth with one hand, trying to contain her screams, but she could not. Running to Bobby, screaming at the top of her lungs, "No, oh God, no," she wrapped her arms around her son's legs, driven by panic and rage, and tried desperately to lift him. She needed to relieve the tension from around his neck so he could breathe, but it was hopeless.

Frantically, she picked up the folding step stool lying on its side where it had landed when Bobby kicked it away and attempted to climb the wobbling steps in an attempt to untie the knot around his neck. In her haste she lost her balance, and the stool slipped from beneath her bare feet, crashing her to the dirt floor.

Looking up at her son's body swaying in mid-air, Betty let out a frantic cry for help that echoed off the barn walls, "Oh, my God! No. No," she continued to scream. "Scooter, help me. Please help me," she pleaded.

The graveyard was on a hill where a Canadian wind from the north was always blowing. The wind whipped Betty's hair in front of her eyes; she pushed the strands away, forcing them behind her ears. Throughout the service, it snowed like it had snowed so many times before in New Hampshire. Fat, lazy flakes came twirling silently down, the kind Bobby used to love catching on his tongue, eventually covering the entire earth with a blanket of wet, heavy snow that would remain for the rest of the winter. There were many friends and relatives around the grave, but Betty still felt isolated, listening to words of encouragement being spoken, but nothing anyone said could lessen the pain she was feeling deep inside.

A crimson tent provided shelter for the casket and the gathering of mourners standing by the edge of the newly-opened grave, the frozen, uncaring earth; Bobby's final resting place. It was an unsettling experience to see the casket suspended on a metal pier above her son's grave where Bobby would spend eternity. The full magnitude of what was taking place hit her like a fist in her stomach, a feeling she wasn't prepared for.

Although she blamed Scooter, believing he had murdered her son, just as surely as if he'd taken a gun, aimed it at Bobby's heart, and pulled the trigger, Betty nevertheless realized she had failed as a mother. She still recalled the night they returned from the auditorium when he had told her, "I love you so much. I'll miss you." Not a day would go by that she wouldn't relive that moment and blame herself for not hearing his cry for help.

The wind had increased, playing havoc with her hair, so she swept it back with her hand once again. Betty felt she was being forced to deal with her suffering without anyone to share the loss of her only child. When she occasionally looked over at Scooter, he appeared to be a statue of a man, rigid without emotion, staring straight ahead. His face appeared to have been chiseled out of stone, acting indifferent to what was going on around him, like he didn't care.

As she watched his profile, tears welled up in her eyes, his silhouette against the gray clouds that hung low over the leafless trees. He looked uncomfortable in his black suit, his eyes shifting left and right, as though waiting for the chance to bolt, as though he'd rather be anywhere than in this cemetery. She couldn't help but wonder how it was possible that a man could be so heartless that he apparently had not loved his son?

All Bobby ever wanted was to hear his father tell him he was worth something, that he mattered, that he was loved and had something to live for; but Scooter had time after time broken his heart, smashed it, crushed it, stomped on it, until her son had chosen death rather than living with the pain.

She listened as the preacher began puffing out cold winter air that looked like cigarette smoke, reciting the words that were meant to help sooth her troubled heart. "I am the resurrection and the life, saith the Lord; he that believeth in me, though he be dead, yet shall he live; and whosoever liveth and believeth in me, shall never die." A tear appeared in the corner of Betty's eye. She wiped it away with the back of her hand. As she listened to the preacher's prayers, she felt empty inside and didn't believe what he said. His words did nothing to make her hatred for Scooter any less.

Bobby was dead and Scooter was the reason. No words could convince her otherwise. She knew what death was and the finality of death. She knew what life could have given Bobby that he will never know. His music, his career, traveling, love, fatherhood and growing old; what could have been and what is now gone. She knew the world would be worse off without him.

While looking at Bobby's father, her chest began heaving like she was short of breath, and realized how much she hated her life and this man who had caused her so much pain. She knew the day would come when she would get her revenge and make him pay for killing her son. Somehow he was going to pay. She didn't have a specific plan, but she knew one would come.

"Honey, you all right over there?" the barmaid shouted from behind the bar, bringing Betty back to the present.

Startled at first, Betty said, "I'm fine," then looking around the room, noticed the men at the bar had left, except for the police officer, who was eyeing her with suspicion.

Her drink had gone untouched. She gathered up her rain jacket and purse and started for the exit. The police officer sitting at the bar continued to watch her closely in the mirror behind the bar, pretending to watch the TV.

The rain had stopped except for the drops falling from the roof. The sun had returned and the air was heavy, hot, and thick with humidity, causing steam to rise from the pavement. Betty slid behind the steering wheel, still shaking from the memory and ugliness of the last days of Bobby's life.

Finding the strength to start the car, she backed out of her parking space and continued her journey back to Barefoot Bay, feeling depressed and angry, and vowing some day she would make both Scooter and Phil pay for what they'd done to her.

CHAPTER 33

SEVERAL WEEKS passed since Kathy and Jimmy had their first unexpected meeting at the bagel shop. They continued to meet secretly each Tuesday morning and took walks along the winding paths of the Indian River together. Over time the relationship intensified and became more intimate.

It felt like they were traveling through a time tunnel, back to the days when they were dating in high school. Jimmy couldn't stop thinking about her. There was something sensual in the way she looked at him, making him feel alive and wanted. She was able to get him aroused in ways that he never experienced in all the years he had been married to Rita.

Jimmy hadn't intended for it to turn out this way, but it did. What started out with casually hand holding, over time turned into hugs and casual kisses as they sat on what they now referred to as *their* bench.

It was mid-morning. They were driving down Route A1A on their way to the motel they'd chosen from the telephone directory yellow pages. The Atlantic Breeze Motel was located in Vero Beach. After careful consideration, they decided it was far enough away from the Barefoot Bay community that they felt confident they'd go undetected.

A quiet tension had developed between them. Although Jimmy agreed to their plan originally, he was now having second thoughts. He was driving, a look of concern on his face. He'd been fighting a mental battle all morning. He wanted to tell Kathy he had changed his mind. The thought of going to a motel and cheating on Rita was bothering him, and the closer they got to the motel, the more Jimmy felt guilty and uncertain.

Kathy could see the worried look on Jimmy's face. Since leaving their cars in the lot across from the bagel shop, he had been acting distant and distracted. She had given a lot of thought to what they were about to do and was determined to go through with it. Wanting to ease his tension, she reached over and gently placed her hand on his thigh. "Nervous?" she asked.

"I guess I am a little."

Kathy frowned. "If you don't think we should, it's not too late."

She wanted to give him every opportunity to change his mind but hoped he wouldn't. The last several nights she had had recurring dreams of them being together and was now looking forward to turning those dreams into reality.

It eased her conscience thinking about being unfaithful to Phil, because, although she had never caught him, she was convinced he had cheated on her. And believing he had had several affairs in the past, she felt justified with being unfaithful to him now.

Over time their marriage had become a marriage of convenience, more like a friendship or business partnership, without any closeness between them. Everything about their marriage seemed to exist along a steady line, never up, never down, never left, never right, never anything, just one boring day after another. She had been forcing herself to think she was satisfied, because she couldn't bear to believe she had wasting her life marrying Phil. Now here she was with Jimmy, the father of her son, the man she now believed she should have married, realizing she may have made the wrong decision.

Jimmy couldn't stop thinking about Rita. He knew she would be heartbroken if she knew what he was about to do. The more he thought about it, the more convinced he was that it was wrong, dead wrong. He realized he was putting his marriage in jeopardy. Rita's image flashed before his eyes, causing him to have second thoughts. He decided to put an end to this before it was too late.

He was about to tell Kathy he couldn't go through with it, when the large sign advertising the Atlantic Breeze Motel appeared on the side of the roadway. He panicked. Reacting on impulse, he drove onto the gravel parking lot, sliding into a vacant spot in front of the office entrance before he had a chance to explain to Kathy he'd changed his mind.

Noticing the strained look on his face, Kathy asked, "Is everything all right?"

He nodded. "I guess so. Yes. I'm all right," he said in a timid voice.

"You're sure?" she asked.

Confused, unsure of what he should do but unable to think fast enough to tell her he had changed his mind, he instead said, "Really, I'm fine."

"Okay then, if you're sure, get us a room," Kathy said. Adrenalin pumped through her, accelerating her heartbeat. She was feeling the same sexual power over him that she felt when they were dating in high school and was anxious to cast her spell over him once again.

Jimmy felt trapped. Seeing the anxious look on Kathy's face made him think he had no choice but to do as she asked. Nervously, getting out of the car, he walked into the motel lobby, trying to remain calm. The air-conditioning hit him when he walked in. The room felt twenty degrees cooler than outside.

It was too late to retreat now. He approached the registration desk on shaky legs and observed a middle-aged woman seated behind the counter talking on the phone.

She looked up, took off her glasses and placed them on her desk. Then peering up at him, she grunted, "uh, huh" and "right" a few times into the phone while holding up her index finger, indicating that she'd be right with him. He looked around the office, feeling awkward and nervous, wishing she would hurry. After what seem like an eternity, she hung up the phone, sighed and approached him.

"Sorry about that," she said, nodding toward the phone. "What can I do for you?"

"I'd like to rent a room," Jimmy said in a timid voice.

The name tag on the woman's chest identified her as Gail, Assistant Manager. Gail observed Jimmy closely. She'd been working the desk at the motel for several years and considered herself an expert at spotting cheaters.

Most men looking for a room at this time of the morning fell into two categories. The cheaters who were having an affair with girls from their work place, or, they were men who had just picked up a prostitute from the boardwalk and needed a room to conduct their business, and Gail was just the girl who supplied the rooms.

This customer was acting nervous enough that she was sure he was one or the other. "It's a little early. Check-in isn't until 1 p.m., but I just happen to have a room available. It'll be sixty dollars, but it has to be cash. I'm having trouble with the credit card machine," she informed him.

Gail lied. She always had rooms available at this time of the day. And there was nothing wrong with the credit card machine. The rooms were available for the cheaters who would use them for a couple of hours, then be gone just as quick as they arrived, in time for her to re-rent the rooms for the evening traffic. Gail liked this arrangement because she kept the cash, destroyed the registration cards, and the management wasn't the wiser.

"That will be fine," Jimmy said, handing her three twenties.

Taking the money and slipping it into her breast pocket, Gail reached over and picked up a registration card from the pile on the corner of the counter and handed it to him. "You need to fill this out."

"Sure," he said, then began filling in the lines on the card.

After Jimmy completed the form and handed it back to Gail, she casually glanced at the information without showing much interest, then handed him the computerized entry key. "Go outside and turn right. It's the third door down," she instructed.

Feeling more comfortable now that the check-in was over, Jimmy hurried back to the car where Kathy was waiting. He showed her the key, then started the car and drove three doors down.

He no sooner left the office when Gail lifted the counter flap and walked over to the window to see what kind of bimbo this novice cheater was taking to the room, something she did on a regular basis. She was familiar with several prostitutes who worked the boardwalk and wondered if this was one of them, not that it made any difference to her.

She had a clear view of the woman seated on the passenger side of the car but wasn't prepared for the wholesome-looking older woman sitting there. She didn't look anything like a prostitute.

Examining the registration form in her hand, she noticed it was made out with the correct automobile registration number, which was usually not the case. The signature said he was James Martin; maybe he was and maybe he wasn't. In any case, Gail wasn't taking any chances and decided she would put the card in the active file draw.

Gail continued watching as the door closed behind them and smiled. There was no luggage. She'd been right. They had to be in their sixties. Imagine that. Guess you're never too old, she thought, walking back behind the counter, registration card still in her hand.

Kathy watched with amusement as Jimmy fumbled with the plastic card, first placing it in upside down, then backward. Feeling embarrassed, and with trembling fingers, he finally was successful. The green light blinked, allowing them to enter.

The room appeared crowded, with barely enough space to walk around the inexpensive furniture. Although small, it was clean with cheap carpeting on the floor and outdated wood paneling on the walls. The floral curtains that hung loosely, framed the window to help block out the light but didn't do much to improve the surroundings. Over each bed was a large Audubon Society print of tropical birds surrounded by lush flowers.

Feeling awkward, they sat on opposite beds, avoiding eye contact. Jimmy was unsure what he should say or do, so he leaned forward and put his elbows firmly on his knees, and unconsciously fingered his wedding band. He didn't feel comfortable. He felt like he was being pushed into a dangerous situation.

After a moment of silence, Kathy sighed softly, walked over, and sat next to him on the bed, letting her hand drift to his thigh. Putting the other hand on his shoulder, she began rubbing it with small circular motions. "I can see that you're still a little nervous."

He felt the warmth of her hand on his thigh. "I've never done this before," he said, looking at her, then slowly turned away.

"Neither have I. But I've been thinking about you, and if I'm supposed to feel guilty, I'm sorry, but I don't. I've missed you and want to be with you again, Jimmy."

Whatever uncertainties Jimmy was having, they weren't shared by Kathy. Right or wrong was beside the point. It was as if she had become another person. A surge of warmth overtook her body. Even if real love wasn't there, the affair was providing her with some relief from the isolation of her marriage, and she intended on enjoying this feeling, even if it was only going to be temporary.

Kathy looked directly at him. Jimmy tried to return her gaze but looked away. "I keep thinking of Rita. Sometimes I think we shouldn't be doing this, but when I look at you, I'm not sure what I want," he said as she continued watching him.

Turning and looking into her eyes, Jimmy could see she was no longer the teenage girl he had known nearly forty years ago. She was now a mature woman, married with a son not much older than his own son. He realized how kind the years had been to her. He detected small lines on the corners of her mouth and around her eyes, but they only added, not detracted from her mature wholesomeness. Her bright blue eyes and full lips still had the ability to draw him in, making him behave in ways he never thought he was capable of behaving.

Afraid she was losing control, Kathy took a deep breath, then let it out slowly. "I've missed you, Jimmy. Please don't let me down. If after today you don't want to see me again, I'll understand, but I need you now," she said, then slowly stretched out on the bed. "Please, Jimmy. I want you . . . I want you now," she gently whispered in a commanding voice.

Rita's image flashed before Jimmy's eyes, but it quickly disappeared. Sitting on the edge of the bed, he watched Kathy reach down and slip off her shoes before undoing the buttons on her shorts. She remained silent as she pulled them off. Jimmy was hypnotized, watching as she pulled her jersey and bra over her head, exposing her breasts, before carelessly dropped the clothes to the floor.

Earlier while waiting in the car, Kathy had wondered if she would feel uncomfortable being naked in front of him. She'd been naked with him in the past, but that was many years ago when her body was young and firm and nearly perfect. Now the years had taken their toll. She realized she'd put on weight and her body was now much softer, her waistline thicker, her breasts lying flat against her chest, but she hoped he would still find her attractive.

The bed squeaked when Jimmy got up, acting like he was in a trance, and began undressing, causing Kathy to shutter. Finally naked, he lay next to her, his erection pressing hard against her thigh. The feeling of excitement was like nothing she had felt in all her married life. It was like she was traveling back in time to when they were young.

Jimmy didn't know what to expect, but soon discovered, instead of a woman who showed little response or enthusiasm for his love making, a woman who remained motionless, stiff and unattached, he found Kathy to be an eager, willing and compassionate partner.

Bending forward, she offered her lips to him; Jimmy hesitated for a moment, then their mouths met, and it felt good kissing him. Kathy didn't care about Rita. She didn't care about Phil. She didn't care about their children or their lives outside of this room. It was Jimmy, and only Jimmy that she wanted.

Jimmy felt the adrenaline rushing throughout his body, when Kathy reached up and brought his lips to her breast. Kathy was now in control as she drew him inside her, and they became one, moving effortlessly together, her body rising and pitching beneath him.

They took their time. This would not be one of those occasions when it's over before it begins. They started slow, unhurried, then gradually the buildup became powerful, and the feeling was electrifying, almost painful. They knew each other's bodies from a long time ago, and there was recognition as they discovered the reunion of that other life, believing they were seventeen again.

"Oh, yes, Jimmy. Yes." She whispered softly. "It's been so long . . . I've missed you."

Kathy's earlier fears of Jimmy not finding her attractive were unfounded. Her body no longer possessed the firmness of her youth, but she still had the ability to completely control him. She knew Jimmy was a slave to his emotions. He would do whatever she asked.

She believed she was reliving the lost love of her past. It felt like a part of her that had been missing, had been found. She was convinced this wasn't just a casual flirtation. She believed she had returned to a place she should never have left and intended on enjoying these moments for as long as they lasted.

When they separated Kathy laid motionless, the skin on her back moist, her breath sounding heavy as she gasped for air. Finally she sat up, raised her knees and wrapped her arms around them, while crossing one bare foot on top of the other. Suddenly life had new meaning.

"That was wonderful," she said, happier now than she has been since Jimmy had walked out of her life.

"I'd forgotten it could be that good," he said.

"Me, too," she agreed. Kathy smiled, thinking she had made a terrible mistake marrying Phil, losing contact with the man she now believed she should have married.

He had meant so much to her then.

And now it was too late.

Or was it?

BOOK THREE

Revenge

CHAPTER 34

CHIEF OF POLICE Ray Barrett showed up in the parking lot of the station nursing a hangover. Last night had been a typical late night at Bottoms Up, and he was now feeling sick to his stomach and in a foul mood. He looked over to where his secretary, Darcy, usually parked her fifteen-year-old, silver Chevrolet station wagon and was happy to see she'd already arrived, which wasn't always the case.

Darcy had a habit of taking days off without giving notice. The next day when she showed up for work, Ray would asked where she'd been, she'd casually dismiss her absence by shrugging her shoulders and saying she'd had something to do, without any further explanation. Whenever he tried to discipline her, she would listen intently, look apologetic, but nothing ever changed. Since hiring her, he had often asked himself why? But after watching her prance around the office, he knew why.

Darcy hadn't been the most qualified candidate to apply for the job when Ray was looking for a girl to fill the dispatcher's position three years ago. Darcy was twenty eight years old. She had long slim legs, which she never hesitated to put on display beneath her slightly too-tight, slightly too-short miniskirt. She enjoyed wearing skimpy, low-cut halter tops that got a lot of attention from Ray. Darcy over did her lipstick and mascara, and chain-smoked one cigarette after another. When she wasn't smoking, she was constantly chewing big globs of gum that made a sharp, snapping sound when she stuck her tongue out and blew air into it, causing it to pop.

Darcy came from a long line of cops. Her father was a cop, her grandfather was a cop before he retired, and she had an uncle who was a cop, all working for the city of Melbourne. It had always been her dream to follow the family tradition of becoming a cop, so when she went looking for work, she applied for the dispatcher's job in Micco with the intention of eventually working herself into a patrolman's position.

Unfortunately for Darcy, Ray had no intentions of offering her a patrolman's position. He was perfectly happy with the way things were and had no intention of giving up the only thing he enjoyed about his job, which was watching her modeling her skimpy outfits around the station.

His mind still groggy from his late night at Bottoms Up, the chief entered the station and found Darcy bent over her desk working. A filtered cigarette hung from a corner of her mouth. Darcy immediately looked up and smiled. She wore one of Ray's favorite outfits, a white sleeveless blouse that hung loosely from her shoulders, allowing him an unobstructed view and a mini-skirt that had worked its way high up on her thighs.

Liking what he saw, Ray casually walked over, eyes cast down the front of her blouse and said, "Good morning," while Darcy made no attempt to cover up. It was times like this he was convinced he had made the right decision in hiring her.

Darcy had heard about the death in Barefoot Bay. She had been thinking about it nonstop all weekend. She, like the rest of the citizens in Micco, after hearing about the possibility of a murder being committed in the Bay, quickly became amateur detectives, swapping theories, sharing imaginary clues and jumping to conclusions that were so far off base they made no sense. She had tried to contact Ray over the weekend without success and had been counting the minutes until she could get into work and get the lowdown from the man with the answers.

"Hi, Ray," she said.

"How was your weekend? Hope it was better than mine," he said.

"Where the hell have you been? I've been trying to get in touch with you. I heard some guy got murdered in Barefoot Bay. Everyone's talking about it."

Ray headed for his office. "It looks like something's going on over there," he said, speaking over his shoulder.

Darcy wasn't about to let him get away without finding out more, so uninvited, she followed him into his office. "Well, tell me what happened," she insisted, sitting down in the chair in front of his desk. "Was it really a murder?" she asked.

"Looks that way," he said.

"Do you have any idea who done it?"

"Don't have the slightest idea."

Ray's head started to throb. He didn't need or want Darcy hounding him with questions he didn't have the answers to. But Darcy wasn't letting him off the hook that easy. Lighting a cigarette, she took a long drag and exhaled in Ray's direction.

Ray had his share of bad habits, but smoking wasn't one of them. He hated the stench of secondhand smoke but decided not to say anything.

"You must have some idea what happened," she said.

Ray hesitated, then clearing his throat, said, "Listen Darcy, I don't have the slightest goddamn idea what happened over there. I'm just now starting to investigate, so don't drive me crazy with all your questions. When I know something, I'll let you know, okay?"

The murder was the biggest thing to hit the town of Micco in many years, and Darcy intended on being right in the thick of things. Inhaling a large amount of smoke, she let it drift out from her mouth and nose while talking. "I just want to help. You don't have to get all pissed off. Besides, I need to know what's going on if I'm going to help," she explained.

His office suddenly became twenty degrees hotter "All I know is that he was strangled, okay? I don't want to talk about it," he said in a harsh voice. Ray's headache was getting worse by the minute, and he felt like he was about to vomit, and the room filling up with smoke wasn't helping. "And another thing, I don't want you smoking them goddamn cigarettes in my office anymore."

Darcy could see Ray was sick and getting sicker, but made no attempt to put out her cigarette. She figured it was best to back off for now but had no intentions of being shut out. "Okay; all I'm trying to do is help."

Ray was having trouble clearing his head. There was something he wanted Darcy to do. He was trying to remember what it was. Then he remembered his meeting with Kathy Gagnon yesterday. "Oh. Listen, Darcy, there is something you can do for me; call Mrs. Gagnon over at Barefoot Bay. The number should be in the directory. When you get her on the phone, give her the number for the County Sheriff's Department. Tell her to ask for a Sergeant Pennie. She'll need to make arrangements to have her husband's remains taken care of. Also, while you have her on the phone, get the address and telephone numbers where she can be reached up north."

"Mrs. Gagnon? Is she the wife of the guy that got murdered?"

"Yes. Mrs. Gagnon is the wife of the man that was murdered."

"How come she's leaving to go up north?"

"I imagine she wants her husband buried there. That's where they come from. Now, will you stop with the questions and call her? Oh, one more thing, while you have her on the phone, ask her if she knows the hometowns of her neighbors, the Pappas's, the Kloskis, and the Martins. If she does, I want you to get the telephone numbers of the local police departments in them towns."

Darcy was frantically writing down the instructions on a scrap piece of paper, happy to be included in the investigation. "If you want, I'll call these places for you. What is it you want me to find out?"

Ray decided he needed to put a stop to her questioning him and volunteering to help. "No! I don't want you to do anything but get the numbers. Think you can do that? Your job is to answer the phones and take care of the payroll. Not play detective."

Then he banged his elbows on his desk and grabbed his head with both hands. He needed time to think. None of this was familiar. It was a living nightmare, and Darcy questioning him wasn't making it any easier.

"I'm going," Darcy hollered, then walked out, slamming the office door behind her.

Ray stared at the vibrating door and waited for the explosion to settle down in his head. He knew that the Gagnons came from Lowell, Massachusetts. He decided to call information and get the number of the police department himself. When he got through, he asked the person answering the phone for any information they might have on a Philip Gagnon.

At first the desk officer didn't recognize Gagnon's name. But when Ray explained that Phil owned an insurance agency, the officer made the connection. He informed Ray that the Gagnon family was well known and highly respected. He sounded shocked to hear the circumstances surrounding Phil Gagnon's death. The officer doubted there would be anything that would be of help, but he'd check, and if he found something of interest he'd call back. Ray thanked him and hung up.

He no sooner returned the phone to its cradle, when Darcy was back. She appeared to have calmed down. She began talking rapidly. "I called Mrs. Gagnon and talked to her son. He said he flew in late last night from Massachusetts. He already called the Sheriff's Department. He said arrangements to have his father sent back north have been taken care of. He also told me if there's something you want to discuss with his mother, you'd better talk to her today because he's driving her back to Massachusetts early tomorrow morning. He gave me the address and telephone numbers where they live. He also gave me a number for a Hennessey Insurance Agency. He said he works there. I also got the names and the telephone numbers of the police stations in the towns that you asked about," she explained proudly, nearly out of breath, placing the handwritten paper with the information on his desk.

"Thanks," Ray said, picking up the paper and examining it closely.

"Is there anything else?" Darcy asked.

Ray lifted his brow, but not his head, then said, "No. I can handle things from here."

Darcy looked like she was about to say something, then thought better of it and walked out of his office, still upset, but decided to let things settle down, at least for now.

SECRETS, SINS & REVENGE

Ray gave himself a minute to gather his thoughts before making the calls. It turned out he wasn't be any better off after making the calls than he was before making the calls. He'd gotten basically the same reaction from the other police departments that he'd gotten from Lowell.

As soon as Ray mentioned the name Pappas, the Pembroke police officer knew the family immediately. He couldn't say enough nice things about them. During the conversation, Ray found out that Scooter Pappas had lost his father in a fire many years ago and had also lost a son tragically when the boy was only twelve years old.

"Did you say his son died tragically?" Barrett asked.

"Suicide; the town's still talking about it," he explained. "This kid had everything. Nice family, good home. Nobody can figure out what could have made him do it," the officer stated.

"How did he kill himself?" Ray asked. He did not like Scooter Pappas but couldn't help but feel some compassion for him, especially learning his son had passed way at such a young age.

"Hung himself; why all the questions about Pappas?"

"We had a suspicious death occur. The Pappas were friends of the guy that died. I'm just doing a routine follow-up."

"Well, you won't find two finer people than Scooter and Betty," the officer said confidently.

"I don't know them personally, but I'm sure they're fine upstanding people."

"Scooter was our first fire chief in Pembroke when the department went full time. He retired recently. His wife Betty worked at City Hall in the Building Department. They go to Florida in the winter now. I guess you already know that."

Deciding he had gotten all the useless information he was going to get from this guy, Ray tried to end the conversation. "Yes. I won't keep you any longer. I'm sure you're busy. Thanks for talking to me," he said."

"If you're ever in this part of the woods, drop in the station," the Pembroke officer concluded.

"I'll do that. Thanks again." Ray hung up before he could respond.

Ray's headache was getting worse, but he nevertheless made a third call, this time to Barnstead, Pennsylvania. It turned out Barnstead was also a small rural town located in the Pocono Mountains. Just as the officer in Pembroke knew the Pappas family, this policeman knew the Kloskis.

The officer in Barnstead told Ray that Stanley worked at the local bank. His wife, Carol, had been the girls' physical education teacher at the local high school for years. The officer didn't know all the details but told Chief Barrett that Carol had resigned shortly after being involved in a serious automobile accident in Vermont that took the life of the school's art teacher. Unlike the officer in Pembroke, this guy quickly gave Ray the information and had no intention of staying on the phone any longer than he had to.

The fourth and final call went to Chelmsford, Massachusetts and was again over in a matter of minutes. The officer knew the Martins personally. He explained the Martins were a typical couple with two children. Jimmy Martin worked for the Chelmsford post office, retiring as head postmaster. There apparently was nothing out of the ordinary or unusual about them. He was off the phone in less than three minutes. Ray couldn't get over how everyone seemed to know everyone in those small New England towns.

Barrett's investigation quickly came to a screeching standstill, not that it had ever really gotten started. He didn't have the slightest idea what to do next. It was now almost ten o'clock. Too early to head to Bottoms Up. He could use a drink, but he knew it would be several more hours before he would be able to get his hands around a bottle of beer. A couple of beers were the only thing he could depend on to make his hands stop shaking and his headache disappear.

He decided instead to drive to the donut shop for his mid-morning coffee. Hopefully it would help calm his nerves.

On his way out he stopped by Darcy's desk. "Want anything from the coffee shop?" he asked.

She looked at him but didn't smile. "No. I'm all set." She leaned back slightly, hindering his usual view.

Ray took this to mean he was being punished; there would be no further looks unless his attitude toward her changed, he assumed. He was well aware that she knew she had what it took to get him excited, and he also knew, she knew just how to use what she had to get what she wanted.

CHAPTER 35

KATHY'S SON, PHILIP, was in the driveway packing his mother's suitcases into the trunk of her BMW. He was anxious to get on the road. It was going to be a long drive back to Massachusetts. Thankfully, the weatherman had predicted good weather for their trip. Once he got the last remaining suitcase in the trunk, he would be ready to get started.

The last piece of luggage didn't seem to want to cooperate. He was trying to jam it in the trunk, when out of the corner of his eye, he noticed a woman walking toward him. "Hi, you must be Kathy's son. I'm Carol. I live next door."

Philip was tall, dark and handsome, just as Carol knew he would be, having seen many photos of him scattered around Kathy's house. His eyes were dark almond, but looked emotionless, filled with a vague emptiness due to the death of his father. He exhaled heavily, forced the last piece of luggage in, slammed the trunk closed, and reached out his hand to her.

"Yes, nice to meet you. My mother's inside packing her travel bag," he explained without much enthusiasm.

"When I spoke to her yesterday, she said you would be coming to drive her home."

"It's too long a ride for her to travel by herself, especially after what's happened to my father."

"There's no easy way to say this, but I'm really sorry about what happened to your Dad," Carol said.

Philip shook his head. "It doesn't make sense. This is the last place you would think something like this could happen."

"The whole community is in shock. Nothing like this has ever happened in the Bay before."

"According to Mom, someone just walked in, beat Dad, strangled him, and then just walked out. It doesn't make sense," Philip said.

Carol brushed several strands of hair from her face. "How's your mother doing? Do you think she's up to making the trip back?"

Philip nodded. "She's actually taken it better than I thought she would."

Carol forced a weak smile. "Right now there's so much going on, she doesn't have time to mourn. Thank God she has you to help her get through this. Do you think she'll be coming back to Florida this year?"

Philip took a deep breath and shook his head. "Not if I have anything to say about it. If I have it my way, she won't ever be coming back to this goddamn place, ever," he lashed out.

Carol was startled by his sudden outburst. Regaining her composure, she said, "The people living here are really very nice. But I can understand how you feel."

"I'm sorry. I shouldn't be taking my anger out on you," he apologized.

Her eyes welled up with tears. "I don't know what to say, Philip, except that I'm really, really sorry."

Just then, Kathy came out of her house carrying an overnight bag. Carol hastened up the driveway, put her arms around Kathy and gave her a friendly hug. "How are you holding up?"

"All right, I guess. I see you've met Philip," Kathy said, placing her overnight bag next to the BMW.

"Yes. He's a good-looking man. Handsome like his father," Carol said.

"I'm happy he was able to get away from the office to drive me home. I don't think I could have made it alone," she said, looking at her son proudly.

"I'm going to miss you, Kathy. Do you think you'll be coming back this year? It sounds like Philip doesn't want you to return," Carol continued, glancing at Philip, then back to Kathy.

Kathy put her hand into her son's. "I'm not sure what my plans are. I doubt I'll be coming back this year, unless Officer Barrett needs me to return."

Philip released her hand and put his arm around her shoulders. "I'd like to see you sell this place and stay home where you'll be safe. I don't want you living in a place where murderers are running around," he said.

Carol reluctantly agreed. "I guess I can't blame you."

Shortly before coming out of the house, Kathy had stood in the middle of her living room, sunlight drifting across the floor from the picture window. She appeared in a trance, looking at the spot where she had found Phil's body. She could still visualize the night she walked in and found him lying on the floor. She couldn't remember if it was the deathly look on his face, or something deep inside that told her he was dead, but she knew immediately.

She had run over, dropped to her knees. There wasn't anything bloody or gruesome about him, just a sense of finality. The biggest shock was his eyes. They were wide-open, the cocky self-assurance she was accustomed to, replaced by a hollow, empty stare. It would be forever burned deeply in her memory. She recalled being frightened, her heart pounding. In a state of panic, she got off her knees and ran out the front door.

"Carol—wait!!" she had screamed.

Carol's car was backing down the driveway. Startled by the sudden outburst, she jammed on the brakes, put the car into drive, and drove back up the driveway. All three women jumped out of the car and came running. Kathy remembered Betty rushing over, getting on the floor and checking Phil's pulse. There wasn't one. Betty slowly turned, looked up and shook her head.

Now, standing alone in the house, Kathy was finding it difficult to believe Phil was gone. Her whole life had suddenly changed. As her eyes traveled around the living room, she stared at the collection of her son's pictures scattered on the walls. In several pictures Phil was standing next to him, a proud smile on his face. His image caused her to think about the day she lied and told him he was the baby's father, and wondered if she had made the right decision. It seemed like a million years ago. In a way, it was.

Had she ever really loved Phil? She wasn't sure. Although there seemed to be something missing from their relationship, there was no denying Phil was strong and reliable, if at times stubborn. At least she knew where she stood with him. Once they were married, their life together, setting up housekeeping in their tiny studio apartment, so small they had to push the kitchen chair aside next to the table in order to open the refrigerator door, the birth of the son he believed to be his, Phil's interest in working at her father's business, had all been events that gave them a sense togetherness, comfort, and security as they worked toward their future.

As the years passed, she no longer thought of her son's real father. She no longer allowed herself to wonder if she had made a mistake. They were making a life for themselves, and Phil, believing baby Philip was his son, was an important part of it. Their life together was not a perfect life, but it nevertheless had been a good, comfortable life, but she doubted there had ever been any real love.

Tears welled in her eyes when she thought about the brief affair she had recently had with Jimmy. At the time it had felt so right. It amazed her how quickly things changed. Just a few weeks ago she was having an affair, a woman her age. What was she thinking? Now she was overwhelmed with grief and wished she could chase their affair from her memory.

As she stood in the middle of the living room, although it had only been a short time ago, she scarcely remembered the affair. In a way it was as if the whole thing had been nothing but a dream.

Why, after all these years did Jimmy have to come back into her life? More importantly, why had she been so stupid to believe that after all this time, with both of them married, she could rekindle the love she now knew had been nothing more than a teenage romance that would have been better left in the past.

Was it because her feelings had been completely selfish? Was it because she thought something was missing from her marriage and had used Jimmy to fill that void? Was it because she believed things would get better between her and Phil if she got rid of the years of sexual frustration she had endured during her marriage? She wasn't sure if things would have gotten better, but she now knew things could have been worse, a lot worse, if they had been discovered.

She was thinking of the injustice of Phil dying. He had his faults, but he didn't deserve to die. She only hoped whoever had done this would someday be caught and punished. But for now she needed to be strong. Her son had loved and admired the man he thought was his father. He would need her support. He was waiting outside to take her home. She was determined to remain strong, and work at putting her life back together.

As she took one last look around the room, a feeling of tension sent shivers down her spine. Everything looked the same, yet not the same at all. She had spent many hours in this room, yet the room seemed suddenly impersonal, like she'd never seen it before. She needed to get out of here. She knew she had to leave right now and start a new life. She would have to do that now that Phil was gone.

Yes, she would move on. Without any further hesitation, she picked up her overnight bag and walked outside, closing the door firmly behind her.

Jimmy Martin looked out his living room window, watching what was taking place across the street. He couldn't make up his mind whether he should go over and say a final goodbye to Kathy or leave well enough alone. Ever since Phil's death, his feelings for Kathy had changed. He wanted to forget what they had done. He wanted to be able to start looking at Rita again without getting that guilty feeling in the pit of his stomach.

He realized now how close he came to losing everything. He loved being married to Rita. He loved his children and was looking forward to being a grandfather. When he thought about how close he'd come to hurting them and losing their love and respect, he became sick with guilt.

He hadn't talked to Kathy since the night of Phil's murder. He wasn't even sure how to approach her or if he should say anything at all. Whatever had happened between them was over. He felt a sense of relief knowing that Kathy was going back home, and he too was getting anxious to return home.

He wished he had never got involved with Kathy. He realized he wasn't in love with her and never had been. It was the excitement of having an affair that had drawn him to her. She had been such an exciting and willing sex partner, something missing in his marriage. He'd spent his whole life walking the straight and narrow, never stepping over the line, never doing anything dangerous or adventurous, so when he began meeting Kathy, he got caught up in the thrill of the moment and taken in with living on the edge. He now realized how foolish and stupid he had been.

Rita had been on an emotional roller coaster ride ever since Phil's murder but had finally gotten a good night's sleep. In fact she was still sleeping. She had spoken to Kathy last evening on the phone, and they'd said their goodbyes. They promised to look each other up when they got back home, but Jimmy hoped that would never happen.

Rita insisted that she didn't want to remain in Florida any longer. She wanted to go home and the sooner the better. Unlike a couple of weeks ago when Jimmy would have tried to convince her to stay, he too was anxious to leave Florida. There was just too much going on here in Barefoot Bay.

As uncomfortable as he felt about facing Kathy, he knew it was the right thing to do. He decided he would walk across the street to say goodbye. Rubbing the back of his neck where it had started to ache from the tension of living a lie these last weeks, he reluctantly left his house and started the long walk across the street.

As soon as she saw him walking toward her, Kathy experienced a combination of fear and uncertain anticipation. Her knees became weak. She couldn't stop her hands from shaking. She realized that Jimmy would be meeting their son for the first time.

As Kathy watched Jimmy approach, she couldn't help but notice the remarkable similarity the three men shared. Thankfully, her son, Jimmy, and Phil had the same features. All three men had brown hair, brown eyes and dark complexions. Although Phil and Jimmy didn't look anything alike, they had enough of the same characteristics and features, that no one would ever be suspicious of her secret.

At the dinner party in January she had gotten nervous when Jimmy held up Philip's graduation picture for Rita to see and commented on how much her son looked like their son, Jason. The closer Jimmy came, the more she could see the resemblance. It was overwhelming. The way he carried himself, the strong facial features, and the soft concerned look in his eyes, left little doubt who her son got his good looks from.

Kathy was unable to speak immediately. She stood dumbfounded, staring at the two men, wondering if it was possible that they might feel any kind of emotional bond.

"Hi, Jimmy," she said nervously when he approached her.

"Kathy, I see you're on your way. I just wanted to say goodbye before you left." Without hesitation, he put his arms around her, hugging her casually.

For a long moment they stayed in this embrace. Taking a step back, but still holding Jimmy's arms, she said with a lump in her throat and her voice trembling slightly, "Philip, I'd like you to meet a friend of mine. This is Jimmy Martin. Jimmy and I go way back to when we went to high school together. He lives in Chelmsford now."

"Nice to meet you, Philip. I'm awfully sorry about your Dad. I'm sure you're gonna miss him." Jimmy extended his hand.

"Thank you. Yes, I will. He was more than just my Dad. He was my best friend." When their eyes met, Philip had a strange feeling of recognition. "Have we met before?" Squinting, he searched his memory.

"I don't think so," Jimmy said.

"You look familiar. I feel like I know you from some place. If you live in Chelmsford, I've probably seen you around town," Philip suggested.

"I worked at the post office for years. Maybe that's where you've seen me. Anyway, I was telling your mother when I saw your graduation picture I couldn't get over how much you resemble my own son, Jason."

"Really? I'd like to meet him. Maybe we could get together sometime for golf," Philip offered.

"I'd like that." Jimmy released his hand. "I'll look forward to it."

"It's a date," Philip said.

Kathy was having difficulty breathing. She could barely draw air into her lungs. She watched Jimmy's face closely and was relieved when their conversation continued, unaware whom he was talking to. Even though so much had gone on between them, Kathy looked on with pride, knowing she had had the opportunity of seeing them together, if only for this one time.

It seemed almost impossible to believe that so much time had gone by since their son was born. She had wondered earlier if she'd made the right decision marrying Phil. But, deep down she realized it had turned out for the best, and was glad her secret had remained a secret for all these years.

There was an awkward moment of silence. Carol, feeling left out of the conversation, asked, "Jimmy, are you and Rita staying for the rest of the month?"

"We're going to be leaving shortly. Rita's anxious to get home and see the kids, and I'm anxious to get back home myself."

"Think you might be coming back next year?" Carol inquired further.

"No. I doubt it. I'm sure we'll both be busy babysitting our new grandchild," he explained in a confident voice.

"I think we had better get going, Mother," Philip instructed. He had obviously had enough of this chit-chat and was in a hurry to get going.

"Goodbye, Carol," Kathy said, giving Carol one last embrace. "I'm leaving the house unlocked. Would you mind locking up later and keeping an eye on things for me until I decide what I'm going to do?"

Carol leaned forward, accepting Kathy's quick hug before stepping back, then giving her shoulders a squeeze before speaking. "Of course I will. Don't forget to call as soon as you get home and let me know that you've arrived safely."

"I will, I promise." Then turning toward Jimmy and looking deep into his eyes, she said, "Goodbye, Jimmy."

He embraced her, knowing it was over. "Bye, Kathy, I'll be thinking of you." He kissed her lightly on her cheek.

Kathy didn't reply. She picked up her overnight bag, walked around to the passenger's side, got into the car and waited for her son to take her home.

Carol stepped forward to give Philip a hug. "Have a safe trip."

"Thanks, I'll make sure mother calls when were safely home."

Philip quickly got into the BMW, started the engine, waved goodbye and headed down Dolphin Drive. As they drove away, Kathy was able to get a glimpse of Jimmy in her side view mirror, his figure growing smaller and smaller. She watched as he raised his hand and waved a final goodbye. She remained looking in the mirror until they turned onto Barefoot Bay Boulevard, when he completely disappeared from sight. She knew she would never see him again and realized it was the right thing for both of them.

As Jimmy headed for home, he had an empty feeling in the pit of his stomach, realizing that someone who had played such an important part in his life was gone forever. But he also realized a huge burden had been lifted from his shoulders, knowing with Kathy out of his life, Rita would never discover what they had done.

He knew now he had never been in love with Kathy, or she with him. Time had flown by, their lives had gone in different directions, and those years as teenagers, their brief affair, all these memories would remain just that, memories that would forever remain a part of a life that the two of them had lived through but was best left in the past.

CHAPTER 36

CHIEF BARRETT sat in his office working diligently on a Sudoku puzzle that was published in the Press Journal that morning. He'd just come back from having lunch at Bottoms Up and was lounging in his chair, stocking feet on the desk. Ray had learned when dealing with things beyond his ability, the best way to handle it was to ignore it. If he was patient enough, the problem usually faded away, then disappeared completely, so that's what he was doing.

He was willing to wait the Gagnon murder case out, push it to the back of his mind, thinking eventually people would find something else to occupy their minds. Unfortunately this was not to be. Ready or not, he was about to find himself being dragged back in.

Ray's first break came when he least expected it. He had no sooner discovered he'd screwed up the Sudoku puzzle, when Darcy came bursting into his office. "There's a woman from Vero Beach on the phone. She wants to talk to you," she said, sounding excited.

"Any idea who she is, or what she wants?" Ray asked, eyes squinting at the newspaper.

"No. She said she wanted to talk to whoever was in charge."

He shook his head. "Haven't I asked you before to screen my calls? Can't you see I'm busy? I can't be bothered talking to everyone who calls here," he scolded her while throwing the newspaper and pencil carelessly onto his desk.

Darcy glanced down at the paper. "You want me to tell her you'll call her back later when you're not so busy?" she asked, sarcastically.

"No. I'll handle it," he said, bending forward to pick up the phone.

"This is Chief Barrett. What can I do for you?" he growled into the mouth piece.

A high pitched, squeaky voice responded. "Are you the policeman that's in charge of that murder in Barefoot Bay?"

"I'm Chief Barrett," he said. "We have an ongoing investigation about a death in Barefoot Bay."

"Well, I was reading about the murder in the paper yesterday morning. It was Sunday's paper. I just got around to reading it," she said.

"What about it?"

"There was a picture of the guy that got killed and his wife on the front page."

The chief was aware of the article because he'd read the same one. The newspaper gave the story front-page coverage. In the center of the page were two large photos directly under the headline, "MURDER IN THE BAY."

One picture was of the Gagnon's house. Yellow tape wrapped around the driveway and front entrance. The other picture was of Mr. and Mrs. Gagnon posing together in a recently taken picture. Ray had seen the picture sitting on a shelf among other family portraits. Seeing the photo in the newspaper had him wondering how the reporter had managed to get the pictures out of the house for publication without his knowledge or approval.

"Yes, I know. I saw the article. Why are you so interested?"

"Well, ever since I saw those pictures, I've been thinking that I've seen that woman someplace before. It finally came to me last night."

"I take it you're talking about Mrs. Gagnon," he said.

"Yes, the wife of the guy that got murdered."

"So what are you getting at?" Ray asked, his patience growing short.

"What I'm getting at is I work at a motel down on the beach. That woman, Mrs. Gagnon, was here with some guy that rented a room on a couple of occasions. The man that registered for the room wasn't the same man whose picture was in the newspaper. It wasn't her husband she was shacking up with."

Ray quickly removed his feet from his desk and straightened up. He looked up at Darcy who hadn't left his office and was standing in front of his desk, popping her gum, listening to every word. She could tell from Ray's expression this call was important.

"Are you sure it's the same woman?"

"Positive! I've been working at the motel for several years. I remember faces. I'm positive it's the same woman!" she said.

Ray's eyebrows lifted. "Think you can identify the man she was with?" he asked.

"I'm sure I could. I've still got the registration cards. The automobile registration plate number was the same number he put on the cards; which isn't always the case. I think you could check with the registry and find out who owns the car."

Ray reached for a pen and piece of paper. "Could I have your name, please?"

"My name is Gail Koppel. I work at the Atlantic Breeze Motel on

Route A1A in Vero Beach."

"You said you still have the registration cards," he asked.

"Right here in my hand. I'm working at the motel now," she said.

"Can you tell me what name this man used when he registered?" he asked.

"He signed both cards, James Martin," she said.

Ray's eyes lit up; Mrs. Gagnon's old boyfriend. "Would it be possible for you to drop the registration cards off here at the station?" Ray asked.

"I'm at work. I can't leave. If you want them, you can come and get them, or I can put them in the mail."

Realizing it would take a couple of days before he received the cards if she mailed them, he reluctantly agreed to pick them up. "How long will you be at the motel?"

"I'm here to six."

"I'm on my way. I'll be there in an hour."

"I'll be here." Gail hung up without saying goodbye.

Darcy was still standing in front of Ray's desk, the sound of her snapping gum echoing off the walls. She knew something was up. "What was that all about?"

Darcy was the last person Ray wanted to share this information with. "I have to go out for a while," he said.

"Where are you going?" she asked, shoulders back, eyes narrowing.

While reaching under his desk for his shoes and looking up at her, he said, "I'll be back in a couple of hours. And another thing, I don't appreciate your hanging around my desk listening to my conversations. Why do I have to keep reminding you your job is to answer the phone, do the payroll?"

Darcy fumed but decided to keep her cool, at least for now. She needed to be in on this investigation. "What if someone calls for you? Where should I tell them you've gone? I thought we were working on this together, Ray? Tell me what the hell's going on," she persisted.

His laces tied, he grunted, "I'll be back in a couple of hours." He gathered up his keys off the desk before walking briskly out.

Darcy stepped back to let him pass and stood dumbfounded with her mouth wide open.

The air was unusually hot and humid for this early in March. The smell of diesel and gasoline exhaust saturated the air. His car's air conditioner had quit working, so he drove with the windows down. The car had been left with the windows rolled up, and it smelled like yesterday's garbage. He made a mental note to clean out his car and get the air-conditioner fixed before summer arrived. But the humid weather wasn't about to dampen Ray's enthusiasm about his first break in the case as he traveled south on A1A.

As surreal as this trip seemed, Ray was energized. He was on a mission, his first break, something he hadn't had before the call from the motel clerk. He had no reason to be optimistic, but he kept telling himself he would find out something today that would be vital in cracking the Gagnon murder case.

The Atlantic Breeze Motel wasn't difficult to locate. Chief Barrett arrived in less than an hour. When he walked into the motel's office, he observed Gail sitting at a desk, talking on the phone behind the waist-high counter; he thought she looked the part perfectly.

Looking up from the swivel chair, she raised her wait-a-minute finger and rolled her eyes at what she was hearing but didn't remove the phone from her ear. Minutes later, after Ray listening to a series of "uh-huhs" and "okays," Gail put her hand over the mouthpiece and whispered, "My mother."

Ray didn't appreciate waiting. He shifted his weight from his right foot to his left, trying to be patient. Finally he heard her say, "Ma, I gotta go. I've got a customer." She hung up and walked the few steps to the counter. In the same thin, high-pitched voice he recognized from their phone conversation, a voice that didn't quite go with the body, she said, "Sorry about that. My mother; she's seventy-five, doesn't have anything better to do, so, she calls me and talks my ear off."

Gail appeared to be a pleasant, easy going woman, but he hadn't driven all this way to talk about her mother, so he ignored her comment. "You Gail?" he asked, his degree of military efficiency fading immediately, feeling stupid for asking, because her nametag was plainly displayed on her ample chest.

"The one and only," she said, pointing to her nametag.

"I appreciate your calling. This information could be important," Ray said.

"I usually don't give out information on customers. We sometimes get people who'd just as soon not have anyone know they stayed here, if you know what I mean. But I thought under the circumstances, this was too important not to notify the police."

"Do you have the registration cards?" Chief Barrett's voice and vocabulary took on the same strong, no nonsense, military tone that he heard on TV police shows, where he got most of his investigating training.

Gail handed over the cards lying on the counter. "Right here," she said.

Ray glanced down, and there it was, his name, James Martin,

automobile license plate number from Massachusetts. "If you don't mind, I'm going to have to take the cards with me. I can mail them back once I'm done with them, if you'd like."

"No need. You can keep them. You might need them for evidence," she said.

"Can you tell me anything about this couple?"

"No. They only stayed for a couple of hours. No luggage. It was before noon when they checked in both times. You've got both registration cards," Gail said, nodding toward the cards that he was absentmindedly flicking with his thumb.

"They didn't leave anything behind by any chance?"

"Not that I'm aware of. If they left anything, the girl who cleans the rooms is supposed to turn it in. I don't remember her turning anything in," she said.

"I can't tell you how much I appreciate this," he said.

"Hope it helps. Like I told you, I don't like to get involved with our customers. But in the case of a murder, I felt I couldn't keep my mouth shut."

Ray kept his features uncommitted, trying not to show he was delighted and excited about walking out of the motel office with his first break in the case. "Thanks again. You've been a big help. I'll be in touch. If there's any reason I need to talk to you again, or if I need you to identify this James Martin, I'll let you know."

"If it's all the same to you, I'd rather not get involved," Gail said.

"Well, if I can help it, I'll keep you out of it. But if I need you to make a positive identification, I might not have any choice," Ray explained, then, walked out.

Driving back to Micco, north on A1A through Orchid Island, Ray was unable to believe his good luck. He enjoyed the smell of the salty air that carried a whiff of high tide whenever the waves broke over the white beach sand.

If Kathy Gagnon and Jimmy Martin were having an affair, and it certainly looked as if they were, there most likely was some connection between these romantic rendezvous and the murder of Mrs. Gagnon's husband. It looked like he had discovered a motive and the person or persons responsible. Now all he had to do was confront Jimmy Martin with the evidence, then see how he reacted. With any kind of luck, he might be able to solve this case before nightfall.

Ray was aware that Kathy Gagnon had gone back to Massachusetts.

He'd deal with Jimmy Martin first. If he got a confession, and if Mrs. Gagnon turned out to be in any way involved, he could always make arrangements to have her returned to Florida.

Ray had never talked to Jimmy Martin. The only time he had observed him was at the Kloskis house the night of the murder. He didn't look like the kind of person who would murder anyone. But he realized sometimes it's the ones you least expect, the quiet ones who surprise you. He was aware that when people became involved in these love triangles, anything could happen, including murder.

Ray had originally felt the murderer would have been the Greek, Pappas. Now there was a guy who actually looked like a man capable of murder—an arrogant bastard, an angry and pissed-off man fully capable of killing another human being.

Jimmy Martin, meek and timid, did not look like a murderer.

Ray continued driving, shaking his head, unable to believe that he had been wrong. But he wasn't about to count Pappas out, at least not until he had a chance to talk to Jimmy Martin.

CHAPTER 37

AFTER GETTING the mysterious phone call from the woman in Vero Beach, Darcy was unable to concentrate on her work. Ray had left the station like a bat out of hell. That call had to be important. She had been chewing and snapping her gum, while smoking one cigarette after another, anxiously awaiting his return. Something was up, and she wanted to know what the hell was going on.

When he finally returned and marched past her without giving her so much as a glance, going directly to his office, she was out of her chair like a shot, following him before he had a chance to close the door. Darcy needed to find out what he had discovered that he wasn't sharing with her.

He had two cards in his hands and a silly smirk on his face. She demanded an explanation. "What did you find out?"

"Nothing," he said.

"Nothing; like hell. You went all the way to Vero Beach, and you didn't find out anything? I might have been born at night, but not last night," she said.

"Let me put it this way —it's nothing that concerns you."

Ignoring his comment, she reached down and picked up the two registration cards Ray had dropped carelessly on his desk. "What are these?"

"None of your goddamn business; now give them to me," he commanded, his face twisting in anger.

Reading quickly, she said, "Motel registration cards! James Martin? Isn't he one of the people you wanted me to get his home town address? Is he involved in the murder?"

Ray reached over and swiped the cards out of her hand. "All right now, I've just about had enough of your interfering. No more questions, understand?"

"I'm just trying to help," she said.

"When I want your help, I'll ask. Until then, just do your job out front," he said.

Darcy was mad and getting madder by the minute. "No need to get all pissed off," she snapped, staring back at him with fire in her eyes.

"I'm not pissed off. I'm in the middle of something important. I don't need your interference, understand?"

"Okay."

"Good. Now that we understand each other, there's something I want you to do; get the telephone number of the Martins in Barefoot Bay. They're renters, so their number won't be in the directory. But if you call their neighbors, the Kloskis, I'm sure they have it."

Even after being scolded, Darcy wasn't one to be put off and wasn't budging until she got some answers. "Okay, but you had to find out something? Can't you at least tell me if this Martin fella is a suspect?"

Ray's head fell forward in defeat. "Please, Darcy, no more questions, just get me the goddamn number, please," he begged.

"Okay, I'll be right back," she said, then made an about face and left in a huff.

Once gone, Ray rolled his eyes to the ceiling. He had been aggravated to the point he was thinking about looking for another assistant but thought better of it. A body like she had would be hard to replace. All the while their heated conversation was going on; Ray kept glancing down at the registration cards on his desk and couldn't believe his good luck. If he could wrap this case up today, it sure would look good with the town fathers. *I might even ask for a raise.*

Several minutes later, Darcy returned with the Martin's telephone number. She tossed the paper carelessly onto his desk. "Here's the goddamn number," she said, and walked out, making sure she slammed the door just hard enough to let Ray know she wasn't finished with him yet.

Ray looked at the closed door and once again wondered why he put up with her, then remembered why. They certainly didn't have the typical boss-employee relationship, but they had actually become friends, so he was willing to put up with her unprofessional behavior; and having a great pair of tits certainly helped. Picking the phone out of its cradle, he pictured her bent over while wearing one of her loose fitting blouses and broke out in a satisfied smile while shaking his head.

Everything was quiet at the Martin's house. Jimmy was reading *USA Today,* relaxed and relieved that he would be going home in the morning. Rita was hurrying around getting packed for their trip. Before Phil was murdered, she had counted the days until she could see her children again. Now, with everything that was going on in Barefoot Bay, she was counting the minutes.

Just as Rita forced one suitcase closed and was in the process of snapping the latches, the phone rang. She hesitated, waiting to see if Jimmy would pick up. After the third ring, it became apparent he wasn't going to answer the kitchen phone, so she walked around the bed and picked up the extension on the night stand.

"Hello," she said.

"Hello. This is Chief Barrett with the Micco Police Department. Is this Mrs. Martin?"

"Yes."

"Mrs. Martin, is your husband at home?"

"Yes. He's in the other room. Would you like to talk to him?"

"Yes, if I could, please?"

Without leaving the bedroom, Rita put her hand over the mouth piece and hollered out through the open door, "Jimmy, there's a Chief Barrett from the Micco Police Department on the phone. He wants to talk to you."

Jimmy dropped the paper on the coffee table, got out of his chair and walked to the wall phone. "Hello," he said.

"Mr. Martin, this is Chief Barrett, Micco police. I hate to bother you so late in the afternoon, but I'd like to talk to you sometime today. Could you stop by the station?"

"You want to talk to me; what about?" Jimmy asked. His mind suddenly flashed back to his affair with Kathy, then he decided it couldn't possibly be that. "Does this have something to do with Phil's murder?"

"I'd rather not discuss this over the phone. I think it would be better if you came down to the station."

"I guess I can."

"I'd appreciate it."

"Where's the police station located? I'm not familiar with Micco," Jimmy asked.

"It's downtown; after you leave Barefoot Bay, go north on Route 1 for about two miles, then take S.R. 510 west until you get to the business district. You'll see the Town Hall on your right. Drive around to the back of the building. You can't miss it," the chief instructed.

Jimmy's mind again flashed back to Kathy. "What's this all about?" he asked.

"I'd rather we talk when you get here," Ray insisted.

There was a moment of awkward silence. "Okay. I'll be right there," Jimmy agreed.

Rita was listening to their conversation on the extension. "What do you suppose that's all about?" she asked, after hanging up and walking into the living room.

"I don't know. I can't imagine what the police could want to talk to me about. It must have something to do with Phil. Just routine questioning, I'm sure. I'd better go over there and find out what this is all about. There's no need for you to come," he said, hoping Rita would decide to stay home.

Rita was as curious as he was, and she wasn't about to be put off. "I'm going with you," she said.

They didn't have any difficulty finding the police station behind Town Hall. They parked next to an older Chevrolet station wagon. When they entered the building, they found an attractive young woman seated at a desk, talking on the phone while chewing gum and holding a cigarette casually between her fingers. Her head was turned away, but as soon as she heard the Martins enter, she ending her conversation. "Listen, I have to go," then slammed the phone down.

Getting up from her desk, her eyes moving back and forth between them, she said, "You must be the Martins. I'll tell Chief Barrett you're here," then quickly disappeared into the back office.

Darcy's voice was full of excitement. "They're here, Ray." She didn't have the slightest idea why Ray wanted to talk to the Martins, but the important thing was she knew she was finally going to get to the bottom of what the hell was going on.

"Okay; tell them to come in," he said, quickly clearing his desk, throwing outdated newspapers, coffee-stained Styrofoam cups, and crumbled sandwich wrappers into the wastebasket under the desk.

Darcy stuck her head into the reception room and announced, "You can come in now."

When Rita and Jimmy walked in, Ray stood and extended his hand, "Thank you for coming. I know it's late in the day, but I think this is important."

There was a brief hesitation, then Jimmy accepted it and gave the Chief's hand a brief squeeze before letting go, but said nothing. Darcy walked over and got a folding chair from next to the wall and placed it off to the side next to Ray's desk, so she'd be looking directly at the Martins. Darcy didn't want to miss any of what was about to take place.

The last thing Chief Barrett wanted was Darcy's interference. "Darcy, I won't need you for anything right now."

Darcy's shoulders tightened as if bracing for a blow. "You don't want me to stay?"

"No. Go back and finish whatever you were doing," he insisted, glaring at her.

"I wasn't doing anything important." She made no attempt at

leaving.

"Darcy, get out of here," Ray commanded.

Darcy looked shocked but immediately got up and walked out, fuming. Ray knew if she stayed, any information she heard would be all over the town of Micco before the sun went down. He didn't want anything getting out, at least not until he was sure that his suspicions were accurate.

Gesturing with an open hand, he said, "Have a seat," indicating the two chairs in front of his desk. Being face to face with Jimmy Martin, he was still having a hard time believing this man was capable of committing murder. He just didn't look like the type.

Once Darcy was safely out of the room, and the banging of drawers had stopped from the front office, Ray turned his attention back to Rita and Jimmy. "Sorry about that."

They didn't respond. They both sat motionless, waiting in anxious anticipation, Rita wanting to find out why they'd been asked to come here, Jimmy hoping it wasn't what he feared.

"I understand you're renting a house in Barefoot Bay," Ray said in a non-threatening, friendly voice.

"Yes. We've been here since the beginning of January," Jimmy said.

Leaning back in his swivel chair, the chief placed the tips of his fingers together like he was about to start praying, giving him an appearance of superiority. Then he brought his fingers to his lips, paused and said, "Do you like Florida?"

"It's okay, but I don't think we'll be back," Rita said. "I don't think Florida's for us."

"Rita misses the kids. We're going to have our first grandchild this June. I know I'll never be able to talk her into leaving once the baby's born," Jimmy added, glancing sideways at his wife.

"We're planning on going home tomorrow, and I can't wait," Rita mentioned enthusiastically.

"In that case, would you mind giving me your Massachusetts address and telephone number in case I need to contact you?" Ray said, picking up a pencil and paper from the top of his desk and handing them to Jimmy.

"Of course not, but what reason would you have for contacting us?" Jimmy asked as he filled out the information, then passed the paper back.

"I'm not sure I'll have to," Ray said, never taking his eyes off Jimmy, watching closely while he wrote down the information.

Ray had been playing good cop. A technique he'd read about someplace. "I'm sure the incident with Mr. Gagnon didn't do anything to boost Florida's image," Ray said.

"I'm still not over it," Rita said, shaking her head.

"I understand you were pretty close to the Gagnons," Ray stated, still watching Jimmy closely.

"Kathy was a school chum of mine. Rita only met the Gagnons when we came to Florida," Jimmy said, feeling uncomfortable with the subject and especially with the way Chief Barrett kept looking directly at him.

"Did you know the Gagnons were going to be here when you arrived?" Ray pressed on.

"No. I was really surprised to see Kathy," Jimmy answered.

"You said that you and Mrs. Gagnon were school chums back in high school. Isn't it true you've become more than just friends since being reunited here in Florida?"

"No. We dated occasionally during our junior and senior years, but nothing serious. After graduating, she went to college, and I went in the Army," Jimmy admitted, knowing Rita was now staring at him with interest.

Ray figured it was time for the bad cop. "I'm not talking about high school. Isn't it true you've been secretly seeing Kathy Gagnon here in Barefoot Bay?"

"Jesus Christ," Jimmy said. "No. Why would you ask a question like that?" he snapped, his voice forced and sounding insincere.

"So you deny it. You haven't been meeting her secretly in Florida," Ray said bluntly.

"I told you, no," Jimmy said, really upset now. "Why have you called us down here, Chief?" Jimmy asked. He was getting bad vibrations about this situation. He wanted to get on with whatever Chief Barrett was getting at.

"I received a call from a motel clerk down in Vero Beach earlier today. Are you familiar with the Atlantic Breeze Motel, Mr. Martin?" Ray said, placing the registration cards down on the desk in front of him.

Jimmy looked at the cards and felt his blood draining to his feet. He knew fear was written on his face, written for all to see, but he couldn't stop it. He knew what this information would do to Rita. Instinctively he picked up one of the cards, glanced at it briefly, realizing he had been caught lying, nervously placed it back on the desk.

"What's this all about?" Rita asked, picking up the other card and concentrated intently on what she was reading. Then she also placed the card back on the desk, while shifting her eyes back and forth between Chief Barrett and her husband, finally settling on Jimmy.

"I'm sorry you had to find out like this, Mrs. Martin." It was obvious from the look on Rita's face she had no idea what had been going on between her husband and Kathy Gagnon. "It seems that your husband has been spending time at this motel with Kathy Gagnon."

"Jimmy, what's this all about?" Rita asked, suddenly feeling sick to her stomach, pleading for an explanation. This was unexpected. When they'd arrived in Barefoot Bay, she didn't know what to expect. She certainly didn't expect this to be happening, didn't want this to be happening.

Jimmy was too upset to answer. He leaned forward, placed his elbows on his knees, and looked at Chief Barrett like he was asking for mercy. Any pretense of remaining calm was lost.

It was difficult for Ray to witness the anguish on Rita's face. He looked down at his desk, giving her time to compose herself. "I'm sorry, Mrs. Martin. But I have to follow every lead that involves anything to do with the murder case."

With the mention of Phil Gagnon being murdered, Jimmy immediately looked up and said, "I didn't have anything to do with Phil's death. I hope you don't think I had anything to do with it? Is that the reason you called us down here?"

When Rita suddenly realized what was being suggested, she lashed out. "My husband's no murderer! I don't know what went on between him and Kathy, but I'm telling you right now, Jimmy didn't have anything to do with Phil's murder." Rita spat out her words, behaving like a mother bear protecting her cub.

"I'm not accusing anybody of anything right now. I have to look into every situation that comes up involving this case," Barrett explained.

Ray always considered himself good at reading people. All during the questioning, he had studied Jimmy closely. Earlier when he had asked Jimmy to fill out the paper with their home address and telephone number, he noticed that Jimmy took the paper with his left hand and he wrote with his left hand. When he picked up the registration card off the desk, he used his left hand as well. There was no doubt Jimmy Martin was left-handed.

According to the autopsy report he had received from the sheriff's department a few days ago, they'd stated the bruises on the left side of Phil Gagnon's face could only have been administered by someone who was right-handed. They had concluded the pressure applied to the victim's neck was also applied by a right handed person, further confirming the murderer was definitely right-handed. This information could not be ignored. He was now uncertain if Jimmy Martin had anything to do with Phil Gagnon's murder.

Now that he had doubts about Jimmy Martin, he wanted to do

whatever he could to help with this uncomfortable situation he'd created between the Martins. "Honestly, I don't think your husband was involved in Gagnon's death, Mrs. Martin," Chief Barrett said.

Rita was sitting on the edge of her chair, nervously twisting a tissue, ready to get up and walk out as soon as the opportunity presented itself. "Then why did you bring us down here, if you didn't think he'd done anything wrong?"

"I had to make sure. When I got this information, I needed to check it out. After talking with both of you, I'm almost sure your husband had nothing to do with the murder."

"What do you mean by almost sure?" Rita said.

"Until I get to the bottom of this, I have to keep my options open. Although I don't believe your husband's involved," he repeated.

Rita wanted out of there as soon as possible. She wanted to get out of there and run away and hide. "In that case, is it all right if we go home? I'm not feeling very good right now," she said; her once olive brown skin now appeared almost snow white, her stomach in knots, struggling not to throw up.

"You can leave. I don't have any more questions," Ray said, looking at the anguish on both their faces and wishing he'd never called them in.

Rita and Jimmy both stood up and were about to leave when Jimmy asked, "We were planning on going home tomorrow. Is there any reason why we should stay?"

"For the time being, you're not being charged with anything, and I don't expect that you will be. There's no reason for you to stay," Ray assured them. "Have a safe trip," he added, feeling his throat constricting and finding it difficult to swallow.

The Martins were no sooner out of the office when Darcy rushed in. She stood hands on her hips, looked him straight in the eyes and asked the question. "What was that all about?" She'd been listening, ear stuck to the door, but unable to hear clearly what had transpired.

Ray was already out of his chair, looking drained, fatigued, and wiped out. "Nothing's going on! Now get back to work," Ray ordered roughly.

A delayed reaction to the interview came over Ray, and his hands began shaking. He felt like he was on the verge of a nervous breakdown. He needed a drink and he needed it now, and wasn't in the mood to put up with Darcy.

After listening to him lash out at her, Darcy rolled her lips inward, then pressed them into a hard line. She didn't have much of a poker face. It was easy to tell when Darcy was angry, sad, or unhappy. She was definitely angry and unhappy now. "Ray, how the hell can I help you, if I don't know what's going on around here?" she said through tight lips, fire in her eyes.

"I never asked for your help, and I don't want your goddamn help!" he informed her. "I'll be out for the rest of the day. I've got errands to run."

Today was definitely not one of Ray's better days. He had been on top of the world just a few hours ago, thinking he had cracked the case. Now he was back to square one. What he needed were a couple of cold beers to clear his brain. Brushing back his thinning gray hair, he placed his badge in the top drawer of his desk next to his gun and slid the registration cards from the motel in next. Without saying another word to Darcy he left the station, slamming the door behind him.

She was following him with her eyes, Ray was sure of it, and not until he left the building did they stop burning into the back of his head. Ray was on his way to Bottoms Up where the beer would put him in a mood where everything slowed down, and he would try to find a solution to his problems; the same place he always looked for answers to questions he couldn't figure out, at the bottom of a Budweiser. He knew the beer bottle would feel smooth, cool, and be full of courage, promise and wisdom.

Darcy remained standing with her hands still on her hips, mouth wide open, glaring at him, as he marched out the door. She was furious that Ray was excluding her from the biggest case that had ever taken place in the town of Micco and was seriously considering looking for another job. If he wasn't going to include her in these police matters, there wasn't much chance of her ever becoming a police officer, so what the hell was the sense in wasting her time working here?

CHAPTER 38

RITA SAT HARD against the passenger's side door, neither of them saying a word. There was no explanation from Jimmy, at least nothing she wanted to hear that would justify what he had done that would make the pain go away. She occasionally glanced at his face and saw a man she barely recognized. She was concerned about their future; that was if they still had a future. Rita could still hear the chief's words being replayed in her mind when he placed the motel registration cards on the desk, and she realized what he was insinuating. These things didn't happen in her world, maybe in other people's lives, but never in her wildest dreams had she expected it to happen in hers.

During the long ride back to Barefoot Bay that seemed to take forever, the silence hanging in the air was heavy, making it hard to breathe. Rita held a damp tissue in her lap and continued kneading it nervously until it was a shredded mess.

She wasn't the only one he'd been unfaithful to. Jimmy had also betrayed their children. Especially now with Elizabeth soon to be giving birth to their first grandchild. One thing was certain, if Jason or Elizabeth were to ever discover what their father had done, it would shatter the image they had of him and forever damage their love. As upset and hurt as she was, she had no intentions of ever telling them. She was going to make sure his betrayal remained buried deep in her mental closet, out of sight, so they would never find out.

Jimmy stared straight ahead, his vision blurred by the tears that were on the verge of falling. He was frightened. He knew once they arrived home, he had to face Rita. He didn't have any idea what he could say that would justify being unfaithful.

The car had no sooner stopped in the driveway when the passenger's door burst open and Rita jumped out, slamming the door behind her. She ran up the carport and disappeared into the house, feeling an uncontrollable urge to scream, throw things and indulge in a fit of hysteria.

As Jimmy watched Rita disappear through the door, he didn't want to follow. He emerged from the car and slowly marched up the driveway and entered the house. Rita was nowhere in sight. The bedroom door was closed. He felt relieved. He didn't feel he had the strength to face her.

Rita laid on the bed, hands clenched into fists, crying hysterically. She tasted the salt in the tears trickling down her cheeks and over her lips, eventually absorbed by the bedspread. She was consumed with self-doubts and overwhelmed with a broken heart. She was reliving the same guilty feeling that she'd felt years ago, that horrible night when her mother walked into her bedroom and found her father naked in her bed.

She felt sick inside as images flickered in her mind of his face, his long, straggling grey hair hanging over his ears, the stink of stale cigarettes and his alcohol breath stinging hot on her face. She could see his dead stare, hungry eyes leering at her and feel his dry, cold hands touching her in places that caused her to shudder in shame. She had suffered with these recurring nightmares of guilt her entire life; a soul-deep sense of shame that reached into the deepest places in her heart.

She had never told Jimmy about being sexually abused. It had always been a carefully guarded secret. She wondered if that had been a mistake. In many ways being raped was worse than being murdered. When you're murdered, it's over. He can't hurt you anymore. But when you're raped by someone who's supposed to love you, you can't ever forget. Never! It was impossible to block out the pain, erase it from your mind.

Rolling over, watching the ceiling fan slowly turning, her face stained with tears, Rita feared her demons were taking control once again, making her feel worthless and a failure as a wife. The things she had done were far worse than anything Jimmy had done, and she always believed she was damaged goods, unclean, and didn't deserve Jimmy's love.

She had never been able to put the physical and psychological torture she had lived through as a child behind her. It had been painful and difficult, being haunted in ways that most people could never understand. The frightening thing about these feelings were no matter how hard she tried, the memories never completely went away.

Rita was suddenly scared. It was her knowing that Jimmy loved her that made it possible for her to climb out of those deep, black holes of depression, where she occasionally had thoughts of suicide whenever she recalled the terrible things she had done. What would happen if Jimmy would leave, walk out of her life, never return?

She couldn't imagine life without him. She was determined not to let that happen. She had loved him for over thirty five years and wasn't going to lose him now. Frightened like she had never been frightened before, but committed to saving her marriage, she knew she had to fight with every bit of strength she possessed to reclaim the man she loved, or her life, marriage and future were doomed.

The time had come to face her demons. Slowly she swung her legs to the side of the bed and dragged herself up. She was lightheaded for a moment as she wiped her tears away with the back of her hand. She was frightened but determined as she took a moment to compose herself. Once the lightheaded feeling subsided, and she felt strong enough to go on, she took a deep breath, let it out, then slowly stood and walked to the bedroom door and silently opened it.

Jimmy was sitting in his chair, staring at the open newspaper. It was obvious he was staring at nothing. She watched the quivering of his mouth. A single lamp burned next to the chair, leaving the room in shadows. From the look on his face, she saw that he was consumed with heartache and pain like nothing he'd ever experienced before.

Rita took several steps, stopped, and spoke his name in little more than a whisper. "Jimmy," she said. He didn't hear her. He continued to stare blankly at the paper. She drew closer and, slightly louder this time, repeated his name. "Jimmy, I need to talk to you."

Not sure if he'd heard his name, he turned his head slowly. Upon seeing her standing there, he dropped the paper, brought his hands up and covered his face in shame. Unable to contain himself, he started crying, turning his face away, unable to look at her.

Without hesitation Rita went to him, falling to her knees. "I'm sorry, Jimmy," she said.

Jimmy was confused, unable to understand what she could possibly be talking about. He was the one who had been unfaithful. He was the one who had the affair and betrayed her. He tried to look at her but couldn't. He struggled to speak, but all he could do was stutter and stammer. Finally, with a great deal of effort, he managed to say, "I'm so sorry, Rita . . . I don't know what to say . . . I love you . . . I've never stopped loving you . . . Can you ever forgive me?"

Rita reached for him and placed her hand on the side of his face, forcing him to turn and look at her. Her eyes were puffed and sore from crying. She was behaving like a woman who was broken but trying desperately to be brave. "Jimmy, you've hurt me more than I could ever have imagined I could be hurt," she said softly.

"I know I have..." he started to say.

Raising her open hand, stopping him from saying anything more, she continued, "Listen to me; I love you. I know I haven't always been the wife I should have been, but I'm going to work hard at making it up to you." She hesitated, gasping to catch her breath before continuing. "But if you ever do this to me again, I'll never forgive you. I don't have the strength to go through this again. Do you understand what I'm saying?"

"So help me God, I never will."

"We're going to go home tomorrow and try to make everything like it was before we came to Barefoot Bay. We should never have come here. It's not going to be easy, but we have two beautiful children, and soon Elizabeth will have our first grandchild. I don't want anything to happen to destroy our family."

"How can anything ever be the same again? How can I ever face you or the children again? What are they going to think of me when they find out what their father has done; I'm so scared, Rita! I'm so scared I'm going to lose you! I wish God would strike me dead right now!"

"Is it because of me? Am I the reason you went to Kathy? I thought she was my friend, but I guess I was wrong. But what hurts most of all is, I feel I've failed as a wife. I haven't been the wife I should have been, but I promise to try harder," Rita said in a quivering voice.

"It wasn't because of you. I don't understand what could have made me do something so stupid. You're the best wife any man could have. I've been sitting here praying that you'll give me another chance. I don't want to live without you."

Rita put her arms around him. Jimmy surrendered himself to her. Her voice became steady as she continued. "I love you with all my heart. We're going to work this out. I don't want to live without you, either."

Finally having the courage to look deep into her eyes, Jimmy lifted his head. When their eyes met, they both could see their love was strong enough to carry them through this. Together they would try once again be the family they had been before they arrived in Barefoot Bay.

Rita looked past Jimmy at the clock on the wall. It was now nearly seven-thirty. The sun had gone down, and the room had turned gloomy when Rita stood, then helped Jimmy out of the chair. Stepping back, she looked up at him with tear-stained eyes and said, "I'm going to bed, Jimmy. We have to get an early start tomorrow. We don't belong here. I want you to take me home."

"I promise I'll spend the rest of my life trying to get you to forgive me," he said.

"I already have. In order to make everything right between us, it has to start with my forgiving you. And one more thing; I don't want the children to ever hear a word about what happened here in Barefoot Bay, do you understand?"

"Yes. I don't think I could ever face them if they knew," he said.

Rita gave him a quick kiss on his cheek, then disappeared into their bedroom.

Jimmy spent the night sitting in his chair. His mind and heart raced.

He would endure the longest and loneliest night of his life; unable to sleep, trying to sort everything out, knowing he'd allowed his physical attraction for Kathy to severely damage his marriage. Rita had never been anything but a devoted, understanding wife and mother, ready to help anyone in need. Everyone adored her. He had almost destroyed everything. Their lives were about to change. Nothing would ever be the same again. He was sure of it. But he was determined to do everything in his power to right the wrong he had caused.

In his mind he kept playing the *if only* game: if only they hadn't come to Florida; if only Kathy hadn't been here when they arrived; if only he hadn't run into her at the bagel shop; if only, if only, if only kept repeating itself over and over again in his mind. Jimmy prayed in time he would gain Rita's forgiveness. She had said she forgave him, but he knew he would spend the rest of his life working to regain her respect. He prayed somehow their marriage would return to the security and comfort they'd enjoyed before he had behaved so foolishly, but doubted it ever would.

At exactly 7:15 the next morning with the sun rising above the edge of the tree line, partially obscuring the faint glow of morning, Jimmy and Rita Martin drove through a thick blanket of white fog heavy with moisture from the warm Indian River, making driving difficult. They passed through the security gates at Barefoot Bay completely different people than when they had arrived in January.

Rita, painfully aware that her life had forever changed, felt emotionally brittle like a pane of cracked glass that could shatter under the slightest strain. She was aware the feeling of security she once had in that other life, a life she couldn't quite remember or go back to, where she had felt safe, had been breached of trust and was now gone forever. Her anger had subsided, and she didn't feel the urge to lash out at Jimmy. But when she had told him she had forgiven him, she hadn't been completely truthful.

She turned and looked out the side window and knew she would never get over his betrayal, because ever since hearing what he had done in the police station, she had been weeping inside like an open faucet. She knew she would never completely forget, and there would always be some feelings of resentment buried deep inside.

Jimmy was sick to his stomach thinking of his family, at least the one he used to have. He squeezed the steering wheel, his jaw rigid, finding it impossible to breathe freely, knowing the feeling of trust and security he had shared with Rita was damaged. Although she had said she had, he realized she would never completely forgive him for the terrible sin he had committed. He was wondering if he would ever be able to look at Elizabeth and Jason again without thinking how he almost destroyed the family he loved.

Looking in the rear view mirror, Jimmy watched Barefoot Bay fading into the background and wished he'd never come to Florida and knew he would never return.

CHAPTER 39

AFTER THE INTERVIEW with the Martins turned out so badly, and the way he had blown up at Darcy, Ray was in a foul mood and couldn't wait to get to Bottoms Up. He intended on bellying up to the bar and doing some serious drinking—the kind a man does when he wants to forget.

The barroom was nearly full when he arrived, but he noticed a stool at the end of the bar was unoccupied. He walked over, looked for Sandy and located her at the other end of the bar, pouring a draft beer. She turned and saw him staring. As soon as she finished ringing up the sale, she nodded her head in his direction, bent over and grabbed a Budweiser out of the cooler.

"Give me a shot of Jack Daniel's," he instructed as soon as she arrived.

Sandy's face dropped. "Jack Daniel's, what's the occasion?"

"None of your business," he said.

"Someone's in a pissed off mood," she said, while reaching for the whiskey bottle on the shelf behind her. "What's new with the murder case, Hon?" she asked, ignoring his unfriendly attitude.

That was exactly what Ray didn't come here to talk about. He knew the town was buzzing with questions, but he'd come here to forget. The last thing he wanted to do was discuss it with Sandy. "Nothing's new. If it's all the same with you, I really don't want to talk about it." When he spoke, he looked directly at her without blinking; leaving no doubt the subject was closed.

Anyone else would have known enough to back off, but Sandy wasn't one to be easily intimidated. "For Christ sake, Ray, it's been almost a week since the murder. You must have found out something by now."

"I told you, I don't want to talk about it. Do me a favor and leave me alone," Ray demanded, tilting his head back and downing the whiskey in one gulp.

Sandy glanced down the length of the bar and realized she was falling behind. Several customers were looking anxiously in her direction. "Okay, Hon, have it your way," she said, then walked away. With a full bar, she didn't have time to argue with him right now.

While staring at the brown bottle cradled in his hands, Ray slowly began peeling the Budweiser label off with his thumbnail. He went over what his investigation had uncovered so far, which was nothing. The more he thought about it, the more he realized he was in over his head. And the last thing he needed, or wanted, was for anyone to be asking a lot of stupid questions, trying to get him to give answers he didn't have.

Ray was here to forget. But things weren't working out that way. After drinking for several hours, the more he tried to forget, the more the murder case kept popping up in his mind. He grew more frustrated and depressed with each drink. He'd come here with one intention in mind and that was to drink enough, so this whole uncomfortable situation would disappear, and he didn't care how long, or how many beers it took.

It was just before midnight when he finally staggered out of Bottoms Up. Driving down Route 1, he was as drunk as he had ever been. Everything in front of him appeared to be moving in slow motion as he watched his headlights struggling to break through a tunnel of dense fog. Finally, after weaving back and forth, nearly driving off the road several times, he managed to pull his car into his driveway.

Safely home, he attempted to get out of his car, but found he'd driven too close to the side of his trailer home. When he opened the driver's side door, the door kept banging into the side of the building. Realizing what the problem was, he decided to crawl across the seat and exit from the passenger side. When he stretched over and pushed the door handle down, it unexpectedly sprung open, causing him to lunge forward, sending him crashing onto the hard packed gravel driveway with a painful thud.

His head exploded with a sudden flash of light and a piercing ringing. The world went completely black. He rolled over in a daze, unable to understand why everything was suddenly upside down. Slowly the stars gradually came into view. With a lot of effort, he managed to grab onto the side of the open door and pull himself up onto his feet. After several minutes, waiting for the dizziness to pass, he felt confident enough to stagger over and leaned against the side of the house. His hand went to a throbbing spot on his skull, where he felt moist, sticky blood trickling down the side of his face. After wiping his hand on his pant leg, he slowly inched his way up the three steps, while slapping at a swarm of mosquitoes viciously attacking his bleeding wound.

Safely on the deck, he opened the door leading into his house and was immediately confronted by Elvis. When the dog saw him, he did a quick lap around the kitchen, his nails sliding on the tile floor, then ignoring Ray, went bounding out into the darkness, heading for the woods.

Ray snapped the kitchen light on. It took a minute for his eyes to adjust to the brightness. He staggered over to the refrigerator to check his supply. Two cases of ice cold Budweiser's were waiting inside. On the kitchen counter sat an unopened bottle of Jack Daniel's, a Christmas present from Darcy that would not remain unopened for long. Satisfied he had enough booze; he grabbed a cold beer from the refrigerator, popped the lid and began pouring the refreshing liquid non-stop down his throat.

While driving home, Ray had decided he needed some time off from work. Get away from everything and everybody. And that's exactly what he intended on doing. Seeing no sense in waiting until tomorrow to call Darcy and inform her of his plan, he went looking for the phone book.

When he pulled the counter drawer out, looking for the directory, it came out faster than expected, sliding off its runners, spilling the contents all over the floor. Frustrated, Ray took the empty drawer and threw it across the kitchen, smashing it against the wall just below the velvet black panther painting over the couch. Getting down on his hands and knees, he searched until he found the phone directory, and with blurry eyes, fingered through it until he located Darcy's number. Struggling to stand, he leaned against the wall and began stabbing at the telephone buttons with his index finger. He found it amusing the way the numbers kept moving, causing him to make two calls that turned out to be wrong numbers. After listening to aggravated, sleepy people rant and rave about being disturbed at this late hour, he finally, on the third attempt, got it right.

The phone went unanswered for several rings. Then finally, "Hello," Darcy said, sounding groggy.

"Darcy? Darcy is that you?" Ray yelled into the phone.

"Yeah, Ray?"

"This is Ray, Darcy. I'm gonna be sick tomorrow. I won't be at work tomorrow," he explained, slurring his words, while the room began spinning.

It had been a long time since she'd gotten one of these calls, but Darcy had gotten enough of them to know what was going on. These conversations usually started out by Ray telling her he was taking time off. Gradually the conversation would turn. He would begin telling her how attractive she was, then, depending on how drunk he was, he would claim he love her.

She had absolutely no interest in him. Drunk or sober, he was just her boss, and these calls in the middle of the night were a pain in the ass. She was hoping this wasn't going to be another one of his long, boring I love you calls. She could tell he was stoned, and she was in no mood to listen to his bullshit at this late hour.

"Sounds like you've had a few, Ray," Darcy said. "And you don't have to yell. I'm not deaf."

"No. I told you I'm gonna be sick."

"You're gonna be sick all right. Sounds like you're already pretty sick." Darcy, still upset about the way he'd treated her earlier, now just wanting to get the call over with.

"I'm gonna be sick, that's all," he repeated, slurring his words badly.

"All right Ray, I get the message. Get to bed. I'll see you Thursday," she said, slamming the phone down.

Realizing his beer was empty; Ray threw the empty can in the direction of the wastebasket next to the sink, but missed. Ray watched it bounce off the wall and roll around the floor, before it came to rest in the corner next to the stove. He had no intention of taking Darcy's suggestion about going to bed. There was plenty of beer in the refrigerator, and he intended to break the seal on the Jack Daniels. It had been a long time since he went on a bender. He was definitely in the mood now. He staggered over to the refrigerator. Reaching in, he got himself another Budweiser; he pulled the tab and began pouring the beer down his throat.

Hearing Elvis scratching and whining at the door, Ray staggered over and opened it. Having taken care of business, the dog came bounding in wagging his tail, excited to see his master. Ray slammed the door shut. Elvis unexpectedly jumped up, putting both paws firmly on his chest, knocking him down. Ray thought that was hilarious. Sitting on the floor, he said, "Whaddaya say, Elvis? I think I'm gonna get hammered. Whaddaya think about that?"

Elvis cocked his head to one side and appeared to be listening. After waiting a minute and getting no response, Chief Barrett figured Elvis obviously thought it was a good idea.

With plenty of beer in the refrigerator, a fifth of whiskey on the kitchen counter, and no work tomorrow, Ray began what was going to be two days of serious, non-stop drinking.

Darcy expected Ray to return to work no later than Thursday

morning. When he hadn't showed up by ten o'clock Friday, she began calling his house. After several attempts and not getting any response, she was concerned. There was no doubt he was drunk when he called the other night, but she figured he should've sobered up and been back at work by now.

After 11 o'clock had rolled around and she still hadn't gotten in touch with him, she decided to take a ride over to his house and see what the hell was going on. Patrolman Callahan was scheduled to begin his shift at noon. As soon as he walked in shortly before 12 o'clock, Darcy explained her concerns and plans to check up on their boss.

"Andy, I'm glad you're here. I haven't been able to get in touch with Ray all morning. I'm starting to get worried."

"He hasn't called in?"

"No. When he called my house the other night he sounded drunk. He's called in drunk before, but he's never stayed out this long without checking in. When I call his house, I haven't been able to get an answer."

"If you want, I'll take a ride over. See what's he's doing," Andy volunteered.

"Did you see his car at Bottoms Up while on patrol last night?"

"No. I drove through the parking lot. There was the usual crowd, but I didn't see his car."

"Do me a favor. Watch the station until I get back. There's not much happening," Darcy said, grabbing her car keys and heading for the door.

"Take your time," he said.

The road leading to Ray's trailer home is directly off Route 1. It's no more than a stretch of dirt that runs through a tunnel of Banyan trees with run down mobile homes scattered along the sides. Darcy noticed several homes had abandoned cars sitting on blocks, surrounded by rusted automobile axles lying in knee-high weeds.

She pulled into Ray's gravel driveway with shallow, hard packed ruts, and parked behind his car. She didn't like what she saw. His Ford Focus was parked at an awkward angle and extremely close to the house. The passenger's side door was wide open. She shut her engine off and slowly got out and began looking around. Except for the haphazard way Ray's car was parked, everything appeared normal.

There were no car sounds, no barking dog sounds. She stood still for a moment, listening to the rustling sound of the breeze moving through the trees and watched as crows circled in the sky above. The only other sounds were from a lawn mower off in the distance that diminished as it went behind a house.

Slowly she walked up the three steps onto a shaky wooded deck.

The midday air was hot and humid, despite a slight breeze. She noticed t-shirts, boxer shorts and skinny dish towels hanging on a clothesline attached to the corner of the house that ran to a nearby palm tree. Cupping her hands to the sides of her face to cut the glare, she leaned forward and looked through the kitchen window, startling Elvis, who barked once, twice, three times, *yark, yark, yark*, then went quiet.

She could see Ray lying motionless on the floor. He looked like he could be dead. Without hesitating, she opened the unlocked door that squeaked on its hinges and stepped inside. The musty smell of stale beer, mildew, dirty laundry, and urine made her gag, forcing her back outside. She needed to get fresh air into her lungs before making another attempt at going back in. Elvis suddenly appeared from nowhere, looking raged, barked once, *yark,* and almost knocked her over, eager to get outside and into the woods.

Her eyes began watering. Taking a tissue from her pocket, she covered her mouth and nose and made her way back inside for a better look. Ray was face up on the floor. She noticed a stream of dried blood running down the side of his face; thinking he was seriously hurt, she was about to call an ambulance, but decided against it. If he was just drunk, having the Chief of Police taken away drunk in an ambulance would not look good.

She noticed a dark stain running from his crotch, down his leg, that smelled like he had pissed his pants, which he had. Disgusted with the sight of him, Darcy walked over and kicked him gently in the ribs, then waited. Getting no response, she kicked him again, but this time much harder. He groaned, then, slowly opened his eyes. Darcy was no more than a blurred image. He made an attempt to speak, but couldn't make any words come out of his mouth.

He tried to get up. Staggering like a boxer, who'd taken one punch too many, moaned, wavered, then he collapsed back onto the floor. After two more attempts, and still unsuccessful, he gave up and rolled onto his stomach. Ray wanted to go back to sleep, Darcy wasn't about to allow it. She kicked him again, harder than the last time.

"For Christ sake, Ray, wake up. What the hell's the matter with you? This place smells like a shit house," she complained.

"Go to hell," Ray mumbled into the floor.

He smelled so bad, she was hesitant to touch him, but figured she had to get him up. Reluctantly and with a great deal of effort, she managed to turn him over onto his back. "Come on, Ray, party's over. Time to get up," she ordered.

"Fuck you!" he mumbled, his voice barely audible.

She was sick of his bull shit. She was tempted to walk out and leave him right where she had found him, wallowing in his filth, but reconsidered. "Come on, Ray, I don't have all goddamn day. Get your ass off the floor; time to sober up."

With Darcy's assistance, his head wobbling on his shoulders like a puppet's, he managed to get up and stumble onto one of the chairs next to the kitchen table, his head collapsing onto the Formica table top with a thump, echoing off the kitchen walls.

"Come on, Ray, stay awake. You have to get into the shower and sober up."

"Fuck you," Ray mumbled again.

"Say that one more time and you'll think those other kicks I gave you where love taps."

The smell inside the house was overwhelming. Pinching her nose with her fingers, she tried breathing through her mouth while she went around opening all the windows. After every window had been opened, she began picking up the empty cans that seemed to be everywhere, putting them in a large green trash bag she'd found under the kitchen sink. Taking one look at where Elvis had crapped in the corner and a puddle of pee next to the stove, she decided they were going to stay right where they were. There was just so much she was willing to do. Picking up dog shit and wiping up Elvis's piss wasn't going to happen.

Beer cans were all over the place. She found empty cans on the floor in the bathroom and scattered all over the kitchen table next to a near empty bottle of whiskey she'd given him at Christmas. She decided there would be no whiskey for Christmas next year. She picked up several empties from the top of his bureau, among outdated catalogs, a few "Field & Stream" magazines, receipts from paid bills, losing lottery tickets, and loose change. Removing the two empty Budweiser cans she found in his bed between the sheets, she wondered how anyone could live in such filth.

"You scared the shit out of me. I thought you were dead when I walked in," Darcy said.

Ray had managed to lift his head off the table. He was starting to make sense out of what was going on. His head was pounding, his hands shook, and he felt a terrible pain in his side, like somebody had kicked him.

Realizing Darcy was trying to help, he mumbled, "Sorry. I guess I had a couple too many beers."

"Couple too many beers? I'd say it was more than a couple. Do you know what day it is?"

"What day is it?"

"Today's Friday. You've been locked up in this house drinking for three days."

"Friday?"

"Yeah, Friday; now get off your ass and get into the shower. You stink. I can't spend my whole day here cleaning up and babysitting you."

Ray conceded, looking down at his soiled pants, embarrassed by what he'd done.

Suddenly his stomach started to churn. He was about to throw up. Almost tripping over the broken drawer on the floor, he nevertheless managed to make it into the bathroom. Falling to his knees, he wrapped his arms around the toilet and began throwing up several stale beers. His eyes began watering and the smell of puke made him sicker. Then, with two final wrenching heaves, he began coughing before spitting his mouth clean.

With a lot of effort he managed to stand, took a moment to steady himself, then staggered into the bedroom and stripped off his filthy clothes, throwing them on the floor with his other dirty clothes. Finding a used towel on top of the bureau, he stumbled back into the bathroom and got into the shower. The faucets squeaked and the pipes vibrated when he turned on the water as cold as he could stand it. His legs began to shake as he watched the water running red from the dried blood from his head wound. He cupped his hands and began splashing the cold water onto his face.

When Ray emerged from the shower he looked in the mirror at his skeletal body, bloodshot eyes and ghostly complexion. He shook his head in disgust at the image looking back at him. Opening the medicine cabinet, he found the Alka-Seltzers and shook out two tablets. He dropped them into a glass, added water, and watched the tablets sizzle until they disappeared, then, drank his medicine, hoping it might help him survive.

While he was in the shower, Darcy looked for clean sheets, but found none, so, she remade the bed with the same dirty sheets Ray had been rolling around in the last three days. She'd picked up all the empty cans she could find and took the large green overflowing trash bag out to the utility shed. With the exception of Elvis's messes, which remained right where he made them, the house looked as good as she intended to make it.

By the time Darcy returned from the shed, Ray was in bed and sleeping soundly. Elvis had returned from outside and began following her around the house, giving a series of high pitched whines. Finding a bag of his dog food under the sink, she filled his metal bowls with water and food. Darcy glanced around the kitchen one last time, noticing the counter drawer on the floor, bent over and picked it up. After attempting to slide it back onto its runners, she discovered it was warped and no longer fit; she placed it on the counter, shook her head, and walked out the door, happy to be the hell out of there.

It was shortly after dark when Ray woke up, shaking and shouting. He bolted up in bed and began rubbing frantically at his face. "Jesus!" he screamed. "Get off me!"

"Spiders!" he shouted, his voice echoing off the walls. "Fucking spiders," he sobbed, large tears rolling down his cheeks. After a few minutes he began to calm down, though he continued to weep deep sobs. "Oh, those fucking spiders," he mumbled. "I must be going crazy."

He began rocking back and forth, shaking all over, the itching was unbearable as he franticly slapped at the spiders crawling on his body, on the sheets and walls. "I've got to quit. I can't keep going through this."

These nightmares were becoming more and more frequent, insistent, irritating and maddening. He realized he had a problem. There was no longer any doubt, he needed help. He was going to join the local chapter of AA. This was something he had considered doing in the past, but he had always changed his mind and never followed through. This time would be different.

"Yes, I'm gonna join AA," he promised himself before pulling the sheets up to his chin and closing his eyes, hoping and praying the spiders would not attack again.

CHAPTER 40

FOR TWO DAYS and two nights, Ray fought the urge to have a drink. The previous week was now just a fuzzy blur. When he woke up Saturday morning the slightest movement in bed caused a wave of nausea, his head hurt so badly he didn't dare move, not even an inch. He remembers Darcy was at his house. He also remembers her finding him passed out on the kitchen floor, his pants soaked with urine. The humiliation and embarrassment he would suffer when he sees her later this morning at the station, isn't anything he's looking forward too.

It was now Monday morning. His hangover was behind him. He felt great. He hadn't had a drink since . . . he wasn't sure, maybe Thursday? He was feeling healthy now, and he liked the feeling. It's too bad he didn't feel healthy when he drank. He felt good then, but not healthy. But that was all in the past. It was a new day and a new Ray. He was going to quit, and this time he meant it. He had been thinking all weekend about joining AA, but changed his mind. He decided he didn't need their help. It was just a matter of making up his mind to stop, which he had, then, doing it.

While driving to the station, he kept thinking about the reception Darcy was sure to greet him with. Pulling into the parking lot behind Town Hall, he noticed her silver station wagon parked in its usual spot. Getting out of his Focus, he walked into the station and found her sitting at her desk wearing a blouse that came up to her neck. Not a good sign. Smoke was drifting up from the cigarette lying in the ashtray on the desk. "Good morning, Darcy," Ray said, his voice sounding strained.

Darcy didn't answer, didn't even look up. It was obvious she was upset. Ray pretending it was just another work day; asked her, "Darcy, I forgot to stop for coffee; do me a favor and run out and get me one."

The words were no sooner out of his mouth, when, he realized he had made a terrible mistake. "What do I look like, your servant? It's not enough that I cleaned up that pig pen you live in, now I'm expected to run out and get you coffee. I'm just supposed to answer the phone and do the paper work, remember? Isn't that what you told me last week?" she spat out, glaring at him. "And another thing, I really think you should do something about your drinking."

"That's all in the past," he said.

"I hope so. I've never seen anybody as drunk as you were. When I found you, you were passed out, piss stains running down your pants. You looked and smelled like some homeless alcoholic living on the streets," she spat out, fire in her eyes.

Embarrassed, he looked down and away. "I don't know what got into me. Trust me, I've learned my lesson I'll never do that again." He hesitated, then, continued, "Look Darcy . . . I know it's been rough around here lately. I appreciate your coming over and helping out. I've been kinda in a bad mood lately, and I apologize for the way I've been acting. I've got a lot on my mind with the murder case."

Her expression softened. "How come you never tell me what's going on around here? I know you have a lot on your mind, but I can help if you'll let me."

Having her help was the last thing Ray wanted. "I know you want to help. I'll be sure to keep you informed from now on."

She shook her head. Thinking it would do no good to continue being angry, she asked, "Just a coffee, or do you want a bagel, too?"

He was happy to see her attitude changing. "Why don't you get me a plain bagel with cream cheese, and get yourself something, too," he said, nodding toward the ten dollar bill in his hand.

"Okay, so you promise to let me know what's going on from now on?" she asked.

"Yes."

She picked up her car keys off her desk and snatched the money out of his hand. "You better. I'll be right back," she said and went marching out of the office.

After she left, Ray went into his office and collapsed in his swivel chair. He leaned his head back, trying to remember where he was with the murder case. It didn't take long before he realized he was no better off today than he was before talking with Jimmy Martin. The only positive thing to come out of the Martin interview was he'd eliminated him as a suspect. This left Pappas. He was the only other logical choice. After Darcy got back, and he finished his coffee, Ray was planning on going to the Pappas house and having a talk with Scooter Pappas, and see what if anything, he could find out.

After breakfast, Betty slipped into a revealing two-piece bathing suit and headed for the patio out back to work on her tan. Now, whenever she thought about Phil, which was most days, turning it around in her head, the feeling of being used and mistreated was no longer unbearably painful. All that remained now was just a dull, bearable heartache, reminding her of how stupid she had been.

She was reading the John Grisham novel "The Summons," and relaxing on the lounge chair when Scooter came home from his softball game. She could tell by the look on his face he was in a foul mood and about to spoil what had been, until now, a quiet, relaxing morning. It didn't take long before she realized how right she was.

"I can't figure out what's the matter with me. I haven't gotten a decent hit in three games. We're in third place now," he said through tight lips as he collapsed in the chair across from her.

Scooter was the team's star player. Lately he had gone into a terrible slump. The whole team looked to him for leadership. When he was playing well, the whole team played well. When he went into a slump, which he was now in, the rest of the team seemed to fall apart.

"It's only a game. Why do you let it get you so upset?" Betty asked.

He didn't immediately answer. Scooter sat massaging his temples, staring straight ahead at nothing in particular. "We lost eight to six. This is the third game we loss in a row," he said.

Watching him closely, Betty could see he was having one of his migraine headaches. "Still getting those headaches?"

He nodded. "Yeah, I think it's my eyes. I have a hard time seeing the ball, never mind hitting it. Maybe I'll go to the eye doctor when we get back home."

"Why wait until you get home? It could be something more serious than your eyesight. The sooner you have yourself looked at, the better," she suggested.

"I don't think it's serious. Besides, our insurance doesn't cover us in Florida, unless it's an emergency."

"So go to the emergency room and tell them you think you're having a stroke. They'll check you out. The insurance will cover it," she explained.

He didn't have any intentions of going to the hospital. He'd never been seriously sick a day in his life, and refused to believe he had a problem now. "I'm not having a stroke," he answered sharply. "I've been like this for a while now. A few more weeks won't make any difference."

Betty wasn't so sure. She'd been reading articles on the warning signs that appeared when someone was a candidate for having a stroke. Scooter had been complaining lately of getting headaches for no apparent reason. He'd just mentioned his vision was blurred. If that wasn't enough to convince him to see a doctor, his feeling tired all the time, along with complaining about weakness on the right side of his body, especially his arm should have been enough to convince him.

But, she decided if he wasn't concerned, why should she be? "You can do whatever you want. I still think you should have yourself looked at," she concluded, then went back to reading.

Feeling miserable, he decided Betty should join him, and wasn't about to let her off the hook that quickly. He unexpectedly asked, "Have you heard anything new on Phil's murder?"

Her mood changed. "Haven't heard a thing," Betty said, glaring at him, not liking the question, knowing what was coming.

"If you had to make a guess, who do you think killed him?"

"How the hell do I know?" she spat out, returning back to her book. "Just shut up and leave me alone."

Scooter never passed up the chance to ruin her day. He knew how easy it was to upset her with the mere mention of Phil Gagnon's name. She tried to pretend she wasn't interested, but he could see her fuming behind the book. "I'm serious, Betty. Who do you think murdered the stud of Barefoot Bay?"

It wasn't enough that he was in control during these confrontations; more important, he wanted to make damn sure she knew it. Knowing he had this kind of power only served to stimulate him. "You know what, I'm glad the bastard got what was coming to him. I'm sure he must have been cheating on Kathy, screwing around with some guy's wife; when a man fucks with another man's property, he deserves what he gets," he said, never taking his eyes off her.

"Is that what a wife is? A man's property?" she asked, not liking the direction their conversation was going in.

"Yes."

She looked over her book with disgust in her eyes. "Can't you talk about something else? Even better, shut up and leave me alone."

Scooter wouldn't let it go. He had gotten to her, and he knew it. "I think half the women in the Bay had their sights set on him, including you. It was only a matter of time until he screwed around with the wrong guy's wife."

Betty raised a hand above her eyes, shading her face from the sun. "What's that supposed to mean?" she said, snapping her book closed.

He leaned forward in his chair. "What . . . do you think I'm blind? I could see the way you looked at him. You couldn't take your eyes off him. Don't deny it," he insisted.

They held a five-second staring contest. "Are you crazy? I was never interested in Phil," she lied, speaking faster and with a higher pitched voice than usual. Unable to return his stare for long, she lost her nerve and looked away, feeling a knot growing in her stomach. She felt like a child that knew she was about to get punished.

Scooter sat quiet for a moment, then, "I'm not stupid, you know," he lashed out, his eyes unblinking.

Did he know? At first she thought he was just trying to upset her, but suddenly his personality had gone from teasing to angry, and it showed as his eyes became small and hard. She was fairly sure he was just guessing, trying to see what her reaction would be. She forced herself to stay calm, although her heart was pounding wildly in her chest like a jackhammer.

In as steady a voice as she could muster, she said, "You can believe anything you want. I don't care what you think."

"Well, it looks like little Betty is upset," he said, mocking her. "Well, it really doesn't make any difference now, does it? It's funny how some things work out. Someone like Phil goes through life thinking he's got the world by the ass, thinking he's got it made, and the next thing you know, he's dead. Of course you still have your gay girlfriend Carol if you ever decide to switch teams," he said, then sat back and watched her reaction.

"What the hell are you talking about now? I swear, sometimes I think you're losing your mind," Betty hollered back.

Scooter shook his head. "I just figured you might want to try something different now that Phil's gone," he continued, enjoying how much Betty hated it when he purposely tormented her; especially since she had little choice except to tolerate his cruel remarks.

"Why do you always have to be so mean? You don't know what you're talking about. I never was interested in Phil. And what's Carol got to do with anything?"

"Nothing, but are you trying to tell me that Carol's not a dyke? Just look at her. If she's not a lesbian, my name's not Scooter."

"So what if she is? She's my friend, and I think the world of her."

Betty couldn't deny what Scooter was saying. She'd thought the same thing herself about Carol. As far as his comment about switching teams, she thought being on Carol's team surely couldn't be any worse than the team she was now on, but she kept quiet. Arguing with him was a waste of her time, breath, and energy.

"I was just thinking maybe you two would make a nice couple, that's all," Scooter said with a hearty laugh.

Their eyes locked. Betty again looked away first. She had had enough. She rose quickly to her feet. "I'm not going to sit here any longer and listen to any more of your bullshit!"

She knew she needed to get away. She threw the novel on the

wrought-iron-and-glass coffee table next to the lounge chair and walked into the house, leaving Scooter sitting alone with a satisfied look on his face.

What Betty wasn't aware of, was, Scooter had followed her. She had just walked into the bedroom and removed her bikini top when she turned and saw him standing in the doorway. She almost screamed. She put one arm across her chest and sucked in her breath, before covering her mouth with her hand.

He stood rigid, letting out short, trembling breaths that sounded like he was gasping, his migraine apparently forgotten. His glaring eyes seemed to be broadcasting rage, sex and power. He remained staring at her with a first-class hard-on. He had no intention of wasting it. "I have to give it to you, you still look good in a bikini," he said, taking in her naked chest. Scooter liked what he saw. He had always liked showing her off, letting people know what a good looking piece of meat he had married, and relished in the fact that she was all his to devour whenever he was hungry, and he was hungry now.

Seeing the look in his eyes, she tried to walk by, heading for the bathroom, but he blocked the doorway and grabbed her by the shoulders. "Where do you think you're going?" he demanded.

She was frightened, knowing what he wanted. It wasn't what she wanted. She put her hands flat against his chest, trying to keep him away. He grabbed her breast firmly with one hand and it hurt. With his other hand, he reached behind her neck and pulled her toward him and kissed her hard with his mouth open. He began sucking on her bottom lip like he was hungry and wanted to eat her alive.

When he pulled away, she pleaded, "Scooter, please, I don't feel good."

"I don't care," he said.

"Tonight, I'll feel better tonight. Please, Scooter, not now," she continued to beg.

Completely ignoring her plea, he released her breast, pushed her onto the bed, then, reached down and forced his hand between her legs, pulling her bikini bottom down around her ankles. Then, he forced her knees apart, before pushing himself inside her with such force it caused her to cringe in pain. His heavy breathing began echoing in her ear, his mouth wide open against her neck, sucking on it like he was trying to inhale her.

She felt her body go rigid. "Stop it, Scooter," she cried out. "Something's wrong. It hurts."

He had forced her into a position Betty wasn't comfortable with. He wasn't comfortable with it either. But the fact that it hurt her, made him grow harder and more determine not to pull out. He held her wrists together and forced them above her head. She tried to wrestle herself free, but he was too strong.

Scooter grunted and began breathing like he was gasping for air, while Betty struggling to contain a scream. He continued to force himself in further and began pumping like a wild animal, harder and harder, while his breathing came faster and faster until he came.

Within seconds, now that he had gotten what he wanted, he seemed to lose his strength. His body relaxed, and he rolled off her. Betty looked at him with hatred written all over her face. "What the hell is wrong with you? It hurt! I asked you to stop." Her bikini top was lying next to them on the bed, the bottom bunched up around her ankles. "Why do you always have to be so goddamn mean? I told you it hurt."

His eyes held no remorse, no guilt, no mercy, just a fierce understanding that this was the way it is. "Sorry," he said.

She stared him down for a few seconds. "No," she told him. "No, you're not."

He ignored her. "You've still got it, Betty. After all these years you still got what it takes to turn me on. I don't think I'll ever get tired of your pussy," he said, a huge grin on his face, then stood up and pulled his shorts and pants up, tucked his baseball jersey in, turned and walked out, feeling like a real man, a man that took and got what he wanted. He enjoyed knowing she didn't want him touching her. That made it better, made him savor the power he had over her. It was just so much more enjoyable abusing her that way. He never got tired of it.

She watched him leave. She felt violated, raped by her own husband. Throughout their marriage, he had slowly but surely stripped away her self-esteem, killed her pride and independence. But enough was enough. He wasn't going to get away with it any longer. No fucking way. Through clenched lips, in a voice low enough so Scooter couldn't hear, Betty said, "God help me, some day, when I get the chance I'll kill you."

Shortly after Scooter left the bedroom, Betty hurried into the bathroom. She needed to wash the smell and damp feeling of his sweat off her body. She took her time under the shower, hoping the warm water would wash away the unclean feeling of that bastard's body rubbing against her skin. After scrubbing herself clean, she stayed in the bathroom, vigorously applying moisturizing cream over every inch of her body.

Satisfied she had eliminated any trace of him; Betty just finished buttoning the last button on her lose fitting, flimsy housecoat that hung halfway down her thighs, ready to continue this goddamn ugly day, when she heard the doorbell ring.

CHAPTER 41

CHIEF BARRETT RANG the doorbell and waited, feeling uncomfortable, not sure what to expect when he confronted his prime suspect, Scooter Pappas. Betty answered the door wearing a housecoat that clung snugly to her naked body beneath. Ray stood, gawking. She wore no makeup. Her hair was loose and damp. She had a fresh just-out-of-the-shower-scent, and her blemish free skin made her look younger than she was. Most women in Barefoot Bay had left their girlish figures behind years ago and wouldn't have been caught dead answering the door dressed like this.

Betty wasn't expecting anyone and was surprised to see a police officer at her door. Seeing him in his uniform sent her memory back to the morning she had stopped in the barroom along the river. She recognized him as the same officer that had been sitting at the bar impatiently waiting for his lunch, while closely observing her in the mirror above the bar the morning Phil had told her it was over.

"Hello, Mrs. Pappas. I hope I'm not coming at a bad time," Ray said, struggling to maintain eye contact.

"No. Please come in. Have a seat, officer," she offered, motioning toward an empty chair in the living room.

"Is your husband home?"

"Yes. I'll tell him you're here. He's out back."

"Thanks," he said, before sitting on a leather recliner.

Moments after Betty went out back to inform Scooter they had company, he entered. "Officer Barrett, what brings you here?" Scooter asked in a harsh tone. From the look on his face it was obvious he wasn't thrilled with his unexpected guest.

Before he had a chance to answered, Betty asked, "Would you like a glass of ice coffee, Officer? I've got a fresh pitcher in the refrigerator."

"Thanks. That sounds great," he said.

Scooter sat directly facing his uninvited guest on the couch. Leaning forward, he picked up a pack of Marlboros off the coffee table, pulled a cigarette from the pack, lit it, inhaled, and threw the pack back onto the coffee table. Looking Ray squarely in the eyes, he purposely exhaled smoke in Ray's direction. "So what brings you here?" Scooter repeated.

Ray pretended not to notice. "I'm looking for help gathering information with my investigation into the Gagnon murder case."

They stared at each other in silence for a moment, then, feeling uncomfortable, Rays eyes dropped to the glass top coffee table. "What makes you think we can help?" Scooter asked, smoke drifting from his nose and mouth.

"I'm really not sure you can help. I'm trying to talk to everybody in the neighborhood who knew the Gagnons. I'm hoping somebody might know something, or, possibly have seen something that could help," the Chief explained.

Betty returned, carrying a tray of ice coffee. She placed it on the table between them. "Help yourself; Officer," she said.

"Thanks," Ray replied.

"If you'll excuse me, I'll go get dressed," Betty said and quickly walked into the bedroom.

Ray's eye's followed her until she disappeared.

Watching Ray closely, Scooter said, with a smirk on his face, "Don't get any ideas, that's my property. She belongs to me, and I'm not sharing."

Ray felt his face go red. "I'm sorry. I didn't mean to stare. Your wife is very attractive."

Without replying, Scooter reached for the pitcher of ice coffee. He appeared to be having trouble lifting it off the coffee table. After making two attempts to pick it up, he grunted and with a strained look on his face, put it back down. He immediately began rubbing his upper right arm with his left hand.

Ray's mind went back to the autopsy report. "Hurt your arm, Mr. Pappas?"

"Must have pulled something this morning playing softball," Scooter lied.

Unconvinced, Ray continued. "Maybe you should have it looked at," he suggested.

"Maybe you should mind your own business. It'll be fine. I'm sure you didn't come here to discuss my health," Scooter said, while crushing his cigarette out in the ash tray.

"No, I didn't come here to discuss your health. I understand you and your wife were close friends with the Gagnon's. I'm trying to get at the bottom of what happened by talking to people that were friends with them," Ray said, his voice trembling slightly.

Betty had returned and sat on the sofa next to Scooter. She was now wearing a pair of dark blue shorts and a light blue top. Ray felt more comfortable. "I don't know how we can help," Betty said.

"I'm not sure you can. It's hard to believe something like that could happen here," Ray said.

"Why are you so surprised? People would be shocked if they knew half the shit that goes on in Barefoot Bay. We mind our own business. And as far as the Gagnons are concerned, we knew them, but didn't stick our noses into their personal life," Scooter spat out.

"I was hoping you might have noticed something, anything out of the ordinary that might be of help. Maybe Mr. Gagnon had recently had an argument with someone, anything like that. Did he have any enemies?" Ray enquired.

"No. Everyone like him," Betty said.

"Not everyone. He's dead, isn't he," Scooter said, smiling at his wife." If there was anything going on with the Gagnon's, it wasn't any of our business. You're wasting your time talking to us," Scooter blurted out, turning his attention back to Ray.

Chief Barrett decided he definitely didn't like this big Greek. The more time he spent talking to him, the more convinced he was that this guy was a bully, capable of almost anything if he lost his temper, even murder.

Struggling to remain calm, Barrett replied, "Well, I suppose you're right. It's just that nothing like this has ever happened in Barefoot Bay before. The people living here are awful nervous, as you can imagine."

"I know. I'm still shocked," Betty said, glancing over at Scooter, then back to Ray. She was sitting with her knees together and her hands in her lap, watching out of the corner of her eye the throbbing pulse on Scooters temple and the clenching and unclenching of his fist, his eyes narrowing, and knew he was getting ready for a fight.

"I understand you were with Kathy Gagnon the night her husband was murdered," Ray said, nodding toward Betty.

"Yes. I went with Kathy and the other girls to bingo over at Saint Luke's Church," Betty explained.

Gathering up all his nerve, knowing Scooter wouldn't like the question, Ray asked, "What about you, Mr. Pappas? Where were you Friday night?"

He was right, Scooter didn't like the question. His prolonged silence together with his dead stare, were sure signs of anger. The fight was on. "Where the hell do you think I was? I was right here watching television. Who the hell do you think you are, coming into my house accusing me of having something to do with Phil's death?" he lashed out.

It was obvious by the tightness of Scooters jaw and the fire in his eyes that the mood between them had become extremely tense, and Ray was scared. "I'm not accusing you of anything," Ray said, squeezing his glass of ice coffee.

"You goddamn better not be," Scooter said.

The temperature in the room suddenly felt like it had shot up to a hundred degrees. "I'm not. I'm really not. I'm sorry if I offended you, Mr. Pappas," Barrett apologized, his voice jittery and several octaves higher than normal.

Ray was now feeling intimidated, discouraged, beaten and extremely nervous. He was looking for the exit, feeling like a trapped rat in need of an escape route. He wanted to be out of there; he wanted to get in his cruiser and drive away as a fast as he could, away from Scooter Pappas.

"I'm sure the officer has to ask these questions, Scooter," Betty interrupted, knowing the extent of her husband's temper when provoked.

"Well, he can go and ask his goddamn questions someplace else," Scooter spat out, his left fist clenched in anger. He had had enough of Barrett. It was time to send him on his way.

Chief Barrett stood and swayed for a moment before steadying himself. "I don't know what you're getting so upset about, Mr. Pappas. I'm just trying to do my job. Maybe we can talk another time when you've calmed down some," Ray pleaded.

Scooter was next to get to his feet. "Get out of my goddamn house," he demanded, pointing in the direction of their front door.

Shaking out of control, partly out of anger, but mostly out of fear, Ray headed for the door. Betty also got up and began following him, apologizing. "I'm sorry, Officer. Scooter hasn't been himself lately."

"I understand, Mrs. Pappas. Everyone's on edge since the murder," he said, his voice quivering.

"I'll let you know if we think of anything that might help," Betty said while opening the door.

Micco's Chief of Police didn't reply, but once safely outside, he practically ran to his patrol car. He couldn't get the cruiser started fast enough. As soon as the engine roared to life, he put it in gear and hit the gas. The tires squealed as he went streaking down Dolphin Drive, glad to be getting away from that crazy Greek son-of-a-bitch, Scooter Pappas.

Arriving back at the station, Ray found Darcy working at her desk. Still shook up from the Pappas interview he walked by her without saying a word. Darcy made no attempt to talk to him either. Safely inside his office, Ray threw his keys onto the desk, sat in his swivel chair and gave out a loud sigh. With the door shut, he leaned back and began going over his talk with the Pappas's, a look of defeat written on his face

The thing that stood out most was the injury to Scooter's arm. That easily could've happened in a confrontation with Gagnon the night he'd been murdered. When Ray asked about his whereabouts that night, instead of just answering the question, Pappas had acted like someone with something to hide. There had to be a reason.

Earlier, when Betty answered the door, he remembered she was the woman who came into Bottoms Up a couple of weeks ago. He recalled she was alone and appeared to have been crying. After she walked out, Sandy said that she hadn't touched her drink. He remembered thinking at the time that her behavior seemed odd. Barrett wasn't sure if any of this meant anything, but there were definitely too many unanswered questions to be ignored.

The one thing Ray was sure of was Scooter was his man. He didn't have any solid evidence, but he was sure he was right. He didn't know how, but somehow, he'd find a way to prove it. He just needed to get a break. It was over a week since the murder. He had no motive and the only evidence so far was nothing but speculation. But he did have a suspect. His problem was he was afraid to go anywhere near him.

He had a lot to think about. If he didn't get to Bottoms Up soon, he was convinced his head would explode. Ray needed a drink and needed it now. He remembered making the promise this morning that he would give up drinking, and he still intended too, but just not today. He would definitely go on the wagon tomorrow. Right now he needed time to think. He was heading to Bottoms Up, where he always did his best thinking when he had a drink in his hands.

CHAPTER 42

CAROL AND BETTY made arrangements to meet at Baker's Bagel Shop for no other reason than an excuse to get out of the house and do some chatting over coffee. Talk about the Gagnon murder had quieted down in the Bay. Seniors were going about their business, just as they had before the murder. Originally the case got front page coverage in the Press Journal, but it had been pushed to the inside pages, and now people infrequently discussed it.

Driving down Route 1, Carol turned left onto Indian River Drive. She noticed a lack of traffic due to the absence of the snowbirds that had started their migration north. Realizing the winter season was rapidly coming to a close, she knew it wouldn't be long before Betty would be returning to New Hampshire, too. With Kathy and Rita gone, and Betty getting ready to leave, she felt depressed, thinking it would be a long summer with only Stanley to keep her company.

Carol parked her Jeep Cherokee Wagon across the street from the bagel shop. She noticed Betty's car parked several spots to her right. This was unusual for someone who was notorious for being the last to arrive. Immediately upon entering, Carol saw her friend sitting in the corner booth. After giving Betty a quick wave, she got in line and waited to place her order. Within minutes she had her coffee and bagel securely in her hands and walked over to join Betty.

Betty was scanning the Barefoot Bay Tattler, a free community newspaper. Carol sat in the booth across from her and took off the plastic cover from her coffee. "You're early," she said.

Betty folded the paper and dropped it on the table. "Yeah, I had to get out of the house. Scooter was having another one of his headaches. He wasn't sure if he was going to play ball this morning. I don't like being around him when he's in a bitchy mood, which is most days, so, I saddled-up and got out of Dodge as fast as I could."

"What's his problem?" Carol asked.

"What's not his problem? He's always bitching about something.

Ever since that cop Barrett stopped over last Monday, he's been a real pain in the ass."

"What did he want? What did he say that got Scooter so upset?"

"Nothing much, he just asked a lot of dumb questions. I don't think that cop has any idea what he's doing. I don't know who was shook up more. You should've seen the look on the cop's face when he left. He couldn't wait to get away from Scooter. I don't blame him. I wish I could," Betty said.

"Well, at least your husband talks to you. I think Stanley has finally completely lost touch with reality. He's been talking to his imaginary friends like you and I are talking now. And another thing, he keeps complaining that he's cold all the time. Did you know that's a sign of someone who's schizophrenic?'

"No."

"Really, I remember reading that somewhere. Have you ever noticed when you see pictures of people like that, they always have their arms wrapped around themselves. I'm telling you, he's starting to turn into a real head case," Carol complained.

"Have you heard anything from Kathy?" Betty asked.

"Yes. She called yesterday. Everything is as good as can be expected. You can imagine the talk among her relatives and friends about Phil's murder. She sounded fine. Thankfully she has her son to help her."

"Do you think she'll be back this year?" Betty asked.

"Not this year, that's for sure. Her son wants her to sell the house. He doesn't like the idea of her living in Florida alone, especially after what happened to his father. I don't think she knows what she's going to do," Carol said.

"I guess you can't blame her son for not wanting her to come back here. I know their close; she email's him every day when she's in Florida," Betty said.

Mentioning Kathy's son brought back painful memories of her son's suicide. Just last night Betty had had another one of those recurring dreams. She had dreamt about Bobby dragging the stepstool to the center of the barn, then throwing the rope over the beam. She could see him vividly placing the loop over his head before pulling the knot tight around his neck; then, just before kicking the stool away, Betty woke up shaking, her nightgown drenched with sweat.

"I know Kathy really likes Florida. It'll be interesting to see if her son's able to convince her not to return next year," Carol said. "I'll miss her if she doesn't come back."

"She really is nice. I hope she'll be back," Betty said, feeling hypocritical, thinking about the affair between her and Phil.

"I suppose you'll be heading back up north before long," Carol said.

"Don't mention it. Thinking about going back makes me want to throw-up," Betty confessed.

"It can't be that bad."

"Oh, yes, it can. I wish the hell I could stay here. I can't stand living on the farm. I can't stand my mother-in-law, and I especially can't stand that son-of-a-bitch Scooter," Betty said, looking down, her gaze fixed on the coffee in front of her, wetness accumulating in the corners of her eyes.

"I never realized you hated New Hampshire that much. I didn't know that things were bad between you and Scooter, either. Sounds like somebody's not very happy," Carol said.

Unable to control her emotions, everything that had been bottled up inside for years came forward and Betty began spitting it out, like an emotional dam had broken and all the heartaches of her life came forward.

"It's been awful, Carol. I can't start to tell you how much I've gotten to hate him. My whole life has been a nightmare. I should have never married him. He enjoys being cruel, like some boys enjoy torturing their pets, always taunting and teasing them; how they enjoy hurting them."

Carol leaned forward, elbows firmly on the table. "Did he ever hit you?"

"No. Mostly he just likes to humiliate me. When we first got married, I tried hard to be a good wife, but nothing I did satisfied him. All he ever did was make me feel stupid. After a while, I began thinking he was right. So I thought maybe if I worked a little harder, maybe try a little harder, but I finally realized that no matter how hard I tried, it would never be good enough. Maybe I am stupid and can't do anything right."

Betty took a deep breath and continued, "I wanted to believe I was a good wife most of the time. But there was always something wrong; something inside of me that constantly reminded me that I was incapable of doing anything right. I'd lie in bed at night wondering what was wrong with me. It seems like I don't know who the person inside me is, but I do know I've grown to not like her."

"Don't talk like that. You're not stupid, and you're a wonderful person. I can't see why you stayed with him all these years if you've been so unhappy. There must have been some part of your marriage that was good. Trust me you don't have to live like this. There're other ways," Carol said.

Carol was caught completely off guard by this outburst. She was surprised but knew better than most people that things aren't always what they seem on the surface. Until this moment, Betty had never given her any indication that she was unhappy with her marriage. "Listen to me, there's nothing wrong with you," Carol said.

"Do you know what it's like getting up each morning, watching the years go by, hating your life? It's an awful way to waste your life when you discover soon after you get married you've made a terrible mistake. But you don't know how to get out of it, so, you spend your life living with a man you don't love," Betty said.

"I know," Carol said, thinking of the years she'd spent married to Stanley, when she should have been with Robin. "You're not the only one. I also made a terrible mistake marrying Stanley."

"You did?"

"Yes. I knew I didn't love him even before we got married." Carol confessed.

"Then why did you?"

"I thought it might change me."

"Change you?"

"Yes, change me. I'm a lesbian, Betty, but you probably have already figured that out," Carol said, raising her eyes, watching for her reaction.

Their eyes locked and Betty never looked away. "I didn't know for sure, but I was pretty sure," she said.

Carol closed her eyes briefly, before re-opening them, happy that Betty had acted unconcerned and indifferent to her confession, then, said, "I guess I was lucky compared to you. Shortly after I married Stanley, I found someone. Being with her was the ultimate joy, the purest of pleasures."

"What happened to her?" Betty asked.

Recalling the worst day of her life, Carol was fighting to hold back her tears of guilt. She explained, "An accident; I lost her in an automobile accident. I was the one driving."

"I'm sorry, Carol. I didn't know."

"Looks like we both messed up. At least I did have someone to love, and that someone loved me back. It sounds like you've never experienced real love," Carol said.

Slowly, Betty picked up her coffee and took a long, slow swallow. "It's just not that I don't love him, I've hated Scooter almost as long as I've been married to him," she said, putting her cup down and began tracing the rim with her finger.

"Hate can be a terrible thing. If you let it, it will eat you up."

"Haven't you ever hated anyone?" Betty asked.

"No. I've disliked a lot of people, but never hated them."

"Well, I hate that bastard. I've spent hours thinking of ways to punish him, get even."

Carol leaning forward, unable to believe what she was hearing, asked, "Why get even? If things are so bad, why stay with him? Just leave."

Betty's throat tightened. But she forced herself to continue. "I'm afraid to do anything. I don't know where I could go. I've never been out of New Hampshire before coming to Florida. I've always been scared to go on my own. I wish I was strong enough to stand up to him. Maybe everything would be different, but I've always been afraid it could get worse," she explained, her tears flowing freely.

Carol could see pain written all over Betty's face. She didn't reply right away. She studied her closely from across the table. What she saw was Betty is beautiful. Her beauty was now being tarnished by the pain lines at the corner of her eyes, but it's still there in her face. She couldn't stand seeing her friend suffering like this any longer and immediately moved to the other side of the booth.

She put her arm around her shoulders and said, "It's going to be all right, Betty. If you don't want to go back to New Hampshire with Scooter, we'll find a way for you to stay here."

"You don't know what he's like when he gets mad. I'm scared of what he might do," Betty sobbed. "Oh, God, just listen to me. I'm sorry, Carol. I don't want to drag you into my problems. It sounds like you have enough of your own problems with Stanley," she finished quietly, shaking her head in despair.

"It's too late! I'm already in. There are ways to handle guys like Scooter. They have this thing called divorce, in case you haven't heard. Don't worry. We'll get in touch with a lawyer. He'll know what to do," Carol said in a strong, confident voice.

Betty felt like a hundred-pound weight had been lifted off her chest. "Are you serious? Do you think we really could? I'm not sure if I've got enough nerve to do anything like that alone."

"Don't worry. You're not alone any more. Guys like Scooter like to scare people. Well, he doesn't scare me. We'll fix him," Carol said, "Just hang in there for a couple more days. Next week we'll go see a lawyer, and if you have to, you can always stay at my house until we send Scooter back to New Hampshire by himself."

"What would Stanley say if I stayed with you?" Betty asked.

"Don't worry about Stanley. He's so busy talking to his imaginary friends he probably won't even know you're there. Maybe we can get a group rate from the lawyer and send them both on their way," Carol said, removing her arm from Betty's shoulders.

"Don't I have to file for divorce in the state that I'm from?"

"I'm not sure. We'll find out what needs to be done when we talk to the lawyer."

Betty looked up from her coffee and found Carol smiling at her. A too-long moment passed, then, Betty smiled back. "Sometimes I think I'm getting to hate all men," she said.

Carol had always found Betty to be extremely attractive, but never really appreciated just how beautiful she was until now. Whenever they were out in public, Carol noticed when men passed by, every one of them would take a sideward glance at Betty. Carol watched men with wives and children staring, taking in the sight of her, their imaginations automatically undressing her. They couldn't seem to stop themselves.

She knew what they saw. She knew Betty was beautiful. Carol had always admired how soft she was, no hard places, curves that seemed to defy gravity. Her breasts still looked firm, her tiny waist flared to her hips, and she had a perfectly rounded bottom. Even with a tear stained face, she looked beautiful. It must be wonderful, she often thought, to go through each day knowing that wherever you went, everyone would look and admire your beauty.

Carol had been listening to Betty's story with increasing anxiety, interest and sympathy, and her comment about her hating all men didn't go unnoticed, but something else was seeping into her thoughts. Because she wasn't aware of how unhappily married Betty was, Carol had never given much thought to their being together. Now, after hearing her complaining about Scooter, and realizing that Betty could soon be single, combined with the remark she'd just made about hating all men, Carol couldn't help but wonder if it was possible, it was probably unlikely, but maybe it was possible.

Once they finished their coffee, Betty seemed to be in better control. The subject seemed to be exhausted, and for a moment neither of them spoke. They cleaned off the table, wadded their paper napkins into small balls and dropped them in their Styrofoam cups, when Betty said, "Will you really help me? I'll do anything not to have to return to New Hampshire with Scooter; but I'd be too scared to go through a divorce by myself."

"Don't worry. We'll take care of this together. I promise. It won't be that bad."

"Thanks Carol. I can't tell you how much I appreciate this," she said and gave her a genuine smile, the kind that comes from someone who really appreciates your help.

There was a short pause while they gathered their thoughts. "What are you doing for the rest of the day?" Carol asked.

"I'm still a little nervous about all of this, but I'm also excited. I think I'll take a ride to the Indian River Mall and go shopping and buy myself something. I need time to let everything settle in. Want to tag along?" Betty asked.

After depositing their trash into the container next to the entrance, they left the bagel shop and were walking across the boulevard, when Carol said, "No. I better go home and see what's happening at the insane asylum," rolling her eyes toward the sky. "He's driving me crazy. Every so often I hear him talking to someone named Rocky."

"Who's Rocky?"

"Who's Rocky? I don't have the slightest idea. Someone out there in the twilight zone, I guess. I don't know how much longer I can take it. I've got to get Stanley to a doctor. He's becoming more depressed and despondent with each passing day. Most days he sleeps twelve hours, and some days more."

"Sounds like you have enough of your own problems. Listen, Carol, if you don't want to get involved in my problems, I'll understand."

Carol put her head back and gave a deep-throated laugh. "Don't worry about me. In case you haven't noticed, I've got big shoulders. We're gonna work everything out. I promise. Us girls have to stick together," she said cheerfully. "Over the years I've been called a loser, a bitch, and a dyke, but nobody ever accused me of being timid." Then her voice turned serious, "You know Betty, I love you, I'd do anything if it would help make you happy."

Betty's eyes widened slightly and Carol saw something in them that might have been confusion, curiosity, or fear . . . or all three. While this awkward statement hung heavy in the air, their conversation was abruptly interrupted by the wail of an ambulance rushing some unfortunate individual to the hospital. They looked in the direction of the commotion and waited until the screaming ambulance was out of hearing range.

"I know you would. And I'm really going to need your help going through this," Betty said.

Carol, looking slightly uncomfortable with her statement, said, "Give me a call tomorrow. I'll check around this afternoon and see if I can find us a good lawyer."

"Okay, I'll call you and thanks for being a friend," Betty said, while wrapping her arms around her, giving her a firm embrace.

Carol had been feeling so alone lately, all the pain of losing Robin came flooding forward. She couldn't get used to being alone. When Betty embraced her, the hug offered more intimacy than she had felt in years, causing Carol to experience a slight involuntary ripple of desire throughout her body. "Okay. I'll talk to you later," she said.

Satisfied they had said everything that needed to be said, at least for now, both Carol and Betty got into their cars and drove away in different directions.

As Carol backed out of her parking space, she could feel the rapid beating of her heart. Losing Robin had left a void in her life that could never be filled. But now, suddenly and unexpectedly, she wondered, could it be possible that she had once again found someone she might be able to share her life with?

She had every intention of seeing where their relationship might lead. She also knew that the chances of getting into a loving relationship with Betty were slim. Betty had never showed any signs of being a lesbian. But it was possible that part of the reason she couldn't make a go of her marriage was, deep down inside lurked another Betty, a bi-sexual Betty. She would have to be careful. She didn't want to lose Betty's friendship if she was wrong.

CHAPTER 43

THE TIGHT FEELING in her chest, a feeling she'd been living with since marrying Scooter, had begun to loosen, melting away, making breathing more comfortable as she made her way south on Route 1, heading for the Indian River Mall, thinking, *Is it possible? With Carol's help, could I finally be free of him?*

It was still early. There were plenty of parking spaces available in front of Sears. Betty wasn't looking for anything in particular. She just needed a little time to herself. If she saw something that caught her eye, and the price was right, so much the better. After about an hour and nothing catching her attention, she left Sears and headed for Wal-Mart, another one of her favorite stores where she usually could find a bargain, but after browsing for a while, once again, found nothing.

While driving from one store to the next, her mind kept going back to her conversation with Carol. Betty admired her strength and knew she would need her support going through with getting a divorce. Scooter often said he was sure Carol was a lesbian. Now there was no longer any doubt. Rather than be uncomfortable with this information, Betty felt closer to her.

Beneath Carol's masculine exterior beat the heart of a sensitive, caring, true friend, something Betty found lacking in the men she had known throughout her life. The brief affair she had had with Phil, thinking he loved her, was meaningless. She had been a fool. He had only been using her. She now realized her thinking he loved her was like a mirage in the desert; she had been so thirsty for love, anyone's love, she had imagined his love was real.

It was easy to talk to Carol. Betty was not good with people in a one-on-one situation. Talking openly about her personal life was not something she did. But with Carol she had poured her heart out, told her how miserable her life had been married to Scooter, and felt a sense of relief confiding in her. Remembering the statement she had made, *"I love you and I'd do anything if it would make you happy,"* along with the hug she had gotten earlier, felt reassuring.

It had been years since anyone said I love you. It felt good hearing Carol say it. With Carol, she was convinced her feelings were honest and sincere. She certainly felt more comfortable and enjoyed her company more than any man she'd known. The strong attraction she had towards Carol made her wonder if her feelings went deeper than just friendship. She began thinking, Could it be possible . . .?

No, she couldn't be. Or could she? After all, she was no kid and would have known by now if she was attracted to other women, wouldn't she? Could it be that she had gotten to be this old and not known . . .? That is, if she is. How could that happen? The question was did she want to know? Was being attracted to women such a terrible thing, suddenly pop into her head? Just thinking about it scared her.

She began wondering if all these years she'd actually been trapped between two different selves: an unhappy straight woman, verses a woman underneath, a woman who might have just been awakened. Betty bit down on her lower lip, continued thinking about it a while longer, and felt confused. She shrugged her shoulders and decided to push it to the back of her mind, at least for now. She knew if she continued down that road she wasn't sure where it might lead and if she would be able to turn back, and that scared her a little. Actually it scared her a lot.

Her final stop was Macy's, where she found an attractive, light green, blouse that would go perfect with the matching shorts she'd purchased a few days ago. Realizing it was getting late and satisfied her shopping trip hadn't been in vain, she headed for home. When she arrived, Scooter wasn't anywhere in sight. He must have decided he was well enough to play ball. But he should have gotten home by now. He always comes directly home after each game, she thought.

Anxious to see how her new blouse looked, Betty went directly into the bedroom. She got out of her jersey and tried on her new purchase. Satisfied with the image looking back at her in the mirror, she slipped it off, took a small pair of scissors out of the bureau drawer, clipped off the price tags, and hung the blouse carefully in the closet.

Looking at her watch, she realized it was nearly noon. She headed for the kitchen to make lunch. As she passed through the living room she noticed the red message light on the answering machine blinking. In her haste to try on her blouse, she walked past without noticing it.

She pressed down the message button. The familiar pre-recorded female voice sprang to life, "You have one new message," followed by a clicking sound, then, another female voice came on. This voice she didn't recognize.

"This message is for Mrs. Pappas. This is the Sebastian River

Medical Center. Your husband has been taken to the hospital in serious condition. Please call or come in as soon as possible. Thank you." The machine gave a series of short clicks, then, went silent.

Betty quickly walked into the kitchen and located the telephone directory on the counter beneath the wall phone and looked up the number, then began punching it in. While waiting for someone to pick up, her mind cleared and she felt she knew what had happened. "Hello, Sebastian River Medical Center, Mrs. Brighton speaking. How may I direct your call," the efficient sounding voice said.

"My name is Betty Pappas. I received a call that my husband was brought to the hospital."

"Yes, Mrs. Pappas, that's correct. Dr. Phelps is with him now. I suggest you come to the hospital as soon as possible."

"Could you tell me what's the matter with him?"

"I'm sorry, but I'm not allowed to give out information. I can only tell you he's in intensive care. I think it's best if you come in and speak with Dr. Phelps directly."

"Could you at least tell me how bad he is?"

"You're going to have to come in and talk to the doctor, Mrs. Pappas."

"All right, I'm on my way," she said and hung up.

Minutes later, Betty was driving over the Saint Sebastian River Bridge, wondering if the ambulance she'd heard earlier could've been the same ambulance that had rushed Scooter to the hospital. Arriving in the parking lot, she found a vacant space in front of the main entrance. She entered through the two large glass doors that parted automatically and began walking down a short hallway where an older woman sat at the information desk. A plaque on the desk identified her as Mrs. Brighton.

"I'm Mrs. Pappas. I spoke to you earlier."

"Yes, Mrs. Pappas. I'll inform the doctor that you're here," she answered, while reaching for the phone. "You can have a seat and the doctor will be with you shortly," she continued, indicating with her free hand towards the vinyl couches and chairs in the waiting area.

Betty began walking toward the light avocado green waiting room, then hesitated to let an old man pushing a walker with tennis balls attached to the legs, shuffling down the hall, pass by. Sitting in an empty chair against the far wall, she waited impatiently and watched nurses who no longer wore white polyester uniforms or caps on top of their heads, scurrying about in the pajama tops they wear today, over silly looking baggy pants and sneakers.

After what seemed like an eternity the doctor appeared, walking hurriedly down the corridor. He was wearing a lab coat with his nametag, Dr. Phelps, M.D., above the breast pocket. She was impressed with how young the doctor looked. He had strawberry blonde hair, a captivating smile that showed signs of concern, and walked with an air of confidence.

"Mrs. Pappas? I'm Doctor Phelps. I just left your husband. I'm afraid he's had a massive stroke," he said, his voice sounding level and courteous.

"How bad is it?" Betty asked.

The doctor shook his head. "Not good! Not good at all."

"Where is he?"

"In ICU, he's not conscious." The doctor hesitated, as if making a decision, then, continued, "Could we talk in my office for a few minutes before you go in to see him?"

"Sure. Is he really that bad? Is he going to live?" she asked, as they walked side by side down the corridor, passing rooms with patients lying in steel hospital beds in stages of drugged sleep. The sounds of her heels were the only sounds echoing off the walls. They eventually came to a room on the right with a small brass plaque with the doctor's name on the door.

"It's pretty bad," the doctor admitted, shaking his head.

Once they entered the small office, the doctor pointed toward the vacant chair in front of his desk, "Have a seat." Betty sat on the plastic chair, bracing herself for what was coming.

His voice was filled with compassion, but firm. "I'm sure you have a lot of questions. But let me begin by being perfectly honest with you, he may not make it, Mrs. Pappas. I'm afraid your husband's suffered a massive hemorrhaging of the brain. A blood vessel ruptured and there's been extensive bleeding."

"He's still alive, isn't he?"

"He's still alive, but just barely," he said, then waited for her reaction. She sat mute. He was expecting some show of emotion, but got none.

When she responded, it was in a flat, uncaring voice. "What are his chances?" Betty asked.

"It's hard to say right now. The next twenty-four hours will be critical in determining what your husband's condition will be when he comes out of the coma . . . if he recovers at all. From what I understand, your husband was at the ball field in the Barefoot Bay Retirement Community when he suffered this stroke. By the time the medics got to him, the damage was already done," he explained.

Dr. Phelps was surprised to see so little reaction. Usually, whenever he delivered this kind of news to the relatives, they'd break down crying, or at least look worried or concerned. Mrs. Pappas was showing almost no signs of caring. Instead of asking questions, she kept looking toward the door, like she wanted their conversation to end so she could leave.

She remained sitting quietly, arms folded defiantly across her chest. "I find it difficult to believe that your husband didn't have any warning signs, Mrs. Pappas. Didn't he say anything or give any indication that something was wrong?" he said, watching her closely with eyes that missed very little.

"Yes. He's been complaining about headaches lately."

"Is that all?"

"No. He was also complaining about blurred vision and numbness in his right side, especially his arm."

"Didn't you realize that these are warning signs that something is wrong? Didn't it occur to you that you should've had your husband examined? I suspect he suffered other minor strokes before this morning," the doctor gently scolded.

She shook her head. "I told him he should go see a doctor, but he refused. He said he was going to wait until we got back to New Hampshire. My husband's not someone you can reason with when he's made up his mind," Betty explained, speaking defensively.

"I'm afraid it's going to be quite a while before he's able to travel. It's too early to know the exact extent of the damage. I've been honest with you, it doesn't look good. Even if he does recover, there's no telling what condition he'll be in."

Betty remained silent.

"If you'd like, you can drop in to the ICU room. But, I must warn you, he won't even be aware that you're there," he said.

"Okay. I guess I should see him while I'm here," Betty agreed.

Having no reason to prolong this conversation, the doctor stood, indicating their talk was over. Betty followed his lead, and the doctor put his hand on her shoulder, gently guiding her out of his office. "You'll have to excuse me. I have other patients to look in on. You'll find the ICU Room plainly marked down this hallway on the left. There should be a nurse in the room with your husband. I'm sure we'll be talking again soon, hopefully with some good news," he informed her, then, walked briskly away in the opposite direction.

When Betty stepped into the dimly lit room, she noticed a faint smell of antiseptic. A catheter was attached to a bag under the bed and saline dripped from the IV tower with the sedatives necessary to keep Scooter stable. A respirator had taken over his breathing. She could hear the even beeps of the electronic machine sending reports from the several electrodes attached to his chest sending signals to the EKG monitor. A nurse was seated next to Scooter's bed, watching closely.

Betty stood there feeling uncomfortable, awkward, and unsure of what she should do. She suddenly felt tired and hungry. She'd been in the hospital since shortly after noon and couldn't recall if she had eaten lunch. There was a chair against the wall, but she didn't feel like sitting. "I'm his wife," Betty informed the nurse who turned slightly to see who had entered.

"I'm afraid he isn't awake, but you're welcome to stay as long as you'd like," she said in a hushed tone.

"I'll only be a minute," Betty assured her.

When she stepped forward, she wasn't prepared for what she saw. It was amazing, almost surreal; the man she had feared and caused her so much pain was lying helplessly in bed. Scooter was taking shallow breaths, while his eyes remained closed, his arms slack at his sides. He looked frail and helpless lying there fighting for his life. She noticed how thin and pale his face was. She hardly recognized him. He was now just a shadow of the man he'd been only this morning. She knew she wouldn't be here long. She also knew she should feel sad or upset or . . . something. But she felt nothing, nothing at all.

With the sound of the EKG monitor echoing steadily in her mind, Betty was trying to sort out how this would affect her plans. It was like a bizarre trick had been played on her, but it was no trick. It was real. Her only concern now was what condition he would be in when he recovered, if he recovered, and what effect it would have on her plans to divorce him.

After several minutes the feeling of being confined in a small room without windows became unbearable. The air in the room felt stuffy, too stuffy. She didn't know what to say or do and was feeling awkward and uncomfortable. Slowly retreating, walking backwards toward the door, she said to the attending nurse, "I think I'll be going." Betty shrugged her shoulders, turned and quickly walked out.

In the hallway, Betty collapsed her back against the wall, quivering, thinking she was living a real life soap opera. All these years she had feared him, hated him, but now, knowing he may never wake up, she had all she could do not too weep with relief, realizing one way or another, she would finally be rid of him.

While driving home, Betty's mind was on autopilot. The trip from the hospital seemed vague, as if it wasn't really happening, more like floating in a dream. Arriving home, she entered her house and found that the rooms appeared larger with an empty, hollow feel to them. She suddenly felt exhausted; her legs were weak and she let her body collapse onto one of the stools next to the breakfast bar. So much was going on.

Her stomach started groaning. She needed to get something to eat. She hadn't eaten since earlier this morning at the bagel shop. It was a struggle, but she managed to drag herself off the stool and walked to the refrigerator. She quickly made a sandwich and was slowly munching on it, pondering her future, when the phone startling her. She considered not answering, she was in no mood to talk to anyone, let the answering machine get it, she thought, but reconsidered and walked over and picked it up.

"Hello," she said.

"Mrs. Pappas?"

"Yes."

"This is Doctor Phelps."

"Hello, Doctor. Is everything all right?"

"I'm afraid not," he said.

"What's wrong?" she asked.

Dr. Phelps sounded compassionate but business like. "I'm sorry to have to inform you that your husband passed away a short while ago."

For a moment there was an empty silence while Betty repeated in her mind what the doctor had told her. Although she thought she was prepared for this call, when it actually came she felt her knees weaken, and she slowly walked backwards and lowered her body onto the breakfast stool.

"But I just left there," Betty said.

"Yes, I know. The nurse told me it was only seconds after you closed the door that he stopped breathing. She tried to revive him, but by the time she realized it was hopeless and he had passed, you had already left the hospital."

After a short pause, Betty regained her composure and said, "At least he didn't suffer long."

"From the moment he had the stroke, I can assure you, he never felt the slightest bit of pain. The damage to his brain was massive. Had he lived, chances are he might not have been able to walk or even talk," the doctor explained.

"He wouldn't have wanted to live like that. Do you want me to come back to the hospital?" she asked, her eyes began to sting, trying to hold back tears, all of a sudden feeling sad and unable to understand why.

"There's no reason for you to come back today. I'm sure you can use some time by yourself. Tomorrow will be soon enough," he assured her.

"I'll be there in the morning."

"See the receptionist when you arrive. She'll direct you to who you should speak with."

"Okay," she said and hung up.

Rubbing the back of her neck, Betty continued to stare at the phone. How she'd often wished Scooter would die. The truth was Betty Pappas wanted her husband dead. She often imagined how she would kill him herself, even dreamt about it. But now that her prayers had been answered, she was confused and sad. *Why did he have to be so cruel? All I ever wanted was to be treated with a little kindness.*

Then the memories of how hateful he had been to their son crept back in. The image of Bobby's lifeless body hanging at the end of the rope, his once beautiful face a horrible shade of blue-gray, the hollow, frightened look in his empty eyes—all came flashing back and she realized nothing would have changed if Scooter had lived. Any regrets she had just felt about his dying, immediately faded away. *Thank God he's dead. I hope he burns in hell.*

She was finally free of that bastard. Everything was going to change and she knew exactly what she was going to do. First thing in the morning she'd have to make the call to her mother-in-law to inform her that Scooter had died. Betty wasn't looking forward to that conversation. Mother Pappas adored the ground her son walked on. She wouldn't take the news very well.

Losing her son would be tragic, but what was about to follow would be just as tragic. She, like Betty, had always depended on Scooter to handle their affairs, including paying her bills, running their farm and taking care of their family business. Her mother-in-law had always been confident that as long as she was alive, Scooter would be around to take care of her. That was about to change. He was no longer alive and Mother Pappas wouldn't like the changes that were going to take place.

The first thing on her agenda would be to get in touch with attorney Caraganis, the family lawyer. She would tell him to begin liquidating everything she owned. And Betty now owned everything.

Years ago, after Scooter's grandfather died, he had convinced both his mother and grandmother to put everything in his name, including the farm and business. Betty remembered while in the lawyer's office, signing the legal papers. Attorney Caraganis explained she had rights of survivorship in the unlikely situation that Scooter died unexpectedly. Well, he'd died unexpectedly. She now owned the farm and everything that went with it. She could sell everything, including the farm, construction business and anything else they'd owned if she wished, and that was exactly what she intended on doing.

Unfortunately for her mother-in-law, this would mean moving off the farm which she'd called home for her entire adult life. This was the only house she'd lived in since she married Scooter's dad. Being told now, after all this time and at her age that she was being forced to leave by her daughter-in-law would surely break her heart. Betty didn't care.

Scooter had been no fool when it came to making a buck. He'd realized that small New England farms were becoming a thing of the past. He also knew he could make more money by developing his land than farming it. So, he had had the farm rezoned to residential several years ago. It would be an attractive investment for developers.

With part of the money from the sale, she intended to give Mother Pappas enough money to relocate. Betty was aware that state run housing for the elderly was available in Manchester, close to the Greek Orthodox Church her mother-in-law attended. With the Pappas' political influence with the town's selectmen, she felt confident the old lady wouldn't have any difficulty securing a place to live.

Tomorrow would definitely be a busy day. After the call to Scooter's mother, she'd have to return to the hospital and sign the necessary legal papers. Then she'd make arrangements for Scooter's body to be shipped back north. Also she needed to call Carol. She'd tell her she no longer needed a divorce lawyer. Once the calls were made, she would start packing for the long ride back to New Hampshire alone.

One of the features Betty loved most about her Florida home was her bathroom. It was large and modern with a deep Jacuzzi tub. All she wanted to do now was take a good, long soak in the warm water and enjoy the scented bubbles while drinking a glass of wine.

She left the kitchen with a glass of wine securely in her hand and walked as if in a trance to her bathroom, stripped, leaving her clothes in a pile on the floor. The tiled walls rang with the sound of water pouring into the tub. The steaming water created a mist on the mirror as she poured a large dose of liquid lilac scented bath soap under the faucet and watched the explosion of bubbles cover the surface of the water.

It was time to say goodbye to the old Betty Pappas. She was finished with her meek and passive ways. She worked her wedding band back and forth until it slipped over her knuckle and off her finger, closed her hand around it and squeezed the ring like it was responsible for all the years of her miserable life, then threw it in the wastebasket next to the toilet.

Giving a sigh of relief, she drew in her breath and held it while sinking naked into the warm water. She pushed the button on the side of the tub and watched as a sea of bubbles swirled around her body. She reached over and picked up the wine from the side of the tub, leaned back and took a long sip. The combination of wine and warm water made her feel good, clean and free.

She closed her eyes and fantasized about her new life. She wasn't sure how to start fresh, be someone else, but start over she would. Her past was behind her. There wasn't anything she could do to change that. But her future was entirely in her own hands now. She was definitely going to change that. For the rest of the afternoon, she would relax and savor this glorious feeling of freedom being the new Betty Pappas.

She closed her eyes, leaned her head back and began to cry.

CHAPTER 44

Two weeks later

IT WAS THE END of another routine, boring, uneventful week. The sun was casting a long, soft light along his office floor. Ray was sitting at his desk, reflecting back to the Gagnon murder case. As far as he was concerned, he had solved the case, it was over, and everything was back to normal.

He was in the process of cleaning off his desk, covered with Styrofoam cups with left over coffee still in them, old newspapers and wrappers from his morning bagels, when Darcy marched in with Patrolman Andy Callahan close behind. These Friday afternoon social meetings had become routine. Nothing of importance was ever discussed, because with the exception of the recent murder case, which Chief Barrett considered solved, nothing of importance ever happened in Micco.

"Looks like you're on your way, Chief. Getting ready to call it a day?" Andy said, collapsing in one of the two available chairs in front of his boss's desk. Darcy sat in the remaining chair, withdrew a cigarette from the open pack in her hand, lit it, took an unhealthy drag, and exhaled the smoke in Ray's direction.

"For Christ sake, Darcy, do you have to blow that smoke in my face? From now on I don't want you smoking in here," he insisted.

Darcy ignored him and kept right on puffing.

"Any plans for the weekend?" Callahan asked.

Ray continued frowning at Darcy as he unpinned his badge and deposited it in the top left-hand drawer in his desk. "Not much; same old shit; a few beers at Bottoms Up. Probably go fishing with Elvis. You know, same ole', same ole'," Ray related matter-of-factly.

"What happened with going on the wagon? Thought you said you were going to quit," Darcy said, smoke drifting from her mouth.

"I did stop for a couple of days, but after thinking about it, I decided what I really had to do was take control of the situation. I know enough now to stop before I've had too many. That's the secret, knowing when to quit" he said, watching Darcy's smoke drift in his direction.

"After the way I found you that morning, I thought for sure you'd smartened up," Darcy said.

"Sometimes you can be a first class pain in my ass, you know that? Can't you forget about that one time? It's not like I get plastered every night. And put that goddamn cigarette out," he commanded.

Darcy turned toward Callahan. She shook her head. "I've never seen anyone that drunk before in my entire life," she said, once again ignoring him.

Ray's face was flushed with anger. "Just drop it, okay. Women like you are the reason I never married. I don't want to listen to you nagging me all the time. Jesus Christ, a man has a few too many once in a while and you won't let him forget it."

Darcy being Darcy never knew when to shut her mouth. "Once in a while! I wish I had a dollar for every time you show up for work hung over. I've seen homeless alcoholics sleeping in alleys in better shape than you were that morning."

Ray shook his head, getting madder by the minute. "In the first place, it's nobody's goddamn business if I drink. In the second place, I just have to watch myself. I've learned my lesson. I know when I've had enough," he said. "Now, just drop it."

"Sure you do. I've heard that bullshit before," Darcy continued.

Realizing a battle was brewing, Callahan decided he'd better change the subject before things got out of hand. "It's been quiet around here lately now that the snowbirds are beginning to head back north," he interrupted.

Ray drew in a deep breath and eased back into his chair while continuing to glare at Darcy. When he finally spoke, his voice was calmer, more in control. "Good, that's the way I like it," he said, then picked up yesterday's newspaper and deposit it in the trash container next to his desk. Under it he found the Gagnon murder file where it had laid untouched, collecting ketchup, mustard, and coffee stains for the last two weeks. The folder was thin and contained little information.

Now that the case was closed, he no longer had any use for it, so he picked it up and was about to put it in the file cabinet when Darcy noticed what he had in his hand. "Anything new with the murder?" she asked.

"What do you mean new?' It's over as far as I'm concerned," Ray snapped.

"Still think it was that Greek, Pappas?' Callahan asked.

"Think! I know it was him. I'm positive of that." Ray said; the folder still in his hand. "No sense in beatin' a dead horse, and in this case, the dead horse is Pappas. Once he died from that heart attack, or whatever it was he died from, that was the end of the investigation."

"How do you know for sure?" Darcy asked.

"When you've been a cop as long as I've been, Andy, you'll understand these things a little better. I was hot on his trail and he knew it. Just about to make an arrest when the son-of-a-bitch up and died on me. I had accumulated a lot of solid evidence. I had him running scared. Wouldn't be surprised if his knowing I was about to throw his ass in jail for killing that fella wasn't what scared him into having the heart attack. Trust me, Pappas was our man," Ray boasted, ignoring Darcy, while glancing confidently at Callahan.

"Guess you're right, Chief."

Ray continued. "Oh yeah, you don't spend as many years as I have in law enforcement without learning a few things. It's just something I've acquired over time. I had him on the run, no doubt about it. You get so you can tell just by watching a fella. He had the look of a murderer. You know, Andy, you're a bright young man; you could learn a lot by watching how I handle things around here. It won't be much longer before I retire and chances are you'll be sitting in this chair someday," Ray complimented Callahan, continuing to ignore Darcy.

"I'm keeping my eyes and ears open, Ray. I've learned a lot from you over the years and I want you to know, I really appreciate it," Andy said.

"That's what I like to hear, Andy. Keep the good work up."

"Doesn't look like that Gagnon woman will be coming back to Barefoot Bay," Callahan informed Ray.

"Really, what makes you say that, Andy?" Ray inquired.

"Couple days ago, when I was making a routine run through the Bay, I noticed a "For Sale" sign in the front of her house. The Pappas house looks vacant, too, but there isn't any sign in front of it. Now that her husband died, I wonder if she'll be back."

Ray shook his head. "Don't know, don't care. I wish all them goddamn snowbirds would stay up north where they belong."

Glancing down at his watch, Callahan decided it was time to get back to work. He got up, stretched his arms, reached for the ceiling, and yawned. "Guess I've wasted enough time in here. Since I'm on the clock, I suppose I should get out on the road," he said.

Darcy was following the conversation closely but remained silent while watching Ray. Although they'd had their moments, she was seeing her boss in an altogether different light lately. It seemed that right after

Scooter Pappas died, he seemed to relax and was easier to get along with. It was like old times once again. There was no denying he was lazy. He had a drinking problem, no doubt about that, even if he wouldn't admit it, but she had gotten used to him and was learning to like him in spite of his faults.

After Patrolman Callahan walked out, Ray got out of his seat with the Gagnon file in his hand and headed for the file cabinet. Once the folder was in the drawer, he slammed it shut and turned, took one look at Darcy and said, "I sure could use a beer and I don't want to hear any preaching from you. In fact, how about you and me going to Bottoms Up and celebrating. Having a couple of beers with your boss to celebrate can't hurt."

Darcy took a long, last puff on her cigarette, reached over and took the remaining used Styrofoam cup from Ray's desk, and dunked the butt in the left over coffee. "And just what would we be celebrating?"

"We have a couple of things to celebrate," he said.

"Like what?"

"Well, like solving the Gagnon murder for one."

"We didn't exactly solve it," she said. "It's not like we made an arrest and got a conviction."

Ray nodded. "That's true. But we would have if he hadn't died. We both know Pappas did it, and we both know it was only a matter of time before I'd have nailed him, and I wouldn't have been able to nail him without your help."

Darcy furrowed her forehead, unsure if she agreed. "Guess you're right. So what's the other thing we'll be celebrating?"

"You're aware that a developer is putting in five-hundred new homes on the other side of Micco Road across from Barefoot Bay," he said.

Darcy looked confused. "I don't know a thing about it, but what's that got to do with anything?"

Ray was unable to keep from smiling. "Well, with all the development that's going on in this area, it means more work for us. And more tax dollars for the town. I've been talking to the town manager about spending some of that tax money on hiring another patrolman," he said.

"And?"

"And, he agreed. I've recommended you for the job. He wasn't too keen on hiring a woman at first, but I explained you'd make an excellent policewoman. I was informed earlier this morning that he spoke to the councilmen and got the okay. When the next Police Academy class starts, you'll be in it."

"Are you serious?"

"I'm serious," he said. "So what do you think; a couple of beers are in order to celebrate?"

Darcy was out of her chair in a flash, ran over and gave him a long hug. "Thanks, Ray. I can't tell you how much this means to me."

Darcy pushed away from him, brought her shoulders back, pushed her chest out and smiled. "It's close enough to quitting time. Give me a couple of minutes to close up, and I'll meet you at Bottoms Up."

CHAPTER 45

SEVERAL DAYS PASSED since Carol heard from Betty. She called when she first arrived back in New Hampshire to let her know she arrived safely, but that conversation had been brief. She hadn't heard anything since. Minutes seemed like hours, hours like days and days crept by like weeks. Carol was lonely. Ever since Betty went back to Pembroke, she had been fighting the sensation of swimming against a strong underwater current of loneliness, with only Stanley in her life.

Stanley's mental health was deteriorating rapidly and she was concerned and frightened. He no longer just sat quietly and stared into space, mumbling softly to himself. For the past several days he would have sudden outbursts, making high pitched wailing sounds that resembled an injured animal caught in a trap, followed by loud arguments, screaming at people who existed only in his mind. Carol was convinced he had all the symptoms of a classic schizophrenic. She knew she couldn't go on living like this much longer. Something had to be done, and soon.

Carol was in the bedroom getting dressed for her exercise class at the Sebastian Gym when the phone rang. She quickly pulled her loose fitting sweatshirt over her shoulders and nearly tripped over the corner of the bed in her haste to answer the phone; hoping it was Betty.

"Hello."

"Hi, Carol. It's Betty."

"I can't tell you how good it is to hear your voice. How's everything going?"

"Good. It's been pretty hectic around here, but everything's finally coming together."

"How did the funeral go?"

"As good as could be expected. Scooter's mother cried and carried on throughout the entire wake. She all of a sudden looks old, and tired, fed up with life. She's taking Scooter's death hard. She worshiped him. When I saw her walking into the funeral home, she looked kind of shrunken . . . shrunken and brittle and confused. She walks with a cane now. She's all stooped over and her clothes seemed to hang on her," Betty explained.

"It must be tough losing your only son. I feel bad for her."

Images of Bobby flashed before her eyes. "There's nothing any worse," Betty agreed. Then she regained her composure. "I think everyone in New Hampshire showed up for the funeral. There were firemen, policemen and politicians from every town and city in New Hampshire in attendance. Everyone kept saying what a wonderful man Scooter was and how sorry they were for my loss. If they only knew what he was really like."

"I would have never guessed he was as bad as you say he was."

"The man you saw in public and the man I lived with were two different people. He was a cruel man that enjoyed hurting people that were weaker and more vulnerable than he was, and couldn't fight back. But now he's gone. He's really gone," Betty said, laughing slightly.

"You sound like you're doing all right. You don't sound too broken up," Carol said.

"I'm not. I've wanted it to happen."

"Betty, stop talking like that."

"It's true, Carol. I've been floating on air since he died. I wanted him out of my life. And now, thank God, he's gone."

"You didn't make it happen."

"Sometimes I think I did. Maybe my wishing so hard caused it to happen. You know what's so funny? I don't feel a thing. Do you think there's something wrong with me? If I was a good person, wouldn't I feel bad? At least feel something?"

"There's nothing wrong with you. You're still in shock, that's all," Carol said.

"I really don't have anybody now, except you. I know you'll be there for me," Betty said.

"I'll always be here for you, you know that. I can't wait to see you." There was a short, awkward pause. When Betty didn't respond right away, Carol continued. "So when will you be coming back to Florida?"

"Won't be much longer; I finally got most of the legal stuff straightened out."

"Have any problems?" Carol asked.

"Actually, yes, I had a problem with the family attorney, Caraganis. He wouldn't handle things for me. He said he'd been the family attorney for over thirty-five years and has known the Pappas's all his life and couldn't be a part of selling the farm from beneath Mother Pappas. He felt forcing her out of the only home she's known for the last sixty years would kill her. I told him I didn't care. You should have seen the look on his face when I told him that. He kept trying to convince me to mortgage the farm. He said if I did, I'd have plenty of money to live on, and when the old lady passes away I could sell the property, pay off the mortgage and still have plenty left."

"You didn't want to do that?"

"No way; I told him I wanted everything sold. I just want to put Pembroke behind me and the sooner the better. So he said find another lawyer."

"What did you do?"

"Found another lawyer. The talk around town is I'm a heartless bitch. So I went to Concord and hired a Jewish lawyer. His name is Bernie Goldstein. One thing about those Jews, they're smart when it comes to money and I feel I can trust him."

"I'm sure you can. Sounds like every thing's falling into place," Carol said.

"Yeah, he told me he would take care of everything and for me not to worry."

"Do you have a date when you're heading back?" Carol asked, sounding anxious.

"No, shouldn't be long though. The realtor said he's got two building contractors looking at the farm. He said developers don't just buy land anymore. They buy views. The Pappas farm has plenty of scenic views. I'm not waiting for the place to sell. Goldstein said it's going to take some time to get all the legal work cleared up, but said I could go back to Florida whenever I want to. He said, even the actual passing of the papers when the property sells could be taken care of through the mail. I can't wait to start heading south on 95. And when I do, I'm not looking in my rear view mirror."

"I'll be glad when you get here. I need a friend. Stanley's driving me nuts," Carol confessed.

"Still babbling too himself?"

"He's worse than ever. I have no idea what goes on in that head of his."

"Do you think he needs to see a doctor?"

"Do I think? I know he does."

Betty laughed then changed the subject. "Heard anything from Kathy?"

"Not much. Last time I talked to her she said she's not coming back. In fact there's already a FOR SALE sign on her lawn," Carol said.

"Too bad, I'm gonna miss her. I better get going. I still have plenty of things to do. I just wanted to let you know how everything was going."

"Okay. I'm glad you called. I really miss you. I'm counting the days until you get back," Carol said, sounding depressed.

There was a pause. Thinking they'd been disconnected, Carol says tentatively, "Betty . . . you still there?"

After a few seconds go by, Betty says, "I'm still here. I really miss you too." Then, there was another pause. "Carol, can I ask you something?"

"Of course you can."

"Well, I've been doing a lot of thinking. I don't quite know how to put this. I'm actually scared to bring it up."

"Scared; what are you scared of, Betty?"

"I'm not sure. When did you first discover you were a . . . a lesbian? What I mean to say, is, ever since Scooter died, I've been wondering if I was ever attracted to him. I know I never loved him, but I don't think I was ever attracted to him as a man," Betty meekly explained.

"I was in high school when I found out I was more interested in girls than boys. Don't misunderstand me, I loved hanging around with the boys, but when I fell in love, it was a woman I wanted to share my life with," she said.

"That's the problem. Before I met Scooter, I'd never even thought about sex, boys or girls. When Scooter came into my life, I was kind of pushed into dating him, then, marrying him."

"Haven't you ever been attracted to men?"

"I did have an affair once," Betty confessed, but didn't go into details.

"You did?"

"Yes. Then, I discovered he was just using me. I did think at the time I loved him, but now I wonder if I was just looking for someone to love me, anyone," she continued. "Except for that one time, I've never even thought about sex with men, never found them sexy or attractive. I've always felt more comfortable around women. I guess what I'm asking; do you think I could be a lesbian, or, maybe bi-sexual?"

"I don't know what to say. I imagine you should have known by now, if you are. I suppose it's possible you've been bi-sexual all these years and not known. I'll admit I've been thinking lately that you might be."

"So, you think I am. If you felt this way, why didn't you say something? It frightens me to think I might have wasted my life not knowing who I am."

"Because I wasn't sure; I didn't want to do anything that might jeopardize our friendship. When you get back to Barefoot Bay will discuss it further. Until then, finish up your business and try not to think about it."

"I can't stop thinking about it, and I can't wait to get back to Florida and see you," Betty quietly replied.

Since Betty went back to New Hampshire, Carol felt like she'd been walking around holding her breath. It had only been with Robin that she could let go, be herself, and that's what she needed now. After the statement Betty just made, Carol finally allowed herself to exhale.

"I'll be waiting," Carol whispered, then hung up.

CHAPTER 46

SHORTLY AFTER GETTING off the phone, Carol retrieved her car keys from the key holder on the kitchen wall, heading for the gym when she heard Stanley muttering to himself. Quietly at first, then his rambling got louder. Soon, his high pitched voice began filtering through the house from the screen room. She had just about come to the end of her rope with him. *Enough is enough. It's time to put an end to this madness,* she thought.

She had noticed lately the stress of his life had left him with dark circles under his eyes and an ashen complexion. He was now living exclusively in a world of make believe. On the few occasions when they spoke, Stanley would mumble incoherently and gaze back with a strange look on his face, then drift away to places where only he existed.

She realized she had two choices. The first was to let him be, after all, he wasn't hurting anyone and appeared content in his world of make believe. The second choice was to get him help. It was true he wasn't bothering any one, but what about later? Could he become dangerous? Stanley was a huge man, nearly three hundred pounds. She knew his mind was a ticking bomb ready to explode. If he became violent, Carol knew she would be in grave danger. She felt she really didn't have a choice. His sickness had to be dealt with, and the sooner the better.

Carol went looking for him. She found him sitting on his lounge chair, his hair was uncombed and he hadn't bothered to shaving in several days. He was slumped forward, rocking back and forth, his arms wrapped around his body like he was in a straightjacket, involved in a conversation with an imaginary person called *Rocky*. She decided she'd had enough. Taking a deep breath and letting it out slowly, she approached him. "Listen, Stanley, we need to talk. Something's wrong."

Stanley gave no indication Carol was even there. He continued to rock back and forth, his moaning and squealing becoming louder. "Stanley, for God's sake stop that and listen to me. It's just not normal for a grown man to behave like you're behaving. I think it's time you got some help," she spat out.

Getting no reaction, she moved closer and began speaking in a louder but more in control voice. "You need help, Stanley. You can't continue to sit out here by yourself, talking to people who don't exist," she said, then sat on the edge of the lounge chair across from him and bent forward in a nonthreatening manner.

Stanley turned and gave her a hollow, vacant look. It appeared he was looking through her, rather than at her. He began squinting. "What? Leave me alone," he insisted.

She remained calm, but her words still came out harsh. "Don't you even know you're talking to people that aren't real?"

"Just leave me alone," he repeated.

It was apparent that Stanley was in far worse condition than she realized. His eyes appeared empty, yet she sensed there was something hidden there, and Carol didn't know what it was. She knew she had never seen this look before. Whatever it was appeared to be tearing Stanley apart from the inside.

"You have a problem, Stanley. These people you're talking too aren't real. Their only in your imagination," Carol explained, keeping her voice nonjudgmental and nonthreatening.

Carol gazed into his face and took a deep breath. *I need to get this right. Don't sound angry, go easy,* she decided. "I want you to listen to me, Stanley," she said, gently placing her hand on his arm. "I'm going to make an appointment with a doctor when I get back from the gym. I want you to go see him."

Stanley's mouth moved for several seconds before any words came out. "I don't need to see a doctor."

"I'm talking about a psychiatrist, Stanley. You need help. Don't worry, I'll go with you. Everything will be all right," she said, continuing to speak softly.

He hesitated, caught his breath, looked down at his lap and began to pout, his eyes filled with doubt. "I don't want to see a psychiatrist. I won't go."

Carol could see she wasn't getting any place with him. She didn't want to provoke him any more than she already had. It was evident Stanley was in serious need of help, more help than she was capable of giving, but knew she couldn't go on living in the same house with a man who constantly talked to people that only existed in his mind. She had to get him to a psychiatrist.

Carol had been going to gym class infrequently. But she was going this morning. She needed to get away from Stanley. She gently placed her hand on his shoulder, her voice low and compassionate and said, "I've got to be going, Stanley. I'm already late for gym class. I want you to think about what I said. We'll talk again when I get home." She quietly walked out of the screen room, then out of the house, feeling depressed and confused. She felt like a stranger in her own home, a stranger who didn't belong here and needed to escape.

Alone, Stanley started trembling. He pressed his fist to his ears, his feelings for Carol confusing and complicated. He thought he loved her, although he wasn't sure. It wasn't just his feelings for her that confused him; it was life itself that was unbearable. His life had slipped into a black hole where he could see nothing, feel nothing and want nothing more than to be left alone.

Then the voice spoke. The voice was echoing through thin air; from outer space, where only Stanley went. He heard it clearly some days and more clearly others. Today it was very clear. It said, *Looks like we have a problem.*

"Did you hear what Carol said?"

I heard everything. I've been right here all the time, the voice in his head said.

Stanley's face began to twist. He choked up momentarily. A thin line of drool escaping from the corner of his mouth, then fell on his chest when he spoke. "I'm scared, Rocky. I don't want to go to the doctors."

You might not have a choice.

"Do you think she can force me to go?"

Sure she can. All she has to do is tell the doctor you're crazy. Then they would come and take you away, put you in a hospital.

Sweat appeared on his forehead, while his body went cold. He felt overwhelmed and frightened of what he didn't understand. "I'm not crazy. I don't think I'm crazy. Maybe I am crazy. I don't know if I am or not. Do you think I'm crazy?" He began rambling.

Don't know if you're crazy. But if the doctor says you are, they'll lock you up in one of those insane asylums.

"What should I do, Rocky?"

Maybe it's time for me to have a talk with Carol, like I had with Phil.

Stanley straightened up; his eyes moved around the screen room. "I never wanted you to kill him. I don't want you to hurt Carol."

Phil should have never done those things to you. That was his mistake. We don't take any shit from anyone. You know that, don't you, Stanley?

"Yeah, I know, Rocky."

The night Rocky had gone next door to the Gagnon's to confront Phil about his taunting Stanley, things got out of hand. Stanley certainly hated Phil but never intended for Rocky to kill him.

Stanley and Rocky had been sitting out back in the screen room, just as they were now. Stanley had gone into detail about how he'd been humiliated by Phil in front of Scooter and Jimmy the day of the golf match. Stanley was nearly in tears. It was then that Rocky decided he'd had enough of Phil Gagnon.

Without hesitation, Rocky was out of the house. The sun was down and there was no moon to replace it. He went undetected, hidden by dark clouds, walking with confidence, headed to the Gagnon's.

When he arrived, he banged on the door in a rage. Phil startled and not knowing what the hell was going on, opened the door and found Stanley Kloski standing there with a crazed look in his eyes.

"What the hell do you want, Stanley? It's kind of late to be visiting, isn't it?"

I want to talk to you, asshole, Stanley spoke in his Rocky voice. Then he walked directly at Phil, causing him to retreat backwards into the living room.

"What the fuck do you think you're doing?"

Listen to me, and listen good; if you ever pick on Stanley again, I'll kill you. Do you understand?

Phil didn't know what to make of this crazy situation. Stanley looked frightening and talked in a voice he wasn't familiar with. Phil might not have understood what the hell was going on, but one thing was definite—he wasn't going to let Stanley Kloski threaten him. "I don't know what this is about, but I'm telling you right now you loser, get the fuck out of my house, or I'll throw you out on your ass."

Phil then put his hand on Stanley's chest, attempting to push him backwards toward and out the open door. Rocky's face became hard with anger. Without warning, he smashed Phil with his clenched fist squarely in the face with such force it sent him reeling backwards, helplessly out of control. Struggling to remain standing, Phil dropped his shoulder like a football player trying to take down the quarterback and attacked.

Rocky easily stepped aside and grabbed Phil by the throat with one hand and slammed his fist against his jaw with the other. Phil collapsed onto the floor, hitting the back of his head full force on the edge of the coffee table.

Rocky felt blood rushing to his head, and his heart was pounding out of control at the sight of his victim lying helpless before him. Without hesitation, he pounced on Phil with his full weight, both knees straddling him, seized him around the throat and squeezed with all his might. Phil began gasping for breath, and his body twitched before it finally went limp.

Don't you ever fuck with Stanley, do you hear me? Don't you fuck with him, the voice shouted, drool falling from his mouth, landing on Phil's face as he continued to squeeze, digging his fingers deeper into his victim's neck, causing his throat to collapse, depriving him of the air he needed to breathe, until Phil lay motionless on the floor.

The silence in the room was suddenly absolute. The air had the deadliness of a morgue. Convinced that Phil would no longer be a problem, Rocky slowly got to his feet, looked down at the lifeless corpse stretched out at his feet and smiled triumphantly, then calmly walked away, slowly closing the door behind him.

"I don't want anything to happen to Carol," Stanley insisted.

Just what do you want, Stanley?

"I'm not sure. I just want to go someplace where everyone will leave me alone."

You know what will happen to you if that cop, Barrett, ever finds out what happened to Phil, don't you, Stanley?

"What?"

He'll lock you up for Phil's murder. That's what.

Stanley shook his head. "No, you're the one. I didn't do it. You're the one that did it."

Don't matter. You remember what happened with Tony in the school yard. Everyone will blame you. If you don't end up in jail for Phil's murder, Carol's going to have you put in one of them insane asylums.

"I don't want to go to jail! I don't want to go to the insane asylum! What should I do, Rocky? You have to help me," Stanley said, really scared now, while two lines of clear snot began running out of his nose.

The voice asked, *Did you mean what you said, Stanley?*

"What?"

You said you wanted to go where everyone will leave you alone. Is that what you really want? If that's what you want, Stanley, you know I'll help you, the voice said, not so much ordering him as coaxing him.

The voice in his head continued. *You know what you should do!*

"What should I do?"

Listen to me. It's time for you to end it.

Stanley began kneading his forehead with his thumb and fingers. What the voice in his head was suggesting was frightening, but only for a moment. For years he had been haunted by thoughts of suicide. There were days when he was fine, but most days he just wanted to close his eyes and end it. The weight of his life was just getting too much for him to bear. He knew that he couldn't go on living like this. He had no idea what death would be like, but often thought it couldn't be worse than life.

"Would it hurt?"

The voice seemed to be echoing throughout the screen room. *Won't hurt a bit; all you have do is go get Carol's sharp knife from the kitchen, make a slit across your wrist.*

A strong and powerful feeling flowed into him. Suddenly he wasn't afraid. Stanley decided that death was what he wanted. He leaped to his feet and began pacing in circles. "I'm gonna do it," he said in a trembling voice.

Without hesitation he marched triumphantly into the kitchen. Although there was no logical reason to be doing what he was doing, something more powerful than logic was in control. For the first time in his life, he knew he would have the courage to do what needed to be done.

Stanley returned to the screen room and collapsed in the lounge chair. Tears of hopelessness and frustration were burning his eyes. The knife had a handle of polished stainless steel and a blade sharper than a razor. Taking a deep breath, his hands shaking slightly, he put the sharp edge against his pale white wrist and began applying pressure. He moved the knife back and forth until he saw blood. He was amazed at how painless and easy it was. He continued sliding the knife back and forth on his other wrist until blood began gushing out.

In a hypnotic state, he watched the bright red blood flow freely against the whiteness of his wrists. It began running down his hands and fingers onto the floor, the left hand redder than the right. With a sigh of relief, he let the knife slide from his fingers, making a dull thump when it landed in the syrup-like pool of blood at his feet.

Stanley leaned his head back and waited for the relief to come that would free him from his terrible life. He believed there was something out there beyond this life, something beyond his understanding, and he knew whatever it was, it was waiting for him.

The corners of his mouth twitched slightly as he took in a deep breath, then slowly let it out. He realized death was coming for him. He remained perfectly calm as the voice in his head said in a soft whisper, *it's okay, it's time.* It was becoming hard to breathe, but his mind suddenly became fiercely alive, and he felt a great weight being lifted from his shoulders.

Finally at the end, at the very end, after everything he'd been through; the haunting voices trapped inside his head, the feelings of not belonging, being born a bastard and the frustration and lonesomeness of never being loved, magically disappeared. His arms hung limp at his sides as he relaxed. There was no longer any rocking back and forth, no out of control sobbing. He had finally found peace.

Taking one last breath, he closed his eyes and felt more happiness and contentment than at any other time in his life, knowing death was the only way he would ever be free, asking only to be left alone to slip into a place of eternal sleep where no one could reach him and nothing could hurt him.

Book Club Topics

1) If you were in Kathy's situation, pregnant but unsure who the father is, what would you have done?

2) After Scooter loses his father in the fire, he becomes bitter and hateful. Do you understand and sympathize with his behavior?

3) After children are sexually abused, as Rita was, do you think they can ever have a normal sexual relationship again?

4) Do you think Doris was right by not divulging the circumstances under which she became pregnant?

5) Do you believe that Carol and Robin's love for each other is as meaningful and fulfilling as those of straight couples?

6) Carol and Robin discuss the fears of gay teenagers being discovered in high school. Do you think these fears are unfounded today, or do they still exist?

7) When Scooter forces Betty to have sex with him against her will, is this rape even though they are married?

8) After Scooter dies, do you think Betty mistreated her mother-in-law by evicting her from the farm?

9) After Rita discovers Jimmy has been unfaithful, do you think their marriage can survive?

10) Do you think Jimmy shares responsibility for the affair, or was he seduced by Kathy?

11) Kathy believes Phil has been unfaithful to her in the past. Does his having affairs justify her having an affair with Jimmy?

12) Was Stanley's mental illness caused by years of loneliness and isolation, or do you think his mental illness would have developed regardless of his upbringing?

13) Can you understand why Stanley chooses to commit suicide?

14) What situation in the novel was the most emotional for you?

About The Author

D. L. Bourassa was born in Lowell, Massachusetts. He is married and the father of two sons. He and his wife are retired and now reside on Florida's Space Coast where they are enjoying the warmer winters.

Secrets, Sins & Revenge is his second novel. He is presently working on his third book.

Author contact: dlbourassa@gmail.com